To
Chris Pallan,

I hope you like
the book

(signature)

Osceola

Thomas R. Stubbs

Cover Art: Kelly Barrow

authorHOUSE®

AuthorHouse™
1663 Liberty Drive
Bloomington, IN 47403
www.authorhouse.com
Phone: 1-800-839-8640

First published by AuthorHouse   11/16/2010

ISBN: 978-1-4520-9392-5 (hc)
ISBN: 978-1-4520-9391-8 (sc)
ISBN: 978-1-4520-9390-1 (e)

Printed in the United States of America

This book is printed on acid-free paper.

Certain stock imagery © Thinkstock.

Chapter One

I couldn't sleep. Heaven knows I tried, but I just couldn't sleep. I had gone to bed early, like Dad said, but all I could do was lay there. It's amazing the number of strange things that can run through your mind when you're trying to sleep. I had never had problems before, but I was just too excited now. I was going hunting in the morning. It's true; I had been hunting a lot before and never had any problems sleeping the night before. In fact, one of my favorite pastimes was hunting deer, turkey, squirrel, and all of the other smaller game animals that lived around our cabin. But I had never gone hog hunting. I still couldn't believe that I was being allowed to go hog hunting.

Last night after supper, a couple of hours before dark, we had just finished eating, and my mother and sisters were clearing the table when Dad looked at me and said, "Boy, you better get your guns, clean them up, and load them. We're going hog hunting in the morning." Now Dad wasn't one you would argue with much—in fact, not at all.

I immediately sprang up and went to the fireplace on the right-hand side, and took my Pennsylvania rifle from the pegs where it had lain and my old Ethan Allen Pepperbox pistol and brought them over to the eating table. Carefully, I moved the candles on the table off to the far side and laid the guns there in front of the little bench stool on which I sat. Then I went to the wood cedar chest next to the front door, which was on the opposite side of the cabin from the fireplace, and got out my pouch with my powder flask, lead bullets, and other supplies. I brought these over to the table and sat down, took the ramrod from the barrel of the rifle, and attached a piece of cloth and began to dry and clean out the barrel. Of course the barrel was clean. We were taught by Dad always to make sure and clean our equipment well after we were finished with it and before we put it up. I knew the barrel was clean, but it was always a good idea to swab out the barrel to remove any excess oil that might cause it to misfire, and so I proceeded. I swabbed out the barrel, picked out the nipple of the musket to make sure it was open, and then swabbed out the barrel again. While I was doing this, I kept a careful eye on my dad. He hadn't said anything since then, and certainly I wasn't about to question why I was being allowed to go hog hunting.

My older brother, William, was allowed to go for the first time two years ago, when he was fifteen. I had begged and pleaded then that I should be allowed to go, but Dad had insisted that I was simply too young. I had pointed out to him that, although I was ten and William was fifteen, I was, at least I thought, nearly as big and nearly as strong and almost as good a shot. But Dad had stood firm, and my pleas had come to no avail. Dad always said hog hunting was too dangerous for a youngster. No matter how much I pleaded, it didn't have any effect. I wasn't sure just what had changed, but I wasn't going to ask. I looked from my dad to my mother and could tell by the look on her face that she didn't approve. One thing you didn't do was argue with my dad, and my mother certainly would never contradict him in our presence. But from one look, you could tell that she was not happy with the idea. Possibly because of the looks he received, Dad suddenly went on to explain further.

Just then he said, "I reckon the boy has grown up enough that he should be able to keep up. He's got a good head on his shoulders, and he knows how important it is to do what he is told." Dad said, while looking at me with a piercing expression, "Remember, boy, hog hunting is dangerous. You have to keep your wits about you at all times and do what you're told." I supposed this is why he was allowing me to go hunting with them now. Previously, even though I was nearly as tall and strong as William and certainly as capable, possibly Dad just doubted whether I could keep my wits.

Dad kept a careful eye on me as I prepared to load the rifle and the Pepperbox. I placed my finger over the nipple spout of the powder flask, shook it several times to break up any powder that may have clumped, and then turned the spout down, pushed the lever to the side to let the powder fill the spout, and carefully poured the powder from the spout into the measurer. I carefully measured out forty grains of fine black powder and poured it down the barrel of the musket. Then I took out the lead ball and wrapped it in the finely waxed cloth and placed it in the muzzle and pounded it home with the ramrod. Then I got up and took the rifle back and put it on the pegs next to the fireplace on the right-hand side. We wouldn't actually put a percussion cap on the nipple until we left in the morning. Dad never allowed us to have loaded guns in the house. He always said it was too dangerous, but he said that since we were getting up early in the morning, we should load our guns tonight while it was still light and put them up out of reach where it would be safe.

Then I sat down again to carefully load the old Pepperbox pistol. It was my newfound pride and joy. Dad had just given it to me a few months before. Before that, it had been his. At one point in time, it had been his most prized possession. It was a heavy, clumsy thing that had six barrels that rotated when you pulled the trigger. It wasn't really a work of art and had no fancy engravings. The barrels were six inches long and of thirty-six caliber. I don't know just how long Dad had had it or when he bought it, but now it was mine. It loaded from the barrel like the old Pennsylvania rifle. I carefully measured out thirty grains of black bullets, poured them down the barrel after having placed the percussion caps on the nipples, and proceeded to load the lead balls and tap them down carefully. I only loaded five, leaving the last barrel under the hammer empty. This was a safety precaution that Dad always insisted on. When the trigger was pulled, the barrel block would rotate and the hammer fire down on the new barrel that was loaded. But there was always a chance, even with the trigger down, that, if it was dropped on a loaded chamber, it might discharge, or at least I'd been told that. No one wanted to experiment and find out for sure. Dad had always been proud of it, possibly because few other people owned anything like it. Living where we did on the frontier and being rather isolated, Dad always felt it was necessary to be well armed. He had always called the Pepperbox his "backup." It was something to fall back on in any emergency.

All that changed a few months ago when we visited my Uncle Aaron at his trading post near the junction of the Osage and Missouri rivers. Uncle Aaron had been excited to show Dad a selection of new weapons he had received. There were some unusual-looking rifles and some revolvers that he had just acquired. Dad was fascinated by them. We owned an assortment of the fine Kentucky long rifles, acquired over many years. We also had several large single-shot pistols and a couple of old, heavy muskets. But the firearms Uncle Aaron had were new rifles unlike anything we had ever seen.

When Uncle Aaron showed Dad the bright, shiny brass Henry Rifles, Dad's eyes had shone nearly as bright as the brass on the rifles. Uncle Aaron explained how you could load fifteen cartridges in the tubular magazine and work the lever to load and eject the cartridges. He helped Dad load several cartridges and work the lever until the magazine was empty, and I could tell Dad was fascinated. We had gone outside and watched as Dad and Uncle Aaron practiced with the rifles. I had known that Dad would be unable to resist.

On returning to the store, Uncle Aaron brought out the new Colt and Remington revolvers he had acquired. He explained how to load and fire them, and once again, we went outside where he and Dad practiced with the new weapons. I had been absolutely itching to get to handle them, but no such luck. Apparently, I was too young. My older brother, William, and my cousins took turns with target practice. Even Isaac and Jacob, our neighbors and hired hands, were allowed to try out the new weapons, but not me.

In the end, Dad had bought a Remington revolver for himself and one for William, along with two extra cylinders. Dad had thought the Remington was sturdier than the Colt and, besides, he liked how the cylinders could be changed out quickly. He also bought himself a Henry rifle and one for William. Isaac and Jacob had purchased one Henry and one Colt revolver.

I had been extremely disappointed that I wasn't fortunate enough to get any, but Uncle Aaron had sold us the last he had, and besides, Dad and Isaac had spent far too much of our precious cash money anyhow. Every year we made the weeklong trip by keel boat to Osage City where Uncle Aaron had his trading post. There we sold tobacco, hemp rope, furs, and whatever else we could for cash money. We then purchases supplies and spent a week visiting our cousins and friends. Most of our cash money that was necessary to live on for the rest of the year came from this one trip, and Dad had spent a good portion of it on these weapons. I was sure Mother would never let him hear the end of it.

When we had returned from out keelboat trip, Dad had surprised me by giving me the old Pepperbox pistol. He had been explaining to the mother how much better the rifles and revolvers were, insisting that they were much easier to load and that they were much more accurate. He had been extremely critical of the Pepperbox, explaining how clumsy it was, how hard to load, how it had no sight to aim, and how at more than ten feet, you couldn't expect to hit anything. I'm not sure it convinced her, but what was done was done and no sense crying about it.

Now the Pepperbox was mine. I had carried it with me constantly over the next several months. Dad wouldn't let me load. It was a waste of powder and lead practicing, but I practiced anyhow. I would draw right hand, left hand, point at targets high, low, and to my left and right, and then pretend to pull the trigger and afterward carefully squint and study along the top of the barrel to decide whether or not my aim was true enough to hit what I was pointing at. It was kind of like shooting my bow and arrow, which I could do left or right handed. We had grown up shooting our bows, and aiming them was an automatic action, almost instinctive. Accuracy was only gained by lots of practice, and I was good at it, much better than William or my good friend Abel, Isaac's youngest son, who was my age. I was even better with my bow than Dad. I was sure I could do as well with the Pepperbox. The hardest part about aiming the pepperbox was adjusting to the trigger pull. It took a lot of pull to rotate the barrel block and raise the hammer. This made it hard to aim till it actually fired. I found it best not to even try to aim it until I could tell from the spring tension that it was ready to fire. Because of all my playful practice, I was sure I could accurately fire it.

Now as we sat at the table, Dad watched me carefully as I loaded the Pepperbox. First, I placed the percussion caps on the nipples and then carefully measured out and poured the powder down one barrel at a time. Then I wrapped the lead ball in waxed cloth and carefully rammed it down before proceeding to the next barrel, carefully avoiding pointing it at anyone.

I could tell Dad was pleased with my attention to detail, and after I had loaded it, I placed it high out of reach of my sisters and younger brothers and returned to the table and watched as Dad loaded his Remington revolver and Henry rifle. The Henry rifle was easy to load. You simply opened the end of the tubular magazine and dropped the cartridges in.

The Remington's were more difficult. Like the Pepperbox, they loaded from the barrel end of the cylinder. You first had to place a percussion cap, then pour in the powder and the shot, rotate the cylinder, and press the ball home with the rod that pivoted down from the barrel. Then you had to seal the cylinder with a piece of beeswax to prevent any flash back of powder, which might cause multiple cylinders to fire off.

I could tell, while watching Dad load his weapons, how proud he was of them. Dad actually possessed few thing he could call his own. What we had was used and shared by all. But these were his! Maybe that was why Mother, surprisingly, hadn't been as upset as I thought she would be.

"Yes, sir," he said as he finished loading. "With these, those old hogs won't have a chance." Then he looked at me again and said, "Remember that hog hunting is dangerous."

I thought then that he would go into the story that he especially liked to tell about the great Caledonian boar hunt that had happened in ancient Greece. Dad had a wealth of knowledge about history, especially about ancient Greece and the Bible. And we were always excited when, in the evening, around the fireplace, he would tell one of them. But instead he simply looked at me again and said, "Remember, boy, hog hunting is dangerous. When we go, we will be going hunting in line. Isaac and Abel will be to the left about thirty yards, and your brothers, William and Jacob, will be thirty yards to the right. Remember, we keep in line. Your job is to keep your eye on the men to your left and make sure you don't get ahead or behind them, and my job will be to look to the right and make sure that William and Jacob are staying. I want you within arm's reach. I want to be able to reach out and touch you at all times, so stay right by my side. Keep your rifle up with your right hand on the butt and your left hand on the stock, keep the barrel pointed up and to the left across your chest at all times. Never shoot at an animal that is running between us. You always shoot straight ahead or slightly off to the side but never directly between us. You walk softly, carefully, and you stay within arm's length. Your main goal is to be quiet. No talking. No whispering. No questions, and do what I do when we find the hogs. You hear me?" All I could do was say yes sir and nod vigorously.

Then Dad said, "Let's get off to bed now. We're going to be getting up early, and you need to get your sleep."

I didn't really feel like that was too likely. It was just starting to get dark. I went upstairs to my room and carefully laid out all my equipment. I put my pouch there with the flask of gunpowder, my lead balls and my percussion caps, my waxed cloth, and all of my other utensils. I got my belt with my hunting knife and the holster for the Pepperbox and laid them next to the pouch. I took out the hunting knife that had belonged to my grandfather. I tested the sharpness of it and looked it over. At one time, it had been a truly fine knife when my grandfather had first bought it. It had a Damascus steel blade that had once been nearly six inches long but now was hardly more than four inches and was once quite broad but through continued sharpening over years, the width was now about a third less than the original width, which corresponded to the loss in length of the blade. I liked to admire the wavy pattern in the Damascus steel blade and the rosewood handle with a fine wavy silver inlay, which I thought made it appear to be the finest knife I'd ever seen. I placed it back in the sheath and laid it next to my bed, ready to get up and leave in the morning.

I then got out my deerskin hunting pants and pulled them on. They were exceedingly tight; in fact, they were nearly too tight. We needed to make another pair, I was growing so quickly, but this would have taken time, and so we always seemed to put this off. Besides, you wanted the pants to fit as tight as possible because the legs of the pants would slide down inside my hunting moccasins. Dad preferred moccasins that came up over the calf nearly to the knee where we tied them with the cord string. Ticks were a real nuisance around our farm, especially out hunting through the brush and thickets. By having tight-fitting deerskin pants placed down to the ankle and moccasins that came up to the knees, it would prevent the nasty little varmints from crawling up your legs.

I then laid out my long-sleeved cotton undershirt and my leather hunting jacket and got my boots out. I call them boots, but they really weren't. They were a type of heavy moccasins that my dad says he thought up. Whether he invented them or not I don't know, but they were certainly like nothing I had ever seen. We made them ourselves. They were quite easy to make. They were made out of hog skin, which was considerably thicker, stronger, and more durable than deerskin but nowhere near as comfortable. The boots were made by putting on your hunting moccasins and putting your feet on a rounded or rather somewhat oval-shaped piece of leather, marking the inside about a quarter of an inch from your toes and your heel and the sides of your foot, and then turning it over and making a deep crease to correspond to the marks on all sides. Then a rectangular strap from the toe and the heel was cut that was long enough to come up over the top of the foot to about three inches or a little bit more above the ankle on both the front and the back. Then a wedge was cut out of the front and the back of the oval so that the sides could be bent up and firmed to come up above the ankle but about three inches less lower than the front and back straps. Then we hand-sewed the sides of the flap, front and back, to the sides and in front where the leather had been left long and then trimmed to fit. They were folded over the top of the foot and sewn together again in front. This gave them a very funny, almost comical look, and for that reason, I would never wear them anywhere where someone else could see, but Dad said these served a very useful purpose. The deerskin hunting moccasins were soft soled, and walking through the rough, rocky ground that we would be hunting on, you could bruise or even cut through the deerskin and lacerate your foot. So we slipped these on over the top of the moccasins by grasping the strap in front and back and pulling them on. Then we had a piece of heavy cord that we used to tie them just above the ankle snugly. They were somewhat clumsy, but they were certainly effective. The deerskin moccasins were so much harder and more elaborate to manufacture that Dad insisted we take care of them as much as possible.

I debated as to whether or not to take my hat. It didn't look like rain, but you could never tell. Besides, the hat had a brim in front that was about four inches long, which was certainly beneficial with hunting into the sunlight to cut the glare and keep the sun out of your eyes. It was a funny-looking hat. It was also of Dad's design. It was made from a round piece of soft deerskin that was folded down over the top of the head, almost like a bow, and came down to just above the ears and just above the eyebrows in front. Then an oval- or egg-shaped piece of hog hide was cut. It extended about four inches in front of the forehead and about six or seven inches behind, being about four inches on each side of the ear. A hole was cut through this that would allow the deerskin hides to be sewn to the inner edge of the hog hide so that when the hat was placed on your head, the brim of the hog hide was just above the ears but extended out in to the back enough to keep the back of the head and neck dry. There were holes on each side of the hog hide so a cord could be placed through, and usually we bent the sides of the hat up over the top and tied the cord together over the crown so that it gave it a look almost like the sides of a canoe. I decided

I would take it, mainly for the protection it offered from the sun in case we happened to be hunting later than I thought that we would.

Having laid everything out carefully, I crawled into the bed next to my younger brother, Jesse, and tried to go to sleep. I said tried to go to sleep, but it was impossible. It was just after it had become good and dark, probably no more than eight o'clock and seldom went to bed that early. So I lay there, tossing and turning. Dad could tell you to go to bed, but he couldn't make you go to sleep.

It's amazing how strange things kept running through my mind. First I wondered just why we were going hunting this early. Usually it was well up in mid-October before we would do it. Possibly it had something to do with the unusually cold temperatures we had had lately. About a week ago, it became quite cold, dropping down into the forties at night, and yesterday we had had a heavy frost on the grass. Dad had commented then that it looks like the weather would be brisk for several days yet. This was probably the main reason for going hog hunting at this time. We always waited until the fall, until we had good cold weather before hunting or doing any type of butchering. One needed the cold weather to keep the game from spoiling. If you hunted during the heat of the summer when the temperatures were well up in the nineties or even hundreds, the game would spoil before you had a chance to get a good cure on it. I suspect the unseasonably cold weather was the main reason that we would be hunting in the morning.

Other thoughts kept running through my mind. Just how dangerous was hog hunting? Dad had always said that hogs were the most unpredictable of all animals. He said that the hog, when injured, will like as not charge you as to run. Deer would always run and weren't considered dangerous at all. Bears, most of the time, were not considered to be dangerous unless you surprised one unexpectedly or came between the sow and her cubs. Dad always said that there was nothing to worry about with bear hunting. If you snuck up on a bear and put a shot in him when he wasn't expecting anything, his first reaction was to take off in whatever direction he was headed as fast as he could. But a hog, like as not, would stop, spin around, look, and charge anything that he thought might have caused his pain. That prompted me to think of the story that Dad always used to tell—I couldn't believe that he hadn't gone into it yesterday evening—about the Caledonian boar hunt.

Let's see, just how did that story go? It had happened at least a thousand years ago in ancient Greece. A goddess had been offended by a Grecian king because she had been overlooked during some religious celebration and hadn't been given any offerings. So she had sent a giant boar to devastate the kingdom. Dad said the boar was as big as a horse and weighed over a thousand pounds. Old Roscoe, our tame boar, Dad always estimated weighed over probably 350 pounds. He was by far the biggest boar I had ever seen, so I couldn't imagine a boar weighing up to a thousand pounds, but maybe boars were bigger in Greece, wherever that was at—someplace over in Europe Dad always said.

Anyway, this big boar was said to slip into the villages of these ancient Greeks and tear down the huts to get to the people inside. Supposedly it would slip into the villages, even in broad daylight, and make off with children and other farm animals. I thought this was rather suspicious behavior for a hog. I had never heard of hogs being predatory, but despite that, Dad had always insisted the story was true.

Anyway, this hog had been such of a nuisance and such a threat and so dangerous that a bunch of Greek heroes from different towns all throughout Greece had gotten together. I don't remember the names. Dad always seemed to do that, but maybe he just made them up. Apparently one was named Laertes. He was the father of another Greek hero named Achilles who would fight in some war against the Trojans years later.

All of this seemed very fascinating. I wished now that I had paid closer attention and could remember all the names and characters and remember the story better, but it was all a blur.

Anyway, the heroes had gotten together and gone off on the boar hunt, which had been successful, although not without considerable misadventure. Several of the heroes had been killed. Some had been killed, Dad liked to remind me, by accidents. Even though the Greeks hunted this big hog with bow and arrow, apparently some had been accidentally shot with arrows and others had been killed by the boar, which seemed to repeatedly be charging and mauling people. But it had finally been killed, to the great celebration of the villages all throughout the region. Dad always said at the end of the story, "Now, boy, how would you like to go boar hunting with a bow and arrow? Those old Greeks were really men."

I agreed. It took a lot more courage than I had had to go after a boar with just a bow and arrow.

I thought about that and thought about old Roscoe. Even though he was tame, we never took any chances with him. We tried our best to avoid him. His job was to breed hogs on the two sows we had, and he was best left alone. Of course, we always fed him, him and the sows, whatever scraps were available. But otherwise, we kept out of arm's reach of him.

I thought about that. I thought about how big he was and agreed that I really didn't think I would want to go up and poke him with a spear. Obviously those ancient Greeks were brave. It's funny how things like this kept running through my head. I was supposed to be going to sleep, but I just couldn't do it. I got to thinking about William and myself and Dad and even Jesse. I was satisfied that the reason I had been allowed to go hunting was probably because Dad felt it was safe enough with these new weapons, but yet he hadn't let William go until he was fifteen, and I thought maybe that probably wasn't all of it. William, even though he was seventeen at this time, five years older than I, really wasn't much bigger. William seemed to take more after my mother. He had the same sandy reddish hair as our mother did and the same white, white skin as Mom.

I seemed to take more after my father and my great-grandfather, Standing Bear. At least Dad always said that I reminded him of Standing Bear. Standing Bear had been an Osage warrior. Of course, that's kind of silly to distinguish him as being an Osage warrior. All Osage men are warriors.

Dad always liked to tell the story about how an Osage boy couldn't become a man until he had gone out on a raid, an expedition, or a quest to kill one of their enemies and to bring back proof of this. Only after having killed another man could an Osage become a man, and only then would he be allowed to take a wife. Standing Bear apparently had been a very noted warrior. It seems he got his name from his exceptional height. All Osage were tall. Dad always said that it was part of their culture that only the tallest and strongest were allowed to take wives and have children. He said it was selective breeding, something that the Indians had discovered, he didn't know when. It was something that had been practiced by Europeans for years, but most people thought this only applied to breeding the strongest horses, cows, hogs, sheep, or other animals.

Dad always said that that's one reason the European nobility only married people from their own class. He says the Europeans had once been nothing but raiders and warriors and the strongest, most fit, and most capable had become the most noted warriors, and so it was by only taking wives from the nobility or the stronger warrior class that they ensured that their children would be selectively bred. I didn't know whether this was actually a conscious thought or not, but it sounded good.

Anyway, Dad said the Osage intentionally, by law or by custom in their tribe, only allowed the tallest and strongest to breed. Dad said that Standing Bear had been nearly six-foot-five, something around nineteen and a half hands, I believe, and I am sure he was. Probably I did take after Standing Bear. I was exceptionally tall for my age, and I had dark black hair and the same hazel eyes as my mother and William; but my skin wasn't alabaster white, as I had heard one of the townsfolk describe my mother's skin. My skin was dark and well tanned. William had coloring like my mother. My younger brother, Jesse, seemed to look a lot like me, with dark hair and dark skin, but he had dark eyes. My two sisters had the same sandy reddish hair and hazel eyes and light coloring as my mother.

Yes, I determined, it was probably the fact that I was nearly as big and strong as William that convinced Dad that it was safe for me to go hunting. Now all I had to do was to keep my wits, stay in line, keep my gun up and pointed to the left, stay within an arm's reach, and walk softly. I had been thinking about William and Jesse and mom and dad and my great-grandfather, Standing Bear, and for some reason, this prompted me to think about my grandfather, Aaron, and all the rest of my family.

My grandfather had moved to this area of the Osage River Valley some time I think in the mid 1820s. He traveled by keelboat up the Mississippi with Abraham and Sara, Isaac's parents, looking for a place to settle. They had come to the junction of the Osage River south of St. Louis and had decided to move west down the Osage. They started the farm here for reasons I'm not sure of, but I suspected this was because there was no one else in the area except Indians and a few travelers. They had made the same yearly trips down the Osage to the trading post that belonged to a French fur trader who had been there for I don't know how many years. It was he who had married the daughter of Standing Bear, and at his post, my grandfather apparently had become infatuated with his youngest daughter.

I don't know how many spring trips grandfather made back and forth to the trading post, but on one of these trips, he managed to persuade my grandmother to marry him. Her name had been Angelique. Apparently this is a common name for French people, but I had never heard anyone else to ever have that name. My grandfather's name had been Rubidoux. I had no idea how to spell this, but that's the way my dad always pronounced it. Apparently that's a French name. He had had the trading post there for years, but it now belonged to my uncle, Aaron. This was Dad's older brother.

I supposed I got to thinking about this because I had been thinking about my great-grandfather, Standing Bear, and now my mind just kept wandering along this line. I was fascinated by the way names kept recurring. I was told that my great-grandfather's, who was left in England, name had been William. Grandfather's name had been Aaron, and I think, once upon a time, someone told me that he was named after his grandfather. Grandfather's oldest son was Aaron, my uncle, Dad's oldest brother, and he had two sons, Robert and Aaron also. Then there was my father, Thomas—I'm not sure where that name came from—and his youngest brother, William. My father had named my oldest brother William, and I had been blessed with his name, Thomas, and my younger brother had been named Jesse, which I think was the name of one of my ancestors who still lives back in England. William had two sons named Thomas and John. There were a slew of girls in through there. I know that my father had sisters named Angelique, Mary, and Elizabeth who had moved away from our farm on the upper Osage back down to the region of Jefferson City, and some had even moved up to some place called St. Louis. We managed to lose track of them over the years. I know they were all married, but I couldn't tell you the names of their husbands. I know that my uncle Aaron, besides his two sons, had daughters named Katherine, Anna, and Susan. I have two sisters, Mary and Elizabeth, and I think that William had daughters also, but they all lived in Texas, and we heard from them but rarely.

My God, what time was it getting to be? I knew it had to be late. It seemed like I had laid there for hours. It must be one or two o'clock in the morning by now. Would I never get to sleep? I suppose I must have, because the last thing that I remember was thinking about names, but suddenly I woke up, hearing my name and feeling a rough shaking by my father. "Time to get up, boy. Time to go hog hunting."

CHAPTER 2

I woke up with a start. I don't know when I had finally fallen asleep, but I was certainly wide awake now. I immediately got up, still wearing the tight-fitting deerskin leather pants that I had gone to sleep in, rushed downstairs and no further than out to the outhouse to relieve myself and then hustled back to my room. I sat down on the side of the bed and pulled on my over-the-calf deerskin moccasins and cinched them tightly and then pulled on my hog skin leather boots by the front and back straps. I got up then and put on my cotton long-sleeved undershirt and tucked it in well below the hips and tied my rope belt tight. This was another precaution to keep those dang ticks out. Then I pulled on my leather hunting shirt and took down my knife belt and cinched it tight around my waist. Grabbing my old leather hat, I rushed downstairs and went immediately to the wall to get my guns from the pegs, but Dad stopped me and said, "Have some breakfast first, boy, before you go."

It was only then that I noticed that Mother had already gotten up and had prepared breakfast for us. "Eat up, son, you're going to need your strength, and it may be awhile before you can get much to eat."

I gulped down as much as the oatmeal and bacon as I could, washing it down with milk from the jug, and while I was doing this, Dad went outside to finish cinching up and saddling up the horses. They had already been saddled up the night before, but he went down the line and tightened up all the cinches. When he came back in, he said, "Now get your gun and let's go."

I went to the right of the fireplace and took the Pepperbox and slipped it into my holster. This had been constructed from lambskin with the wool on the inside. Dad said this always helped to keep the barrels lubricated with the lanolin from the sheepskin and kept them from rusting, and this was a great way of keeping the gun protected. It also seemed to me that it let the gun slide in and out easier, since the wool lubricated it. It just seemed to make things go faster.

I grabbed my rifle and went outside and took the leather pouch that Dad gave me, which he told for me to fasten across the knob of my saddle. I call it a knob because the saddles that we had were homemade. They had no wood frame to them. The only wood in the whole contraption were for the stirrups and a little stick-like piece that was encased in leather on the front of the saddle next to the withers. The saddle was nothing more than a piece of hog skin cut flat. The undersurface had a piece of sheepskin that was sewn around the edges and across the middle to the hog skin. There was no cantle, and there was no saddle horn. It was just a strap of leather. It did have two stirrups coming down each side that helped us mount. The stirrups also helped us balance while riding, but it was nothing like the fancier saddles that could be bought at the trading store or even in town.

I grabbed a handful of hair on the horse's neck with my left hand, which also was used to grasp the stock of my rifle, grabbing the piece of wood that was sewn into the leather just above the withers, and placing one foot in the stirrup and giving a strong jump, I mounted up. We then proceeded out single file down to the Osage River to the south. It was still too dark to see, but having crossed the river to the south side, we rode over the flat ground that we farmed. Then, just a few hundred yards west of Jacob's farm, we crossed the Osage again. We then proceeded along the west or north shore of the Osage, depending on how the river was curving at the moment.

Dad went first. Our old hunting dog, Buck, traveled in front. Dad had picked him up and carried him across the river on the withers of his horse, but as soon as we got to the side where we planned to hunt, he placed Buck down and let him start. Buck was Dad's favorite old dog. Buck was a golden yellow, short-haired dog. He had the most beautiful yellow eyes I had ever seen and the most intelligent look about his face you could imagine. He had large, triangular, erect ears, which he would point at you when you talked to him, and a way of cocking one ear over when he listened that Dad would laugh at and say, "Look, boy, Buck's on to something."

Also, Buck was the most affectionate dog I had ever known. He just loved to be played with and would become so excited that when he wagged his tail, he shook his whole body from the shoulders down. But Buck was definitely Dad's dog. No matter where we were, or what we were doing, when Buck saw Dad, he bounded to his side and wouldn't leave. Apparently he had been born about the same time I had. Dad had worked diligently to train Buck when he was a pup, and he often exclaimed how intelligent Buck was. Buck never strayed more than a few steps from his side under any circumstances. He never growled loudly and certainly never barked. When aroused or excited or frightened, he would emit a slightly louder growl. When exhibiting more of a curious, questioning attitude, there would be a weak whining noise that Buck emitted. Dad said that that's one of the reasons he liked Buck so much, because he never really barked or raised cane like most dogs. Dad really hadn't had to try to train him much to learn these qualities. It seemed like it was more of a natural instinct for the dog. Dad said when Buck had been young, he also had stayed close at heel, never wandering off and charging through the brush, searching and hunting on his own, but seemed to be content to stay by Dad. I think they had some special type of affection or bond that, although rare amongst humans and animals, is not altogether unheard of.

At this point, Buck went ten to fifteen feet in front of Dad's horse, and we went in line. I followed Dad on my horse, keeping close but certainly not within arm's reach. I was followed by Isaac, who was followed by his youngest son, Abel, who was my age. Abel and I were the best of friends and always were side by side, whether we were working in the fields, swimming in the river, fishing, or hunting. Now Abel followed Isaac, followed shortly by William, and bringing up the rear was Jacob. Jacob was several years older than William. I don't know just exactly how many, because for some reason we placed little emphasis on birthdays. My mother did have a family Bible in which she recorded our birthdays. It seemed like it started off with my great-grandfather, but the only entry next was my grandfather and grandmother and then Dad and us. Any of my aunts and uncles, certainly my great-grandmother's brothers or sisters, even my grandfather's brothers and sisters, were not on the list, which made it somewhat confusing, but then it was just a family Bible, and there really wasn't enough room to list every relative. But I do know that Jacob was a few years older than William and growing up, and they, likewise being the closest in age, had been best of friends. I suppose that's why we hunted in the order that we did.

We continued westward up the river, still way before daylight. I tried my best to keep alert, watch for signs, listen, smell, and stay quiet. Staying quiet riding a horse in the dark really wasn't very easy, but we weren't too concerned at this point because we were depending on Buck to let us know when we came in range of any hogs. We continued on in this fashion. Dad had always said that hunting was more about being alert at all times than anything else. He had always said that when you hunted, you had to make use of all your senses. He said that the most important sense was actually hearing and that you would usually hear your game or your enemy long before you could hope to see them. He also said that smelling was of great importance. That always seemed strange to me. I knew that animals had a great sense of smell, at least some of them, and some better than others, but I never thought much of a human being able to smell.

When we hunted, we usually always went into the wind to try to allow it to blow our scent away from any game that we might be coming on. Dad said that since the game was upwind from us, often we could smell it before we could see it. I'm not sure how accurate that was, but I had never been hog hunting. Dad always maintained that hogs have a strong odor and you could certainly smell them before seeing them. He also said it was the same with bear, but certainly the deer, coon, turkey, and rabbits I was used to hunting really didn't exude any aroma.

Nevertheless, I kept my ears open, listening carefully, sniffing constantly, and watching studiously. All I could hear were the horses and the bushes we brushed as we went through. All I could smell were the horses and the faint aroma from my buckskins. I couldn't see much of anything since it was still way too dark. We traveled on in this fashion for what seemed like hours but probably wasn't more than one or two when just as it was starting to get light, just as it was getting to where I could make out outlines of trees on the ridges, I began to notice a faint trail that we seemed to be following. About this time, Buck let out his curious whining noise, and we came to an abrupt stop. Dad dismounted first, and the rest of us continued to sit our horses. He went forward, bent over next to Buck, and looking and feeling carefully on the ground, suddenly stood up and walked back to us and said, "Hogs." Then he whispered,

"Dismount, tie your horses to the tree. Make sure and get the rope head high so he won't get his leg across it and get tangled and let's go."

I started to bring the pouch that had the ham and biscuits that mother had prepared for us, but Dad whispered, "Leave it. We probably won't be eating. You can go for the rest of the day if necessary without eating." But he did take the leather waterskin, slipped the loop over his neck and shoulder, and proceeded. Isaac and Abel grabbed their water skins and started off to the left, and William, with Jacob, went to the right respectively. I took my place at Dad's left side, gun up across my chest with the barrel pointing in the air, and waited until everyone was in position. It was still too dark to judge thirty yards, so I suspect to begin with we probably weren't more than fifteen or twenty yards apart. Then Dad bent over and whispered to Buck, "Get 'em."

Buck ceased his faint whining, put his nose to the ground, and started forward. We walked as careful as possible. Dad and I were on the faint trail, and I tried to walk as close as I could, keeping within arm's reach, keeping my gun up and pointed in the air to the left and trying not to make any noise, watching my feet where I put them so as not to step on any limbs, twigs, or rocks to turn my ankle and taking care to slip around any blackberry brambles or other brushes or bushes that might catch against my clothes, snag me up, or make noise. This was practically impossible since Dad was walking down the main part of the trail and I was off to his left. Sometimes it was necessary to move slightly behind him to get through the brush but immediately when possible I moved up and even in line to the left.

I kept a careful watch to my left to keep an eye on Abel and Isaac and never paid much attention to my right, although I occasionally did to see that we were in line with William and Jacob. In this fashion we moved forward for what seemed like another hour or so. By this point, the sun was coming up enough that you could make out pretty clearly everything around you, at least out to a distance of maybe a hundred yards. Beyond that, it was still too dark to see much. As we moved slowly, stealthily forward, I imagined I was more alert, more in tune with nature than I ever had been.

There. What was that? A brief, melodious chirping, and a soft flutter of wings. But I knew immediately. It was only a cardinal flicking through the branches. My eyes rushed to the spot, and I instantly picked him out as he hopped and flitted from one small branch of the Dogwood tree to the next. Even though the leaves of the Dogwood were a range of deep purple and brilliant red, I had no problem picking out the perfectly camouflaged cardinal. Hey. What was that sharp, barking noise? Now it was followed by an angry scolding chatter. My eyes jerked quickly to the top branches of a large oak, whose leaves were starting to turn brown; there, in the upper limbs, was a large, round nest of leaves and twigs and on the edge of the nest, the angry red squirrel, who was warning us we were now in his territory. Suddenly my eyes rushed to the left, drawn there by the soft, sad coo of a lonesome mourning dove. I had no problem instantly locating him as he sat softly on the dead, dry lower branches of a red cedar tree. Ouch! The back of my Dad's raised hand suddenly connected to the right side of my forehead as he waved backward for me to stop. About that time, Buck, who was never more than ten feet in front of Dad, stopped suddenly, gave his whining noise, and then proceeded to a deep-throated growl but still so soft that it could barely be heard. Dad and I moved up cautiously just behind. Dad looked carefully to the right and managed to make out William and Jacob, and I looked carefully to the left, recognizing Abel and Isaac.

Abel had his bow and arrows. His Dad had the Henry repeating rifle that he had bought and his Colt, and they were in position to the left. William and Jacob were in position to the right. William had his Henry and his Remington revolver, and Jacob had his double-barreled Pennsylvania rifle. This at one time had belonged to Isaac, who had been given it by his father, Abraham, who in turn had received it from my grandfather many years before. Abraham had passed it down to Isaac, who now passed it down to Jacob.

This double-barreled Pennsylvania rifle was rather unique. I hadn't seen one like it anywhere in the countryside where we lived. My grandfather had got it from the trading post that his father-in-law owned years back—I don't know how far back—and had given it to Isaac's father, Abraham. There were two barrels, one over the other, and when the first one was fired, they could be rotated so that the bottom barrel was now on top and it could be fired again. Like I said, my family always believed in having the best weapons available at the time. I think that my grandfather had given it to Abraham because he hadn't been able to afford any handguns. My grandfather had carried a Pennsylvania rifle that he passed down to my father, who used it diligently, cared for it meticulously, and passed it down to me just this spring after they had made the trip to the mouth of the Osage where he had acquired the Henry and Remington revolvers. Grandfather had also carried a large Waters muzzle-loading pistol and a small two-barreled English matchbox pistol.

Moving carefully forward, making no noise and following Buck's lead, we gradually and carefully advanced. Buck was certainly aroused. Dad must have felt that the hogs were close, although I couldn't hear, smell, or see anything. But he whispered to me, "Do what I do, boy, and stay behind me." We advanced carefully. I continued to look left and right to make sure we were in line and saw that William was following slightly behind Jacob and Abel was following behind Isaac. In this fashion, we advanced slowly. Dad would study the ground and seemed to carefully pick out his path. We would move forward, staying behind the biggest tree that we could, and get up to the back of the tree, peek around it carefully, and then slip around the sides in front of it, still keeping in its cover. With the tree directly to our back, we would move forward a short distance and then move left or right to line up behind another big tree that gave us protection as we advanced up behind its cover, got in directly behind it, peeked around, looked carefully, and then slipped around the sides up to the front of it. We would then move slowly forward, carefully and soundlessly, watching our steps and keeping all senses alert. I listened, sniffed, and watched but could sense nothing. We would move forward, suddenly move left or right a few feet to line up behind another big tree, and then advance again.

We did this several times over what seemed like eternity but probably wasn't more than a half hour. Buck, at this point, was staying right next to my father's heels. He wasn't leading, but he wasn't getting behind either. We moved forward slowly, and then my dad raised his hand to indicate stop. I couldn't smell, hear, or see anything, but I knew they were there. At this point, we were directly behind a large tree, and I peeked out to my left, then peeked out to my right, while Dad peeked out to the right. I still really hadn't seen anything, but then I recognized some faint movement. There, maybe thirty to forty yards directly ahead, was a huge old boar. He looked entirely black. This didn't strike me then as being particularly unusual although, thinking about it later, it did because most of our domestic hogs would wallow in the mud along the river and carried a brown layer of dust and dirt on them. I suppose he must have swum across the river at some point in time, washing off all the dirt, and it was still cool enough that he hadn't wallowed in it since then, but there he was, big and black and evil looking. I couldn't take my eyes off of him.

I knew that we weren't going to shoot him. This boar obviously looked dangerous, and besides, he was certainly too big, too tough, and too rank for good eating. I was looking carefully for a smaller hog, one that had been born last year. I could tell about what size that would be since we had hogs at home and you could certainly tell. We sold them off every year once they reached the second summer of their life. I was looking for one about this size, good eating size, but hadn't managed to discern one yet. Dad had explained to us previously that he would fire the first shot no matter what, and no one ever questioned Dad.

I wasn't watching to the left or right at this time. I didn't know whether Isaac, Jacob or William had seen anything or not. It didn't matter about Abel; he was certainly too far away. This big old boar was thirty to forty yards in front of me, and if the hogs were in his immediate vicinity, as Dad had said previously that they would be, since hogs always stay close in packs, then I doubted there would be anything in reach of Abel's bow, especially through this brush.

Abel and I were both excellent shots with the bow, having used those from the time we were old enough to pull one. We had made our own bows that we took great pride in. William's was a good bow but certainly at a distance that probably was more on fifty to sixty yards. Since he was off to our left and diagonal to where the boar was, it was unlikely that he could have hit anything. It was while I was thinking this, peering for the hog that was the proper size to shoot, that Dad's gun suddenly went off, followed immediately by three other shots. I hadn't seen anything to shoot at, hadn't even got a shot, and all of a sudden all heck had broken loose. Hogs were squealing, and you could hear a tremendous racket and crashing in the bushes ahead. There was one other quick shot, and then things were quiet, except for some thrashing and pounding of hoofs up the hills heading away from us.

No one said anything. Dad carefully slipped around the tree to his right. I slipped around the tree to the left and came up within arm's length, the rifle up across my chest, barrel in the air, and started moving forward. Things were quiet. We walked forward carefully for the next thirty yards or so, where, over just the slightest of dips in the ground, I was able to see a nice-sized hog lying still and motionless. I hadn't been able to see any hogs myself, probably because they were just barely out of my sight down below the lip of a bowl-shaped, shallow sinkhole. I had picked out the big boar because he was so big he stood up above it. Isaac, William, and Jacob, being off on each side and on slightly higher ground than Dad and me, since we had been walking up the faint trail that followed the nearly dry creek, obviously had been able to spot them, but to me they had been invisible. I stood there admiring the fine hog my father had shot, and looking left and right, I picked out three others that were closer to Isaac, William, and Jacob and knew that they had all succeeded. Four shots, four hogs, but no, there had been five shots. I looked around carefully but didn't see any others.

For some reason, my eyes seemed to fix on the blackberry thicket immediately to my front. This was maybe fifteen yards in distance, certainly no more. I thought possibly it had run in there and was looking carefully when suddenly my eyes seemed to be drawn to a certain spot. At this point, I couldn't really make out why, but then suddenly I realized what I was seeing were two huge, bright white, shining ivory tusks. Looking slightly above them, I seemed to be staring into the red, beady eyes of that enormous old black boar. It was just as I recognized what I was seeing that suddenly his whole head came into view. I jerked my rifle up, aimed right at the one red beady eye that seemed to be staring directly into my soul, and without thinking or even aiming but seeing only that eye, I fired, and without another moment's thought, I dropped my rifle down to the my left side and snatched at my Ethan Allen Pepperbox. Just as I brought it up and fired, my head seemed to pound with the reverberations of two quick shots from my father's Henry as he seemed to pick up the danger we were in and react. That hog had seemed to keep coming and then suddenly went nose first into the ground, rump over head, and laid still.

I never got off a second shot with the Pepperbox. I had it pointed straight at him, and my eyes were fixed motionless on him. I waited for the slightest tremble, struggle, or attempt to get up and then saw that he slowly seemed to shrink some in size with a faint exhalation of air. He shivered once and let off a horrible stench. I realized he was dead. He had just urinated and passed a stool, shivered, and expired. Now I knew what Dad meant by you could smell them before you could see them, because it certainly was a rank scent, but I had barely noticed it until that moment. It was surprising I could have gotten close as we had and not smelled it.

I hadn't really even seen them or heard them. I certainly never even saw them. Maybe I hadn't been old enough to go hog hunting after all.

I still stood there motionless, hardly daring to breathe, and only moved after Dad walked forward. We walked up side-by-side to the boar's rump, and then Dad walked carefully around to the front, bent over, and looked down. He felt with his fingers at the boar's snout, looked up to me, and said, "Nice shot, son." Only then did I dare to move. I walked around to my right, came up on Dad's left side, and looked down as he pointed and felt at the boar's forehead. "Here's where your shot went, just right in the right eye." Then he pointed to the boar's left eye and said, "Here's where I got him with my first shot, just above the left eye."

Then, looking at him carefully, he stood up and moved back to the shoulder area. The hog at this point was lying on his left side, and he said, "Here's where my second shot got him, right at the joint of the left shoulder."

I replied, "I was aiming for the right shoulder." At that point, you couldn't see whether I had been successful or not, but you could see my Dad's face light up as he beamed down at me.

"Good, boy, good," he said. He had always said that if you were charged by a creature, the first shot should be a killing shot or an attempted killing shot, and any other shots you got should be to break him down, aiming for the shoulders or joints to cripple him so that you could bring them up short before they got to you.

With that event over, we laboriously tried to roll the boar over. My dad was a big man, but even he wasn't having any success with that. At about that time, I noticed that Isaac, Abel, Jacob, and William had come up on each side. I was shocked. I hadn't seen, heard, or smelled them getting close, but suddenly there they were, so close they were slapping me on the back. Isaac and Dad grabbed the boar's legs on the left side that were on the ground, and William and Jacob grabbed the right legs, and we rolled him over. You couldn't really see it, but looking carefully and feeling, we found the spot where my little .36 caliber Pepperbox slug had taken the boar right in the left shoulder joint. The wound from my father's .44 Remington had been easily apparent, but the .36 didn't make nearly as big an impression. Possibly it was because of the size. The .44 slug is what 20 to 25 percent bigger than a .36, and besides the .36 we loaded with twenty grains of powder, but Dad put thirty grains of powder when loading his .44 Remington. The effect was noticeable and obvious, and it convinced me that there was probably more to my dad wanting the Remington than I had realized.

The main thing he complained about the Pepperbox was the fact that it had no sights and couldn't really be aimed; at least he always said it couldn't really be aimed. He had bought it as a last line of defense, always saying that you did your killing with the rifle and only used the Pepperbox when you were out of time and your enemy or game was so close that you couldn't get your rifle loaded. Then you just pointed the Pepperbox in the general direction and blasted off all five shots as fast as possible. The Remington had sights and could be aimed, and Dad said it was pretty much effective in shooting even after thirty and forty yards. However, we had never tried shooting it at that distance, mainly because ammunition was scarce and really could only be obtained in town infrequently, if at all, or else at the trading station my uncle owned, so target practice with it had been impossible.

Dad looked at me again, smiled, and beamed, "Nice shot, boy," and then he was quiet. I think that he was surprised that I had hit where I had aimed. He probably felt it was just a lucky shot. I never bothered to explain that I knew it wasn't luck.

Each of us went to the hogs that had been shot. William and Jacob went to find the ones they got slightly to the right, and Isaac and Abel went to the left. They found four shot hogs, but William insisted that he had shot one other. I thought there had been more than four shots; it seemed like that to me. It really had been hard to tell because it seemed that they all came as one, so it was just a rolling thunderous sound, but then I recalled there had been one other shot a second or two later. William had said after he shot his first hog, he saw another one take out and he had brought his gun up and taken a shot at it. We then went to left and right in a circle, crossing and overlapping each other until on the other side of the blackberry bramble we finally found a trace of blood. Obviously William had been right, he had hit another pig, but it wasn't anywhere to be seen.

Dad looked up at Isaac, and their eyes met. Isaac said, "I reckon I'll go get him." Dad said, "That's fine." Isaac was an excellent tracker. Even Dad wouldn't claim to be any better, and besides, I think Dad felt obligated to take control and direct us into preparing the hogs that we had.

We went back to the other side of the blackberry bramble, went up on each side of the hogs, starting with the smaller ones first, and slit their throats. Then with Abel and Jacob on one side pulling the legs to the left and William and I on the right, we proceeded to gut and clean them. Stretching them out, we made an incision from crotch up to throat, splitting the chest cavity and disemboweling them. After having cleaned the four smaller hogs, we started on the big boar. He certainly was a tough, smelly thing, much more rank than the smaller hogs that we had killed. It was all that we could do to roll him on his back and pull his legs apart so that we could begin to clean him. His skin was so tough that even Dad's sharp hunting knife seemed not to pass through easily. Of course, he had already cleaned four other hogs, and possibly the blade was getting dull. Finally he had split the hog's abdominal and chest cavity and gutted him when Isaac came back carrying the fifth smaller hog that William had shot and that he had already gutted and cleaned out by himself. I knew this was much more difficult to do and commented on it, but Isaac said, "You didn't expect me to carry all that back to the clearing here, did you?"

Dad looked up at me at that moment and said, "Why don't you go start a fire, boy?"

I don't know why he always called me boy. It was either boy or son. Sometimes when he was proud or affectionate, it was son. He usually called me son whenever we went to town and usually called me son when we were at home with mother, seldom calling me by Thomas, but otherwise it was usually boy. When working in the fields, fishing, hunting, or out alone, it was always boy. I suspect that when I got older, he would start calling me Thomas, since he always called William by his first name, and I suspected that Jesse would someday be "the boy."

I immediately rushed off to start the fire like Dad had instructed. I suspected that he wanted to see how quickly I could get it going. First I searched around and found some old dead cedar branches and gathered them up. I gathered up a bunch of dried cedar needles and put them in a big pile. I then took some of the smaller cedar branches and drew out my Damascus-bladed knife that had once belonged to my grandfather. I began whittling off shavings as fast as I could. Once I had a good mound of shavings on top of the pine and cedar needles, I took the smaller twigs of cedar that I had gotten, leaned these over the shavings and needles in a teepee-type fashion, and continued to pile these small twigs in a circular fashion, leaning them up to where they met at the point until I had a good mound of twigs. Then I bent over, knelt down, and took my flint and steel from my accessory pouch, and when Dad wasn't looking, I poured just a half a spout full of black powder from my flask on top of the shavings, put the flask away in the pouch, and struck the flint on the steel. It only took a couple of blows until a glancing spark flew down, hit the powder, and in one quick puff, which I had hoped that Dad hadn't seen or smelled, because he hated wasting black powder, it flared up in the shavings, and my little mound of twigs was rapidly ablaze. I let it burn until it was going good and then placed bigger sticks across it and then followed them up with even bigger sticks, then finally some logs.

It was just at this time that William and Jacob got back to camp with the horses. Dad had previously sent them back down the trail, and I'm sure they hurried and made a lot better time down than we did coming up, moving as slow and carefully as we did hunting. They rode up on their horses, leading the rest, and got down. They took the ropes that had been stashed on the saddles and looped them around the hind legs of the hogs. Then we drug them over, and throwing the ropes over various tree branches, we hoisted the hogs up in the air, tied the ropes off, and let the hogs hang and bleed out as much as possible before heading back to camp.

While we were doing this, I noticed that Dad had been preparing some sharpened sticks. He had been busy prior to that with the hogs, and I hadn't really paid much attention to what he had been doing. Now that they got back with the horses and the saddles, he went to the food pouch that he had left on the saddle. I had thought that we had just had biscuits and ham pretty much in them, but Dad proceeded to remove a small slab of bacon and several onions and, arranging these on a flat rock, he took slices of liver and heart that he had made, placing a piece of bacon on the spit. He spit the bacon at one end of it and pushed it down a few inches, then put on a piece of heart, an onion, some liver, rolled the bacon up and pierced it again and slid the arrangement further down the stick, put on another piece of liver, onion, bacon, and heart, and wrapped the bacon up over this again, pierced it, and laid it on the flat stone surface. He made up maybe a dozen pieces like this and then went to the fire, handing each of us a spit and we sat down around the fire and roasted our lunch. I have never been much for liver, heart was okay, but not my favorite, but there was something about cooking it over the cedar fire with onions and bacon sizzling that made it all taste exceptionally good. We finished our two spits of hog and onion. Then I peeked in the sack and found a piece of ham and some biscuits. I finished off the meal and washed it all down with water from the skin.

We all sat around the fire, kind of laid back on our elbows, and just laughed and talked. William began to brag about what a great shot he had made. He said his first shot had killed the hog dead and had just dropped in place. He had seen the second one take off and brought the gun up and fired once. He knew he had hit it. It swerved off to the left, and he thought it had gone through the blackberry bramble, but apparently it had gone into the blackberries and holed up. I think that it had been in there with the boar; maybe it felt safe with the boar. All the rest of the hogs had headed off for the hills, squealing and thrashing, but this old boar apparently had stayed in the blackberry bramble. No one had shot it before, and I guess it was just like Dad always said, that hog hunting was dangerous and that hogs were unpredictable. They were as apt to charge as not even if they had been shot at or disturbed. Certainly this hog had not been shot. It had run into the brambles, apparently thinking it would hide. Maybe it had only charged when it realized that I had seen it, even though I hadn't really realized what I was seeing at the time. I could still recall just tusks and those beady eyes. I could say I hadn't really realized that it had been a boar until I saw the whole head, but I had only seen the head because he was in full charge at the time. From the time I first saw it until the time it was all over could only have been a couple of seconds. I didn't say it, and no one else did either, but I think that Dad and maybe even Isaac realized that I had got off two shots before Dad got off one.

Maybe they could tell what I was thinking, because about that time Dad looked at me again and said, "Mighty fine shooting, son, mighty fine," and I knew that he was proud. We sat there and talked some more. Abel had said that he thought about taking a shot with his bow at the same hog that his dad was shooting at but then was afraid that if he moved to turn and line the bow up, that maybe he would scare the animals and maybe, if he drew back and held it before Dad shot, he couldn't hold his pull long enough to keep a steady hand, and so he just watched. But he was still profoundly excited and profoundly pleased by the whole adventure. After resting here for about an hour or so, letting the hogs hang and drain, Dad said, "Well, it's time to go."

I got up and poured what was left of the water in the waterskin over the fire. I kicked it apart and stomped on the embers, poured some more water from Jacob's skin over it, and then went to help them as they maneuvered the horses under the pigs still hanging from the tree, lowered them down across the rump of the horse, and secured them to the saddle and cinched them under the horse's belly with ropes around their feet. The old boar was much too big for any horse to carry. Dad said he probably weighed four hundred pounds. Certainly it was the biggest hog I had ever seen. He was much bigger than Roscoe, and with that, the thought went through my head that if this hog weighed four hundred pounds, those Greek hogs from Caledonia must certainly be huge. It had pressed upon me again how brave those old Greeks were to hunt such creatures with bows and arrows. It also dawned upon me how maybe they only hunted out of necessity. I think that the only reason they went after that Caledonian boar was the fact that it was more or less a case of self-defense.

I wondered what we were going to do about getting that old boar back to camp, but Dad had sent Isaac off, who returned with two long, fifteen-foot cedar poles.

He chose my horse. Taking one pole, he put the smaller end up next to my saddle, and with some rope, he tied it to the leather above the right shoulder. Then with some more rope, he tied the pole to the back cinch about mid-part of the belly of my horse. I think he chose my horse because it was the oldest and tamest animal in the bunch and possibly also because I was the lightest person in the group. I then adjusted the pole on the left side of the horse. Finally we took some rope and tied the cedar poles together in several places throughout their length, down to about two feet above the ground. At last we managed to get the hog by each leg and drag him up and onto the travois. Then we tied his back legs to the cedar poles on each side of the horse's rump, and we were ready to go.

I decided not to try to ride my horse back but elected to lead it. I had never drug a travois before. I felt certain that the old mare was calm enough she wouldn't get excited by the hog or by the poles rubbing or beating against her flank, but I wasn't comfortable about that even. Besides, I figured she was actually old enough that she didn't need to be carrying all that weight, and anyways, I was much too excited. I just didn't feel like riding.

Father took the lead, and Isaac followed. Abel and I were one behind the other, followed in the rear by Jacob and William. In this fashion, we headed back down the faint game trail that we had been following and came out down along the banks of the Osage where we had started. We were still on the north or west side of the river, and we stayed on it and followed it back to the cabin.

Along the way, it seemed that I could take in all the detail that had been missed on the way up. It turned out to be a bright, sunny day, although it was still exceedingly cold. It was only mid-September. Usually it didn't seem to get this cold until mid-October or so. I expected that's why we had gone hog hunting earlier than usual. The trees were just starting to turn good. The sycamores were bright and golden yellow. The redbud and dogwood trees were taking on their usual reddish hues. The redbuds were pretty much all red-leafed, but the dogwoods were purplish reddish on the edges but still green in the center. The sumac and some of the other shrubby bushes had gone bright red. The oaks and hickories were starting to turn golden yellow but still had a good degree of green in them. Some had actually gone brown. As expected, the walnuts when we passed them had already become completely brown, and several were lacking most of their leaves.

Passing along the bank, looking across the river, I was just constantly amazed by the beauty of the Ozarks where we lived. I could think there was no finer place at all. Off to the right was the Osage river, rumbling clean and cold over the rocky bottoms, and closest to the river was a profoundness of blackberry bushes and other bushy, thorny plants. Large clumps of bushes, weeds, and wild hemp lined the banks in places, but we kept farther north or west, closer to the face of the bluffs where here there was little underbrush and a well-defined game trail, actually more of a hunting trail. I had never been far to the west, but I suspected this road, if that's really what it was, path was more like it, was traveled by people following the Osage east and west. There were keelboats that went up and down the river, but most didn't go any further up than Osage except for us. The Osage actually became too shallow and rocky not far from where we lived, but nevertheless, it was a good means of travel further west where it opened out of the Ozarks mountains into rolling plains and more open ground. Over sixty, seventy miles or so west, the ground was open, and I knew that people went north and south a lot easier there since there weren't as many trees and no mountains or ravines, and the bluffs were easier to maneuver through.

We followed on down the Osage and came in closer to our farm. We passed the mouth of the canyon that my grandfather had enclosed with a split rail fence and reinforced on each side with Osage orange bushes, all except for the gate area. It was a unique design that my grandfather had come up with. He had chosen the valley because it was open pretty much only at the two ends—where it came out at the Osage and where it came out several miles further north. It could be entered and exited relatively easily only in these two places. Here he had first put a split rail fence by taking rails and stacking them in a zigzag fashion, one upon the other, enclosing it to the center from each side. Then at the apex of each angle, he pounded posts through to keep the rails from being dislodged, either in or out. Then he planted Osage orange saplings.

There was an expression that was commonly used in those days about how an Ozark orange hedge would be cattle high, hog tight, and man tough or something like that. It's amazing how I had heard it several times but couldn't seem to remember just how it actually went. I knew it had something to do with the fact that the hedge would be high enough that cattle couldn't jump and tight enough a hog couldn't work its way through, but I don't know what man-proof meant necessarily, or maybe it wasn't man-proof. He built these at each end of the canyon and any place that he thought was easy enough that cattle could maneuver up and get out. It had taken him years to accomplish this. He had done the same further downstream right next to our cabin. Our cabin was in a little saddle on the low end of the bluff, which came kind of like a finger down between two canyons on the big bend of the Osage. I say big bend because we had two big bends right next to the property but Dad typically called this the big bend.

On each side of our house was a canyon. The one that we were passing now, where the cattle were, was easily three times as large as the other, but the one that was east of our house is where we kept the horses. Our grandfather had built the same split rail, hedge apple type fence to block it in, and we kept the horses there. That's also where we kept our milk cow, as well as the few goats, sheep, and donkeys we owned. This was because it was closer to the house and easier for us to get to the animals and also because grandfather felt like the horses were more valuable and more apt to be stolen.

With our cabin on the west end of the bluff and Isaac's cabin directly across from ours about two hundred yards and somewhat downstream in the canyon, people would have been foolish to come close to where we kept the horses. Because of that, with old Buck and the other couple of dogs we kept at our house, and the dogs Isaac kept at his, we felt secure with this arrangement. We had a third quite small little canyon that grandfather had boxed in at each end, in which we kept the hogs. Through the center of each of these canyons, a small creek ran. The one where the hogs were at was more of a trickle. It couldn't be called a creek, it's more of a trickle, but the other two were a foot deep and three or four feet wide at most times. This ensured that our animals had a sufficient supply of water all year round.

As I said, we passed the canyon where we kept the cattle and soon came upon our farmstead. We passed by the tanning hut, passed by the grindstone, and came up to the cabin. Directly behind the cabin was the root cellar somewhat west of this, but behind the cabin also was the smokehouse. The outhouse was more in front of the cabin but also off to the west, while the corncrib and dry storage hut were off to the east and back of the cabins.

As we came in sight of the cabin, Dad let out a loud yell, and my mother, two sisters, and brother came hurrying out to see the results of our little expedition. Everyone was excited and babbling, talking about the hogs, amazed by the size of the boar, and just pleased to have us back. Mother looked at Father and gave him her knowing look, and you could see the disapproval that was still in her eyes. She said, "I thought you weren't going to shoot any boars."

Dad simply replied, "We had to." Mother's eyes widened even more. She knew what that meant, but she didn't say anything.

We took the hogs over next to the rack, where we cleaned and prepared animals. What I meant by this is that we had a couple of posts pounded deep in the ground with a crossbeam supported across this, and we threw the ropes of the hogs up over the crossbeam. We pulled them up to where they came from the back of the horses hanging by their feet with their heads just a couple of feet off the ground and tied them off there. There was only room for four, so we took the other hog and the boar to a big chestnut tree that grew closer to the river, and throwing the ropes over the strongest limbs, we hoisted them up there to hang. Then we got down to work.

I was still so excited that all I wanted to do was talk and tell everybody about the big adventure, but I knew that would wait for later. Now we had business to attend to. While we had been gone, Mother had been busy getting everything ready. She had taken the big iron pots out of storage and had lit fires in the front yard around them and filled them with water. She had set up the tables in the yard and gotten out the meat grinders and the casings and her ingredients for sausage making. Now everyone stood around and waited to get started.

After we had the hogs hanging and adjusted at the proper length, we began the food preparation. We made a circular cut around the top of the hams on each leg, front, and back, and then began peeling the skin from the back of the rump, down over the flanks, and toward the head. My younger brother, Jesse, and I would hold on each side of the skin diligently while Dad, carefully using his skinning knife, fleshed the skin from the big old boar. He said he felt that it was important to get him skinned so he could start to cool as soon as possible. This was one of the reasons why they didn't like to hunt big boars. Dad always said that the hams were too big to get a good cure on and their skin was so tough, they seemed to get hot a lot sooner than anything else, and there was a good chance of them spoiling before you were done. This was also the reason why we only hunted hogs, or anything else, for that matter, that we were planning to preserve for the coming winter late in the fall after things had gotten cool.

It had warmed up slightly. It was probably mid-afternoon, two or three o'clock, and we were in somewhat of a hurry to get things done as soon as possible. Still, I don't think it was much more than the mid-forties. We got the skin off the boar about the same time that William and Jacob and Isaac and Abel got theirs skinned. Dad said, "Take the skins down and put them in the urine barrel in the tanning hut, boy," and I did. The tanning hut was built farthest to the west away from anything else, probably because it smelled all the time. It wasn't just the animal skins, but it was the barrels of urine.

I'm not sure that anybody else tanned hog hides in this fashion, but my Dad did. Throughout the months or so preceding the hunt, we had a couple of forty- to fifty-gallon barrels that we would use to store urine. The fresh hides that had been skinned off the hogs were taken down and put in the urine barrels and left overnight before we took them out to the log that we used to scrape them. I hated scraping urine-soaked hog's hides, but that's what we did. Dad said the urine would help to loosen up the hair on the hog and also would help soften any flesh or membranes attached to the inner surface of the hide. Skinning the hogs the way we did was a rather difficult preparation. A lot of people would kill the hogs and throw them in boiling water first to help loosen the hide before they fleshed it off the animals, but we didn't have any containers big enough to scald the whole hog in, and so we had to laboriously scrape the hide off from the pigs while they were still hanging. This was a rough job and left a fair amount of flesh and membranes on the inside of the skin, as well as all the hair that was on the outside. Dad said that soaking them for twenty-four hours or so helped to loosen the skin and the hair and help it come off. I'm not sure just how well that actually worked because scraping and cleaning the hides after that was a laborious process, but that's what we did.

After having skinned the hog out while he was still hanging from the frame, we removed the lard casing. That's the fat that holds the intestine. We threw it into the large pot so it could be rendered into lard. Then we made a cut down the middle of the back into the backbone and sliced over each side of the backbone. Then we took the hog down from the frame and laid it on the plank bar, removed the head, and spreading the body cavity open, divided it on each side of the backbone to split the hog in half. Then we cut the two halves into three pieces, separating the shoulder from the ribs and the ribs from the loin. Then we sliced off the piece for the bacon and took it down into the root cellar, rubbed it down good with salt, and left it. We also took the hams down on the plank table in the root cellar and covered them and rubbed them down good all over with salt. These were the cuts that we intended to smoke and preserve for the coming winter. The tenderloin as well as whatever other lean meat that we had, mother would cook to make into sausage.

While we were busy butchering the hogs, mother took the sections of rib cage and covered them with a mixture of one-third molasses, one-third honey, and one-third cider vinegar and put them over the fire to cook. The tantalizing smell of barbecuing ribs was something that caused my mouth to water with anticipation, but it would be a while yet before we could eat.

While we were still butchering and fixing to cure the meats, Moses, Isaac's other son, arrived. Moses lived with his two sisters, Sarah and Miriam, on the edge of town, where they ran a small restaurant and laundry service. It was usually them to whom we sold our domesticated hogs and any other game that we had when it was in abundance and we felt we couldn't preserve and care for it properly. They greatly appreciated all the fresh meat. The ribs and other cuts of meat we didn't feel were needed, Moses loaded up and took back to town with him, intending to pay father and Isaac later in cash money after they had served the freshly prepared pork to the townspeople who frequented their little restaurant.

Isaac had several other sons and daughters, some of whom I had never even met, but they had elected to follow their cousins downstream to Jefferson City and to places beyond. Of all Isaac's children, only Jacob, Moses, Sarah, and Miriam had chosen to stay around Osceola and our farm. Jacob's cabin was in the flat ground bordered by the big bend and sat on a small rise about six hundred yards across from our cabin and a bit east.

The ribs were cooking up nicely. We had finished with most of the butchering. The meat that mother was planning on making into sausage we had taken down to the river, placed in baskets, and set the baskets to soak in the cold Osage River water. This water was usually always extremely cold because it was spring fed from several places, one being right where our cabin was; but there were other springs just a little bit further upstream. Even in the warmest of weather, the water was cold, and with the week's chilly temperatures never getting much above forty, the water seemed even colder than usual. We suspended the closed baskets with rope into the water and let them soak for the next hour or two, having done this with several repeated trips during the process of the butchering. The baskets that had been soaking for the longest, about two hours or so, we brought back up to the house, where mother and my sisters, along with Rebecca, Isaac's wife, Abel and I began grinding the sausage. We used tenderloin as well as any other strips of exceedingly lean pork ground it up and then re-ground it into smaller pieces and then ground in the fat. Mother always insisted that the best balance was about one-third fat to two-thirds of exceedingly lean meat.

After having ground the meat and fat, mother would take and mix in the salt, some ground dried sage, ground black and red pepper, some ground cloves, nutmeg, and a little bit of sugar. This was one of her favorite recipes, but she liked to experiment. Sometimes she had mixed in onion and garlic, sometimes with the salt and pepper. Sometimes she would add thyme with the onions and pepper, and sometimes I think she just threw in a mixture of anything that had done well in the herb garden that year.

A good portion of the sausage that she fixed up, we placed down in the root cellar, spreading it out thin so it could cool and intending for it to sit and cool overnight. Others of the sausage she cooked and browned nicely and put in crocks, covered with a layer of several inches of melted lard, and then covered that with the lid with the rubber seal and fastened it securely before putting it in the root cellar. The lard, when it cooled, would solidify and form a seal, and this sausage would stay reasonably fresh for several months. The sausage that was intended to be placed in the gut casings and smoked was felt to last longer, even a year or two.

It was hard work, but it went faster because the whole family was together doing it. Father, mother, my two sisters, and my two brothers and Isaac's whole family worked side by side. We laughed and joked and kidded around. Mother had taken a big pot of green beans to boil, threw some hog jowls and onions in, and between ribs and green beans and biscuits that she had made that morning, we ate to our hearts' content.

By this time, it was getting really quite dark, but father insisted that we pick up any scraps or any remains and clean up the yard, then take these down in baskets to feed the domesticated hogs. Abel and I made several trips the nearly half mile down and across the creek in front of Abel's house and then down the east bank of the Osage to the hog pen and threw the bones and any other remnants to them. Hogs had no qualms about eating other hogs, and everybody was full and content.

We made our way back up to the cabin, but mother wouldn't allow us to go up and go to bed without washing first, so we went to the room, removed our clothes, grabbed a towel, and went down to the river for a quick dip. Standing in water knee-deep, we soaped up and then dove in and swam a few short laps. We came back and got our towels and walked back to the cabin and went to our rooms for bed.

Our cabin was actually divided into three main sections. The section where my mother and father lived had been originally built by my grandfather, and as his family grew, another similar cabin was made just west, straight in line with that and separated by about twelve to thirteen feet by a breezeway. The only doors to the cabin faced each other, east and west, directly across from each other.

When my dad was young, he and his brothers had slept in the west cabin. Their sisters had slept upstairs in a loft of the west cabin. The east cabin had been for my grandfather, Aaron, and his wife, Angelique. Later, when my parents were married and after my grandmother had died, grandfather gave the east cabin to them and he moved into the west cabin and shared that with my brothers and sisters. The girls, for some reason, were always given the loft to sleep in. I don't know whether it was because the loft was felt to be safer or because it was felt to be warmer in the winter, but the girls were always allowed to sleep in the loft. But that was okay; the loft was also a lot hotter during the summer.

Sometime fifteen or sixteen years ago, Dad had built a roof and sidewalls enclosing the breezeway. It was left open, from about waist high up to the roof line, but had big shutters that could be raised and lowered to close in the sides in bad weather. In warm weather, Mother did most of the cooking on the fireplace in the breezeway and raised the shutters up to where it essentially opened to air on two sides. During the winter, most all the cooking was done in the fireplace in the east cabin. There wasn't a fireplace in the west cabin, so in the wintertime we often got quite cool, but we would usually put on our warm bed clothes in the east cabin, run across the hall to the west cabin, and dive quickly under the covers. So, it didn't really matter much if it had heat or not. Once you were under the covers, you were warm.

I remembered thinking about this as I went back across to the west cabin, and put on some light nightclothes. I put the wet towel on the hook to dry and crawled into bed to go to sleep. It had been a great adventure that day, and as I lay there, I was thinking I wouldn't have any problems going to sleep since I was tired to the point of exhaustion. But somehow a thought that had subconsciously nagged at me all day came, uninvited, to my mind. I had imagined that I had been acutely aware of everything as we had hunted along the trail through the woods. I had recognized every sound and every disturbance around me, and I had been quick to visualize its cause. But why was I looking for cardinals, doves, or squirrels?

I had known instantly from the sound alone; why was I looking to spot them? We were hunting hogs, not birds. After Father's upraised hand had so abruptly stopped me, it had taken a few seconds for me to spot that old boar even though he was in plain sight. And worse, I had never sensed the other hogs, even though I knew they must be close. I had been surprised, when the shooting started, to find they had been that close!

I couldn't believe that I hadn't smelled, heard, or seen them. And worst of all, I should have known exactly where they were. The way the ground straight ahead, and off to each side, sloped down and to the center should have told me that we were on the lip of a broad, bowl-shaped sinkhole. And especially from the way Buck was acting, it should have been obvious right where the other hogs were. Maybe I wasn't such a good hunter after all.

CHAPTER 3

I awoke the next day feeling pleasantly tired and still somewhat sleepy. I was wide awake but seemed to lack the ambition to get up. As I lay there, I suddenly realized how much later in the morning it was than I had expected. Usually we were up just as soon as it started to turn light and were busy doing chores, but it was now definitely a bright morning, and still we hadn't been roused up for chores.

I hustled up and woke up William and even Jesse, who was still apparently sound asleep, and we hurriedly dressed and rushed over to our parents' cabin. My sisters had already gotten up and slipped down from the loft above us and were over there, having already eaten breakfast.

When we came in, my dad looked up and smiled and said, "About time you boys made it up."

Mother started sitting plates of hot biscuits and fresh sausage, gravy, and fried eggs on the table for us, and we slowly started to consume breakfast. Usually breakfast was somewhat of a hurried affair, but this morning it seemed very relaxed and at ease. We ate slowly and talked and chatted. My dad seemed to be in a particularly good mood, and Mother, who had been rather sullen for the last day or two after Dad had announced we were going hog hunting, was quite cheerful and smiling and beaming happily.

We had a very relaxed breakfast and then went outside to finish up with whatever chores were left from yesterday. We went down into the root cellar where we had placed the hams, shoulders, and sausage and other meats for curing. We had given them a rubdown with salt the day before, being very careful to work the salt into any open place where the meat was exposed. The large hams and cuts from the boar Dad had slit down the inside from top to bottom to open the meat up down to the bone, and we had thoroughly rubbed salt in this area. Usually we didn't do that with hams, but he said the large cuts were needed to get the salt to the center of the hams so they could cure. Some people actually skin the hams, but we, at least on the smaller hogs, always left the skin on. The larger boar, we had peeled the skin from the hams at the time we initially skinned him, and this was to let it cool quicker and also to get the salt through that old thick hide better.

We rubbed every piece of meat down with another layer of salt. Salt was hard to come by, and Dad insisted that we not waste any, and so every day for the next week or so, we would go down and rub salt over every layer and every inch of exposed meat. In a few days, we would be lighting up the fires in the smoke house to let it heat up and dry out so that we could start smoking the meat.

Then we turned to the sausage. We loaded it up and took it outside, where my mother and the girls had set up the meat grinders on the plank table, and we re-ground it to make it finer and also to mix the herbs in better. Then we started stuffing the casings. We would stuff the casings, then twist them every foot or so and tie it off tightly with twine or cord and then take the sausage back to the root cellar to hang up for the next couple of days until we decided to smoke them. Usually we would smoke sausage in two or three days, then maybe a week or ten days later, after the salt had a chance to set, we would hang the hams and shoulders up to smoke them also.

The next week or two we would be busy curing and smoking the meat, in addition to our other chores. We finished up salting, stuffing, and hanging the meat about one in the afternoon. Then we cleaned everything up and put it away and gathered up any remnants to take to the hogs.

The afternoon was a leisurely affair. All the boys went down to the river for a swim. The big bend in the river, as we called it, was shallow, and this made for a nice ford, being no more than three feet at the deepest and having a very rocky bottom, which allowed us to cross from the north to the south side. About a mile south, downstream, the river made another bend to the east at the base of a steep, high bluff. Here the rushing water had scoured out a deep hole, and this is where we preferred to go to swim. We could climb the bluffs and swing out or jump into the deep water. Just how deep it was, I'm not sure. I know that it was quite deep. It was all that I could do to dive to the bottom and then get back up to the top with one breath, but we had never actually measured it. I suspected it was a good twenty to twenty-five feet deep. At that time it seemed to me to be almost a terrifying depth to descend into, because near the bottom it was black and you could imagine any type of creature living there. It's strange the things you can imagine when you're young.

The day was quite uneventful. After swimming, we went back home and while it was still light, cleaned and oiled our guns. Surprisingly, yesterday Dad hadn't insisted, as he usually did, that that be the first thing we do when we got home. I suspect it was because I had only fired one shot through the rifle and one shot through the Pepperbox and they had only fired a couple of shots each through their weapons. Probably they had cleaned theirs and just hadn't mentioned the fact that I had forgotten to clean mine. But having given the guns an oiling and having removed the lead from the Pepperbox and unloaded it, I placed them back up on the pegs next to the fireplace.

I had no sooner put my guns up when there was a light knock on the door followed, almost immediately, by a faint rustling noise as the door opened and Abel came storming in. He was carrying his bow and arrows, and since Dad had no further chores lined up for us just then, he agreed that we could go practice—as long as we took Jesse. I rushed over to the west cabin and got my bow and quiver, and the three of us headed down to the ford, crossed over the Osage, and came to the flat ground around the tobacco barn. Along the north side of the barn, which was walled down to the ground, we had set up several straw stuffed gunny sacks as targets. Abel and I each selected our separate targets and carefully aimed and released one arrow after another, till we had each fired ten. Then we approached the targets to retrieve our arrows and compare results. Each target had three different bull's-eyes to aim at since we didn't want to fire too many arrows at the same spot and take the chance of splitting a perfectly good arrow. We laughed and joked about whose arrows were closest. Abel insisted that he had won, and I think he had but wouldn't admit it. Then we walked back and fired another ten arrows, this time left-handed. When we checked the results, I had definitely won.

Jesse had been insisting that he be allowed his turn and had been very patient about it. So we moved closer, to where he could hit, and let him have his turn. Abel and I took turns trying to teach him how to hold the bow, place the arrow, pull the string to the exact same point, and sight before quickly and smoothly releasing. Over the last year, we had practiced often with Jesse while he used a small bow that Dad had once made. Now he insisted that he was six years old and wanted to use the bigger bow. He insisted on using Abel's bow, which surprised me. I think Jesse knew how proud Abel was of his bow, and nothing else would do. He was only six, but he was strong enough to bend the bow enough to flip an arrow fifteen feet or so. He often hit the target but not hard enough to stick the arrow.

We let him shoot till he was tired of it then moved back and shot several more groups of ten arrows ourselves. Then we finished up taking turns as one would throw a sawdust and wood chip bag as the other tried to hit it. We always made sure the wall of the barn was in line to serve as a backstop so we didn't lose any arrows. Our practice arrows had metal "Bodkin points," as Dad called them, because our flint-tipped hunting arrowheads would break against the barn. Chipping arrowheads was a pain! That's why we always used the metal tips for practice. As he watched us, Jesse became quite excited and insisted on trying to hit a tossed target but couldn't come close, so we persuaded him to try for the targets again. Again we coached him on how to carefully draw the string back to the same precise point, keep the left arm straight, sight down the arrow, and fire. This was the same technique that Dad had impressed on us when we were learning. Practice, practice, practice. You had to be precise in technique, and only after thousands upon thousands of shots did it become automatic and instinctive.

Both Abel and I were capable of drawing, aiming, and firing without apparent thought. We insisted that eventually Jesse would also be able to do it. Abel flexed his biceps and laughingly told Jesse, "Just feel these. When you are old enough to have muscles like these, you won't have any problems shooting pigeons out of the air." And with this prompting, we immediately got into a wrestling match to see who was strongest, with Jesse throwing himself on top of us, as Abel and I tumbled and rolled across the ground. Only after we were thoroughly worn out did we head back to the cabin and were sent straight back to the river to clean up by my mother, who wouldn't let us eat before we had bathed. Shortly after we returned, we were joined by Isaac, Jacob, and the rest of his family. We had supper, and that evening we sat around in the breezeway between the two cabins until quite late, using the light from the candles to visit and talk . This was our last day of leisure. The next day we were up at the crack of dawn again. Dad felt we had gotten behind on the farm work. We went down and turned and rubbed the salt on the meat cuts again, ate breakfast, and then crossed over the river and started working the fields. We went through the tobacco field and flipped the tobacco stalks that had already been cut and were laying to do their preliminary drying from front to back so that they could dry better. We usually let them dry in the field for several days before the final backbreaking job of actually storing them in the tobacco barn.

This was one job that I truly hated. Hanging tobacco was backbreaking work. First we would go through the fields with oak stakes about six feet long. The younger kids would go through and drop the stakes about every six or seven tobacco stalks and then the older children or the adults would follow along, take the stakes, plant them on an angle in the ground, then fix a little spear tip to the stake and pick up the stalks and impale them on the oak stakes. Working them down to near the ground, usually six or seven stalks were put on. You needed to leave a little bit of space between the stalks so they could dry, and you needed to have something that you could actually lift. After having walked through the whole field and impaling all the stalks on the oak stakes, then we would hitch up the wagons to the mules, go through and lift the racks of tobacco, place them on the wagon, haul them to the barn, and then, through a rather ingenious and laborious method, hang them up to dry.

The tobacco barn was maybe twenty-five feet long and twenty feet wide and maybe as high as thirty feet in the center. The roof's line sloped down gradually for half its length and then angled down steeply toward the ground. Ours was left open, at least below the roof line on each end. Between the roofs, up in the apex, it was boarded in to keep rain from blowing through, but the idea was mainly to let the tobacco hang in a dry place where it could get a lot of breeze to let the green leaves dry out and age and cure.

Usually Dad would drive the wagon and the rest of us would work from the back of it. Driving the wagon through in the center of the building first, we all would climb up on the back of the wagon, grasp the rails that were affixed to the rafters, and clamber up to the top of the barn. The rafter beams were about three to four feet apart. They were also about four feet above one another, and so climbing up and bracing our feet with legs spread wide on the rafter beams, and holding with one hand to the rafter beam above us, we formed a pyramid of young boys and strong backs.

Dad usually took the impaled tobacco stalks, handed them to the person above, who passed them to the person above him and so on up to the man on the top where the stalks would then be settled on the rafter beams. The man on the top had the least amount of work because he would only get one out of every seven or eight stakes. Obviously the man on the back of the wagon did most of the heavier lifting and also suffered most of the grief. Not that there were any serious accidents doing this—it's just that occasionally stalks of tobacco slipped off the stake and would fall on the person below. Certainly all the dust and dirt and small insects showered down continuously on the lower people. The people on the top rafters main worry, besides the height and flimsy rafter beams, were the occasional wasp nest that would be hanging from the ceiling. Bumping into a wasp nest while busily engaged in hanging tobacco thirty feet in the air was not an occurrence that was pleasant to anticipate.

Usually the youngest, lightest, and probably weakest were assigned the higher places. Maybe that's why it seemed that for several years I had always been at the very top. I expected when it got to be time to hang the tobacco this year that maybe Jesse would be top man, but he was probably still too small to handle it.

We had finished turning the tobacco in the fields, and then it was time to go back to the house to grind the sugarcane. We had finished a day before the hog hunt with cutting all the sugarcane and taking it across the river to the cane press that Dad had set up here. The cane press could be taken down and moved from one place to the other, and Dad frequently would take it to neighbors' houses to help them press their cane.

He chose a relatively flat area on the north side of the ford to set it up. He had one of the old mules tied on one end of the sweep, and the boys made continual trips back and forth to the corncrib to bring down the stalks for pressing. I called it the corncrib, but it was kind of a universal outbuilding. It was similar to the tobacco barn but not as high and not as big. We used it to store corn, primarily, in a similar fashion to drying tobacco. Once the corn had been harvested from the field, the husks were pulled back off of the ears and tied together while still green over some stakes made of oak, naturally, and then were hoisted up into the top of the barn, and hung from rafters to dry.

We had finished harvesting and hanging the corn a couple of weeks before that and had cut the sugarcane and stacked it a few days after having hung the corn. We had put it in the corncrib, where it would be protected from any moisture, and had intended to take it for pressing within a couple of days of actually cutting it. I think possibly it was because of the cold temperatures and desire to go hog hunting that we had put off pressing the cane for a day or two longer than usual, but now we carried it in small lots down to where Dad had set up the press and watched as he fed the sugarcane stalks between the rollers and watched the syrup roll out and dribble slowly down the spout and into the barrels. It was our job to keep the stalks coming and take the pressed stalks away, hauling them down and across to feed to the hogs on the other side of the river, and keep the barrels coming, removing them as they were filled and replacing them with empty barrels and sealing the lids on the barrels all in one continuous and unbroken process so that Dad's job was to keep feeding these stalks through the grindstones.

We worked late into the evening doing this and quit just in time for supper again. There was always some work to be done on the farm, always something to be harvested, canned, dried, hung, plowed, hoed, or cultivated. But still I remember it as the happiest time in my life. Things were good, and nothing could be better. We lived in pretty much isolation. True, there was a town eight or ten miles away, but we would go for usually several weeks without seeing or talking to anyone except for Isaac's family, who lived directly across the river to the east and his son, Jacob, or his other son, Moses, who came from town every few days, probably about twice a week, looking for anything that we had to sell to feed the clients at their little café and guest house in town.

We all worked hard and were a close-knit little family. Besides my older brother, William, and my younger brother, Jesse, Abel was probably my best friend. In fact, I think he was actually my best friend. We were roughly the same age and, when working in the fields, usually we were side by side. Any free time we had, was usually spent by Abel and I swimming in the river or hunting, tracking, or trapping together. I had told him everything I thought, and he pretty much always told me how he felt and any of his little life's concerns.

Right now we didn't have much free time, although whenever we had a chance to talk, usually in the evening before bed, we would make plans for what we were going to be doing in the next few days. Abel was informing me that he was planning on working on his bow further. A few years ago, we had decided to make our own Indian bows. Dad had told us how this was done years before and we had watched as he had made one for himself and one for William and we had begun the process ourselves. I had chosen red cedar for my bow. I liked the looks, the contrasting colors of white and red, but Abel had been more conservative, choosing a standard hickory tree to make his bow.

We had cut the six-inch trees and let them age for a couple of months, trimmed them down, and split them and begun the laborious process of shaving and tillering the bow. I thought we had done a surprisingly good job. I thought our bows looked well enough, if not perfect, but Abel had decided that his was too primitive. Abel had elected to make a perfect bow. He had taken the time, and the trouble, a couple of months ago, to ask me to help him recurve the bow. I had watched carefully as he dug about a foot-deep trench in the ground, lined it with pebbles from the river, poured water to cover the pebbles, and then tamped in about an inch of dirt on top of the pebbles. Then he placed his bow, which we had worked so hard to fashion and which I felt was an achievement in itself, on top of the ground, covered it with another layer of dirt and pebbles, poured in a little more water, and then raked hot embers from the fire that he had built a foot or two away, over the entire trench.

I watched, amazed, thinking that surely that would wreck the bow. I had not seen this done before. Dad had described doing it, but it sounded too risky to me. After a few hours of letting it steam, he had taken the bow, and this is where I was able to help. He had placed it centered on a limb about the size of his upper forearm, and under each tip, he placed about a thumb-sized stick. Then he stepped on the precious bow, centering his feet between each of the logs, which supported the bow as I took a wet rag and sponged down the bow from a bucket of cold water from the river. I kept this up until we felt that the wood was entirely cooled, and then Abel gingerly and carefully stepped off to admire the result. I was amazed that it had actually worked.

We let it set for a day or two and then had tested it out by re-stringing it and shooting it. It required a little bit of work, a little bit of shaving on the tillering board, but surprisingly, it shot as good as ever. While we sat around this evening, after working in the fields, he was talking about backing the bow with sinew and planed on even painting and decorating it. My thought was to leave well enough alone, but Abel always was a very inventive and creative person, and if there was anything that you could do to make something better, he was all for it. Thus, we had spent the last few days working in the fields, playing, and socializing in the evenings.

Dad announced it was time to go to bed, and as we slowly got up to hustle off to our rooms, and Abel and his family started to walk back to their cabin across the river, Dad had said that we should be planning on getting up early in the morning to travel in to Osceola. We hadn't been into town for well over a month. It was hard to believe, but it was probably closer to two. Mother liked to take time every third or fourth week to go in to attend a meeting and church at the little community of Osceola.

Once a month after the morning church services, they would have a community lunch. We had missed the last one. It had been necessary to skip church at this time to proceed with the harvesting of all the various crops, but it appeared that things were under control at this time, and Mother was quite insistent that we would be heading into church and planning on having the lunch social tomorrow.

I certainly looked forward to attending church. It's not so much the preaching and the exhortations to good living that we got, but after church there was always the lunch social and a chance to talk with other boys living in the vicinity, play games, and admire the young girls. The last few meetings admiring the girls had seemed to be more important than playing games, and at this point in time, I didn't think that there was anything that I would be more interested in.

CHAPTER 4

The following morning, we woke up early. Dad and William went to hitch the mules to the wagon, Abel and I rounded up a couple of extra horses to saddle, and mother fixed breakfast while we got ready for the trip to town. With the wagon hitched and the horses saddled, we ate a quick breakfast and then were off. William and Jacob decided to ride. Isaac, Rebecca, Mom and Dad, and the girls rode in the wagon, but Jesse, Abel, and I took the canoe. I thought it was much more fun to paddle to town in the canoe. It was shorter, and you never know what adventures you would have along the way, but we all planned on meeting up once we got to town.

We had had to get up early to head out to town because the church services started about nine. None of us owned a watch, so it was only a guess as to what time it actually was. Mother hated to be late and was absolutely insistent that we get started early, so usually we were there long before service started. By wagon it was about a ten-mile trip.

To get to Osceola from our house was kind of an adventure of itself. I preferred to go by canoe, but the times that we had gone by wagon were equally exciting. We would cross the ford at the big bend, head south around the bend to where Coon creek came in to the Osage, and head east from there. We crossed the Osage just below where the Sac River made the sharp, snake-like turns before entering the Osage, and then came to Osceola from the south side of the river. On these journeys, Dad remarked continuously how when he was young there was nothing between our house and Osceola. In fact, at one point in time when grandfather had first settled there, there weren't any other people even living at Osceola or in the vicinity; at least that's what I had been told. But on these trips by wagon, Dad would remark continuously whenever we came across a small farm or even a plowed field or met people on the road at how things were developing, how many people were moving in, and how the area was prospering. I myself hadn't been able to notice this and hadn't been aware of the changes that Dad had seen over the years. It seemed to me that even on my first trip into Osceola, most of these farms had been present, although I could definitely tell the changes that had occurred in Osceola itself.

When we had arrived in town, Dad liked to point out the different buildings and relate stories about them. He would never fail to point out an old log building that he said had been the first hotel built in the area. He was quite proud of the courthouse that had been built down the street a short way from this. It was two-storied, one of the few two-story buildings I had ever seen that actually had a complete upper floor. Our cabins had lofts in them, but you couldn't stand up in the lofts, and they didn't occupy the whole roof line. This had two complete stories and even an attic-type area on top. It was made of frame lumber and had a tin roof, and there was a picket fence around the courthouse in which people often gathered to sit and talk. Further down the street he liked to point out the Pollard house on which he said construction had started the same year I was born. Other buildings had sprung up around these, and I never ceased to be amazed on coming in to town how it seemed like, on every trip, there were new buildings and more people and just the general sense of prosperity.

One thing I liked about going by canoe was that it was a lot faster. We always played a game, thinking we were racing the wagon into town. I know the wagon had a lot farther to go since they went well out of the way south and east and then back north but that, it seemed, never decreased our enthusiasm for the race.

With Abel in the front of the canoe, Jesse in the middle, and me in the rear, we paddled furiously heading for town to be sure to be the first ones there. Also, it seemed like the lack of supervision was something we enjoyed once we got to town. We could walk freely, admire buildings, and just in general enjoy a sense of mischief that wasn't possible if Mother and Dad were anywhere in the vicinity.

When we got to town, we walked the streets and peered in various shop windows, most of which were closed since it was Sunday, and stopped by the establishment that Moses, Sara, and Miriam ran on the west side of town close to the river. Sara was the oldest of Isaac's girls who had elected to stay in the territory. I think she was around twenty-six or twenty-seven, although I never paid much attention to the birthdays, especially of people older than me. Miriam was a year or two younger. And Moses, the oldest of Isaac's two sons who were still living in the territory but not at home, lived there with them. The girls ran an eating establishment, and Moses provided food, vegetables, and other things for the table. Moses frequently visited our cabin, buying produce or other excess goods for the inn, did some trapping, took care of the garden that they had made around their establishment, distilled a little corn liquor to be sold in town or to guests in their eating house, and in general kept himself busy. I often felt that one of his main jobs was just keeping an eye on the girls and keeping them from being harassed by customers at the establishment.

They did have a couple of rooms that they rented out to people passing through town, but beings how the Pollard house had been built a few years prior to their establishing theirs, and definitely was nicer looking, it had acquired a reputation that induced the more privileged or affluent people to stay there. I suppose that Moses' eating establishment, maybe I should call it Sara's eating establishment, had a rather rough reputation. But we enjoyed stopping in and visiting there as we awaited the arrival of my parents. It did seem to me that for some reason there was a much bigger bustle and stir of excitement around the town than I had noticed before. It seemed like the last time we had been here was four, five or six weeks ago, and things hadn't been particularly excitable then. Yes, there had been talk of the war that recently had started. Usually on visiting town I was more interested in playing with other children and old acquaintances and just enjoying the games and mischief that children can get into.

On that last occasion I had been distracted by the talk that was going on between the adults. I heard them talking about Mr. Lincoln's war. Some people were in favor of it, and other people thought it was an encroachment on their rights. The exact reason for the war wasn't quite clear. I had been there listening to the conversation by myself. My parents hadn't been around, and none of the other adults, so it just seemed to occupy my interest, but I wasn't sure that I grasped the total extent of the difficulties. This seemed to be something that was going on out east and involved a bunch of other states that I hadn't really heard of much previously.

I know my grandfather had originally worked on a plantation in Georgia and had moved west along the Tennessee River, ending up in Memphis, Tennessee, and had lingered there for a year or two. He had served in the war of 1812 with Andy Jackson down at a battle against some Indians in Alabama. After that, he had moved down to around Natchez, Mississippi, so I had heard of these states, but other states, such as Rhode Island and Connecticut, were unknown to me. But this all seemed like a long way off, and although it was a curiosity, when I asked Dad about it later, he really hadn't wanted to talk much of it. His only reply on the occasion was, "It's really none of our business what goes on there. We have enough to do to keep ourselves busy here."

Today it seemed that there were a lot more people in town than there had been the last time I was there, and they certainly seemed a lot more excited. We wandered down south and west toward the crossing where Mother and Dad would be coming into town with the wagon. We waited until it was alongside and then hitched a ride on the tail, probably overloading the two poor old mules pulling the contraption with all these people. We rode as far as Dad would allow and then were forced off and told to walk beside the wagon and arrived eventually at the church that my parents had elected to attend.

It seems there were finer church buildings that had been erected. I think they had even erected one since the last time we had been in town, but this was the first church that had been set up in the territory. It was just a small log contraption and had a big extended front porch. Some of the people were able to sit inside, but most people sat out under the porch. With the windows and door open, you could clearly hear the preacher and get instructions. I expected to hear the usual sermon delivered about love your neighbor, repent your sins, follow the Ten Commandments, etc. But surprisingly, the preacher could only talk about the war. The extent of his sermon went along the lines that we should pray to God for guidance for the politicians, for the wisdom to love one another, to realize that war was not something that God approved of, that all men were brothers and certainly there were better ways of resolving differences than through violence. That seemed to be pretty must the gist of his sermon, as best as I could remember.

After the sermon was finished, the folks broke up into smaller groups. Most had brought things to cook. Some people who lived in town had brought prepared items, already cooked. The fires that had been erected in the cooking pits around the picnic area had been kindled before church and were now in fine beds of coals. Women began to cook on the open pits whatever meats they had brought. Food items were spread out on the tables. The kids bustled around happily playing, at least the younger ones.

I was still intent on discussions of this terrible war that seemed to have broken out. Several men, including my father, were engaged in a rather serious discussion on the events of the war and recent happenings. It seems that there had been several battles over around Springfield, Missouri, at a place called Wilson's Creek, which had resulted in a possible victory for the rebel forces, in that the union forces had retreated. It seems there were several other skirmishes or confrontations in and around that area.

But things seemed to be quiet where we lived, and a lot of the men, including my father, felt that it was best to ignore these events. Certainly common sense would come to bear and people would remember the teachings, especially the ones we just heard in church, and settle down to discuss and resolve their hostilities. There were a couple of men in the group who seemed determined there was no way the war could be stopped at this point short of freeing the slaves.

This seemed rather dramatic to me. I know I had heard Father talk about this subject before. There had been slavery in the United States for hundreds of years. He had always maintained that slavery wasn't something that the United States had invented. The slavery question actually came into being because slaves were imported both by the French and by the English when they were colonies. If it was anybody's fault that slavery existed in the United States, it was the fault of the British and French governments. He was quite proud of our country, as I know our grandfather had been. He maintained that the United States had dealt with this question when they ratified the Constitution, that it was a stumbling block to ratification and that, if they hadn't resolved on compromise, the country would never have been formed. Apparently several states in the south depended on slavery for their existence, and this wasn't necessarily so in the northern states. Father had always maintained that the southern states had only accepted ratification after being assured that slavery would not be compromised. He said every time that congress met after that, the slavery question had come up, and it had resulted in numerous proclamations or laws being passed in attempt to limit slavery.

I know that I had heard him talk previously about how he didn't see a lot of difference between slavery and indentured servitude. My grandfather had come over as a young boy, not much older than I was at this time, and had worked for seven or eight years for a plantation owner in Georgia before he was given his freedom. He had saved every bit of money that he had been able to and set out on his own. In fact, Father raised this thought at this time, but a couple of men who were quite hostile and outspoken seemed to rapidly disagree with him. I had actually never seen these people before. I didn't know whether they were members of the community who had recently moved in or just strangers passing by. But they maintained that indentured servitude was for a period of only seven or eight years while slavery was for life. One of them actually made the proclamation that he wouldn't expect any different thinking from a man who owns slaves. This seemed to raise my father's ire. We didn't own slaves. True, Abraham had once been a slave of my grandfather, but he had been freed after working for a period similar to the indentured servitude of my grandfather. Isaac and all of his children had been free men, but when father pointed this out, his reply was that there were blacks still living on our plantation, and they were pretty much slaves whether we called them free or not. Father had pointed out that several of Abraham's and Isaac's sons and daughters had left and moved away but that Miriam, Sara, Moses, and Jacob still lived there of their own free will and that there was nothing keeping them if they wanted to leave. This really didn't seem to convince this, I'll call him gentleman, although I really don't think he was.

About that time mother came, and seeing the rather heated discussion that had developed, announced that it was time to eat, and her influence seemed to break up the discussion. People moved away and went to enjoy the lunch. Usually after eating we stayed around and visited and associated with the people in the community for several hours before returning home. But today Father rather abruptly announced that he thought we should go and stop in on Moses and Sara to see how they were doing. We did this often after church and lunch but usually not until later in the evening. I think Father was more intent on leaving these people who were gathered so as to avoid any further discussions.

When we arrived at the eating establishment, it was fairly quiet. There hadn't been many customers in the eatery that afternoon mainly because I think that even strangers decided to take advantage of the free church luncheon. Initially we talked pleasantly with Moses and his sisters and discussed their business, anything that they might be needing, and what we could provide, but after only a few minutes, the discussion evolved to the war and the recent events. You could tell father was still quite upset because he brought up the idea of slavery and seemed to be offended that people considered him to be a slave holder. I hadn't ever given the question a thought.

Abel was my best friend, and I believe my father's best friend was Isaac. Growing up, I know that Dad considered Abraham to be like an uncle and Isaac to be like a brother. He was quite proud and overjoyed with the birth of all of Isaac's children. Jacob and my older brother, I thought, were best of friends, and like Abel and I, they always seemed to be together, whether working, hunting, fishing, or just being engaged in whatever activities young men found pleasing at the moment. Yes, Abel was black and Jacob was black, but that hadn't seemed to matter at all. Apparently throughout the country that wasn't necessarily so. I guess it's a good thing when you grow up on your own and can live in your own private world. You can form your own attachments and your own little social organization without influence, emotions, or input from others.

Things had certainly changed recently. It had always seemed that Osceola was growing and that people were coming in, but now I wondered if things hadn't been much happier just a few years ago. A few hours later, we decided to head back for our plantation. I had never considered it a plantation. I had never heard that word applied to anything like what we had. From what my grandfather had said, the plantation he worked on in Georgia was huge with a big house made of stone and wood and big columns and pillars and several thousand acres of ground, all maintained by the slaves. Ours was nothing like that. We had laid claim to no more than a thousand acres. I don't think I ever really considered how much land an acre was. I just knew that the two valleys and the big section of ground enclosed between the bends of the river that we farmed looked like a huge amount of land. We had no stone and framed plantation house, no pillars or columns, just a two-room log cabin connected by a breezeway, a tobacco barn, a corncrib, a smokehouse, a root cellar, and some other assorted outbuildings. But apparently, this was enough to make us, in the eyes of some people, wealthy plantation owners.

These thoughts all went through my mind as we paddled the canoe back, as quick as we could, home. Usually the trip home was rather leisurely. Paddling against the current, although not difficult, required effort. But this time it seemed that we all put our backs into it and arrived much quicker even than the wagon that the others brought back. When we got back home, there wasn't much further discussion. We did a few minor chores and went to bed, possibly, earlier than usual.

That evening, once again I found it hard to sleep. I think the only time in my life I hadn't been able to sleep well was before the hog hunt. And now, just a few days later, I again was finding it hard to sleep. I kept thinking about slavery and whether or not we actually had a plantation to call home. And the thought went through my mind, for the first time, as to just how Abel and Jacob and the girls felt about it. Did they feel like they were slaves? Did they resent us? I found that hard to believe. We had always been smiling, happy, and cheerful growing up, and I couldn't see that anything was wrong in the arrangement. But I guess I had never asked their thoughts on the matter. Of course, shortly before I fell asleep, I determined that they really hadn't even considered the matter because it wasn't something that was ever even discussed. Now it seemed to be a question that lingered in my mind. I determined to talk to Abel about this the following day and finally drifted off.

CHAPTER 5

The next day, we were up early at the crack of dawn again, had breakfast in the main cabin, and then went down, crossed the stream, and finished staking and hanging the tobacco. Over the next few days, we completed the cane pressing and cooked the juice down into the thick, golden brown syrup. We finished up other chores around the cabin, and on Wednesday, we went out in an expedition through the woods gathering up acorns, hickory, chestnuts, and walnuts. We put these in large sacks and took them back for storage in the corncrib.

The week passed quickly. There was always so much work to be done around the farm. I had heard my parents discussing whether or not we would be making another trip into town for a church meeting on Sunday, but apparently one meeting about every month was all my father felt was necessary for church. Besides, I thought that he wasn't in any hurry to get back to town after the last encounter. Sunday came. We did some light chores around the cabin that needed to be done, gathering eggs from the chicken house, milking the cows, but then once these were completed, the rest of the day would be pretty much ours to spend as we wanted.

That morning we had Bible lessons. We only had one book in any of the cabins, and that was the family Bible. The days that we didn't go to church, Mother usually made us sit around the table in the main cabin and read lessons from the Bible. We would take turns reading a page. Even Jesse, who had just turned six sometime earlier that summer, was struggling through his pages in the Bible. The older ones of us, after having read the pages, one after another, would be required to write them down as Mother reread through them. In this fashion, she taught us both to read and write. She would say a word, and we were expected to write it, and she would read on through the next couple of words as we did our best to write them down. Spelling was something that we were supposed to have picked up by having read the page in the first place and reading the word out loud, looking at the spelling. We were expected to remember it so that when she read it, we could write it down. This actually worked surprisingly well.

We usually did this on Sundays, but Mother would do it as often as she could. Some weeks we only read and wrote lessons once, others we would do it three or four times a week. This seemed to be somewhat seasonal. In the winter, when there wasn't much to do as far as chores and when the weather was too brisk for even being outside much, it seemed that we had reading and writing lessons on a nearly daily basis. Mother was quite proud that all of her children were able to read and write, which is something that was actually fairly uncommon along the frontier.

After lunch, we went down to swim in the river. It was getting quite cool, but it had warmed up to probably the mid-forties that afternoon, and the water temperature was never much warmer than what it was now, even during the summer, so we elected to take one good long swim again before the temperatures became so brisk that it was painful to do that. The river was our most important asset. We bathed in the river, fished in the river, used it to grow crops, and for Isaac and Jacob, it was their main source of water. We were fortunate to have a small trickle of the stream to come out from the limestone bluff behind our cabin and in which grandfather had carved out a deep basin and then cemented an even higher rim around the limestone to hold water. He had then built up a rock and cement wall, enclosing an area of about six feet square. The excess water came under the wall and trickled down to join the creek that ran between Isaac's cabin and ours. In this spring house is where we stored the vegetables that didn't dry and keep well, as well as the cheese and milk.

We spent most of the afternoon swimming and then went back up to the house, dried off, and dressed. We spent the rest of the afternoon sitting around the main cabin and just visiting, making plans for what we were going to do next week and discussing the war that inevitably came up as a topic. Dad still didn't wish to talk about this much. He felt that it was a far-away event and shouldn't concern us, and the least said, certainly the less done, the better. I think this was another reason that he seemed determined to avoid any further visits to town.

I had found out that William had been approached about volunteering to go off to serve, which infuriated father. He felt that William was much too young to be involved in military service. He hadn't quite reached the age of eighteen yet, and besides, it wasn't any of our business. I know Grandfather had served in the War of 1812, as he called it. And I know that my dad's younger brother, named William, had gone off to Texas when he was not much older than my brother William to fight in some troubles that they were having down there. Apparently he had elected to stay, and he and his family were now living there.

While we were discussing this bit of family history and recent events, we heard a noise and commotion in the yard. I think we had been too wrapped up in ourselves and the discussions of family history that we hadn't realized that someone was coming. Dad got up to walk to the door about the time that we heard someone call out hello to the house. Dad opened the door and took but maybe one step outside and froze. I could see his body stiffen as he jerked to a halt, which drew my eyes which seemed to fix on him. What happened next I can still see clearly. There were several gunshots. Dad twisted, turned, and staggered back into the room and slammed the door, throwing himself hard against it. And as he slid to the ground, knocking the latch to fall into place, I could see that he was bleeding from several places. His left hand clutched up at his upper abdomen. There was blood running down from his right chest also. He seemed to look directly at me and said, "You, boy, get the young ones to the tunnel."

I knew precisely what he meant. Living in isolation on the frontier and having served in the Indian wars with Andy Jackson, and probably from conversations he had had with my great-grandfather, John Rubidoux, about his life on the frontier, my grandfather had always felt that it was best to have a plan for survival. He seemed to pass this on to my father. They had dug a tunnel under the main cabin, which was hidden by a trapdoor, actually just a plank three-by-three-foot false floor that was under a bearskin rug under the table in the center of the room. This went down about five feet and then connected to a crawlspace that led to a concealed room behind a false wall in the root cellar.

When I was a child, it seemed that father was always insisting that we have practices. At that time, William, being the oldest child, on command would clear the table and the bearskin rug, jump down in the tunnel, and lead the other children single file through and into the false room behind the wall in the root cellar. I had always considered this to be a game and thought it was somewhat silly and ridiculous, but nevertheless the crawl through the tunnel in the dark was quite an adventure.

Arriving in the little hidden room, we could imagine snakes and other varmints having taken up residence there and laughed and giggled while listening carefully and watching for any type of strange movement. When we were youngsters, it was always raiding Indians that Father seemed to worry about. We hadn't had one such drill for years. I think that maybe father had become relaxed and confident. After all, the territory was becoming civilized; there were new settlements all around us. And we were only eight or ten miles from Osceola, where nearly three thousand people lived.

I hurriedly cleared the table and the rug, lifted the trapdoor, and was about to jump in the tunnel when Father called out at me, "Take your guns, boy, and don't you come out of there until I come to get you."

I couldn't believe that I had almost forgotten the most important thing, something to defend myself with if necessary. I ran to the door where Father lay and looked at him, not believing what I was seeing. He already looked white, like he was struggling to stay awake, and like he was having problems breathing, but his only other word to me was, "Go, and don't come out until I come get you."

I opened the chest to the left of the door, grabbed my belt and hunting pouch, and then ran to the wall and grabbed the Pepperbox and my percussion rifle and ran back and leaped into the mouth of the tunnel. Mother assisted Jesse down the tunnel while I crawled out toward the root cellar. Elizabeth went next, followed by the oldest of the girls, Mary. The tunnel suddenly became completely dark as I realized that mother and William had placed the false door back in position and were covering it with the bearskin and the table.

I crawled rapidly through the tunnel. I could hear Jesse, following behind me being encouraged by Mary, who was bringing up the rear. Suddenly I arrived at the hidden door at the root cellar, coming up so quickly that I dislodged it with my forehead. This let in very little light. The root cellar was underground and was as much airtight as we could make it. But Father had made a connection up through the roof of this hidden room that opened into the little flowerbed, which covered the root cellar on the outside and that they had decorated with an assortment of rock arrangements. This let in a very little amount of sunlight and a very little amount of fresh air. This little room that we were now in was no more than six feet long, four feet wide and four feet high. I suppose it was a good six to eight feet underground. In this, at all times, we kept stored a minimal amount of survival gear and our extra money.

There were candles. Mary begged that I light a candle so we could see. On a little shelf on the wall that separated our hidden room from the main root cellar, I felt with my hands until I located the small pouch that had a brass container that carried flint and steel as well as a few wooden matches. Striking one of the matches, I lit a candle. We were all there in the room, all that were coming, I knew that. I replaced the wooden door that I had knocked down with my forehead, leaned back against it, and studied the faces of my two sisters and younger brother. It seemed their eyes were wide open, and their mouths were wide open, and they were staring at me in horror.

Jesse could only whimper. Elizabeth kept repeating hysterically, "What's happening, what's happening?" Mary only stared at me. She knew what was happening as well as I did. It seemed like it had been years since we had practiced this escape maneuver, but I knew what to do next. Hadn't Dad impressed that upon me already? The last words that he had said were, "Don't come out until I come get you." This had been a plan determined, I think, by my grandfather. In the event of Indian attack, the younger children were to go through the escape tunnel into the root cellar while grandfather and my grandmother, Angelique, and the older sons were to fight them off till the end, the end being when all in the cabin were killed or the cabin was so well in flames that they could escape through the tunnel, feeling assured that no one would follow into the cabin to be able to discover the tunnel that led to the rest of the family.

I knew that it was my job, at this point in time, to protect the rest of the kids. I felt confident that we would only be here a short while. I had no idea who was apparently attacking the cabin, but surely this couldn't last long. Father had managed to successfully bar the door. I remember the way he looked and thinking that it would be miraculous if he survived. I had seen animals we hunted wounded with such wounds, and they never survived. But William and Mother were there to care for him. I knew there was nothing further I could do in that regard. With the door barred and mother and William to defend the cabin, surely it would only be a short time until Isaac and Jacob came, and probably even people from the town. So, although I was quite worried and distraught, I tried my best to appear calm and reassuring.

To Elizabeth's continual whining of what happened, my reply was, "I don't know, but it'll be all right." I reached out and took Jesse's arm and pulled him toward me while we sat, hugged and huddled on the floor of the cabin watching across at Mary and Elizabeth six feet away on the other side. How long we stayed here, I really don't know. It seemed that there were several flurries and volleys of gunshots that we could hear, but faintly. The root cellar was deep, and the walls were thick and heavily built. There was the one slanted oak door, on the top of the entrance, that led to a flight of stone steps, down the stone tunnel from the top of the root cellar to a cedar-lined door that was vertical, closing the root cellar off from this tunnel. There was the root cellar itself, which was stone lined with shelves along each wall and barrels of perishables stacked in the center as well as a plank across the top of the barrels on which other sacks of produce stood. Then there was the wall that we were behind, which was also made of stone, the walls being lined with cedars and with a small trapdoor under the lower shelf that entered into our room. We took care not to put anything in front of this small door, but its presence was not really discernible. Because of the rock in the walls and being underground, the root cellar was extremely cool but also extremely quiet.

Try as I could, I wasn't able to pick up much in the way of noise to tell what was happening. It did seem that there were flurries of gunshots followed by quiet, followed by other rapid bursts of firing, then a period time to make you think it was all over, and then continued rapid flurries of shots. At some point in there, after the second or third outbreak of firing, I thought I detected a smell of smoke. Over the next several minutes, this seemed to become quite more powerful. I thought that possibly they had fired the cabin and expected that soon Dad, Mother, and William would be arriving through the tunnel. I listened carefully for any noises in the tunnel and even put my ear down to the trapdoor to listen better. I could hear nothing to indicate that they were coming. The wood smoke smell grew stronger, and still I felt that they must be coming soon, but about that time, I heard another volley of shots and thought, no, they must still be in the cabin fighting off the attackers who for some reason seem to be exceptionally persistent. I reasoned that possibly the attackers had fired the corncrib or maybe even the outhouse.

I wondered why this was still happening. Surely Isaac and Jacob would have come by now and with these defenders, and my parents on the inside of the house, no one would dare face such an resistance. Several times it was in my mind to remove the door and crawl back through the tunnel to see what was happening, but every time I determined that I was going to, a thought would come that the last words Father had said to me were, "Don't come out until I come and get you."

I realized that if I went back down through the tunnel that probably Jesse would be right on my heels and that the girls would be panicked and who knew what would happen. So, I left the door in place, leaned against it and listened, and smelled. I couldn't see anything because about this time the candle had gone out. I reasoned that for that little nub of candle to have gone out, at least an hour had to have passed, because a candle that size should have lasted for an hour. It seemed that it was exceedingly stuffy in the little secret room. It had grown completely dark. Crawling beneath the little pipe that extended up to our hidden air hole, I reasoned that it was well past sundown by this time. I thought surely it was safe to come out. People from town, riding hard, would have arrived by now.

It had been probably five o'clock when this had all started. It must be eight by now. Surely it was safe to come out, but about that time there was another flurry of gunshots. I determined I wasn't going to think and worry about that anymore, I was going to stay here until Dad came to get me. But the thought kept going through my head that Dad would probably never come to get me. I didn't think that he could have survived those wounds, but he was tough and determined, and you never wanted to put Dad down.

I went back to sit against the door to the tunnel, hugged Jesse in my arms, and stared across to where the girls were. I couldn't make them out in the darkness, but I could tell they were still there and still watching me. No one spoke. Sometime later, I could tell that Jesse had fallen asleep. I put his head on my shoulder, leaned my head on the top of his head, closed my eyes, and sat there throughout the long night. Once again, I don't think I slept. Gradually I became aware that it seemed a little bit lighter in the secret room. I could tell that there was a faint infusion of sunlight through the pipe and knew that the sun must be well up by now. I could hear nothing else. There was still the strong stench of wood smoke, which had a little different odor than usual.

I determined that whatever had happened must surely have ended by now. I figured that Dad wasn't coming to get us, or Mother or William either. I couldn't understand why Isaac or Jacob or someone hadn't come, but I didn't know. The uncertainty became palpable. I couldn't stand it anymore. I had to know. I know what I feared more than anything. I was so afraid of this that I even said a prayer that when I came out Father would scold me, maybe even beat me for not staying till he came to get me. I was praying for a beating, but I wouldn't get one. My biggest fear was that everyone was dead.

I removed the trapdoor between the walls of the root cellar and crawled out. I told Mary to stay there until I came to get them. I slipped to the cedar door, listened, and smelled carefully. I felt like I was on a hunting expedition at this point. I slipped the door open quietly, crawled up the stone steps to the oak door that lay diagonally across the top of the root cellar, and tried to peek through the fine cracks there, which was silly because the cracks were too slight to allow any means of seeing in or out. I put my ear to it and listened and smelled. Everything seemed quiet. I lifted the edge of the door only a fraction so I could see out from under it on all sides. I could see nothing. I could still hear nothing except logs crackling as they burned slowly. I could see the edge of the corncrib, which laid directly across from the door, and knew that it hadn't been burned, but the smokehouse and the cabin were obscured by the top of the root cellar and by the door that I was lifting so that I could see nothing in that direction. I lifted the door further and further until it was high enough that I could stick only my head out at the bottom of the door next to the ground and looked toward the river and the cabin. It was gone. There was only a smoldering pile of rubble with the chimney standing on the left or east side of the cabin. I lifted the door slightly higher and stuck my head out farther to look in all directions. I was looking, listening, and smelling. There was a strange smell, almost a cooking smell. There was a heavy smell of wood smoke. The only noise that I heard was the crackling of the logs as they burned and occasionally collapsed in further, but there was no one in sight.

I looked up toward the east, to the sunlight, and reckoned it must be close on to nine o'clock by this time. Where were Isaac and Jacob, where were the townsfolk? Surely this couldn't have happened to us. I would have thought that, being within ten miles of town, certainly people would have heard the shooting and come to investigate. There had obviously been a lot more shooting than what you would expect from anyone, even on a hog hunt. There had been a lot more shooting than you would expect if someone was hunting in a pack and had come upon a large flock of wild turkeys. Why wasn't anybody here?

I slid back in, shut the door, went back to the false wall and stuck my head in there and told Mary, Elizabeth and Jesse that they should stay here. I said that I didn't see anybody outside but I was going out to investigate and they should stay here until I came to get them. Mary was quite insistent that they should come out, but I told her that I would go and only me. That way, if there were people here and they found me, I could possibly convince them that I had been hiding in the root cellar and if they had looked in the root cellar, that they just hadn't seen me. But surely no one would believe that all four of us had been there. I told her to stay there in the hidden room, keep the door shut, and stay there until I came back.

I had managed to load my guns in the dark last night, but I left them there. I reasoned that if anybody was still around, that I in the open probably wouldn't be able to do much even with my guns, and if no one was there, I didn't need them anyhow. Besides, Mary and Elizabeth both knew how to shoot, and I felt that they needed the weapons more than I did.

First, I went to the cabins. The roofs were caved in, the walls had fallen in. There were still heaps of smoldering logs and ash. It was not blazing but more of a smoldering glow from the logs that were still on fire. I could not see or recognize anything in the ruins of the house. I prayed that my family had made it down to the tunnel and were hiding in the tunnel, but if that were the case, why wouldn't they have come out to the secret room? I walked around the remains of the cabin several times staring at it and then decided to walk in wider circles away from the cabin and around it.

I could make out a lot of horse tracks, several patches of blood, and then I noticed two, no, three bodies lying on the edge of the clearing around the house and just on the edge of the brush. I hoped and prayed that these were my parents. Although they weren't moving and appeared to be dead, I still wished that these were my family, but I could tell by the looks of their clothes that they were strangers.

I don't know why I hadn't spotted them first. I suspect it was because my attention was directed directly at the cabin. All that father had told me about looking, listening, and smelling seemed to flee from my mind whenever I needed it most. If I hadn't been able to notice these dead bodies, what made me think I could notice if a live person was hiding in the brush waiting to ambush me? My whole attention had been directed on the cabin and on anyone that might be still in the flaming embers of the cabin. I don't know why these bodies were directly on the edge of the clearing around the cabin. I couldn't guess that there had been more than three people to attack the cabin. Had my parents killed them all, and why were they here? That caused me to wonder if there was anyone else here and why Isaac or Jacob hadn't shown up. I suspected that when all this started, Isaac had done the same as my Dad had ordered us to do. They also had a crawl space going from their cabin to the root cellar behind their house. I suspected that he ordered Abel and his wife, Rebecca, through this tunnel to take refuge in the root cellar, and I thought that he would have come to help. Jacob lived over half a mile, probably close to three quarters of a mile, across the river directly south of our house on a small rise within the low ground in the bend of the river, but surely he would have heard the gunshots and come to investigate. There didn't seem to be anyone else around.

Curiosity got the better of me, and I slipped through the woods, going tree to tree, watching, listening, and smelling.

I gradually, carefully, and skillfully approached Isaac's cabin. Possibly it was a little too late, but gradually I was beginning to truly comprehend what Dad had always said about hunting, "Be silent, look, listen, and smell." It was important in hunting to discover your game before they discovered you. I hadn't seemed to be able to discover the hogs until Dad had pointed them out to me. I hadn't seen the bodies of the people that attacked our cabin, even though they were actually in plain sight, until I determined to actually search for them. If you were going to be a hunter, you had to do better than that. You had to be aware of your environment at all times.

I came down to Isaac's cabin, I think, totally unawares. It was quiet, but as I slipped up onto the porch and approached the front door, listening carefully, I could pick out a hush of voices within. Initially I couldn't make out the voices. I wasn't about to give myself away. It could be other villains in the cabin. But as I listened carefully, I was able to recognize Rebecca's and Miriam's voices. They seemed to be discussing something, but I couldn't make out what it was. I thought about knocking and entering but decided to remain where I was. I approached closer, put my ear to the door, listened carefully, and finally could make out Moses' voice. I still wasn't able to pick up the gist of their conversation, but they didn't seem to be panicked and didn't seem to be in any danger.

I knocked carefully and stood there waiting until the door was opened. Jacob came to open the door. He looked at me quietly, not saying another word. Initially I watched him and peeked into the room. I could see that the rest of the family was gathered on the opposite side of the room, around the only bed, on the main floor. I could tell someone was in the bed but couldn't make out for sure who it was. I looked around the room carefully, and could pick out Rebecca, Sara, and Miriam. I saw Jacob and Moses and finally could see in the corner of the room opposite me, to the left of the bed, Abel, as he sat in the corner hunched over.

I had never seen Abel look so despairingly. He had his hands folded across his knees and seemed to be rocking back and forth. I knew that it had to be Isaac who was in bed. That had to be bad. I had never seen Isaac in bed. In fact, I had hardly even seen Isaac sitting down. He always seemed to prefer to be up and walking. Even in the evenings when the rest of us would be sitting on the porch, he would be standing up leaning on the wall. I had never seen him on his back.

Jacob looked at me then and said, "Where have you been?"

I told him, "Well, naturally, we have been in the root cellar."

He said, "Well, I know that, but I thought that you would have been out long before that."

I looked at him and said, "Dad said to stay there until he came to get us."

Jacob shook his head knowingly. I'm sure he had heard the same thing from Isaac when he was young , and I think he realized that, if a similar situation had occurred, he wouldn't have left that root cellar none too soon either.

I asked him what had happened, and he said that he didn't know for sure. He had been in his cabin and hadn't noticed any riders. He said he was relaxing after having completed some chores, was cleaning up some and just getting ready to come across to Isaac's cabin to see what was for supper. He said he hadn't noticed anything when he left the cabin and was probably almost halfway across the fields to the Osage River crossing that led to our house when he had heard a flurry of gunshots. He said that he had immediately turned around and ran for home.

He hadn't brought any weapons with him. He didn't know what was happening, but he just had an instinctive fear that it wasn't good. He said he had run all the way home, got his double-barreled Pennsylvania rifle down, and loaded it and had loaded up his Colt, none of which were kept loaded. This took a little time and then he said that he had left the cabin heading toward our house where there continued to be gunshots in volleys, followed by quietness. He said he had come to the river, slipped across it, and gotten to the brushy area along the path to the east side and came up the bank between our house and his father's house. He said he had done this thinking that possibly he would meet up with Isaac. He said by this time he could still hear shouting and an occasional shot and he started smelling a strong odor of wood smoke. He said that he had heard a couple of brief shots off from his right in quick succession and felt that his dad was over there shooting at the raiders around our house.

By this time it was probably nearly six and was starting to get dark. He said that, in fact, it was dark enough that he really couldn't tell where his father was. He thought that it was his father shooting at people that were around the cabin and that they were probably to the west side of the cabin staying out of range. He determined not to move any closer to his father's position or where he thought his father was, because in the brush, and the gloom, he might well get shot by his own dad. Therefore, he moved more back to the west and up toward the clearing. He crossed the trail that led to our house where there was a stand of blackberry brambles on both the east and west side of the road, crawled through the brambles, keeping low to the ground to avoid thorns, and crept up toward our house.

By this time he said the house was pretty much in flames. He felt that the attackers had realized that the only firing that was coming from the house was coming from the main cabin, since the cabin where William, Jesse and I and the girls lived had been quiet throughout all this time. Jacob said he felt like they had spent a good deal of time throwing brush and debris in and firing this part of the cabin. I remembered the pressed sugarcane stalks. We hadn't gotten around to hauling all of them down to feed to the hogs, and there was a good pile of pressed and dried stalks that were there, off to the left of the cabin, where we had cooked down the juice to make the cane syrup. He said that they took these, shoved them through the windows, threw torches in, and got this portion of the house burning intensely and would then throw torches into the breezeway between the house. We kept kindling wood there, as well as stacks of oak wood, for the fireplace in the breezeway on which Mother cooked during the summer, and he said they got these mounds of kindling and firewood going fierce. This would pretty much have blocked the only exit from the cabin.

He said there were still shots coming from the cabin when anyone exposed themselves, but the raiders would rush forward and throw flaming cane stalks on the roof and against the walls. He said that there were occasional shots coming from the east, from the top of the little crest that led down to the river that went between ours and Isaac's cabin, and he felt that was his father firing from there. He said he opened up from where he was and gave several quick shots. He said he fired both barrels of his Pennsylvania rifle and drew out and fired once from his Colt. This caused the people who were taking shelter behind the western end of the cabin to move around to the north out of sight. But he said for some reason they seemed intently determined to continue firing the cabin.

He said by this time it was good and dark, so that outside the flames from the cabin, beyond the edge of the clearing, you really couldn't see anyone. He said the cabin was too far gone. He knew that no one was coming out of it. He thought that, as his father had explained to him, once the cabin was well up in flames, the defenders of the cabin would go through the tunnel to the root cellar and take refuge there in the secret room, so he wasn't all that concerned that the cabin was in flames.

He said he backed away from the cabin down toward the river, hiding as much as possible, and was actually thinking, at that point in time, that he might head toward town to see what was delaying Moses. He said he got down close to the river when he noticed noises coming from the west and upstream. He said he could make out the sound of hoof beats and the splashing, faintly, of water. He said he dropped down on the riverbank and watched carefully as several riders came down. He said he never bothered to call out or give them any warning. They were coming from the west and, from what he could tell of what he had seen, he recognized what he thought were the shapes and outlines of horses and people that had been around the cabin earlier when it had been light enough to see. He said he pulled out his Colt, which still had five shots in it, aimed in the center mass of the group, fired all five shots in quick succession and lifted up his Pennsylvania rifle, and fired it once. Then, since they had taken off, splitting in all directions, some going across the river, some going back up the river, and some apparently heading back up toward the house, he saved his one shot, slipped into hiding again, and lying on his back under brush, wriggled away from the banks of the river and proceeded to reload his Colt in the dark. Apparently that was the last of the fighting that I had heard. He said after that there hadn't been any shooting.

He stayed where he was for another couple of hours and then went up carefully to the cabin. He said he crawled to the west of the road and came up from the west of the cabin thinking that, if there was anyone still lingering, he would see them before they saw him. He then moved down toward the cabin, which was still aflame, circled north of this, and actually passed right behind the root cellar and in front of the spring house, to the top of the low bluff that led across the creek to Isaac's house. He said he stayed here and watched toward his house and the area where he thought his dad had been firing from and didn't notice anything. He said everything seemed to be exceedingly quiet, and so after a bit, he had called out, "Dad, I'm coming out," and had walked out into the clearing and into the light that came from the flaming cabin, where he was clearly visible and then walked directly to where he thought his father had been firing from.

He found Isaac. Isaac had been wounded several times. Apparently he was too weak to even be able to call out loud enough to be heard, but he was still sensible enough to realize that it was Jacob approaching. He said that he had lifted Isaac across his shoulder and carried him back across the creek to the cabin. I don't know for sure how old Jacob was. I know he was two or three years older than William, but Isaac was an exceedingly big and strong man, and it surprised me that Jacob had been able to lift him across his shoulders and carry him back to the cabin by himself, especially across a creek and up a slight, but somewhat treacherous, embankment. He said that he had carried his father in, put him in bed, covered him up, given him some fresh water to drink, and gone to the root cellar to fetch Abel and his mother. They had done their best to bandage and bind Isaac's wounds and staunch the bleeding.

At this point, I hadn't been able to approach close enough to see Isaac. I was still standing in the doorway looking into the room, but I could see that he was still moving faintly; at least I thought it was him. It seemed that you could see the blankets raise and lower occasionally, and sometimes there would be a flurry of movement as he waved one hand or motioned. During all this time, Abel hadn't moved. He was still sitting on his stool in the corner hunched over, rocking gently back and forth as he clutched his knees. Rebecca, Sara, and Miriam were standing about or sitting on the bed surrounding their father, and Moses was sitting at a chair at the table. He hadn't said anything throughout this period of time. My first thought was that he felt guilty for not having come to help. I thought briefly that if he had gotten there in time, he and Jacob could have driven off these attackers and possibly have saved my family. It's strange that I thought "saved my family" because I really didn't know where they were. I suspected, but I didn't know. They hadn't been in the root cellar. Possibly they had shown up there now. It's hard to believe that I hadn't thought about Mary, Elizabeth, and Jesse for the last couple of hours. To my way of thinking, they were safe in the root cellar, and they would stay there until I came to get them, which is precisely what I decided to do at that time.

I had told Jacob where I was going, and turning around, I went back across the creek and up the hill to the root cellar. I threw the oak door wide open and went down the stone steps and through the cedar door. I got down and whispered that I was coming in, loud enough to be heard, and after Mary had replied, I pushed the trapdoor down and they crawled out. Mary was still carrying the Pepperbox, Elizabeth had my rifle, and Abel came out last, carrying my belt with the holster and the Damascus blade. The Damascus blade he held in his right hand, the holster in the left. He was ready for a fight.

The first thing that Mary asked when they were out was, "Where's Dad, where's Mother, where's Dad, where's William?"

My reply was, "They haven't come through the tunnel to you?"

She said, "No, I haven't heard anything."

I told her then, "Well, I don't know where they are."

Her eyes widened, and a look of shock came across her face, but she didn't say anything. Jesse seemed to look at the two of us, back and forth and back and forth, and had a quizzical look on his face but not one that showed alarm. Elizabeth was still repeating her inevitable question, "What's happening, what's happening?"

It seemed like that's all she could say. She had kept repeating that question all throughout the night, so I felt obliged to tell her, "Someone attacked the cabin and burned it to the ground. They shot Isaac, and I think he's going to die. I haven't seen Mother, Dad, or William, but the cabin is burned, and I'm afraid they are too."

She immediately broke down in tears, crying and sobbing hysterically. I know I shouldn't have said that the way I did, but I didn't know how else to say it. It was best to say it and get it over with, and besides, I felt that she knew anyhow what had happened. It had happened just like I feared from the moment I first saw Dad shot, from the moment I started smelling smoke, from the moment I heard the additional volleys of gunshots. I felt like I knew what had happened then, and I think that they should have known too. But still, I have felt bad ever since then that I said it so bluntly and directly.

CHAPTER 6

We crossed down to the bluff and across to Isaac's house, knocked on the door, and entered. Mary and Elizabeth ran immediately to the bed and took their positions, sitting around it, next to Miriam and Sara. Rebecca was surprisingly up and preparing something to eat. She was an excellent cook, and it seemed that she felt that one of her main jobs in life was to be sure that everybody was fed. Besides, I don't think she knew what else to do at this point in time. I spoke up and suggested to Moses that possibly he should go to town and fetch help. There was a man there who proclaimed to be a doctor. He treated men, women, and children and any other animal or creature that knocked at his door. I didn't think that there was much he could do for Isaac, from the look of him, but I hadn't been close enough to check his wounds either.

Moses looked up at me, having not moved from the chair at the table where he had been sitting the whole time, and said, "There is no town." I was amazed. I couldn't understand what he had said. How could there be no town? There were nearly three thousand people living in Osceola. I thought this but never spoke out loud. He looked at me, and speaking slowly, he stated that he reckoned the people who burned our cabin were a group that had strayed off from the main group that had attacked Osceola.

I couldn't believe that someone had attacked Osceola. We were only ten miles from town and had heard nothing; we had had no indication or warning, so how could that have happened? But Moses went on to explain that sometime during the night Saturday, an alarm had sounded in the town that raiders were coming from Kansas. He said some of the people had hastily gathered together to defend the town. He said sometime around midnight out south and west of town fighting had broken out and that the result of the fighting was that most, or a good portion, of the people from Osceola had fled northeast toward the river and abandoned it. He said that sometime Sunday morning, the raiders from Kansas had come into town, which, by that time, was emptied pretty much except for women and children. He said that they had promptly begun looting the town, taking anything of any value. He related that they even managed to steal a piano that he thought came from the Pollard Inn. He said he had watched as they had been loading it on the wagon.

There had been two pianos in town, one at the inn and another at the bigger church in town, so he didn't know for sure where it had come from. He said anything that could be taken, was. He said after most of the houses had been looted and probably most of the things that were valuable had been confiscated, that these people began drinking and shooting randomly at anyone they saw, which prompted him to head back toward his cabin where his sisters were. He said he did this slowly and carefully, hoping that no one would shoot him. He said he watched, while he slipped back toward the cabin, as these raiders set fire to the town and after having reached home, he would occasionally go out on the porch or watch through the windows as it seemed that the whole town went up in flames.

He said he felt like they had been powerless to do anything. He thought there were probably almost a thousand people who raided Osceola and that probably half of the townsfolk had abandoned Osceola before they actually entered. Since the initial fighting occurred about midnight, there was mass confusion, and he felt that people weren't able to take any possessions with them and it was hard to be organized. He thought that some families were separated, some staying in town and some fleeing northeast. In the daylight, when the actual burning took place, there wasn't really any fighting or any defense put up by the townsfolk at all. Apparently they simply watched as the whole town was burned. Moses said that their cabin had been spared, possibly because this was on the very west edge of town and possibly because it was commonly known that the people who owned the cabin were Negroes. Moses said that although pretty much the whole town was burned, there was an isolated house left still standing, but everything else was in flames. He then seemed to have nothing else to say.

Jacob said that he had carried his father back to bed and helped bind the wounds, and after he felt that everything was safe, he had headed toward town looking for help. He related that he had fetched down one of the horses, not bothering to saddle it, ridden as fast as he could to town, and was shocked at what he had found. He said he went through the rubble and the flames, looking to see if he could find the doctor or find someone who could be of help, and had then gone to Moses' cabin. This would have been apparently sometime Monday morning. He said he found Moses and the two girls safely boarded up in the cabin. It seems they were determined to protect what they had or maybe just to protect themselves. They didn't have a tunnel to the root cellar behind their house, so they were armed with whatever weapons they had for defense.

The girls each held a shotgun. Moses had a shotgun and a rifle musket, and they each had a muzzle-loading percussion pistol. I guess since they lived in town, they hadn't felt a need for any more sophisticated protection than that, and possibly they couldn't have afforded a Henry rifle or a Colt revolving pistol. Anyway, they had hitched up their wagon that Moses had used to haul produce and other goods from our cabin to theirs for their eatery. This was a fairly small wagon, but it was sufficient to carry Moses and the two girls back out to our place. There, Sara and Miriam did what they could to comfort their mother and to care for Jacob. Everyone seemed to be at a loss as to what to do next. Moses didn't speak much or didn't seem to be able to move far from the chair at the table. He finally announced that he reckoned he would go back to town. I think that he was worried that if they left their little place of business too long unguarded, that it would be burned and raided.

Anyhow, he headed back to town on the horse that Jacob had ridden. That made three trips to town for this poor animal in one day, but I don't think anyone was particularly thinking too clearly at the time. He left the wagon for Miriam and Sara in case they wished to come back. We seemed to be at a total loss for what to do next. Mary mentioned a couple of times, "What about mom and Dad?"

I told her that I had walked around the cabin briefly and hadn't seen any sign of them. She looked at the smoldering rubble of what was left of our house from off the porch of Isaac's home and said, "Maybe we should look again." I decided that was a reasonable suggestion.

I left Jesse and Elizabeth there, with Rebecca and her family, took my Pepperbox and my musket, borrowed one of the shotguns from Sara and gave this to Mary, and we headed across the creek. We came up to the house and walked around it from each side, looking in. There was no sign of my parents, but I didn't expect you would be able to see anything either. We searched along the top of the hill next to the bluff and then went through the trees and bushes toward the river on the west of the house. We noticed the three bodies lying on the edge of the clearing in the brush but were surprised to find two more down on the gravel banks in a level spot just before the ford of the river.

Apparently Jacob's shooting had been much more effective than he had supposed. I thought no further of the bodies lying there. We walked back to Isaac's cabin, and when we entered, the first thing that struck me was that nothing had really changed. Jacob still sat at the table, and Abel was in the corner by the left side of his father's bed weeping. Jesse sat a few feet away from him, leaning back against the wall clutching his knees. Sara and Miriam sat on the foot of their father's bed, and Rebecca was up to the right of the bed at Isaac's left side trying to get him to drink some broth or water. He didn't seem to be able to. He would mutter and groan weakly and coughed and choked occasionally, but I wasn't sure that he was even aware of what was happening around him.

People seemed to be unable to think of anything else to do. I went and sat next to Abel on the floor by his stool and did my best to be supportive. Nearly everyone in the room was weeping, although quietly. I noticed this, and the sight of it made me want to shed tears, but my mind kept thinking that there was something else we should be doing. Perhaps it was just the grief, but I was unable to weep.

It gradually became darker in the cabin. Candles were lit around Isaac's bed, and Rebecca moved to the small fireplace to the right of the bed, which was under the center of the roof, and with help from Mary and Elizabeth, prepared a meal. After having eaten the brief supper that she had fixed, she resumed her position next to Isaac, and Mary and Elizabeth cleaned up what there was to be cleared. The rest of the evening, and it seemed all through the night, people held their position lingering around the bed on which Isaac struggled to breathe and stay alive.

The next two days passed in pretty much the same fashion. Abel didn't seem to be capable of moving from his father's side. Jacob remained rooted, sitting at the chair next to the table. Rebecca occasionally arose to prepare brief meals. No one seemed to want to leave the cabin. There was a restlessness upon me that I couldn't explain. While everyone else seemed to be gently weeping, I still was incapable of shedding a tear. Several times a day I would get up to walk out across the creek, around the cabin, through the woods, down to the river. I kept searching for something. I am not sure what it was. I told myself I was hoping to find traces of my parents and William, but I knew that was going to be impossible. I would occasionally go to the smoldering ruins of the cabin. I would probe it with a hoe that I got from the corncrib, but it was always too hot to attempt to search.

Finally, on early Wednesday morning, the third day after the attack on the cabin, Isaac passed away. We had been expecting it. I knew it was inevitable. It seemed like anytime in the last twenty-four hours he could have passed. There were times when I thought he had because it seemed that he went so long between breathing, but then he would rouse, take a few breaths, cough, struggle, and seem to revive. His actual passing was barely noticeable. He seemed to just exhale softly, shuddered and barely moved, and then was gone.

I had been sitting on the floor next to Abel's knee. He had thrown himself to his knees next to his father, weeping inconsolably. I gently helped him to his feet, took him in my arms, and hugged him much the way my mother used to hug me. Jesse came up to my left side, and I grasped him with my left arm, and the three of us hugged each other, weeping. Abel shook vigorously. Copious tears ran down his cheeks, and his sobs were able to be heard throughout the cabin. Jesse wept softly. It seemed that everyone else in the room was weeping to some extent—everyone except me. I looked from one person to another around the room, looked up and studied the ceiling and the loft, looked around at the floor, and looked at Isaac lying dead on the bed and wished there was something I could do to put an end to this sorrow and emotion, but I could think of nothing. I thought I should be weeping like everyone else, but the sobs would not come. After what seemed like hours, Abel seemed to collapse. I assisted him back to sit on his stool next to his father's bed and left the room.

I went outside across the creek to the corncrib on the hill where our cabin had stood. I searched around and found a long-handled shovel. Inwardly I was in a rage. This should not have happened. I was furious.

I felt the need to strike out—to hurt someone—but what could I do? I then walked past the cabin to the west, down a gentle slope and arrived at the small graveyard where our family had been buried. The graves of my grandparents were farther to the west. There were two flat boards that served as tombstones that had my grandfather's name and the date of his death. We didn't know for sure the date of his birth and really didn't know for sure where he had even been born. My grandmother's grave was slightly east of that. In-between there was a smaller grave with a single crossed pair of sticks as a marker. There was no name on this grave. I had always been told that this was the grave of one of the children that my grandmother had borne. There was no name or no plaque on the grave. My father had always said that this was because grandmother, being half Osage Indian, had refused to allow the child to be named. I didn't even know whether this had been a male or female child.

Apparently it was an Osage custom not to name children before they were a year or two of age because so many children died as infants. I had actually thought that this seemed a reasonable custom. Certainly it seemed to be a family custom of ours to pass the same name down from grandfather, and uncles, to parents and siblings. I had come to this deduction due to the incredible number of Aarons, Williams, Thomases, Roberts and Johns that came up whenever my father had been talking about his relations. It was always hard to keep them straight. If the Indians had used up all their names on children who died, maybe they couldn't have thought up more.

To the right or east of where my grandparents' graves lay were the graves of Abraham and Sara. Like my parents, they had a plain wooden plaque with their names and date of death. Birth dates seemed to have been something that had been forgotten throughout the course of their lives. Just east of Sara's grave, I began digging another grave. I had never dug a grave before, but it seemed that I had heard talk about this and the idea was six feet high and six feet deep. I took the shovel and broke the sod in a rectangle about three feet wide and six feet high. After having broken the sod, I scooped it off by angling the shovel in a shallow fashion. My intention was to replace the sod after the grave was dug. I had managed to proceed about a foot deep throughout the length and width of the grave when Jacob arrived. He had a short-handled shovel and a pickax. I soon realized why he had the pickax. It seemed we had only gone down a few more inches when we started encountering large rocks. The Ozarks region was one of valleys and of tall sandstone, limestone bluffs and shallow layers of dirt. I suspect that the location for the graveyard had been chosen initially because it was softer dirt in this area than most.

Finishing the grave was quite difficult. We never made it down to six feet. At about four feet down, we came upon a layer of limestone or sandstone that seemed to cover the whole length and width of the grave. Jacob left me to extend the length of the grave. He felt that we would need probably another foot in order to get the coffin in. While I finished the last remaining touches on the grave itself, Jacob walked back to the side of our cabin. He took some of the planks from the corncrib that we used to set up the table in front of the house when we were making hams and sausage and formed these into a rather crude, and rough, casket. He had this completed as well as the lid by the time I arrived back from the graveyard, and we carried it down across the creek to the cabin.

Rebecca had wrapped Isaac's body in the blankets that had covered him before he died and had fastened them snug around his corpse. We carried the coffin in and sat it on the bed next to him and then gently and carefully placed his remains in the casket. We carried this outside and sat it on a couple of benches that we had arranged on the porch, and Jacob fastened the lid securely. Sara and Miriam said brief prayers. I was asked to say a brief prayer and muttered something about how God should protect and treasure this good man and show him a peaceful life in the hereafter, or something to that effect. I couldn't think of much to say. I know it only took me less than a minute. I supposed that I had been asked to say something because I was now the unofficial head of our family. I certainly wished they had asked Mary, because she was much more thoughtful and insightful and never seemed to be lacking for a word to say.

We had planned to have the actual burial service at the cemetery in the morning. Rebecca and the girls went down to the river to clean up while Jacob, Abel, Jesse, and I remained at the cabin. We sat around the table and talked briefly. No one seemed to have much to say. I felt that we should be doing something, should be making some plans. I thought there must be something we needed to do as far as work around the home site but could not get my thoughts to go any further in this direction. I think I was incapable of coming to any further course of action other than searching until I could finally locate my parents' remains. It had been at least seventy-two hours since the cabin had been torched, but it was still much too hot to search through the ashes, embers, and remains of the cabin.

When the womenfolk had returned from the river wrapped in blankets, we politely left the cabin and wandered around outside and across the creek and through the woods. We walked down to the river, squatted at the edge of the bank and washed our hands and arms up to the elbow and made our way back to the cabin. By this time the womenfolk had dressed and Rebecca was hard at work preparing a rather sumptuous meal for supper. We sat at the table and waited for supper silently. Rebecca fixed a splendid meal, but we ate pretty much in silence.

That evening we spent sitting around the table. No plans were made, and very little discussion was held. Rebecca kept incessantly busy cooking and preparing further things to eat, but she put these up and stored them for the following day. It was customary when someone died to have a large meal and have neighbors and friends to attend the burial service. I think that Rebecca was planning on having a lot of folks to eat the next day, but I wondered how many people there would be to attend. I suspected that probably only Moses would be there, if he would even leave their establishment in town for the occasion. I knew he would, but there was always a lingering doubt. He worried, cared, and worked as much around their small business place as my dad did about our farm. There, he was the boss and the proud proprietor. It wasn't something that he would neglect, even in this situation.

I offered to take the canoe to town to fetch Moses back, but Rebecca said that it would be best to wait until the morning. She thought that it may be dangerous to go after dark although we had made this trip to town by canoe several times after dark. Then I remembered there was no town. Possibly it would be dangerous traveling after dark.

We all went to bed that evening. Rebecca and her daughters slept in the bed in which Isaac had died. They had turned the straw mattress, laid a quilt over it, and slept on top of the quilt in the clothes in which they had dressed after having bathed in the river. My two sisters and Jesse slept in the loft. Jacob, Abel, and I found convenient places on the floor, threw down some featherbeds, and slept on them. It was another cool night, but with all the humidity in the cabin and the low fire glowing in the fireplace, we were warm enough without any blankets or covers.

The following morning, we were up at sun break. Rebecca was fixing a large breakfast, but before we could eat, she announced we had to clean up. The boys all took the lye soap, towels, and a change of clothing, went down, and swam and bathed in the river, then dried off and dressed. We returned to the cabin for a heavy breakfast of pancakes, eggs, bacon, and fried potatoes with onions. Jacob was intending to saddle up a horse and go to town to meet Moses, but about that time Moses arrived by horse from town. I suppose he had come to check on his father and felt that he had somehow instinctively known that this morning was the day we had planned for the funeral. He didn't seem to be surprised that Isaac had died and didn't say much as he sat at the table. He didn't ask many questions and seemed rather withdrawn and taciturn. Rebecca asked if any of the townsfolk might be coming to the services. Moses replied briefly that he didn't suppose so. He didn't seem to be inclined to volunteer to ride back to town to ask either and suggested that we should just proceed with the services.

We carried the coffin to the grave that Jacob and I had dug and covered it with dirt and replaced the sod. We could always erect a name plaque and date later. Rebecca said some prayers and read from the Scriptures. Apparently at some point in time they had actually agreed and concluded on some ceremonies. Sara and Miriam led the group in singing some songs that they had chosen, and then my sister Mary gave a brief prayer.

We then walked back past the remains of our cabin and went down to have a noon lunch. I paused briefly to take my hoe and probe through the embers of our cabin. I felt that it wasn't safe to begin a search through the rubble until at least tomorrow. It was surprising how much heat and glow a burned cabin could put out and for how long. There wasn't actually much heat coming off now, but when I stirred through the ashes, it seemed to kick up smoke and occasionally red embers. Things would just have to wait.

When I returned to the cabin and the rest of the family members, for I included Rebecca and her children as being family, were just beginning to eat the food that Rebecca had set out on the table for the general dinner. Everyone seemed a little more talkative, but there was still an intense gloom that hung over those gathered. I think it was Jacob who mentioned something about the boarding house and café that Moses managed. In one of the first attempts at humor, he said something like he was surprised that

Moses would be leaving it abandoned for this period of time. Moses replied that it was no longer there either. It seems that he had continued to attempt to prepare meals for people from the town that had been burned and to go on with business as usual. Apparently sometime Tuesday evening, around dusk, a group had gathered outside of his establishment, and he hadn't noticed until they rushed through the door that they were armed. They had kept him covered as more people came, entered the cabin, and made off with everything of value. All the food had been taken, the root cellar and smokehouse cleaned out. They had taken every cooking utensil, any bedding, and any clothes—pretty much everything—and had left the place totally ransacked. They hadn't burned it down, but Moses felt that they may as well have. It seems the only thing they hadn't taken was his rifle and shotgun, one of which he kept pointed at them with the left and right hand, and his knife.

Things certainly made no sense to me. Apparently Osceola had been burned by raiders from Kansas who, I think, were just intent on stealing and looting as much as they could. They did this under the pretense of fighting a war against slavery. I thought that Moses' building had been spared because it was on the edge of town and because he was black and these raiders had been determined to punish the good folk of Osceola because people in this area seemed to either support slavery or not be willing to take any action against it. Moses' place was one of the few places that hadn't been looted, raided, or burned. Possibly the townsfolk now raided his home from a sense of revenge.

I thought about this considerably but concluded that it likely had nothing to do with revenge but just a feeling of necessity. If Isaac's cabin had been burned, if the smokehouse, root cellar, and corncrib had been burned and looted and we had absolutely nothing left, maybe I would feel justified in going to town and raiding any establishment or any person that still had anything worth eating, worth wearing, or worth stealing for my own survival. I thought this was possible but then determined it was not likely. Even under circumstances of having nothing, I felt that we could get by without harming our neighbors. We were capable of making bows, arrows, or hunting spears, baskets for trapping fish in the river, and of scouring through the woods for any edible plants, berries, or nuts, even at this time of year. It would be difficult but not impossible to survive, and stealing and raiding from one's neighbors was something that I felt we could never do.

That evening, Thursday evening, once again was spent quietly. No one seemed to be able to make any plans or discuss much of anything. Rebecca puttered around the cabin, tidying up after cooking, tidying up the room and the bed, and just piddling around in general. Moses, Jacob, and I went outside to sit on the benches on the porch. Abel and Jesse sat on the edge of the steps, and we just seemed to stare out through the woods. Occasionally someone would make a remark, but this rarely elicited any further conversation or discussion. I had taken, several times a day, to just walking around and probing at the cabin site. Earlier that day, I had elected upon a plan. I had carried a couple of wooden buckets on a pole down to the river and had made several trips fetching water, which I threw as far as I could into the ashes on any spot that looked like it might still be hot. The only thing I could think at this time was that I needed to find my father, mother, and brother so that I could place them in the family cemetery. I thought that doing so might bring some sense of peace to the family. I couldn't seem to plan any further than that.

The following day I dressed in my buckskins with my leather moccasins and my stiff leather boots, found the hoe lying next to the cabin site, and proceeded to step through the ashes, searching carefully with the hoe in front of me. I would rake through the ashes and burned logs. Things seemed to be going well. I hadn't noticed any sparks or smoke, but as I proceeded to work deeper into the ashes, I felt a sudden intense burning on the inside of my right ankle. Leaping, skipping, and jumping, I rushed to the cleared area around the cabin site and tore off the boot to see a piece of ember about the size of a small acorn that was glowing intensely red in all directions. It had apparently worked up over the top of the leather boot, down next to the leather moccasin and burned a hole completely through the moccasin and was now stuck to my skin. I knocked it off and then proceeded to take off my moccasin and rushed down to the creek between the cabins. I stepped out into the water that wasn't much more than ankle deep and began rubbing and stroking at my foot. There was already a large, weepy blister arising.

I carefully walked to the cabin, where Rebecca tended to my injury. First, she scrubbed it down with lye soap, removing the top of the blister over the burn. She then rubbed my whole foot, even up to the knee, with the lye soap, rinsed it off thoroughly, and then went out to the spring house and fetched a hunk of cheese. This cheese seemed to be a specialty that my grandfather had enjoyed. It was also something that we kept for medicinal purposes. She scraped the white, filmy mold off the top of the cheese, mixed it in some butter to make a paste, and then applied a thick, heavy layer of this mixture over the burned area and for several inches in all directions. She then wrapped my foot fairly snugly with some clean white muslin cloth. The rest of the day I spent pretty much inside the cabin with the rest of the family.

Jacob and Moses would go out and disappear for a while on their own and then return, but no one asked them what they had been doing. Abel seemed to be unable to leave the corner of the room in which he had sat and lingered while his father had died. It seemed that we were incapable of any happiness. It seemed as if there was never going to be laughter and joking again. Everyone seemed to be absorbed in their own thoughts, and mine mainly consisted of my parents and my determination to see that they were buried.

Rebecca refused to allow me to go back and wade across the creek. She said with my injured ankle I shouldn't be wearing moccasins and shouldn't be getting it wet. Perhaps she was right, although twice a day she insisted that I soak my foot in a basin of salt water, after which she would scrub it thoroughly with the lye soap, rinse it off, and reapply her butter- mold medication. Before she applied the salve, I continually inspected the burn. It had taken on a grayish-white appearance in the center of the burn, surrounded by a half an inch of a fairly intense red. The

grayish-white area didn't seem to hurt when I poked it, although the reddish area was intensely painful.

The following morning, I felt determined to make another attempt to explore the burned site of our cabin. After my foot was bandaged, I had dressed again in my leathers, put on the old leather boots, gone down to the creek, and taking a running leap, cleared it. I approached the smoldering ruins of our cabin site. I picked up the hoe where I had dropped it a few days ago and began stirring the embers around the edges of the cabin. Reaching out as far as I could from the edges toward the center, I determined that there wasn't any smoke or glowing embers within reach. Then I stepped carefully out and began working my way through from one side to the other. Having crossed from east to west and north to south, scraping through the ashes and bits of charred wood, I finally realized that I had found no evidence of remains of either my parents or my brother.

For a moment I felt relieved, thinking that possibly they had escaped after all, but if that had happened, where were they now?

I knew there was only one other place to look, and I approached the entrance to the tunnel. Here ceiling beams, rafters, and shingles had fallen in, and the floor had caved in around it. This seemed to produce a deep pit that was filled at least halfway with ashes and burned pieces of wood. I was concerned that this might still be smoldering down deep toward the bottom. Rather than lower myself down into this pit, only to experience hot embers like I found the day before, I made several trips down to the river with the two buckets on the sling. I continued to dump buckets of water for the next hour or so until I felt like the pit had to be a foot deep in water. I then began pulling out any charred timber that was there until the bottom appeared to be just a soupy mass of wet ashes. I fetched the long-handled shovel and began scooping out as much as I could. I didn't wish to drop down into a two-feet-deep pile of what would amount to be lye ashes.

I continued using the long-handled shovel to scoop out as much of the debris as I could. Finally I had no choice but to drop down into the debris that remained at the bottom of the pit. I squatted down on my haunches and felt with my hands. It wasn't long before I encountered pieces of bone and evidence that indeed this was the final resting place of my parents and brother. I felt an odd mixture of relief and repulsion as I removed long bones and skulls and other evidence of my family's demise. Some of the bones still had remnants of tissue and charred flesh.

Jacob had come to assist me in this endeavor. He had assisted removing soaked ash and charred wood remnants with the shovel, and now I tenderly handed up pieces of remains to him. He would take them, collect an armload, and then carry them out of the ashes to the clearing around the cabin site. I kept searching with my hands and feet. I tried to use my feet as much as possible to avoid getting the wet ash remnants on my hands since it seemed to dry the skin out rapidly and I even started feeling a tingle as if it might be burning. Often I would wash my arms and hands off in a bucket of water that we had set by the side of the pit. I thought about wearing gloves, but any gloves would become wet in a short period of time, and I felt this would just add further to the skin irritations.

I was determined to remove any bony remnants that might be left and kept searching, and suddenly I was surprised to feel something exceedingly hard, rounded, and long. Perhaps I had been searching for this as much as I had for my parents' remains, because I knew instantly what it was. Clutching it almost with relief, I lifted up the Henry rifle that was badly burned, charred, and discolored. The beautiful walnut butt looked more like a large piece of charcoal. It had split along its length. I handed this up to Jacob and continued feeling with my feet and hands, and quickly I located the two Remington revolvers. They were in as bad of shape as the Henry. I wasn't sure that any of them were worth retrieving. I wasn't sure that they would function or that they could be of any use. Nevertheless, I handed them out, and then, feeling relieved and convinced that no further remains were covered here, Jacob assisted me out of the pit.

We laid everything I had retrieved from the pit, along the clearing just outside of the ruins of the cabin, and walked down across the creek to Isaac's cabin. We requested towels and some goat milk-honey soap that my mother was particularly fond of making, and which she seemed to reserve for the womenfolk. Rebecca had a good supply of this on hand. I had felt that it wasn't a good idea to use the old lye soap that most of the men preferred, since it actually seemed to clean better, because it was hard on the skin and hair. I felt I had had enough of oak ash and caustic lye material for the rest of my life. My hands were red, dry, and irritated. I didn't think that my feet would be too badly damaged or the burn that I had on my right ankle would be affected since we had been careful to scoop out as much of the ashes as we could so that the ashes remaining in the bottom of the pit hadn't come to over the tops of my boots. Just for precaution, we had wrapped my feet and lower legs up to the knees, covering the tops of the boots in all corners carefully with several layers of old gunnysack and leather. This had worked adequately to protect my feet and legs. It was just my hands and forearms that felt like they might require medical attention.

Jacob and I walked back to the ford at the river. All we carried at that time was a tub of the honey milk soap. We were intending to bathe in the river, but as we neared the shore, my eyes were drawn west to the five bodies that lay piled here. I had refused to go to the trouble of burying these raiders. I felt it was insulting and demeaning to bury them on our property. I decided it wasn't fitting to commit their corpses to the water to float downstream to the town and pollute it. I had elected just to leave them there on the shore.

I had noticed over several days how they had bloated, swelled up, and discolored, and how the birds and other small animals had begun to feast on the remains. Suddenly I had an uncontrollable impulse. I sat the soap down, walked out toward the nearest body, grasped it under the shoulders, around the chest and the armpits, and lifted it up and began dragging it along the bank eastward. Jacob looked at me and said, "What the hell are you doing, boy?"

I smiled at him. I think I even laughed for the first time in the last week. I said, "We haven't fed the hogs for a week." I continued dragging the corpse along. He said nothing further, simply nodded his head, walked over, and grabbed the corpse around the knees, and lifted it up.

While we were struggling toward the hog coop, Moses came down the path. He saw us off to his left and set down the change his clothes and towels that he had been bringing and rushed over. His only question was, "What are you doing with that?"

I told him again, with a laugh in my voice, that it was time to feed the hogs. He said nothing but stepped forward and put his right arm around the hips and between the three of us, we hauled the first one down. When we arrived at the hog pen, there were only a couple of small hogs present. We heaved the body over the gate of the fence and were amazed that within a few seconds it seemed every hog we had had arrived on the spot. They seemed to communicate by some sort of squealing, grunting noise that it was time for feeding. I didn't stick around and stand there and watch to see the hogs consume their meal but immediately went back to fetch another. This time Jacob grabbed the corpse around the chest and under the shoulders and armpits, and Moses took it around the hips and I was relieved to only have to carry the feet and knee portion. We made three more trips in similar fashion. Once we had heaved the last of the corpses over the pen, without taking a further look at them, I turned and walked back to the banks of the ford.

Without bothering to undress, I waded out in the river up to my waist, dove under the water, and swam back and forth as far as I could up and down river, only coming up to take a breath of air as necessary and continuing to swim laps back and forth submerged. Jacob and Moses had likewise walked out to the center of the river and were swimming. I then walked back up to the shore and struggled to remove the wet leathers and wrappings and bindings and just tossed them as far as I could out into the water downstream. When totally naked, I grabbed the soap, marched out to my waist high, and starting with my hair, face, and ears, I worked down. I tried to wash every crack and crevice on my body. I closed my eyes and washed my eyelids. I washed inside my ears. Jacob shared the soap with me and, while I soaped my upper body, he even washed my back and then I, his, and Moses'. We would occasionally dunk completely down under water and then stand erect, only to begin the process of scrubbing again from hair down as far as we could all the way around.

Then, we walked in toward the shore to where it was just between ankle and knee deep and washed the rest of our bodies. Finally I went to sit on the very shore, on the fine pebbles and gravel, and washed my feet. I washed between each toe. I very carefully washed around the burn on my ankle and scrubbed repeatedly. Finishing this, I walked back out in the center of the stream, lathered my hair up again and my upper body, and then swam several laps. I swam until I was exhausted and could swim no more.

Jacob and Moses had walked to the shore and were standing there watching me, drying their bodies, but hadn't begun to dress yet. I swam to the ford, walked out to the edge of the gravel and sat down. Sitting there in water eight or nine inches deep, I just laid back, with my head in more shallow water and began to laugh. I laughed for what seemed like hours. It seemed to be a high-pitched cackling type of laugh. I felt such intense relief, almost joy, I couldn't quite explain it. Finally, I actually became dozy. I began to realize that I was probably becoming hypothermic by this time and that the cold was having this effect on me. I stood up stiff and could barely hobble, but once again, I waded out to deep water, dove under, and walked to the shore. There, I dried off and wrapped the towel around me, and we headed back to the cabin.

Once I got inside the cabin, Rebecca hurried me to sit in front of the fire, and she soaked my foot in hot salt water and then applied her cheese mold and butter remedy to my foot. While she was doing that, I took a good look at it. The central area of the skin that had been dry and grayish in color had now become rather a slimy, grayish-looking wound. The area of redness seemed to extend for about an inch in all directions around it. It wasn't particularly any more tender than it had been. She was quite upset at me that I had been in the pit with all this lye ash, but I knew that it hadn't really caused any problems since it never managed to penetrate the wrappings, my moccasins, and my boots.

Before she began to apply the cheese and butter ointment, I stopped her. I went and fetched my Damascus-bladed knife. The point of this had narrowed down to where it was almost needle sharp. I got another knife from the kitchen and sat down. With the pointed edge of the Damascus blade, which was intensely sharp, I sliced through the skin completely in the center of the burn. This released a thin, watery reddish fluid. I then put the edge of the other knife under this to lift it up and taking the Damascus blade, I made quick, slicing flicks of my wrist to cut the obviously dead skin away from the skin that appeared whole. Occasionally I cut too far and would slice through quite sensitive skin. The pain was nearly unbearable, but I felt that it needed to be done. After having raised up an edge of the dead skin, I took it with my fingers, and using the tip of the Damascus blade, sliced off the dead skin in its entirety. I then repeated this procedure on the upper half of the piece of dead skin until I had debrided it. Then, I soaked the foot again in the salt water solution, and only then allowed Rebecca to cover it with the salve. She wrapped it up carefully.

I continued sitting there naked except for the towel wrapped around me and some blankets draped over my shoulder but now felt considerably warmer, even sleepy. I got up and went to the corner behind the screen of blankets that Jacob and Moses held and dressed myself. Then, once again, I went and washed my hands with water and honey-milk soap. My hands and forearms were quite red and irritated, and Rebecca then used some of her precious butter mold salve to cover my fingers, palms, and back of my hands all the way up to my elbows. This felt intensely good and refreshing. We ate then what had been prepared for supper and went to bed.

The following day, we held services for my family. While I had been searching through the pit and the embers of my house with Jacob, Moses had dug a larger grave than usual. This was to the west of my grandparents' grave. He had also made a single large coffin. He had put all of the remains in the one coffin, not bothering to try to sort them out. I felt that that was a very decent thing to do. I certainly couldn't have told one bone from another, and I felt that, since they had lived and died together, they should be buried together.

After the coffin had been placed in the ground, the womenfolk took turns saying prayers and singing songs. It was quite similar to Isaac's burial. I had thought that once the remains of my parents and brother had been found and properly buried, I would feel a great sense of relief. This actually did nothing to improve my mood or the gloom of the rest of the family and friends that were gathered here. Some things, I think, are too hard to ever totally overcome.

As we walked back to Isaac's cabin, when we passed the burned remains of ours, I suddenly thought about the weapons. I looked, but they were nowhere to be seen. On inquiry, I found that, at some point in time, Moses and Jacob had retrieved them, taken them to the creek, washed them out thoroughly, cleaned out the barrels with soap and water, and used some of the precious solvent that we had brought back from the trading post at Osage City. Then they had oiled them down. I hadn't even thought of them until this point. I then took them and set them around the table in Isaac's cabin and inspected them. They had been cleaned and oiled well. I worked the lever, pulled the trigger to dry fire the hammer, and did this several times. I took a couple of shells and dropped down the tubular magazine and worked the lever, and they did load and eject properly. I didn't fire the guns for fear that, although they seemed to be functioning properly, possibly the steel had been weakened from the heat and they might explode.

I then took the Remingtons. Apparently one of the guns had had at least one or two shots to fire off, as it had cooked in the pit. I think the other gun must have been totally empty. But on this one gun, there was one lead ball that had fired through the cylinder, and striking the frame next to the barrel, it had deformed, flattened out, and lodged there. This kept the cylinder from rotating. Using one of the knives, I managed to cut, whittle, and pry it out. Then, rotating the cylinders, cocking and dry firing, I inspected them. We further cleaned the guns with soap, water, and solvent and oiled them down. The handles were badly burned, split, charred, and cracked, but the guns mechanically seemed to be fine. However, I was not taking any chances and had no intention of actually firing them. I had never been allowed to shoot these guns, but Jacob and my father and Isaac had talked about how tricky they were to care for, so I had a rough idea about loading and maintaining the weapons.

The rest of the day was spent in relative silence. Abel seemed still reluctant to move from his place in the corner to the left of the bed. The womenfolk sat around the table primarily and talked occasionally but rather infrequently. Rebecca seemed to be convinced that there was always something to cook or clean, or just pitter-pattered around in the kitchen. Jacob, Moses, and I seemed more content to sit out on the porch in front of the cabin. We talked occasionally about things that needed to be done, plans that needed to be carried through, but no one seemed able to get up to begin.

A melancholy lethargy had seemed to settle upon the whole group. Rebecca had said repeatedly that we should stay with them. I loved her as a mother, and her sons and daughters were like my own siblings. I knew that we could stay there with them and continue to work on the farm as always, but the cabin seemed small, confined, and close to me. Certainly, we had enough sustenance stored for the winter for the whole group. I had even thought about having Moses go down to town to try to sell off some of the stuff that we had stored, thinking that we had an obligation to help our neighbors, but then I decided against that for fear that, if they knew we had any extra food, they might be drawn to us. They hadn't been above raiding Moses' cabin and stealing everything they had, and I didn't think they would hold us in any higher regard. I actually felt the less we had to do with the town folk, the better.

That evening after we had finished supper, I made the rather blunt announcement to Rebecca that we were going to be leaving in the morning, going by canoe down to Osage City. It was there that my uncle Aaron had his trading post. Initially at one point in time it had been called the Rubidoux trading post, but sometime after Aaron had started running this, after my grandfather, Jean, had died, he started calling it the Osage Trading Post. I think this was possibly because most of the people who had traded there originally were Osage Indians, or because Jean's wife had been a full-blooded Osage. I don't really know how the name came about, possibly because it was on the Osage River at its junction with the Missouri

My brother and my sisters stared at me and wondered, and Rebecca rushed over, rather franticly pleading that we should stay there. Jacob, Moses, and their sisters were pleading also and insistent that we not leave. They reasoned with me that it was getting on toward winter, that it was a long and dangerous journey, and that my brothers and sisters were not up to this. Rebecca hugged me in her arms and looked me in the eyes with a questioning, pleading expression. I didn't know that I could explain everything that I was thinking. I thought, *How do you tell people that you love them but you're leaving? How do you explain to them that the reason you're leaving is because you feel you simply can't stay there any longer?* We had been so happy on the farm with my parents and my siblings and Isaac's family, but now there was such an intense gloom over the farm that I felt that it was impossible to be happy here any further.

For the last week after the raid and the death of my parents, we had been unable to talk or to communicate. We could only sit around and watch as Isaac had died. We could only barely manage to talk as we waited for the embers to cool so my parents' bodies could be found and buried. The whole area seemed to have taken on a sense of loss, disappointment, and despair such that I didn't feel that we could stay. It's hard to explain. I simply looked up in Rebecca's face and said, "I reckon we must be going."

Somehow I think that she could read my mind. She seemed to sense everything that I had thought and merely shook her head and said, "All right."

The rest of the evening I spent thinking about things that we would need for the journey. While I was sitting there thinking, Rebecca came back from outside. I hadn't even realized she had left. She had one of the well-cured hams from last year, which she put in the deep cast-iron cauldron and commenced to boil. It was necessary to boil these well-cured hams for usually at least a day to remove all the salt so they could be edible. She kept the kettle bubbling vigorously all night long in an attempt to speed up the process. She also had some of her white moldy cheese and a crock of butter. She had a sack of apples, some potatoes, and onions in sacks, and one of the less well-cured hams that we had recently started, what, less than two weeks ago? She didn't bother about starting to boil this one, but instead we placed it in a wooden cask, stuffed a few sausages in around it, and sealed the cask tightly.

As we proceeded to gather all that we felt was necessary for the trip, we made plans for how to stow it in the canoe. The canoe that I decided to take was the larger one that Dad had often used to take produce and other items to town to sell for cash money. We took the potatoes and some well-cured sausage and placed it in one of the small casks and sealed it tight.

In another cask, we had placed onions and a few sausages and sealed it tight. In a third cask, we placed the ham that had been curing but not yet smoked. We placed a few sausages in with it and sealed it up tight also. In the fourth cask, we placed some of the white, moldy cheese, some butter, a couple of sausages, and a small stone jar with honey. We got a sack of apples and some of the salted, but not yet smoked, bacon. We placed this in a muslin sack and tied both ends. We filled several leather pouches with pemmican, one for each of us.

Rebecca busied herself baking up biscuits and loaves of hard French bread, as Grandfather Rubidoux called it. She baked a dozen biscuits for each of us and set them out to cool. While we were arranging all the food supplies, we made plans for clothing for the trip. We had nothing left except the clothes that we had been wearing when we were hustled into the tunnel to the root cellar. The weather had continued to turn colder. By all signs, it appeared that we were going to have a difficult winter. A journey by water this time of year would be a bone-chilling experience. This is something we knew from years of experience. Along the river it was much colder and chillier than higher on the bluffs around the house and even across the river in the fields. Something about the damp and mist and fog that usually hung around low-lying areas in the river valleys held in the cold whenever the temperature was brisk. In order to offset this, we needed to have available plenty of warm clothing. From past experience, we knew that heavy wool was by far the best material available to hold in warmth, especially in damp, moist areas, but we had few woolen items.

While Rebecca continued boiling the ham and cooking the biscuits, Sara and Miriam helped Mary and Elizabeth hem and alter some older wool clothing. A pair of old wool pants that had belonged to Isaac were hemmed up for me. They also had an old heavy wool jacket that they rolled the sleeves up and hemmed. Otherwise, these were not altered. The waist that was much too large was simply fitted with a rope belt, and the coat that was also much too large was left otherwise unaltered except for hemming up the sleeves so that I could use my hands without getting the coat sleeves soaked. Another old pair of wool pants that Abel had outgrown were generously donated. They were too big for Jesse, but like mine, the legs were rolled up and hemmed. We fastened a rope belt to cinch them up. Between Sara and Miriam, Jacob and Moses, we were able to gather up enough old and cast off clothing to complete the outfits. We were a ragged and bizarre-appearing group as we sat around dressed up in the clothes we would be wearing for the journey. Slight alterations were made. Mary had a strange-appearing outfit of layered bundles of lighter and heavier clothes. Under the dress she had been wearing when we fled through the tunnel, she wore a pair of woolen long johns that had been altered as best as they could that had previously belonged to Isaac and Jacob. Then, she had a lighter woolen coat that had belonged to Sara that was more for appearance around town than for actual warmth or work, but still, it was wool. By layering up with different assortments of clothing, we felt that we would be sufficiently warm for the journey.

We took two waxed canvas ground sheets and four woolen blankets. We placed the woolen blankets on the ground sheets, folded it, then rolling it up, we tied it up cord. I felt that we had sufficient food and clothing for the journey, and now my attention turned to a means of self-defense. I set about cleaning and loading the Pepperbox and my Pennsylvania rifle. I also gathered up my knife, and each of the girls acquired a knife from the kitchen. I set a small hatchet on the table for the trip and as an afterthought, decided to take a leather punch. This had been quite useful in helping to alter the buckskins that we were wearing. I thought it might be useful on the trip.

As I started to load the Pennsylvania rifle, I had an unusual thought. Abel had withdrawn to the corner where he usually sat and had become even quieter as he watched us gathering our necessaries for the trip. He looked so miserable and forlorn that it tore at my heart. I got up and walked and sat down beside him, carrying my rifle. In the small cabin, it was hard to have any type of a private conversation, but speaking in whispers, we talked long and intently more than we had talked since the tragedy of that Sunday night. Abel couldn't understand why I was intent on leaving. I tried to explain, even though honestly I wasn't sure that I could. I thought about it long and carefully before making the decision. I tried to explain, although we had enough foodstuffs stored in the root cellars and corncrib and spring houses to suffice for nine people, that the cabin was small and crowded. True, Jacob had a cabin across the river, but we hated to split up the group to try to defend both places. Also, I tried to reason with him that, although we had survived the original attack on the family, we couldn't be sure that these raiders from Kansas might not come back. Several of these people had been killed, and possibly they might be looking for revenge, even though with Osceola burned there was no other reason for them to return in that there was nothing to steal and plunder.

I tried to explain that, if this were to happen, if the raiders were to return or if some of the townsfolk from Osceola took it in their heads to raid our cabin like they had Moses', that having the two younger girls, Mary and Elizabeth, and Jesse, would worry and distract us from any defense of the cabin. I tried to explain to him that the main reason I was leaving was to ensure that my younger siblings would be safe. I told him that I felt we were much safer on a trip to the river down to Osage City and my uncle's trading post than we were hanging around Osceola.

He seemed to understand this, but at the same time, I couldn't bring myself to discuss the feelings that were my main reason for leaving. I wasn't sure if I should try to explain that, after what had happened, I just felt that there could be no happiness for us there anymore, and I certainly didn't attempt to explain possibly my own personal reason for the trip. I finally ended up by explaining to Abel that, once I had taken Jesse, Mary, and Elizabeth, I would be coming back. I told him that, after what had happened, we were low on ammunition. Originally, my father and Isaac had bought two fifty-round boxes of the Henry ammunition. All of my father's had been lost in the cabin. We never counted how much ammunition that Isaac had left precisely, but we figured we couldn't have more than thirty or thirty-five shells left. If we had any further trouble at the cabin, we would be limited to the black powder rifle and the single Colt and various old shotguns and muskets that we possessed. It would be hard to make an adequate defense.

Abel seemed to understand everything that I said and became much less reluctant to concede to the leaving in the morning, but I kept assuring him that I would be coming back, and finally he seemed to become satisfied with the decision. Acting on a sudden impulse, I told him that I wished that he would take my rifle. His eyes widened as he stared at me in surprise. He knew how much I had treasured the rifle that had been handed down to me by my father. I explained to him that I wished him to have it. I tried to convince him that I felt it would be more of a liability than a use on the canoe journey because the powder in the rifle would be sure to get damp and would be unreliable if I actually needed it.

He still seemed reluctant to take the rifle, and I then suggested that possibly we should trade. I told him that with all the clothing they had given my family for the journey, the rifle would be a fitting means of paying for this. I told him that I was worried about him and his family and I felt that they would need it to defend themselves if they had any further trouble with raiders. I told him that, as we went further east down the Osage, we would be moving away from danger, but they were apt to be still in the middle of it. Finally I asked if he would trade me his bow. I knew how much Abel treasured this. He had worked for several months on making his bow. We had cut and cured the wood, split out the slabs for the bow, tillered, sanded, and formed it. He had steamed it to reflex it and finally had backed it with sinew and glue made from hoof and hide. He considered it a thing of beauty, and I had to agree. I told him we would be better off on the trip with a bow and arrows than with a rifle that might have damp powder when needed. He was quite pleased and excited that I should feel that his bow was more of a treasure than my rifle, and he finally agreed almost joyfully. Placing the bow and quiver of arrows on the table, I looked over everything that we had gathered for the journey and felt that we were ready.

CHAPTER 7

We went to bed earlier than usual that evening, and once again I found it hard to sleep. The following morning, we were up at the crack of dawn. We bundled and dressed ourselves up in our many layers of castoff clothing. Then Rebecca and her children helped us gather up our supplies for the journey and carried them down to the canoe. I loaded up the canoe carefully according to a plan I had decided upon while I was unable to sleep last night. I took the four sealed wooden casks, tied a rope to each, placed one under the cane seat in the back of the canoe, and tied it to the struts on the seat. Another one, I tied in the front to the cane seat struts. Two I tied to the thwarts in the middle of the canoe. I placed a sack of apples in the middle of the canoe between the thwarts. I tied the one ham in the muslin cloth to one of the thwarts and tied the bacon wrapped in the other muslin to the second thwarts. I then took the blankets wrapped in the waxed canvas ground sheets and tied them to the center thwarts. I gave Abel's precious bow to Jesse and told him that he should keep this up and out of the water and protect it at all times. The four dozen biscuits that had been placed in separate sacks, we tied around our shoulders and suspended from our back. I put the sacks of pemmican and the bread in also. We needed to make sure and keep these up out of the water at all times.

I had taken the Henry rifle and loaded it, even though I was afraid to fire it except in the direst of emergencies, placed it in a leather gun cover, and tied it to the gunnels of the canoe on the inside between the thwarts in a location where I felt that it would not be seen. When I had dressed that morning, I had put on my woolen socks, then my long johns, then my knee-high moccasins. I then put on the hemmed heavy woolen pants, tied the rope cinch around the waist, and fixed my belt with my knife and the leather holster for the Pepperbox. Among the alterations we had made to our clothing last night, I had cut a hole in the pocket of the wool coat to allow me to slip my right hand through the pocket to get to the Pepperbox. We had also taken some sheepskin with the wool turned in and made a couple of pockets on the inside of the coat up across the breast on each side. I slipped the old Remingtons, which we had loaded, into these pockets. The coat was much too large for me, and with all this underneath, it was impossible to tell they were there due to the ruffled, baggy nature of the much-too-big coat. We next put on some wool caps with ear flaps and topped off our costume with the leather hats that we made. I was the only one to have a pair of our heavy hide boots to keep my moccasins dry; but if we were careful, I was the only one who would need them.

Giving a paddle to each of the girls, and Abel's bow to Jesse, I took up my own paddle and shoved off from the shore. We paddled the canoe out to midstream and turned to watch as Rebecca and her children faded from sight. It didn't take long to approach the bend in the river, and they were quickly out of sight. I was in a hurry to leave this homestead and the whole territory in general. We paddled hard and almost furiously, keeping to the center of the river.

It seemed like in no time we were passing the site of Osceola. On the north side were steep stone, rocky bluffs. We kept as close to these as possible since the water was deepest here, but also I had hoped that we might be able to slip by without being seen, and I supposed that, inwardly, I still had a fear that people now might still be living there. Once they had been our friends, and it seemed that everyone had been good, decent, law-abiding folks, and I didn't feel like we had an enemy in the world. Now, I felt that these people could not be trusted, and I was only too anxious to get by without any conversation and if possible, without even being seen. We were spotted by a few people on the shores, but I think in all probability there were few people who even noticed our passing or gave it a second thought. The way we were dressed in an odd assortment of many types of clothing and different layers, I'm not sure that they would have recognized us even if they had known who we were. I think they felt that we were probably just another group of townsfolk who had decided to leave.

Watching carefully as we went by the town site, I felt that most everyone had left anyhow. Still, I couldn't relax until we were well downstream and away from them. We paddled incessantly the whole day. I refused to even pull ashore to stop, to make a fire to cook lunch. Instead, we snacked on the ham. Whenever they felt that they were hungry, we would pull the muslin sack aside, and Elizabeth would shave off some ham. Mary was the oldest and was in the front of the canoe, carefully guiding and watching for snags, ripples, or anything that might upset us, so it was Elizabeth's job to slice ham and hand out the food and paddle, for a little extra speed, as necessary. It was she who passed out the biscuits, sliced the ham, passed the apples around, and allowed Mary and I to paddle pretty much nonstop.

We had coyote fur mittens to keep our hands warm, since the temperature was still hovering around the mid-forties. The coyote skin worked exceptionally well to turn the water away and keep our hands warm. It also helped to protect our hands from blisters, but with the nonstop, continual paddling, nothing could entirely prevent that. We paddled nonstop throughout the day and only decided to look for a place to pull ashore when it started becoming dark. This time of year it seemed that it went from dusk to total darkness almost in the blink of an eye.

On the north shore I spied a small, what I initially thought was an island, hugging the bluffs. In fact, this was a sandbar. It seemed that it was about a half a mile long and maybe two or three hundred feet wide. During the spring and higher water, I'm sure that it was an island because, right at the base of the bluff, there was a channel that, although dry now, would probably fill with water. As we passed around this sandbar, I watched carefully and studied the shoreline. There didn't appear to be any movement. There didn't appear to be any sign that a canoe had been drug up out of the water and onto the bank. As we passed the eastern end, I ordered Mary to turn the canoe suddenly, and we paddled up to the channel that ran along the side of the sandbar at the base of the bluff. We ran the canoe in lightly to the shoreline. Mary, Elizabeth, and Jesse stepped carefully to the front of the canoe and out. I stepped out of the back of the canoe, into the water, and we lifted it up and carried it carefully shore. I wished to leave no trace of a canoe having been taken out of the water there.

We walked along this channel until we were back and hidden completely from the river. I told my brother and sisters to be quiet, and stay hidden and taking Abel's bow and quiver of arrows, I walked back up to the west end of the sandbar and back down. It appeared to be deserted. Mary had inquired about lighting a fire and fixing something to eat, but I was reluctant to do that. No matter how careful you were, wood smoke could be smelled at a considerable distance, and any light from a campfire would probably be visible. I wished to get as far away from Osceola as possible. I felt that it was more dangerous here than anywhere, because people like us who had lost everything in the raid might be traveling or in the vicinity and might not have any qualms about taking what little we had.

So, we ate ham, biscuits, and apples, drank water from the river, and went to bed. Without any campfire, it was apt to be quite chilly, but it didn't appear like it would be raining, so I didn't make any type of a shelter. I also didn't bother about unloading the canoe but left it just as it was, in case we should have any trouble. The plan was for everyone to go to the canoe, and we would set off downstream again. The only thing we removed were the two ground sheets and the four wool blankets. Then we kicked and raked together a mound of dry leaves, which I covered with some small, soft cedar branches for a mattress. Finally I placed the ground sheet to keep moisture out and provide a barrier between us and the earth and then, covering with the two wool blankets, we snuggled up to sleep. Jesse and I cuddled together, while Mary and Elizabeth cuddled immediately next to us. I hadn't slept the night before, and my younger brother and sisters were extremely tired from paddling all day, so we had no trouble in immediately falling off to sleep. It seemed that, although I was deeply asleep, that I still was somehow vaguely aware of our surroundings.

Sometime during the middle of the night I was awakened by a horrid shrieking scream. I jerked awake immediately. Initially I didn't know where I was or what had happened. Then I seemed to think that it was my mother screaming and the cabin was on fire. In truth, I hadn't heard any screaming the night of the raid. I thought that possibly I was just imagining this. Then suddenly there was a scream that seemed close by. This shook me to my bones for I knew that scream. I had actually heard it several times growing up, and Father had explained to me that it was a panther. I hadn't heard one for several years.

Initially they were a lot more abundant around our homestead. Once, several years ago, we had hunted and treed one. Father had been convinced that it had been raiding our precious small herd of cattle. He had found several cattle dead and partially eaten. This had occurred over the space of a couple or three months. Initially father had felt that this was nature at its normal course of events, but after having lost several cattle over several months, he determined that we would have to take action and we had gone trailing and hunting this beast. We managed to tree it, and I can still remember its screams of defiance.

I lay, wide awake, trying to decide what to do. My first impulse was to leap to my feet and draw the Pepperbox. But I realized that was stupid. Any sudden movement like that would arouse the other children and cause a panic. I didn't want them yelling and running around in the dark. I tried to see in the dark but couldn't. I had set up camp at the base of a forty-foot bluff that was topped by tall oak and cedar trees, which leaned out over the sandbar, and since the sandbar was heavily covered with trees, we were in darkness as deep as any cave. I stared into the pitch blackness and tried to make out any movement. I listened carefully and even sniffed hard and intently. I knew big cats had a strong odor, but I could not make out anything. I began to wonder if I had really heard anything; but I knew that I had. None of the others seemed to have heard anything. I listened carefully to their breathing and could tell they were sound asleep. I sniffed, listened, and stared for what seemed like hours, as I lay there clutching my Pepperbox and then suddenly—I woke up. Just when I had fallen asleep I don't know. The last thing I remembered was lying there, nearly petrified with fear. I had never heard it scream again for the rest of the night, but I had imagined every rustle of the bushes, every splash of the river, and every sigh of the wind through the trees was the panther sneaking up on us.

It might have been as early as six-thirty, but I think it was much later since it was already starting to get light even where we were under the trees. I got up quickly and started to look for tracks but never saw any. I fought the urge to explore the sandbar in an attempt to find any trace of the panther. I decided I really didn't want to find it anyhow. I shook the others roughly awake and hurriedly loaded the canoe and carried it to the water. Mary was demanding that we make a fire to warm up and cook something to eat, but I would have none of it. I was anxious to be off, and I didn't want to tell them about the panther or spend any more time on the sandbar. I didn't want to admit that I was still scared, or that I hadn't slept all night. But Mary just wouldn't quit. She was getting mad and being very petulant. Finally I had enough and snapped out, "Shut the hell up and get in the damn canoe."

We shoved off, and I paddled furiously for the next hour until I gradually began to relax. We snacked on biscuits, apples, and ham for breakfast and throughout the morning. Paddling hard, it was probably well past midday before I decided to pull in to a small, shallow sandbar in the middle of the river. The river was fairly wide and deep on both sides of the sandbar but there appeared to be an abundance of dried driftwood on the shore. That, plus the fact that we could see from one side to the other of it without impediment, convinced me that it was safe to stop.

We ran the canoe up on the bank, and everyone clambered out. I had a small fire going in no time while Mary shaved some small slices of the salted bacon into the small frying pan that we had taken with us. She sliced in some potatoes and onions, after having cooked some of the bacon for grease, and then she sliced in some of the ham. It was only then that I realized that I hadn't brought any plates or any means of eating. We sat around in a little huddle, all eating from the same frying pan with our fingers and our knives. After having consumed one skillet full of potatoes, onions, bacon, and ham, Mary prepared two others. These we consumed in similar fashion, sitting in a group and eating out of the single pan.

After having stowed all of our supplies again, we shoved off with the canoe, and feeling much stronger and actually more refreshed than I had that morning when we got up, we continued the journey. That evening as it started to become dark, I found a similar widened area of bank along the high bluffs on the north side of the river. I instinctively preferred the north shore, although I don't know that it made much difference. Osceola had been on the south banks of the river, and I was afraid that stragglers or people wandering away from town might be more inclined to be to the south than the north side of the river, but I knew that didn't probably make much sense. However, this bluff was quite high and could not be climbed. Also, the bank along the edge didn't appear to be more than twenty or twenty-five feet wide, and the bank was probably no more than one hundred feet in length. Passing it, we again made a sharp turn and came up from the east. If we needed to make a quick escape, we would be able to launch directly into the current and be away from the area in no time.

We paddled the bow of the canoe into the bank, where my brother and sisters walked forward and stepped out on the bank while I stepped out in the back. We lifted the canoe up from the water and carried it up and into hiding on the shore. Once again, I walked the island from one end to the other and even crisscrossed through it. I assured myself there were not any panthers on this island. I don't know that there had actually been a panther on the other island. The screams could have echoed anywhere from the bluffs or along the river valley; but one thing I knew was that panthers didn't like to swim and wouldn't be able to scale this bluff, and so, I felt confident that no matter what I heard or thought I heard throughout the night, I could put it aside and actually sleep.

Once again, we ate ham, biscuits, and apples. This evening, after I had prepared the salve of butter and cheese, we ate the cheese and a little bit of the butter on our biscuits. Once the mold had been scrapped off the cheese to make the salve, the cheese would start to turn fairly quickly and, so what had been shaved, we felt necessary to eat. It did not appear that it would be raining any that night, so once again I didn't form any type of a shelter, nor did we unload the canoe. We simply kicked together leaves, cut a few soft green cedar branches, and covered these with the ground sheets and then laid down and covered up with the blankets. The night passed uneventfully, and I didn't wake up again until the early sunlight seemed to shine directly into my eyes through the lids.

Mary won her argument that morning, and once again, we lit a fire. We warmed up while she cooked bacon, ham, potatoes, and onions for breakfast. We finished the rest of the cheese and had some honey on our biscuits, and then we loaded up everything in the canoe and once again set off. We paddled hard throughout the rest of the day. Jesse sat in front of me, in the back of the canoe, and held the precious bow above the gunnels, while Elizabeth, Mary, and I paddled unceasingly. Once again, Elizabeth shaved ham and passed out biscuits and apples for lunch. We would dip the small frying pan into water as we paddled and drink from it. I think that this small frying pan was the most useful item that we had on the whole trip. We used it to cook in, to eat from, and even to drink with.

As we traveled, I kept a watch along both shores and the river itself for the sign of any other refugees. It surprised me that during the previous two days we had only occasionally seen people. We hadn't passed anyone going downstream, which I thought was surprising, but I finally realized that they had all probably left at least a week before we did, or possibly no one else found it necessary to travel by river to leave the area. Possibly the population that had taken up residence in Osceola were not as used as we were to using the river for transportation. I suspect there were a lot of people who had come by road from north or south to move into the town. Possibly they had friends or relatives in the immediate vicinity and had only moved thirty or forty miles away. I couldn't say.

I began to feel much more relaxed and comfortable. Then the thought struck me that if we hadn't been feeling so relaxed and comfortable, those raiders would not have been able to slip up on us as they had. Looking back on it, I realized that Father had possibly been nothing but careless. We had heard old Buck growl but hadn't really thought much of it. We heard horses approach, but that wasn't all that unusual. However, what was unusual was that Father didn't look out the windows to see who was there before he opened the door and walked out. He simply had gone to the door, opened it, and stepped out. He told us never just to open the door or do anything without first looking the situation over. If he had done what he had always done before and what he had always told us and looked before stepping out in the open, he might well be alive. Then the sudden thought hit me that here I was blaming my father for having been killed and having allowed the destruction of our home. I felt quite guilty and ashamed of myself. This caused me once again to become more vigilant and study everything around us as we passed. I couldn't afford to become complacent.

Nevertheless, I couldn't help noticing the beauty of the countryside. The water was clear blue. You could look through it and see ten or fifteen feet down as assorted fish and other water life swam beneath the canoe. Along the banks and shore, the bluffs were gorgeous in an assortment of colors. The golden-centered purple asters that my mother had particularly loved would occasionally be found along the low areas by the river. Also, the various coneflowers were blooming.

My parents often got into arguments about these things. My father kept wanting to call them black-eyed Susans, but my mother would insist that they were actually coneflowers. It seems that they came in golden yellow colors with a rounded center. Somehow they were different from black-eyed Susans. In addition, there was purple clover in patches. These sometimes seem to grow up almost like a small bush two or three feet in height. Then there were plants of a bright orange nature and even a brilliant red. My mother had always called the orange one "Butterfly weed" because it seemed that butterflies seemed to be so intensely attracted to them. We passed the reddish flowers on a long stem that father called cardinal flowers because they were the same color as his favorite bird.

Besides the abundance of flowering plants, even at that time of year, the different-colored leaves on the trees made everything breathtakingly beautiful. The sycamores had gone from a golden yellow to a brown. A lot of the red leaves from the dogwood and redbud trees had already fallen. Most of the oak and hickory had gone from light yellow to dark brown, but this, interspersed with the green pine and cedars, caused a riot of colors that had to be seen to be appreciated.

All of this went through my head as we paddled carefully along the river. It was Mary's job to keep an eye out for snags or submerged rocks and to keep us in the center of the stream by guiding the bow of the canoe. My job was to guide and turn the canoe, either rapidly by a sudden, strong backward paddle or gently by the slow, pushing J-stroke. Growing up on the river as we did, we were all quite competent in managing the canoe, and I felt entirely safe.

That afternoon, it seemed to fog over and become cloudy and colder. I knew we were going to be in for a storm. This was the third day of our trip on the river. I had hoped to be able to travel like we had the previous two days until longer in the afternoon, but I knew it was necessary to find a place for shelter. I kept my eye out for any suitable places to stop. There was a small strip of land at the base of a high bluff I didn't feel was suitable to making camp if it was going to rain. I didn't think it was going to rain much, but you could never really be sure. As we traveled, I noticed an island out in the center of the river. This island seemed to be surrounded on both sides by very deep water and seemed to come up rather quickly and steeply on all sides. We passed by it, and I instructed to Mary to turn sharply, and we paddled up on the other side. The island was higher on the upstream side, with some fairly steep banks. The center of the island must have been at least ten feet out of the water. We then went back down along the northern side to the east side of the island, where it seemed to more gradually slope down to enter the water. Here there was a small sandy, pebbled beach area. I looked at the island for its size and shape and suitability in case we had heavy rains, and I watched carefully for any sign of people. We paddled in to the shore, picked the canoe up, and carried it up into the brush, which was low and thick at this end. We carried it up toward the center of the island where the brush gave way to taller, thicker, and stronger formed trees.

Once again, I put the canoe down, left the kids together, and searched the island over carefully from one end to the other. It, like all the others, was deserted of both humans and animals. It seemed entirely safe. I then went back to the canoe and announced that we would be staying here. You could never know how much it was going to rain or for how long, but I thought it looked like it might last awhile. I found a tree that had blown down previously in a storm. We unloaded the canoe and began to fix a shelter. First, we kicked all the leaves and debris and old bark away from the tree. We didn't wish to have ticks and other vermin in our shelter. Then, taking the small hatchet, I chopped down several cedars that were about the size of my forearm just below the elbow. We took these back to camp and chopped off all the branches to throw up next to the downed tree for bedding. We hadn't taken the trouble to do this the other nights because it hadn't appeared like rain and I didn't think it was that cold, but tonight looked like it was going to be miserable.

After having formed a mound of cedar limbs about a foot thick, we lifted up the canoe and placed it over the fallen log. The canoe was about four feet wide in the center, and we placed approximately the front one third of the canoe over the tree. Then I had found another fallen tree that was only a foot or so in size, and we manipulated this in and lifted up the other end of the canoe to place it on this. Having the upside-down canoe suspended from these two fallen trees, the higher end being about two and a half feet off the ground, we placed all of our supplies under the lowest end of the overturned canoe. Then I braced the cedar poles on the bottom of the canoe, protruding out from one side, and took one of the ground sheets and placed it over the cedar poles and partially over the bottom of the canoe to form a tent. Using the rope that we had brought along, we tied the ground sheet and stretched it out to give us a little more shelter under the canoe. Then we piled the other ground sheet and all the blankets under the canoe on top of the cedar limbs. We dug out a shallow pit, along the edge of the canoe, opposite the tent. It was no more than six inches deep. We lined it with rocks and filled it up with shavings and pine needles and started a fire. While Mary started fixing supper, it began to rain. Shortly after dark, it began to rain hard and continued to rain and blow all throughout the night. I was certainly glad that we had stopped and set up this shelter. Although the temperature got down to where I felt it wasn't much above freezing, we were dry and warm—at least we were as warm as it was possible to be. Winds still blew through the shelter, but because the fact that we were in the center of the trees on the island and the fact that the canoe was not high off the ground and had cedar logs and brush stacked on one side, we were relatively warm. The fire certainly helped.

The following day at sunup, it seemed that the rain had finally stopped. I thought it looked like it was going to clear off. The sun was actually shining, and the fog had lifted before I decided to tear down the camp, load up the canoe, and set off. We cooked breakfast again. We feasted on bacon, ham, potatoes, and onions, a couple of apples, some honey and cheese, and bread and felt fairly refreshed. We were dry and content, the shelter having served its purpose quite adequately. We loaded up and set off. The morning passed without problems. It had become somewhat cloudier but hadn't rained or even drizzled anymore. We had biscuits, ham, sausage, and apples for lunch and washed it down with water from the frying pan. However, shortly after noon, the weather seemed to change suddenly. It became much colder, clouded up, and started raining again heavily. We were thoroughly wet in no time. I knew we would have to stop our journey and make camp again, earlier than I had anticipated, but I determined to paddle on for another couple of hours since we were already wet before looking for a place to make camp again.

Sometime around probably three o'clock, the best I could tell, we had come around a bend with a high cliff on the south and there, to my horror, on the north bank I could make out a large group of people clustered together just away from the river. In the rain and the mist, it was hard to determine just who these people were. We were in the center of the river, as always, and my initial thought was to stay there and paddle on past them and pretend that we hadn't seen them and that they hadn't seen us. But I could tell that we had been spotted. It seemed that everybody on the shore was looking directly at us. As we approached, I stared back. Initially I had just seen men and horses, but then I noticed tents set up further back from the shoreline. In looking closer, I could see through the mist and the clouds that we were coming upon a small town. I didn't know the name of the town then, but I suddenly realized who these people were. They all seemed to be dressed alike. They had dark blue uniforms on. The tents all seemed to be of the same size and general appearance. I felt intensely relieved when I realized that these were soldiers. I didn't know whether they were union soldiers or rebel soldiers, but I could tell from their appearance and their actions that they were fairly disciplined.

I called out to Mary, and we turned the canoe suddenly toward the north shore and paddled in. We disembarked and picked the canoe up and then carried it a short distance onto shore. It was my intention to avoid any discussion with these soldiers. I was somewhat suspicious and distrustful but not actually fearful. We carried the canoe up west of where they were camped and a little bit closer to town. While Mary, Elizabeth, and Jesse unloaded the canoe and turned it over to drain any accumulated water from the bottom of it, I moved off further west and north into the brush along the banks, scouting for suitable wood, logs, and debris to prop the canoe up to form our shelter. I had found some driftwood in the shape of a forked tree that appeared to be adequate to hold one end of the canoe up off the ground a couple, two and a half feet or so, and that was light enough that I could drag it. When I returned to camp, Mary and Elizabeth had accumulated some green cedar branches and some stouter branches to assist in making a roof and barricade for the wind and rain.

As we set about preparing our shelter, we were suddenly, but politely, interrupted. I had been bent over arranging the branches and steadying the canoe upside-down when I heard someone softly clear his throat and speak. "Might I have a few words with you?" he said.

I stood up and turned around to see the man I had taken to be in charge of the soldiers on the bank. He was tall and rather sturdy. He was wearing a bluish uniform with a woolen overcoat that came down past his knees and a cape around his shoulders. He also had a funny, square-looking, billed cap on his head that he managed to pull down to cover his ears. In the mist and gloominess of the afternoon, I could see that he had a darkish colored beard but couldn't make out much more of his face. However, the tone of his voice and the polite manner in which he spoke made me instinctively want to trust him. I'm sure at one point in time I would never have hesitated to trust him, but these were unusual days. I didn't trust anyone. He asked where we were from and why we were traveling on the river at this time of year by ourselves. I could see that he was somewhat concerned. From a distance, the way we were dressed in the odd assortment of clothes that were much too big, it was hard to tell just how young we were, but I think when he realized that, he was even more concerned, and that's what I would call it, concerned.

I was distrustful enough that I answered all of his questions only briefly, although honestly. When he asked why we were traveling by ourselves, I told him we were on our way to Osage City. On further inquiry as to why we were by ourselves, I told him simply that our parents were dead and we were moving there to be with my uncle. My replies were short, succinct, and truthful. I think he realized that we were all distrustful and hesitant to talk with him. He then suggested that our canoe and shelter really wouldn't be adequate for four of us since he expected it to rain hard that night and get quite cold. He offered to let Mary and Elizabeth stay in one of the soldiers' tent. Apparently they had a few extra tents and had already set them up. The girls seemed excited and relieved by this prospect. The tent that he offered was the closest to where we had placed our canoe and was in clear view and seeing the expressions on the girls' faces, I agreed.

The man I took to be an important officer offered to let Mary and Elizabeth have some spare blankets to share so that Jesse and I could more adequately use the four that we had for our own comfort. Mary and Elizabeth had hurried off to the tent to check it out. While they were gone, Jesse and I continued working to set up our shelter, and the man watched us quietly. He did interrupt to ask a few questions but didn't seem anxious to press us any. We got our shelter sufficiently set up and prepared, and I started to gather the kindling and prepare a fire.

The wind had been blowing from the north and west, and the brush and debris that we had gathered and placed over one of the ground sheets had been placed on the upriver side of the canoe to form a barricade. The fire pit that I began to dig was on the uphill, east side, at the edge of the canoe, the ground sheet extending a foot or so past this and covering the fire. I got the fire started and built it up to a low blaze. I didn't pile the wood on excessively high because I didn't wish to scorch the ground sheet. Instead, I made the pit for the fire longer than usual. This would provide a bed of embers for two to three feet along one side of the shelter. Then I began to open the cask to get out food to prepare our meal. The man suggested that we didn't need to do that, that we could certainly join them for supper, which would be ready probably in the next hour or so. I was quite pleased with the prospect of having something to eat besides potatoes, onions, and bacon or ham.

The man politely excused himself and said he would be back when supper was ready to invite us over to share their meal. Mary and Elizabeth returned about that time. Their tent was warm and dry, and they were quite happy about the arrangements. However, there wasn't enough room for all four of us to sit in to discuss the events or make any type of plans and, so we huddled together under the canoe and continued feeding wood on the fire in order to build up a bed of coals for the evening. Mary had suggested that we all go up to the town to see what was there. I was quite reluctant, possibly even afraid. There was nothing that we really needed. We had sufficient food and supplies to make the rest of the journey in safety. I also didn't want anyone to know that we had real cash money. If anyone looked at us, they would have thought that we were destitute and couldn't have had anything worth stealing even if they had wanted to, and I didn't want to let anyone know any better.

Maybe a couple of hours later there was some bugling and racket in the camp as peopled seemed to gather together in the center. A minute or two later, the officer arrived and invited us to supper. It had quit the heavy raining, and the wind seemed to even have died down a bit. We went to see what they had for supper. It consisted of bacon and beans and what they called hard tack. I thought it was the best food we had eaten in a long time. In fact, I thought that mother and Rebecca had never fixed anything near as good. We had no utensils or anything to eat out of, so the man gave us some tin plates and tin cups. We also had some spoons and forks. These, likewise, were made of tin. At home we usually had wooden spoons. We did have a few crude forks but they seemed to have only two tines instead of the three that these did. We ate until we were contented. The man had poured water from some canteens into our tin cups to wash the food down with.

After we had eaten, we felt somewhat content and peaceful. The man began telling us something about their situation. Apparently they were a detachment of union infantry soldiers who had been sent to this small town, the name of which I never asked. I think he mentioned it, but I didn't quite comprehend. The man talked in an accent that I didn't entirely comprehend at times. The longer we sat there, the more relaxed we became and it seemed the more he talked. I actually became somewhat drowsy. I know Mary and Elizabeth did also. The man asked us if we would like to have some coffee. I wasn't sure just what he meant, but I readily agreed. I thought it may have been some type of dessert. He returned from the fire with a large pot with a handle and a spout and poured my tin cup full of a hot steaming dark blackish liquid. I thought that it had smelled wonderful, but the cup was almost too hot to hold, and the fluid was much too hot to drink. The girls related that they felt like going to bed, so they had excused themselves and went off to the tent, which was easily in clear sight.

We were sitting on some high driftwood, well up off the ground, and Jesse was leaning against my left shoulder. The other soldiers seemed to have moved off away from us, leaving the man, Jesse, and myself. I began to sip at the coffee but found it extremely bitter and not to my taste. Jesse wished to try it also, but on the first little sip, he wrinkled up his nose and almost choked. I could tell he felt like I did, that it was much too bitter to drink. I had a sudden thought and suggested that he go to our camp and fetch back the little stone jar of honey. It was over half empty, but I poured a good-sized dollop into the coffee and stirred it with the fork. What had previously been unfit to drink now seemed quite delicious to me. Jesse and I sipped down the whole cup rather quickly and the officer kindly poured us another cup. I think that we had three or four cups of coffee with honey. It seemed the more coffee we drank, the more relaxed we became. I felt relaxed but more alert. I think the heat and the warmth from the coffee helped me relax, and I think the coffee seemed to make me more alert and talkative. Possibly it was that or just the easy manner that this man had in talking to us.

Initially he seemed to do most of the talking. I found out that he wasn't an officer, that he was a sergeant. I found that they had been stationed there because there was a ford in the river that actually wasn't apparent due to the fact that the water was up enough. Apparently they had cavalry assigned with them, but the cavalry patrolled up and down the river. They had been stationed here for the last couple of weeks, and he wasn't sure how long they would be stationed there still. The sergeant began talking about the war and the things that had been going on. Once again, he asked us about our personal situation. I don't know why, but I felt that I could trust him. I told him that we had come from Osceola and that the town had been burned, and people had been massacred by a group of vicious robbers from Kansas. That seemed to surprise him. Apparently the story that had spread was one of a great and glorious victory for a union officer and his army of soldiers. Reports were that they had fought off a large confederate force, had been attacked by another confederate force, and in response had had to burn the town.

Not having been there myself, I couldn't say if that were true or not, and I told him that. However, I followed up with the story that Moses had related to me. I told him Moses actually lived in the town, and according to Moses, after they had gone to bed Saturday night, they had heard a brief exchange of gunfire somewhere south of town that hadn't lasted more than ten or fifteen minutes. He said the following morning when they got up, there were no signs of a fight, no signs of trouble. He said shortly after getting up, all these ruffians from Kansas rode into town. He said there was no fighting in the town, certainly no great and glorious battle. He said this bunch of thieves simply began raiding, stealing, and drinking themselves into a near stuporous mood that rapidly became vicious. He said they randomly shot people and started burning the town. According to Moses, people simply ran, didn't put up any type of a defense, and had watched fearfully as their town was burned and anything of value that could be stolen, was. According to Moses, the band of raiders had withdrawn quietly without being attacked by anyone. He said that no rebel army had arrived that night, and the next day the only people he saw were people who were salvaging through the ruins of their homes looking for anything of value that hadn't been stolen and hoping to salvage something that hadn't been burned and destroyed.

The sergeant seemed shocked and surprised by this revelation. I then went on to tell him about the death of my family and the destruction of our property. He listened intently and never bothered to interrupt, except only occasionally. When I told him about my father being shot and about us escaping through the tunnel, he then asked how I knew what had happened to the cabin and to the house and my parents if I were in a tunnel behind a root cellar. I told him about how Isaac and Jacob had come to help defend our house and most of what I told him had been what Jacob had told me. I told him about how Jacob had approached the cabin and how apparently he and Isaac had managed to kill two or three of the raiders around the cabin. I told him that Jacob had estimated there were at least ten or twelve people in the bunch. I told him how Jacob had described how the cabin was burned and how he had been forced to retreat away from the cabin. I related everything that Jacob had told me.

He then asked me who this Jacob was. I hesitated briefly and I could tell that that caught his attention. I told him that Jacob was Isaac's son, and he asked me what their last name was. I hesitated briefly and then related that their names were Abrahamson. I gave that as their last name. I think the man was somewhat surprised. I don't know if he had heard of anyone named Abrahamson, and I certainly can't say that that was a name I had ever heard used before. I think he thought that I was lying, but I don't think he understood why. I tried to give him the impression that these were our neighbors. I think I was ashamed to tell him that they were free blacks who had once been my grandfather's slaves. After all, he was in the union army and obviously would not approve of slavery.

His kindly manner induced me to keep speaking, and I told him about our trip down the river so far, about the first night on the river, the panther in the vicinity, about the cold, rainy night last night and how we managed to get through it warm and dry. By that time Jesse, who had been leaning on me, listening to the conversation but not interrupting or making any replies, shifted suddenly and nearly fell from the stump on which we had been sitting. I realized he had been sound asleep for the last hour or so. I couldn't believe it, but we had probably been sitting there talking for a couple of hours and Jesse had long since fallen asleep.

The sergeant suggested that I should carry him to bed, which was not a problem, and that he would see us in the morning for breakfast. He offered to let us stay and use the tent until the weather cleared. We had gone off to bed with the anticipation of arising to the best breakfast probably that we had had in weeks, or at least it seemed like weeks.

The following morning we had been awakened by bugling and bustling around camp. It seems like after I had fallen asleep last night, I had heard this bugling, but it hadn't really awakened me. I had slept peacefully until this time. We aroused quickly and hurried off to see what was for breakfast, but it was a good thirty minutes before breakfast was ready. We sat around the same place we had last night, and I was waiting for the sergeant to show up. Finally he did and escorted us over to the cooking pot, where we dished up our breakfast of bacon and beans and hard tack. I still thought it was delicious. The sergeant offered me another cup of coffee, and I asked if Mary and Elizabeth might have some also. I had brought the little jug of honey. We used up the last of our honey that morning. I poured some in Jesse's tin, Mary's, and Elizabeth's and even poured some for the sergeant. He was quite thankful. I got the impression that he didn't care much whether the coffee was sweetened or not, but he acted like the honey was a special treat. That pleased me.

During the night, the rain had ceased, the wind had quit blowing, and it seemed an exceptionally nice, sunny morning. I thanked the sergeant profusely and announced that I thought we should be off on our journey. He smiled kindly and seemed more relaxed and relieved. He said that he felt like the worst of the danger was behind us. There hadn't been any hostile activity this far east, the cavalry patrols had had no difficulty, and that he was confident that within two days we would be in Osage City.

We took our time gathering our things together, loading the canoe, and carrying it down to the river. It seemed that I was somewhat hesitant to leave this spot. We had felt safe, warm, and well fed here, but I knew we really couldn't stay. It seemed like we were dawdling unnecessarily, but probably sometime around eight that morning we set off again. We had finished the first ham, and the second had been taken out of the wood cask. I tied it with a cord to the thwart of the canoe and dropped it over to let it drag through the water. It hadn't been smoked, but it was certainly well salted. Usually we boiled hams for maybe up to twenty-four hours before eating them to remove all the salt, but the best I could think of was to let it drag through the water. Hopefully this would remove the salt from the outer edges of the ham enough that we could slice off some that would be edible. I wished that I had thought to boil it last night while we were in the camp. I think I felt just too safe and secure that I wasn't planning far enough ahead.

We paddled throughout the day, not as hard as we had been because the river was up and we seemed to be moving along fast enough. We mainly paddled only to keep the canoe centered, avoid obstacles, and let the current take us. We snacked on ham throughout the day, with some biscuits and apples. We finished up the last of the apples, but I wasn't concerned because I felt that we were within a two-day journey of our destination. Once again, we didn't stop for our noon lunch but kept on paddling throughout the day.

As it started to become dusk, we pulled in to the south side of the river. There was a high bluff here but with a high piece of ground along the base of it that was well above the waterline. There wasn't much in the way of cover here, but there was a large tree that had been uprooted in a previous storm lying with its top pointed downstream and a large segment of dirt remaining on its roots. We carried the canoe up, lifted it over the tree, and put it up against the trunk. We kicked together some brush, up against the trunk of the tree and from the river side. It was impossible to discern the bottom of the canoe that was showing under the tree. On the downstream side of the tree, its branches intermingled with a large cedar tree. It had snapped off several of the limbs on the cedar tree as it had fallen, but clearing a space under the brush and debris, I felt that it was safe to make a fire. Any smoke would go drifting up through the branches of the cedar and probably wouldn't be noticeable. It was just getting good and dark about the time I finished with these preparations. We didn't bother to build a shelter because it didn't appear there would be any sign of rain.

We all slept well that night. The morning arrived without incident. We got up and fixed a good breakfast using up the last of the potatoes, onions, and bacon. Now all we had for provisions were the hams, sausages, and a few of the biscuits. I wasn't worried because I thought we might actually make it to Osage City that night, and even if it didn't, we could survive well enough on just the sausage and ham even if we did eat all the biscuits that day. We had a little bit of butter and a little bit of cheese left, but no honey.

Throughout the day, we paddled rather leisurely because there was still a fairly brisk current from the water being higher than normal. We snacked on biscuits and ham and consumed the rest of the cheese during the day, not stopping to prepare a meal or light a fire. We really had nothing to cook, and it was warm enough that day that we didn't feel we needed to stop just to make a fire to warm up. It was starting to get dark, but I persisted. I seemed to see things that I thought that I recognized. The bluffs had seemed to be mainly all on the south side of the river now. It seemed to me that was the way it was just before we got to Osage City. I was convinced that at any moment we would come around the bend and be there. It actually started to get full dark, but I was insistent on continuing. One should never let their fears and anxiety or emotions enter into any planning or thinking.

About that time, we felt a fairly hard bump on the bottom of the canoe that wouldn't have been enough to cause us any great concern, but suddenly it seemed that the canoe turned sharply to the right and tipped. It seemed to be skewing to the right and overturning and was almost ready to fill with water. Being experienced in traveling by canoe, the immediate response of all four of us had been to lean somewhat to the left. This was rather treacherous to do because the canoe could easily capsize. If you leaned too far, you would go to one side and over to the other in a hurry.

However, the canoe righted, we took on only a bit of water and we were on our way again.

I knew instinctively how close I had taken us to disaster. I had actually been steering after it was too dark to see, and if we had overturned, we could well have lost everything that we had, although it wasn't much. What was worse, we would have been thoroughly drenched by the time we got to shore, and although it had been warm during the day, it was certainly starting to get cold now. An evening spent on the shore of the river totally drenched, even if we did have a fire blazing up high, would have been miserable. In addition to the fire, I was afraid it would alert any ruffians who might be moving through the territory. I knew that the sergeant had told us that things were calm here and there wasn't really anything to fear, but that was still in the back of my mind.

I immediately headed into shore. I didn't pay much attention to scouting out where we were in relation to bluffs or areas to camp that would be sufficiently safe. It was actually too dark to tell much. We got to shore and carried the canoe up underneath some blackberry brambles where it was reasonably well hidden. We set the canoe down, and Mary got out. Elizabeth and Jesse stayed in, and we shoved the canoe up under the blackberry brambles. Mary and I then crawled in from the back. We hadn't slept in the canoe before, but I felt like it was best at this time. Jesse and I cuddled together in the middle, and Mary and Elizabeth were at each end. I had placed one of the ground sheets in the bottom of the canoe since the canoe had dampness from our near disaster and then placed one of the blankets there. We covered up with the remaining blankets and put the ground sheet over the top, draping over the edges of the canoe. The night passed without incident.

The following morning, we got up and got started with the break of day. The weather had started to look like it might rain again and had cooled off more than it was yesterday. For breakfast, all we could do was eat some of the ham and some of the sausage. At least that was my intention, but when I went to look, the ham was gone. I thought that we had simply hit a snag. Probably there was a tree floating in the current that had been washed away by the high water and I thought we had probably gone over a limb that Mary hadn't been able to see. I suspected that's what actually happened, but in truth, it was worse. The sudden turn to the right and the near capsizing of the canoe had been due to the fact that the ham, dragging through the water, barely submerged, had caught on this snag and the sudden jerk had turned and tilted us. I thought that our quick reactions leaning to the left had kept the canoe from capsizing, but in truth I think what had happened was that the ham had been ripped loose. Anyhow, it was gone.

We finished up what was left of the sausage for breakfast. There was probably more than what we would have usually eaten, but I thought we might as well consume this before we lost it too. I put the empty casks back in the canoe after we had breakfast. They were tied to the thwarts and, if we happened to capsize, they would float and give us something to catch onto and keep us from getting separated or losing the canoe. It seemed like a good idea. We launched the canoe and paddled fairly vigorously. If we had been paddling the previous two days, we may have gotten there already, was my thinking, and now I was determined that we would get there this day.

We paddled for only about an hour, came around a turn, and there in the distance I could see Osage City. We were all intensely relieved and almost exuberant. We paddled harder than ever we had been and seemed to come upon the shore almost skimming across the water. We ran the bow of the canoe up on the shore, everyone disembarked, and grasping the thwarts on each side, we carried the canoe up through the gate and into the fort. It was just as I had always remembered it, just the way I had been picturing it for the last week. We carried the canoe up to the main trading house. Just as we set the canoe down before the steps that led up to the first floor, my uncle came out the door, placed his hands on his hips, and looked us over. I'm not sure he recognized us immediately, but I think he sensed who it was. The clothes we wore were much too large and oversized. We had on the wool caps down to cover our ears, and I think the only thing recognizable about us were the strange leather caps that we always made ourselves and possibly even the boots that I still wore, which I don't think anyone else had ever made or had ever been seen on anybody but us. As we looked up into his face, the only thing he could say was, "What in creation are you doing here?"

CHAPTER 8

We were a miserable little group as we stood huddled around the bow of the canoe, but it was only for a few seconds. No sooner had Uncle Aaron spoken than it seemed that his wife, Susan, his three daughters, and his oldest son, Robert, had appeared on the porch beside him. They seemed to fly down the stairs and huddled around my family, and in seconds Mary, Elizabeth, and Jesse had been rushed and hustled up the stairs and into the house. I call it a house, but in actual fact, it was the main part of their trading post and general store.

The house had been built on a solid stone foundation. How far down in the ground these stones went, I really don't know, but they had pillars that came up and then at the top formed a circular arch. These arches went all around the house as a foundation. On the northeastern end, there was a fireplace where during the summer they did most of their cooking. The area had flat stone paving for a floor. It had solid oak doors that could be closed at night and locked. During the daylight hours, these were kept wide open. At one time this ground floor had served to store a lot of the merchandise that my uncle bought and sold in his business. The floor in which the general store's business was conducted was about ten feet above the ground, built on these stone pillars. The second floor of this building was used entirely for his trading business, while the family lived in rooms on the third story.

Now, I stood on the steps of the porch looking up at my uncle Aaron, the rest of my family being in the general merchandise portion of the store. What was being said and done, I had no idea. My uncle stood on the porch looking down at me, and then he spoke for the second time. I could see a look of concern on his face. He repeated himself, saying, "Well, boy, what are you doing here?"

Fighting back the tears, I managed to tell him about the tragedy that had befallen our family, about the death of his brother, nephew, and sister-in-law, and about the death of Isaac, who was his dear friend and childhood companion. Isaac and my uncle had been roughly the same age and had grown up together as much as Abel and I had. I related how I had left Jacob, Moses, and the womenfolk and Abel in their cabin on the banks of the Osage. I tried to explain to him why I felt the need to come here.

He seemed rather shocked that we had made the journey alone. He kept saying repeatedly that he knew he should have come to check on us. Apparently he had heard of the disaster at Osceola. He said he thought several times about making the journey but couldn't bring himself to do it. Now was actually one of the busier times of year for him, and he felt he couldn't leave his trading post establishment. His sons, Robert and Aaron, were roughly the same age as William and I. Robert was a couple of years older than William, but I'm not sure how many. Aaron was maybe a year or two older than I. He said he thought they could have handled the business but somehow he had been reluctant to leave. He said he could have taken one of his horses and made the journey in about a week or so, but he had been reluctant to do that. He said he kept telling himself that we lived far enough from Osceola, in relative seclusion, and that there was no reason why anyone would have bothered us. He also stated that he felt like my father would have been a tough person to have taken. He said how he always felt that Thomas had been able to take care of himself and that he felt that we were well armed and the house secured and what, with Isaac and Jacob there, that we were entirely safe. He said, still he had been extremely worried and kept criticizing himself for not having come.

This put me in a strange position, having to console him, because I could see how terribly upset he was. "You really couldn't have done anything, Uncle Aaron," I said. "It happened so fast that no one could." I told him, "I think that by the time you had heard of it, if you would have left immediately, we probably would have already left to be on our way down here. We probably would have just crossed paths." I said, "Wouldn't that be too bad if we were here and you were there?"

That seemed to bring a smile to his face and he chuckled briefly. He said, "Well, at least I would have known, and when I got back, I could be relieved to find you here."

I related to him, "Yeah, but you wouldn't have known for at least another week whether we were safe or had met disaster along the river and now, here we are, all safe and sound."

"Well, son," he said, "I suppose I kept you out here long enough. Let's go see what's going on inside."

We went inside to find that Susan and the girls had cooked up a heaping breakfast. They had made pancakes with maple syrup. At home we had always used cane syrup or honey. They also had a jar of strawberry jam. Aunt Susan had fixed bacon, eggs, and potatoes with onions. Aunt Susan had her own way of fixing potatoes and onions. Usually we just fried them in the bacon grease until they were a rather crispy brown. She cooked them this way but then would pour in a little apple cider vinegar and some water, then cover the pan and boil or steam it for a bit. This made the potatoes and onions rather soggy but somehow even more delicious. She had cool milk for us also. I asked if they had ever tasted coffee, to which Uncle Aaron smiled and said, "Coffee isn't for youngsters."

While we sat around eating breakfast, until we could eat no more, Aunt Susan and the girls chatted. I think they must have talked about what had happened to our parents up on the homestead by Osceola before we came in off the porch because it wasn't mentioned again. Aunt Susan seemed to talk incessantly, a lot more than I heard her ever talk before, and they seemed to have a whole range of topics that included just about anything but the raid on Osceola or the present ongoing war.

I was quite anxious to talk about the war, but if I tried to bring it up, the topic was quickly changed. We sat around and visited for a half hour or so, and then Susan insisted on hustling Mary, Elizabeth, and Jesse upstairs. It seems while we had been having breakfast and visiting, they had had one of their hired hands boil up a lot of hot water and carry it up the outside stairs to their rooms on the floor above. She took the kids upstairs and had them disrobe to bathe. Of course, I wasn't there, but Mary related afterward how they had a large brass bathtub. This was big enough to accommodate her easily but was rather crowded when Elizabeth was placed in the tub with her. They said that Aunt Susan and all three of her daughters, Kate, Anna, and Susan, had gathered around and helped wash their hair and backs and bathe them. Jesse had been put in the adjoining room that Robert and Aaron, my Uncle Aaron's two sons, used. A large wooden barrel that would have held about fifty gallons had been filled, and he had been placed in that simply to sit and soak and wash. My cousin, Aaron, helped him.

Robert and Uncle Aaron and I sat around downstairs. It seemed that we had exhausted or at least grown tired or emotionally spent, discussing the events of Osceola and my parents' and brother's and Isaac's fate. We talked about his trading establishment and about the present, ongoing war. I knew there had been a war going on; that much I had learned on the last visit to Osceola before the town was burned. Apparently it had broken out sometime shortly after we left to return from our spring trading trip down the Osage. We had stopped in Osceola on our return trip and had traded off whatever goods we had brought back that we might be able to sell in town and had divided up the pay for the people who had helped us on the trip down the river. In town, we had heard that the disturbance had actually resulted in fighting. When we had been here at the trading post with Uncle Aaron, they had discussed how a man named Abraham Lincoln had been elected president and how the south or some states in the south were threatening to secede or split off from the union, and that was all we knew at the time. Apparently some time before we made it back upriver to Osceola, the south had actually seceded, or at least some states had, and there had been some fighting at a fort somewhere in the south. All of that had been rather disturbing, but it was a long way away. Things were quiet here, and people were still somewhat optimistic that things could be worked out without any further problems.

We hadn't made it back to Osceola for about a month. This apparently had been sometime toward the middle or end of May. It might even have been the first few days of June. At that time, it seemed that there had been some further troubles out east, there had been some further fighting but nothing too serious. There had even been some sort of trouble or riot up in St. Louis. It seems like this was a long time ago and at that time I had been more interested in just playing with the other kids in town and trying to sneak as much of the various types of food that had been brought for the church luncheon as I could.

This time of year was quite busy around the homestead, cultivating, smoothing out the fields. and getting in the plants. We didn't often make it into town. When we had come in next, probably in July, it seemed like there had been even more activity, but it all seemed a long way away and didn't really concern us. It was only when we made the trip in August that Father had first seemed to become quite concerned. Apparently by then there had been fighting actually in Missouri, but up around Kansas City and out on the border with Kansas. That seemed like an awfully long way off to us, and I don't think that anyone else in the family had been concerned. Maybe we should have been more aware of what was happening. If we had, maybe we would have been more alert and vigilant. I had found out for the first time, then, that Osceola hadn't been the only place that had been attacked by these Kansas raiders. Father seemed to go into great detail about how this colonel, Jim Lane, had led his army of a thousand soldiers and had burned and destroyed, not only Osceola but places called Harrison or was it Harrisonville, and Butler and Clinton. My uncle seemed to believe that this vicious, murdering Jim Lane had been responsible for all of these activities.

As we sat there continuing discussions along this line, my Uncle Aaron had offered me a cup of coffee. Apparently after I had asked about it at breakfast, he had had their hired woman make up a pot. We sat there drinking sweetened coffee until it was gone, discussing the events of the rebellion, which seemed at this point to have become a full out and out war involving everyone. About that time, my aunt Susan came down, scolded Uncle Aaron rather harshly for keeping me occupied, and related that the water was getting cold. I was hustled upstairs, disrobed, and was placed in the barrel that Jesse had bathed in. As I sat there in the barrel nearly up to my shoulders and hunched forward slightly, Aunt Susan washed my hair and scrubbed my back.

Uncle Aaron and the rest of the family were gathered downstairs with my brother and sisters, and Susan had left. My cousin Aaron and I sat there for a long time just talking about things in general. He was talking about the trading post and the area around the town that had sprung up just upstream of the post. It had only been about six months since I had last been here. We had spent a week on that occasion, and I had enjoyed immensely investigating around town and around the trading post and going through the hills and woods in the vicinity. To me, it was an extremely fascinating place. I often envied Uncle Aaron's family that they lived here. It seemed so much more exciting than where we had lived in Osceola.

As I sat there in the hot, sudsy water, relaxing and soaking, we continued talking for a long time. Aaron talked about his father's trading post. He talked about all the changes that had occurred around the area. We had always considered Uncle Aaron to be extremely prosperous. In fact, he seemed to be rich to us. Aaron related that in actual fact, the last several years had been almost touch and go. Apparently there is a lot more expense to running a trading post than I could have imagined. It seems like things had been progressing downhill for the last several years. A railroad had been constructed in the area, and it seemed that had taken a lot of business away. Also steamboats that twenty years ago had stopped here regularly now seemed to bypass their trading post and head on upriver to Jefferson City. It seemed that most of their business in trade had been coming from the people who traveled up and down the Osage River. Although it was possible for small steamboats to go a day or two's journey upstream, the Osage was considered treacherous and nearly unnavigable. Whereas the Missouri river looked to be about a half a mile across, the Osage was probably about a quarter of a mile. The Osage was wide and deep at that point, but within a day or two's travel upstream, the limestone bluffs narrowed on each side, and the river where it went through became quite rocky and shallow.

Most of the business on the Osage was still carried out by keelboat, and that's the way we had conducted our trading expeditions every spring for the last forty years or so. Also, apparently when the trading post had been built,

Mr. Rubidoux had relied considerably on fur trade with the Indians. The Osage had been the dominant tribe anywhere south of the Missouri, and Mr. Rubidoux profited greatly from their trade. I was surprised to learn, I think for the first time, that Mr. Rubidoux hadn't actually owned the trading post. Apparently he was someone who just managed it for another trading company. I'm not sure who the actual person in charge of this company was, but after the Osage had moved further west and finally entirely abandoned the state of Missouri and as the amount of furs traded had declined considerably, Mr. Rubidoux had stayed on there, managing the trading post that at this point was more of just a general store. A small town had developed upstream from it. Initially this town was inhabited

Osceola

mainly by Indians, fur traders, and keelboat river men. It was considered a rather tough and lawless town. Now, most of the keelboats had been replaced by steamboats, and the steamboats themselves were being caught up in a fierce type of competition with railroads. Uncle Aaron's business had suffered considerably as a result of these things. Apparently, also Mr. Rubidoux had been strongly offended by the development of Jefferson City. It seems his trading post had been in business for something like twenty or twenty-five years before anyone ever settled in the vicinity of Jefferson City. I think Mr. Rubidoux felt that the settlement should have been around his trading post. After all, his trading post had been right at the junction of the Missouri and Osage rivers, while Jefferson City was merely on bluffs above the river. He couldn't see any particular advantage to the location.

Apparently these were things he said to Uncle Aaron while Mr. Rubidoux still was alive, and my father had been party to these discussions and complaints. Father often said that he thought one big advantage that Jefferson City had over the area around Mr. Rubidoux's trading post was the fact that people felt safer. Apparently the white settlers moving in were somewhat intimidated by the rough and tumble people who lived around the trading post. What, with Indians and French fur traders, riverboat and keel boat men, and just the general rough and tumble frontiersmen who passed through and traded at Great-grandfather Rubidoux' establishment, folks possibly felt safer and more peaceful further upstream. For whatever reason, things weren't going as well as I had always thought that they were for my uncle, and I was surprised to listen to these thoughts by my cousin, Aaron.

After probably a half hour of soaking peacefully in the hot water, we emptied it partway out with buckets, and I stood up and some warm water was poured over my head and shoulders to wash off all the soap. I then stepped out of the barrel and carefully dried and dressed in some new clothes that uncle Aaron had provided. By this time it was nearly noon, and when we went downstairs, we found that Uncle Aaron's assistant, and my aunt Susan, had prepared another large meal. We ate and relaxed, sitting around the table afterward. Aunt Susan didn't want to hear anymore about the troubles of the nation, what with the war and the fighting. It seems like she was determined to move on to happier thoughts. Most of the conversation revolved around my cousins, Kate, Anna, and Susan, and my sisters, Mary and Elizabeth. It seemed that my cousins were quite delighted to have Mary and Elizabeth to join in with them. They talked about the town, about Jefferson City, about traveling and visiting and even about social life. It seemed that, shockingly, they didn't hesitate to travel the distance to Jefferson City just to socialize, go to dances, or go even shopping. My sisters were enthralled by the prospect of whole days spent merely shopping.

After lunch, Jesse, my cousin Aaron, and I went out to explore the fort, for that's what I called it since it's precisely what it reminded me of. Aaron, himself, wasn't exactly sure who had designed or been responsible for building the fort. Apparently it had been built, or at least started, nearly sixty or maybe even seventy years before. At that time there were very few settlers or even traders in this area. Most of the inhabitants were French fur traders, trappers, and Indians. There had been no riverboats and not even any keelboats. Most all traffic was by canoe. Possibly because of Indian depredations or fear of attack during the revolutionary war back in the 1780s or '90s, the fort had been built up stronger and stronger in a gradually progressive manner. The trading post was situated directly in the triangle formed where the Osage River entered into the Missouri. The fort was built to follow the lines of the two rivers as they joined. In its present shape, it looked to me like a square with a triangle added on one side pointing at the confluence of the rivers.

Earthen banks had been heaped all the way around the fort about ten to twelve feet high and fifteen feet, maybe twenty feet thick, at the base, and another ten feet thick at the top. This was primarily to keep the fort from being flooded. It seems that every few years, due to its location, if the Missouri and Osage rivers became high, and all the land around that area would be flooded. It would have to be an exceptionally bad flood to crest the top of these ten- or twelve-foot-high earthen mounds. At the triangle that pointed to the junction of the Missouri and Osage rivers, the trading post came to a point. Here, there was a tower built. Limestone had been placed several feet beneath the ground, and walls of limestone had been constructed, against which the earth of the levee wall had been piled. These limestone rocks, which had been cemented together, extended for four or five feet above the earthen mounds on all sides. From there up were laid a typical log–cabin-style squared oaken blockhouse. This was actually eight-sided. The oak logs laid horizontally, one upon the other, up to the top, which was a good eight feet or so above the palisade around it. On the top there was plank flooring, and a small cannon was situated looking down the Missouri river, which could be turned either up the Missouri or the Osage river. I had never seen this cannon fired. It always seemed like the most impressive and dangerous weapon to me. From the apex or corner, upright posts were driven into the ground about ten feet above the top of the levee. These posts were usually somewhere between eight and ten inches in diameter. They ran at an angle back about fifty feet and there abutted up against two other towers on each side, one being north and the other being more on the east side of the fortifications.

Again, limestone rocks and floors had been used for the foundation up to the top of the levee. Here, squared oak interlocking logs had been built up to the top of the ten feet or so high palisade walls. The last layer of squared oak logs level with the palisade had been left about three feet longer than the rest. These were allowed to stick out from the wall of the palisade into the open ground beyond the trading post and also extended toward the inside of the trading post. Planking had been placed across this, and squared logs would continue for about another three feet outside of the palisades. On the top of the wall, small swivel guns had been mounted. Then, the upright log palisades continued for about one hundred feet toward the southwest on each wall. This formed roughly a square, being one hundred feet by one hundred feet in size, and the triangle facing the confluence of the river had walls about fifty feet long. At the two western corners of the wall were similar towers made to protrude beyond the edges of the palisade walls. Two small swivel guns were mounted, one on each corner.

I was always fascinated by the construction of this fort. Entrance to the fort was through the palisade wall on the southeast side. Here, the trail went up from the Osage River, over the levee, and through a gate in the wall and then down the levee on the inside. Water would have had to have gotten to at least ten feet high or possibly more before it could overtop the levee and come into the fort. Even if it did that, the way my uncle's house was constructed on top of the stone-pillared foundation, the porch would have been above the level of the water, even if it had topped the levee. Apparently once at some point in time water had actually gotten over the levee and up about two feet in the house, but I think this had only happened once in about fifty years.

Jesse was absolutely fascinated. We walked all around the trading post on the inside and then on the outside, climbed the walls, manipulated the swivel guns, and even pretended to be firing the larger cannon overlooking the mouth of the juncture of the rivers. Aaron said that this was called a six-pound cannon because the ball that it shot weighed six pounds. It seemed enormous to me. Jesse couldn't get enough of exploring the fort. We went into the towers on each corner. In most of them were stored powder and shot for the swivel guns or the cannon. These were actually stacked on shelves well above the ground. It seemed moisture could hardly be kept out of these turrets, and it was necessary, in order to keep things dry, to have them on shelves or large tables in the room. The powder and shot was kept behind the stone, actually below the top of the levee. Right at the top of the levee a floor had been constructed in each of the towers.

The large tower at the confluence of the river had a room that was large enough that some of Uncle Aaron's workers and hired hands, and their family, were able to live. Along the north and west walls of the triangle pointing toward the river, there were other log houses for employees and other workers. It seemed that my uncle had a full-time blacksmith there. He was necessary to work on steamboats, do horseshoeing, and any other type of metal repair. He also had a carpenter who worked on wooden barrels, wagons, and wagon wheels. At one time, they had been kept completely busy. The blacksmith still seemed to do a reasonable business, but the man who built barrels and casks, kegs, and wagon wheels had taken to building more elaborate, fancy furniture that they offered for sale. He would make it on order for people who lived in Jefferson City. In addition, there was a woman hired to do cooking and run a small inn. Apparently meals were made, breakfast, lunch, and supper, and anyone traveling or trading could stop in there to eat. There was also, adjoining to this and connected to it, a few rooms that could be rented to sleep in as people passed through the area. They also employed younger women whose job was to help around the shop, helping clean, stack merchandise, and wait on customers. Their husbands were employed, at least part-time, by my uncle to handle, move, and ship merchandise.

The only time I had been to the trading post had been on our spring visits. In thinking back on it, the first trip I had been allowed to make was when I was seven. I made the trip for two years in a row but then wasn't allowed to go because my mother and two sisters came instead. Apparently my mother had made the trip almost yearly with my father just to visit family, but once the children were born, she hated to travel on the river with the small children, and so she usually stayed at home. Sometime after Jesse was born, she took the two girls and went with my father, and I was left at home to watch out for Jesse. We stayed with Rebecca and Abel in their cabin, and my responsibility was to shepherd my younger brother. I can still remember Mother and Father saying that it wasn't proper to make Rebecca take the responsibility for watching little Jesse and that that was my job. The fact that Jesse managed to survive was almost astounding, as I don't consider myself to have been very reliable at nine years of age.

This was Jesse's first trip down the Osage to the fort, as we liked to call it. He couldn't get enough of it. We explored the blacksmith's shop and the cooper's shop and went through the inn and the different towers. We explored beneath the main house and general store, around the stone pillars, and in the different storage rooms beneath, through the kitchen underneath the trading post on the ground floor and all through the trading post itself. We looked at all the inventory, all the goods and gear that my uncle had stored. I had my eye out for Henry repeating rifles or Colts or Remingtons, but it seems that my uncle had sold out of all of these. What, with the hostilities going on and the general fear throughout the population, it seems that he couldn't seem to keep weapons on the shelf. He even related that he had great difficulty in getting them. He had placed orders and been promised weapons, but it seemed they never arrived by steamboat or even railroad.

We explored through the trading post and went upstairs to the area where Uncle Aaron's family lived. He and his wife, Susan, had a room for themselves, Robert and Aaron had a room, Kate, Anna, and Susan had a room, and they had another room that they kept for guests and special friends who might be visiting. The top stairs could be reached through a small stairway that went down and entered into the trading post beneath. There were also stairs coming up on the outside that were built especially to move larger furniture and stuff up to the top floor. The stairs in the house leading down were so narrow that my uncle Aaron had trouble squeezing down them.

We had gone outside and explored around the two big open-air barns that my uncle had. These occupied most of the western two corners of the post. These sat about ten feet from the palisade on the north, south, and west ends. They were about twenty feet apart. Each was about thirty feet in width and about fifty feet long. It was here where great-grandfather Rubidoux and my uncle Aaron usually stored the tobacco, hemp, and other goods that they took in for trade before they in turn sold those and shipped them up or down river. The tobacco was usually hung across the top, and hemp and cotton bales were placed on the ground as well as any other article for trade that Uncle Aaron had taken in. The sides were left open for air circulation. But because there was a ten-foot-high earthen mound around the barns, topped by ten-foot palisades, anything inside underneath the roof of the barn was reasonably well protected from driving rain or wind.

Now the barns were pretty much empty. Uncle Aaron had said that things were bought up as quickly as he got it. Apparently with the war going on, tobacco was at a premium, as well as cotton and hemp. The barns were pretty much empty. Most all of Uncle Aaron's business was now confined to that of a general store. People came there to buy cloth, thread, grocery goods, and whatever other articles that they needed. It was still a considerable distance, I think something like forty miles, to Jefferson City, and so my uncle's post was the largest and busiest for probably thirty miles in any direction. This kept him reasonably busy and certainly ensured a source of income, but it was nothing like it had been apparently when he first took over the business from my great-grandfather twenty years or so ago.

By this time it was starting to get dark and was time for supper. We went in and ate once again, three large meals in one day. This was better than we ever dreamt of eating, even at home. It was certainly a lot better than it had been on the river or in the last week or so before we had left. I think whatever weight I lost in the last two weeks, I had put back on in that one day. That night I slept without a care in the world. I woke up well after it was bright sunlight, surprised that I could have slept that late, but still thinking that I would like to sleep longer.

When I went downstairs, everyone was already up and had been for a while. My uncle Aaron was out and about the fort doing something, I'm not sure what. My aunt Susan, my sisters, and my cousins were busy altering clothing for my sisters. Apparently my cousin Robert was out working with the blacksmith or the cooper, I'm not sure which, and Aaron and Jesse were sitting there waiting impatiently for my arrival. It seems that Jesse couldn't wait to be out to further explore the surrounding countryside. I remember how excited I had been when we first arrived there when I was seven years of age. I had done pretty much the same thing, having spent the first day of our week's visit exploring the fort itself. Then,

I spent the next several days rambling through the woods and the fields around the fort.

A couple of hundred feet beyond the southwest wall of the fort, there was an earthen mound that went from the Missouri to the Osage River. This appeared to be somewhat like the levee on which the fort itself was built. Aaron insisted that he had been told that this had been there when the trading post was first established. I thought that it must have been something that the French had built maybe back during the time of the wars between the French and American colonists or during the revolutionary war, but Aaron insisted that my great-grandfather, Jean Rubidoux, had always said that this had been there before that. Aaron seemed to think that it had originally been built by the Indians. True, by the time I had been born the Osage had moved away from Osceola, a few Cherokee had moved in, but even they had seemed to move farther west into the Oklahoma and Kansas area, but I had never heard of Indians making mounds or fortifications, for that's what this wall appeared to be.

I could remember my own enthusiasm when I watched Jesse running up and down the length of the wall and climbing its sides. Then, we left to walk across the fields and up the steep bluffs that were about one hundred feet beyond this. When we got to the top of the bluff, cousin Aaron pointed out a couple of mounds that he said had been built by Indians. He said that they were extremely old but that the Indians who had lived here most recently continued to use these to bury their important chiefs. He pointed out one that he was told by Jean Rubidoux had been used by one of the principal chiefs that he personally knew as his final resting place. We walked all over the top of the bluffs and climbed the sides, which in places could be quite steep and treacherous, and explored the top of the bluffs. Then we worked our way on down the west side and into the little town that had been built in the flat area along the river, between these bluffs and some other bluffs further south and west.

The little town certainly still seemed to have a rough and uncivil appearance. It didn't appear nearly as neat and prosperous as Osceola had looked in the last few years before it had been burned. Most of the structures were simple log cabins, and there was a rather unpleasant smell about the place. Possibly this was due to being right on the river and hemmed in pretty much on three sides by higher bluffs, but the whole area did seem to be dirty, smelly, and unkempt. I could imagine why people had elected to build Jefferson City in possibly a better location than this.

We walked all through the town, but there wasn't really much that seemed to attract our interest. Finally we walked back to the fort by following along the Osage River. We had been gone most of the day and just managed to make it back about sundown and in time for supper. That evening after supper, we talked until fairly late again. I had told my uncle about the Henry and the Remington pistols. He asked to take a look at them and inspected them. He felt that they were perfectly salvageable. He related there was a gunsmith in Jefferson City who was very, very good with repairing weapons. He instructed my cousin Robert that tomorrow he should take the day off and travel up to Jefferson City to drop these off and have them thoroughly cleaned, inspected, and repaired. In private a little bit later, I took cousin Robert aside and asked him if, when he was there, he could see if this man had any other Henrys, Colts, or Remingtons that were for sale. I related to Robert that I was worried about Isaac, Moses, and the rest of the family still up at the homestead site and intended to go back. I would like to have some other weapons for them when I did. He readily agreed to discuss it and check it out with the man in Jefferson City.

Once again, after I went to bed, I slept delightedly all through the night. For the next week, we continued to relax and enjoy ourselves. It's surprising how good it can feel to be with family. Not that I didn't consider Jacob, Moses and their mother Rebecca and sisters to be family, but things were just so much more relaxed here. It wasn't like having a plan for every day where we can anticipate getting up at the crack of dawn to go plow, cultivate, plant, hoe, rake, or harvest the fields. It wasn't like we had to slaughter, butcher, salt, and smoke meats. At home, every day had seemed to have its chores to do. Here, it seemed that every day we had nothing to do but just live for the day.

After breakfast each morning, Jesse, Aaron, and I would travel, investigating the fort or the surrounding countryside. When we first arrived, we had simply shoved the canoe and all of its contents in underneath the porch. We had taken the quiver of arrows and the bow up and greased and oiled these down. We had let them dry and put them up. Now, possibly because of the experience of seeing the Indian mounds and the wall the Indians had built, Jesse was excited about shooting the bow and arrows. We set up straw targets for him. He would do his best to pull the bow back and let fly and at a distance of about twenty feet, could seem to manage to hit the straw-stuffed gunnysack, but usually the stone arrowhead wouldn't even penetrate. He was quite impressed and excited about how well I could handle the bow and arrows. He was determined to practice until he was strong enough to work the bow himself. I realized it would be several years before he was strong enough to do that.

Jesse seemed so excited about the thought of shooting the bow and arrows and imaging that he was an Indian living around the mounds and the fortifications that I decided he needed some sort of a weapon for himself to pass his time. I let him carry the bow and arrows and began a search for a suitable substitute. I came across a small hickory tree that had a split in the fork just above the ground. The main branch of the hickory was probably no more than three inches at the ground. There was a small shoot that wasn't more than an inch in diameter coming up almost parallel to this. I had taken the hatchet with me and chopped this off about four or five inches below the juncture. Taking it back to the trading post, I shaved all the bark off it, used a saw to trim it up a little bit better, and cut a shallow groove in the main three-inch diameter trunk down to the small branch. I cut the smaller branch off to where it was only about a couple of inches long and shaved and whittled it down somewhat to a point. I then cut it off to where the whole piece was about two feet long.

Then we went out searching along the banks of the river and found another small hickory tree that was about an inch and a half in diameter at the base and maybe an inch up at the top. I cut this off and trimmed it to about six feet in length, split it at the top, and put a piece of sharpened steel in the split and then wrapped it with wet and stretched rawhide. We placed this over the fire overnight to dry, and the following morning Jesse was armed with his atlatl and spear. I showed him how to use this, and he was quite enthused. This is something he could actually do himself. Placing the butt of the spear on the pointed hook of the atlatl, and holding the shaft of the spear while balancing it with his fingers on the club in his right hand, he could take a step forward with his left leg and whip or sling the spear forward. He seemed to never tire of this. He would be slinging his spear with the right arm and then with the left arm, and we went through the woods out along the wall of the old Indian fort with him slinging his spear at anything he could see.

We spent several days in this fashion, alternating shooting the bow and arrows, using the spear, or just exploring along the bluffs and flats along the river. One day we spent taking some line and fishhooks down and at the junction of the Missouri and Osage rivers, throwing the line out into the water and fishing. This was quite easy. We sat on the banks while the line drifted out in the current, suspended on a float on the water over the line, and waited for a bite. We caught several fish throughout the day, which thoroughly delighted Jesse. Most of the time I would let him pull the fish in as I sat there and watched. Of course, we had fished in the Osage River at home, but something now seemed so much more important and so much more pleasing about this time that we spent together fishing.

After about a week's time, my cousin Robert made another trip into Jefferson City, and when he returned, he had my Henry repeating rifle and the two Remingtons. He said the gunsmith in Jefferson City had taken the guns apart completely, cleaned them, inspected them, and had replaced any parts that he thought might possibly have been defective as a result of the fire even though he felt like they would probably have been okay anyhow. He had carved new grips and a new butt stock for the Henry and assembled everything back together. He had then given the guns a good bluing. The Remingtons looked as good as ever. The Henry looked good too except that the brass that had been so bright and shiny and yellow had been blued as well. This gave it a funny greenish-gray appearance. One might think that it actually destroyed the looks of the gun, but I concluded that it gave the gun character. Robert had also returned with one Colt revolver and a Spencer rifle. The Spencer was, in comparison to the Henry, I thought an ugly-looking gun, but if the Henry was not obtainable at this time, it would certainly do better than another percussion rifle.

I took all my supplies back upstairs to our room, which I shared with Jesse and my two sisters, and stored them in the corner in a chest of drawers. The following morning when we went down for breakfast, I broached the subject that I had been thinking about for the last ten or eleven days. I asked Uncle Aaron if I could buy a horse and gear from him. I intended to travel back to Osceola. He seemed rather shocked and almost dismayed that I would be considering leaving, but as I tried to explain to him my thoughts and intentions, he seemed to understand and agreed. I told him that we had had no contact with Jacob, Moses, Rebecca, or the girls since we left, that they were probably worried, had no idea whether we had made it or died along the river. I think he could understand that since he felt so much remorse and guilt that he hadn't come to check on us after he heard about the events of Osceola. I think he could understand why I wanted to get back to let them know that we were all right. I also reasoned that they were now left with one Henry repeating rifle, one Colt, one Pepperbox, a couple of percussion rifles, an old flintlock musket, and a couple of shotguns for their self-defense and I was hoping to take them the Spencer and the Colt for protection.

He actually thought this was a good idea and suggested that instead I should leave the Spencer there with him. He reasoned that he would have better luck getting ammunition for it, which apparently was harder to come by than ammunition for the Henry. They had kept some Henry rifles for themselves, as well as a good supply of ammunition, and he thought he would trade the Henry for the Spencer. Thus, we talked and reasoned out what I would need for the trip and planned and prepared for my departure in the morning. Throughout the rest of the day, we made preparations.

My uncle did sell horses when he could get them. Since the war had broken out, it seemed that horse trading had been a booming business. It seems there weren't very many left in the area, but he did have a small black Morgan horse that he kept for his daughter, Kate. He felt this was a fine, strong animal, docile and mild mannered, but yet strong enough and eager to go. We got a small saddle for it. This saddle was made out of black leather and matched the horse. It had a skirt and a wood-framed contraption, covered in black leather, on its back. What I had called a saddle before was just simply a skirt of leather over the horse's back with stirrups to it, but this contraption made out of wood and covered with leather had a raised swell in front and a raised cantle in back. Apparently this was designed to keep one from sliding backward or forward in the saddle.

We arranged all my gear and equipment and determined that I would be leaving in the morning. Throughout the day, Jesse and the girls seemed somewhat gloomy and despondent. We spent the day wandering around the fort and in the immediate vicinity. I thought that Jesse might actually break out in tears, but I tried to reassure him that I would be coming back, that he would be safe there with his sisters, aunt, uncle, and cousins, and that I needed to go back to check on Jacob, Moses and the rest. He seemed to understand, and although he was reluctant to see me go, he bucked up, cheered up, and made no further protest. That evening, we went to bed rather later than normal, and I was up just slightly after sunup for a large breakfast before loading up and making the return trip.

The following morning, the sun came up bright and shiny and somewhat warmer than it had been. I slept a little bit later than I had intended. I suppose on the one hand I was reluctant, even hesitant, to leave. The time that we had spent here had been quite pleasant and enjoyable. On the one hand, I hated to go. While I got up and dressed and had breakfast, Robert went out to saddle the Morgan horse that I had arranged to purchase from Uncle Aaron. This was a black horse, the only touch of white being on the two right-sided hoofs and a blaze down its forehead. Kate had, rather naturally I suppose, named the horse Blaze.

While Robert saddled up the horse, I went upstairs and finished dressing and loading everything together. I put the clothes that Rebecca had loaned us in a couple of gunnysacks and placed a couple of tins of beef and a couple of tins of beans, two cans of carrots, and three cans of peaches in the sack. I also put half of the ammunition for the Henry and a couple of the powder horns of black powder in each sack. In my necessaries pouch, I packed one hundred of the Henry cartridges and one hundred of the preformed lead balls for the Remington pistols. I put a brass nipple capper in that I bought for Jacob. I bought one for myself, but I suspended this by a cord around my neck and let it hang down on the outside of my buckskin leather shirt. I put some wax patches and a couple of small jars of beeswax in the pouch. I also placed my brass black powder flask as well as one of the powder horns in the pouch. I placed the two extra cylinders for the Remingtons in the pouch, then packed my wool scarf in around this to prevent the metallic instruments from rubbing against each other, and fastened it tightly shut. Then I packed my saddlebags with a couple more tins of meat, a couple of cans of peas and carrots, some sausages, and the last two powder horns. I rolled the two wool blankets up in two of the waxed ground clothes and tied them snugly. Then we carried everything down the outside stairs to the grounds outside the store.

I had placed one of the Remingtons in the hip holster that had held the Pepperbox, which I had modified to fit it. I put the other in the pocket that I had made in the wool coat that I borrowed from Rebecca. We loaded everything up on Blaze and fastened it securely. I had placed the extra Henry rifle that I had bought for Moses in the soft buckskin leather case that I had brought down in the canoe and placed it under one stirrup on the right side with the butt of the gun in the air, and we tied it up and cinched it securely. We had had the Henry that had belonged to my father slightly modified by placing a swivel in the butt and made a sling that fit over the top of the muzzle and tube magazine. I threw this over my head and adjusted it on my left shoulder so that the butt of the rifle was up and behind me but could be brought to bear quickly. When all was ready, I took my final leave.

Jesse seemed somewhat sad to see me go. I could tell that tears were nearly ready to burst out and run down his cheeks. He stood there with his atlatl and the bow and quiver. Aaron stood next to him and patted him gently on the shoulder. My sisters didn't seem to mind much that I was leaving. I think they were adjusting to life in the trading post quite well. Actually, I was a little upset by their lack of concern, but possibly they had such confidence in me that they weren't overly worried. I wasn't quite so self-assured myself. I loaded up and waving good-bye, kicked Blaze into a trot, and we left the fort.

CHAPTER 9

Throughout the next day, I traveled west on the north side of the Osage River. I intended to follow the road that ran along the banks of the Osage all the way back to Osceola. I had never been on this road before, but from where I was starting out and where I had seen it running along the banks of the Osage in Osceola, I thought it would be a good road all the way back home and easy to follow.

The next two days I made good time. I alternately trotted Blaze for fifteen minutes or so, then let him walk, then trotted again for another fifteen minutes and then would dismount and walk and lead him. I decided that the name Blaze didn't fit near as well as the name "Pig." As long as we were trotting, he wasn't too difficult, but whenever we just walked, it was a constant effort to keep his head up. He had been fitted with a hackamore that allowed him to crop grass and chew as we went, and it was a constant struggle to keep his head up and keep him moving. I don't think I had ever seen a horse that wanted to eat so much. About an hour before I felt like it would be sundown, I would be sure and get down to the river to water him good and then travel on for another hour or so. When it started to get dark, I would move back off the road and into what I felt was a secure and concealed hiding place. Usually I would just hobble Pig up and tie his lead rope to a tree about head high. I would sleep at his feet.

Throughout the day I munched on sausage, some biscuits, or hard crackers that I packed in a little sack that hung from the back of my neck. Usually for the noonday meal I would open some of the canned fruit or vegetables. On the third day of the trip, the road moved down the hill and crossed the Osage at a relatively shallow ford. I crossed the Osage and took the road up the hill heading south. When I got to the top of the hill, as far as I could see in the distance, the road seemed to continue going south. I thought this looked like a long way out of my way and went back to the river. I followed right along the edge of the river, or even in the shallow water, avoiding the thick brush that was on the banks. After a couple of miles of travel, the bluffs narrowed in on each side and became so steep that they couldn't be climbed. Here the ground along the banks on the shore of the river faded away and was impossible to travel. I took Blaze out to the center of the river, which seemed rather shallow, rocky, and passable. We traveled for a couple of miles up the river before it started getting deeper. I became concerned that it might become impassable, but yet it seemed like such a distance to turn around and go back, probably five miles or so wasted, that I kept on.

The next hour was spent carefully studying the water and the ripples and trying to pick my way forward. There were places where there were deep pools that we couldn't get through except by swimming, but by studying both banks and the flow of the water, I was able to make my way cautiously forward without getting any water up past the horse's belly. Finally, the bluffs seemed to spread out and I was able to reach the shore and exit the water. After another hour or so of riding, the road came back from the south, crossed the river again, and went up on the north bank. I felt like I had been lucky in not getting everything soaked and ruining my horns of black powder. Also, Pig had stumbled several times on the rocky bottoms of the river, and I was concerned that he might have cracked a hoof and go lame. After I had gotten out of the water, I lifted up and checked his hoofs and was reassured to find he suffered no injury. Once again, I reminded myself that it was better to be cautious and safe than to be sorry. The last time I had taken what was probably an unnecessary gamble, we nearly capsized the canoe. I determined from here on I would simply be sure and follow the road.

The rest of this day and the next four followed without incident. About noon of the seventh day, I found myself approaching the outskirts of Osceola. Before when we had gone by, I hadn't bothered to look, trying to avoid making eye contact with any of the people who might be still residing in the town. This time I carefully studied the town and what few people I saw as I approached and passed through the devastation of the burned buildings and rubble that had once been a beautiful and proud town. I don't suppose there were more than a hundred people in the town. What struck me as odd was that before the town had been ransacked, the white population was so overwhelmingly noticeable that one couldn't really tell how many blacks actually lived in the town. I didn't suppose there had been more than a dozen or twenty black people. But now it seemed like almost all of the white inhabitants had left, while most of the black population had stayed, and that of the hundred people that I saw, probably fifteen were black. I made polite conversation with the people I met but never engaged in much of a discussion. We talked about the tragedy of Osage. They asked how my family was doing. Most people didn't even know about what had happened to us.

As I reached the western outskirts of Osceola, I ran into old Bill. Old Bill was a free black man. He and his family had lived in Osceola for as long as I knew. His kids were all grown, and he still lived with his wife. I knew Bill well. He had once belonged to a man who owned slaves in the town, but he had been freed many years ago, probably before I was born. He lived around the town doing odd jobs. Usually he was one of the polers who made the spring keelboat trip to Osage City with us. Other times during the summer he would work helping us plant, cut, and hang tobacco. He could also always be counted on to help with plowing, cultivating, planting, and hoeing the hemp, sugarcane, and gardens that we put out. He was always ready to do whatever type of work he could find. When other types of work weren't available, he would spend his time cutting and splitting firewood for the people in the town.

I wasn't surprised to find that he was still here. I was, however, surprised to learn that his small log shack had been burned like most everyone else in Osceola. While everyone else I had talked to seemed to be pretty angry and full of hate for the raiders, Bill, if anything, was worse than anyone I had met. He was a freed black, had worked hard all of his life to get ahead and provide for his family. Now, his little log shack and everything that he owned had gone up in flames. He had put together a bit of a shanty from whatever he could salvage and was living with his wife. He was determined not to leave. Bill was someone I felt safe to talk with. I had asked him what the townspeople were doing or what people in that part of the state were doing as far as retaliation against this monstrous Jim Lane. He said that there wasn't any organized type of retaliation that he was aware of. The state at this point was controlled by the union, and there were union patrols passing through the area, although infrequently, but enough to keep people dispersed. It seems that General Sterling Price and the rebel army had been chased clean out of the state. He related that the only activity that he knew of was that that was being conducted by some ruffians who called themselves bushwhackers.

We talked about the bushwhackers, where they were located, and where they seemed to hide out or hang around. He really didn't know much about them but was able to mention a few by name and indicate an area of extremely rough and wooded land around the northern tributaries that fed into the Osage at its origin. He couldn't be any clearer than that. I noted this in my mind and taking leave, proceeded on the remaining ten miles to our homestead.

When I reached the neck of land along the big bend of the river, I turned and headed north, passed Jacob's cabin, and crossed the ford of the river. It was just getting dusk, and riding to the top of the bank overlooking the creek across from Rebecca's cabin, I paused the horse and called out in a loud voice, "Hello" to the cabin. I didn't see anyone. The windows and doors were closed, but a voice answered from inside, "Hello yourself."

I recognized it immediately as Isaac. I called out, "Isaac, is that you?"

He said, "Thomas, Thomas," and about that time the door opened, and he peered out, recognizing me instantly. He opened the door wide, and in a second the whole family had emerged on the front porch. I kicked Pig up and went down the hill and across the creek and came up in the yard outside the cabin and dismounted.

The family was already gathered around me, patting my head and taking hold of the horse's lead rein when I dismounted. They were overjoyed to see me. First, Isaac and then Moses hugged me and shook my hand. Rebecca and the girls each grabbed me, hugged me, and gave me a kiss and never stopped talking or asking questions. Abel was there. He looked quite proud and relieved at the same time. I turned and walked a step forward, and we rushed together and embraced. I thought for a moment he was going to kiss me also, but that was only for women. We turned and walked up and sat on the bench on the porch.

They were full of questions about the trip to the trading post. They were delighted to see me back. They asked about my uncle and his family and asked how Mary, Elizabeth, and Jesse were doing when I left. While we talked, Moses got up and went into the yard and stripped all the gear off Pig. He brought this up and laid it on the porch and then went back to pick the horse's hooves, dry it down, and brush it out good. Then he led Pig down to the creek, let him drink, and brought him back and tied him in front of the house. While he was doing this, Isaac had gone in his house and came back with some neat's foot oil and rubbed the saddle and all the leather gear down well with this. Abel, Rebecca, and the girls and I remained sitting on the bench talking constantly.

After they had finished with the necessary care of the horse and equipment, they came and sat on the edge of the porch, looking up at us, and we continued talking. It was good to be home. I felt now just as relieved as when we had reached the trading post at Osage City. People seemed to be acting almost normal again. While we had been sitting, Rebecca had flitted back and forth into the house, and now she rather abruptly announced that we needed to be getting in and have supper before things got cold. I went in, and we sat around the table and ate a well-prepared and well-appreciated meal.

After supper, I took and opened up the gunnysacks full of the clothing that I had returned. Aunt Susan and the girls had brushed and cleaned this to where it looked, if not almost new, certainly better than it had looked when we took it. I went through the things I had brought back. I gave the other Henry rifle to Moses, as well as the other Colt that I had bought. I gave them four of the five powder horns that I had bought, 150 rounds of ammunition for the Henry, and 50 rounds of precast bullets for the Colts. They had chunk lead and bullet molds to make more if they needed. I also gave Moses the brass capper I had bought for them.

By then, it had gotten fairly late, and we all took off to bed. The girls went up in the loft. Rebecca slept in Isaac's bed behind a blanket hanging from a rope on the ceiling, and the men folk slept on the floor in front of the only door. Pig had been hobbled and turned loose. I felt he wouldn't wander far from the cabin now that he was given free time to wander and graze. I thought that the little pig would probably still be within ten feet of the cabin eating grass. It was a joyous feeling to be home.

I spent the next week visiting with Rebecca and her family. We did some work around the place. Mainly, I just wandered around looking things over and remembering. I would make several trips a day to the small cemetery to say prayers for my parents and my deceased family members. I remembered how good life had been. After a little over a week, I told Rebecca that I would be leaving in the morning. I felt that I needed to go back to Osage City. I told her that I felt that they were certainly adequately armed and were safe enough. I thought that if they had any further trouble, what with two Henrys and two Colts and the other assortment of weapons, they would be able to defend themselves satisfactorily. I could tell that they had been taking a lot of precautions, never being anywhere visible when I had approached and helloed the cabin. They weren't going to be caught unaware as my father had been.

The following morning I arose early, packed up everything we had put together, left the cabin, and went down across the ford. I went for a few miles down the neck of land in the big bend and then, when safely out of sight of the house, I turned the horse west and headed for Kansas. I don't know when I had made the decision to do this. I suppose that it may have come when I had talked to the union sergeant at the ford of the river when we were on our way to Osage City. I had been surprised to learn that it was being given out amongst the union people that Osceola had been a great battle and a splendid victory for Jim Lane. My uncle even seemed to accept this version of events. People were shocked, dismayed, and somewhat offended to learn that it had been nothing but a massacre by an evil, monstrous man bent on personal raiding, stealing, and plunder. Somewhere along this time, I determined that anyone who was capable of doing such things and then taking such pride in his actions, becoming famous and wealthy from his murderous and monstrous activities, wasn't fit to live. Thus, I was on my way to Lawrence, Kansas, to kill Jim Lane. Just how I was going to do that, I had no idea.

CHAPTER 10

I knew that Kansas was to the west and Lawrence was somewhere in Kansas, but other than that, I had no idea where to go. Also, I had no idea how I was going to find Jim Lane once I got there. I had no idea what he looked like or whereabouts in Lawrence, Kansas, he might live. I also didn't know how big Lawrence, Kansas, was. Osceola has been about three thousand people at the time it was destroyed and my family knew a good many of the people who lived there, but certainly there were a lot more people that we didn't know. What would I do in Lawrence, just walk around asking people one after another if they could point Jim Lane out to me so I could kill him? I didn't think that was much of a plan. However, first I had to make it to Lawrence.

When I had left Osage City, the first couple of days I had ridden pretty much down the center of the road, taking only minimal precautions. The farther I went, the closer I got to Osceola, the more careful I had been. It was strange how our territory, that had felt so safe to me growing up, now seemed so dangerous and desolate. The closer I had gotten to Osceola, the more carefully I had ridden. I had taken to riding off the road, staying forty or fifty feet off on one side or the other, and trying to move through the woods as silently and carefully as I could. I had been afraid of anyone who might be passing along the roads. However, moving west from Osceola was still even more terrifying. I didn't know if it was actually dangerous or if it was just my imagination, but I took to riding off the road forty or fifty feet and moving forward, taking advantage of brush and trees and thickets to avoid being seen. I also took to listening very carefully, and if I thought I had heard anything that sounded like traffic on the road in the distance, I would often dismount and lead my horse into cover and squeeze his muzzle tightly so that he couldn't hardly breathe, much less whinny, at the approach of another horse. Most of the time whatever I had heard turned out to be nothing, but there were a few times that people passed on the road. I seemed to feel like anybody who was traveling in this territory was an enemy and it was best not to be seen by them.

As I moved west following the river, I thought about what old Bill had told me in town. He had mentioned bushwhackers moving through the area, raiding over into Kansas for revenge or for loot and plunder, he didn't know which, and the thought struck me that if I joined up with a group such as this, possibly we could gather enough men to raid Lawrence, Kansas, and that in the ensuing commotion, I might be able to find and kill Jim Lane. I actually thought about this and then discarded it because it seemed so farfetched. How could you find one man that you didn't know what he looked like in such a confrontation? However, that thought kept recurring to me.

One thing that old Bill had said was that the bushwhackers seemed to hide out around the forks of the Osage about two days' ride west. I didn't know how I would recognize this territory once I got there. I knew that within a few miles of each other, the Osage seemed to branch into three separate, large creeks or small rivers. Bill had said that the river that ran to the northwest was called the Mari and that it was the largest of the three. I had passed some small streams flowing in to the Osage but always discarded them since I felt that moving as slow and careful as I was, it would be probably more like three days or even four before I got to the region that Bill called the forks of the Osage.

About the mid-afternoon of the third day as I was coming down the southern slope of a western running ridge toward a flat and level area ahead, I heard the sound of horses and moved off to my north. I reined up and watched and listened carefully. Pretty soon I noticed three men moving along the south side of a road, on the north slope from me. It seems that I had been approaching a fork in the road with the branch I was on, running on the south side of a ridge and another branch running on the north side. I was just approaching the convergence of these roads. These men were on the south side of the road on the other side of the ridge and moving, it appeared, much like I was. They were probably still fifty to seventy-five yards away, and I was able to get a fairly good look at them.

They were dressed pretty much like I was, in rough woolen clothing, and appeared rough and unkempt, much the way I myself must have looked. They were all carrying muzzle-loading rifles, and an assortment of gear hung from the saddles of their mounts.

Acting on impulse that I still am not sure that I understand, I called out to them and spurred my horse forward. I know that I put on a show for them, one that I didn't really feel deep in heart. I was much more talkative and joyous appearing. I told them how glad I was to have found them, how I had been riding north to Kansas City. I babbled on about how my family had all been killed in the raid of Osceola and how I had stayed in Osceola hoping that my uncle who lived in Kansas City would come and search for me. I told them that I had only recently given up waiting on them and that I decided I needed to make my way to Kansas City on my own. I told them that people in Osceola were having a difficult time, they were near starvation, and people lived in constant fear that Kansas jayhawkers would return.

I'm not sure if any of the men knew quite what to make of me. I introduced myself to them as Bill King because that's the name of old Bill, the freed Negro back in Osceola, and it was the first name that came into my head. Two of the men didn't seem to even want to talk to me and merely nodded but never bothered to introduce themselves. The one in the lead seemed more talkative and introduced himself as being John Clem. He seemed rather proud of the name, as if I should know it, and indeed I did. Old Bill had specifically mentioned that name as one of the bushwhackers who had been raiding over into Kansas. However, I was careful to act as if I had never heard of him, which seemed to cause him some disappointment. I asked several times if I might be allowed to ride with them, and John Clem replied, "Well, you're riding with us now, what more do you want, boy?"

I was careful not to ask them where they were going or what they were doing but said, since they were headed northwest and I knew that was the general direction for Kansas City, that, if they didn't mind, I'd ride with them as far in that direction as they were going. John Clem replied, "Well, be our guest." And so, we continued riding for the rest of the afternoon.

That evening after dark, we pulled up and made camp. We never bothered to light a campfire and I didn't ask why. I figured they were on their way some place and didn't want to be noticed. That suited me just fine. While we sat around on the ground, relaxing and spreading our groundsheets and blankets, I babbled on more about Osceola and the hard times people were having there. Then I mentioned Jim Lane by name and said I wished I knew where he was; I would like to kill him. That brought chuckles from all three of the men. I think that the two who had been the least talkative thought this was a great joke because they seemed to become more cheerful and talkative and began razzing and teasing me a great deal. One of them jokingly said that he had noticed that fancy gun that I was carrying and then he asked if he might see it. My reply was that the gun never left my hands for any reason. I told him how it had belonged to my father and that I was going to use it to kill Jim Lane.

John Clem spoke up and said, "I thought you were going to Kansas City."

I didn't even pause when I replied, "Well, I didn't say I was going to kill him anytime soon."

That made them all laugh again. It seemed they were taking a liking to me. Then John Clem said, "Well, we have it in mind to go kill Jim Lane too."

I asked if I could come along with them. This time nobody laughed. I could see that they were seriously considering this. Then John Clem said, "Why not?" I was greatly relieved. When I started out, I had no idea how I was going to find Jim Lane or how I would get close to kill him, but suddenly with these three bushwhackers with me, I felt that I was well on my way.

Over the next two days, we rode silently and carefully, much like I had been riding for the previous days before I met them along the banks of the Osage. I suddenly realized from what John Clem said to one of the men that we were no longer actually following the Osage. When I met up with them, I had been on the north side of the river, but actually being on the north side, I had missed the fork to the south and apparently had been traveling along the Mari River for a good portion of the last day. It seemed we were actually getting close to Kansas. John Clem was leading us, if possible, even more carefully than I had been traveling on my own.

On the end of the third full day of travel with these men, just about dusk we were traveling up the road when suddenly I heard a faint movement and rustling ahead. About that time, John Clem and the others must have noticed it, because they all pulled up suddenly and stood their horses still. We moved the horses off the road and dismounted and took the muzzles tightly in hand and squeezed to keep them from whinnying and replying to any horses that were approaching, because I now recognized that for having been the noise that first alerted me. I could make out some riders approaching. It was just after sundown, and I couldn't really tell much about them, but suddenly John Clem seemed to relax and called out. The group that looked like there must have been six or seven pulled up short, and one man replied. John Clem said, "Boys, you make so much noise, it's a wonder you have lived this long." That brought some rather scathing comments. We all mounted up and rode out to join them.

It seems they had arranged to meet here and were going on a raid. This suited me just fine. I knew we had crossed into Kansas at some point in the last twenty-four hours, but just where we were, I still had no idea. We moved silently off the road we had been on, down another road that joined there. It seemed we were headed pretty much directly straight west. We moved on fairly silently for another hour or so when the moon came up. It was a near full moon and was shining brightly so that it seemed like we were nearly moving in daylight. We came upon several small houses, and I realized we were on the edge of a town. It wasn't much of a town. The men rode into town still rather silently, and some dismounted. They immediately rushed up, kicked down doors, and barged inside. There was a considerable amount of shouting, a gunshot or two, and the men would then come rushing back out with anything they had found inside that they thought was of any value at all. I sat my horse amazed.

There were several houses rather close together, and all of these were kicked in and ransacked. Then we moved off a little bit farther north, and I thought we were going to turn and head back the way we had come, but there was one other cabin on the edge of the town that caught their attention. We rode up to it en masse. The others dismounted and stormed through the cabin. I sat my horse out in the yard and watched as they came back from the cabin loaded down with blankets and supplies from within. Just what had transpired inside, I don't know. As the last few members of the group exited the house, they drug and pushed some man in front of them. This man was dressed in bedclothes and seemed shaky and unsure on his feet. A woman rushed out beside them, begging them not to hurt him. She said he was sick and so weak he could hardly get out of bed. John Clem replied that they weren't going to harm a hair of his head. However, they did shove him around and rough him up a bit.

Pretty much everyone had mounted up, and I thought we were preparing to leave. In fact, a couple of people had already left. I was sitting on my horse, where I had remained the whole time, when we pulled up in front of the cabin. I could see quite clearly what happened next. As one of the men started to mount up, he suddenly brought his rifle down and shot the man through the chest as he stood there on the front porch next to his wife. I was stunned and shocked into immobility. The woman immediately rushed up on the left-hand side of the man, and other family members rushed out. A young boy flew to his side, knelt down on his right, grabbed his hand, and bent over. There were other family members there. Everyone was screaming and crying. His wife was hysterical and kept yelling, "You promised you wouldn't hurt him."

John Clem turned and rode back the eight or ten feet to where the man was and said, "Why did you do that? I promised we wouldn't hurt him."

The man just laughed and got up on his horse, and he and the rest of the group turned around and spurred their horses and went flying out of there.

I still couldn't move. I stood my horse and looked down at the dying man and his wife and family gathered around him. The young boy raised his face and seemed to look straight in my eyes. I knew that he was far enough away that he probably really couldn't see me, but it seemed like I could see him clearly and still can. It seemed like his eyes looked straight into mine and he kept screaming, "Why, why, why" as he rocked back and forth there cradling his father. How long I sat there unable to move, I don't know, but then I turned my horse and tore out after the rest of the people.

They had gone, hell-bent, back down the road we had been so careful to follow up till that time through the night. When we got to the main road where we had turned off, I noticed that they were still pounding their way down the road to the southeast in the direction we had come. However, I turned my way north. For another hour, I too went tearing along. Then I pulled my horse up and turned off more to the northeast. Throughout the night, which was still bright moonlight, I moved slowly but steadily in a northeastern direction. Once I came across a pretty well-formed road that seemed to run straight north and south, and I turned up it, walking my horse for an hour or so, and then turned off again to the northeast. I was traveling by moonlight and by the North Star. I had traveled up the road that I had just left, intentionally thinking that, if anyone were following my tracks from the cabin, they would now be lost in the general traffic on the road. When I turned off northeast and moved through the country, I felt secure that no one could have linked me with this group. Why I didn't want to be linked with this group, I didn't know quite for sure.

When I started out, I had this vague notion that I was off to punish Jim Lane and his raiders for what they had been doing. I hadn't counted on anything like this. In my mind, Jim Lane and his jayhawkers were all evil and deserved whatever they got. I think I pictured only vicious, evil, murdering jayhawkers being killed in whatever confrontation might ensue from my actions, but I had never thought I would end up being part of a group that shot down an apparently innocent man on his doorstep in front of his family. The boy's face and eyes kept flashing back into my mind, and the more I saw them, I felt like I could see myself. I imagine that's how I had looked as I stood there over my dying father. My God, how could I have become part of such a thing!

As the sun came up, I kept riding. I was headed northeast. I don't know why exactly. It was possibly because the rest of the group had ridden off southeast and possibly because I didn't feel that I could ride west farther into Kansas. Even riding straight north was taking me into territory I didn't know and in which I knew was in the throes of conflict between bushwhackers and jayhawkers all along the border.

Anyway, I kept heading northeast. It seems that I had been accustomed, over the last couple of weeks of travel, to moving cautiously. I didn't seem to even notice what I was doing. It was a habit I had picked up of moving from cover to cover and from one concealed place to the next without consciously thinking of it. I kept moving northeast, and for most of the day, all I could think about was what we had done and the young boy kneeling there next to his father. I felt so bad and so ashamed of myself. I moved on throughout the whole day, and about the time it started to get dark, I moved off the trail into a good, thick area of concealment. I dismounted and removed all my gear from the horse's back, dried him down well, and brushed him down and picked his hooves. Then I hobbled him and tied a rope that I had brought with me around his neck. I wanted to let him graze and still wanted him close, within reach, in an emergency, so I tied the rope low down around a tree. This would allow him to move in a circular manner and graze. Then I lay down next to the tree and tried to sleep.

Initially I found it difficult, but I think within a half hour's time I had fallen into a rather deep sleep. I had essentially been riding for about thirty-six hours. I seemed to sleep well throughout the night, but in the early morning, I seemed to arouse somewhat yet remained slumberous. It was then that I kept catching glimpses of the group I had ridden with and their actions of the night before. I kept seeing the boy's face especially and the face of his mother and dying father.

That morning I awoke and fixed breakfast. I brushed down Pig, and I inspected his back for saddle sores. Luckily, I still didn't weigh much, and he had a good saddle blanket and saddle and I didn't see any sign of any sores developing. I inspected his feet again before carefully saddling him up. I loaded up and headed still northeast, moving throughout the day. As I rode, I began considering what had happened to me over the last few months. Suddenly Jim Lane didn't seem quite as evil as I had imagined him. I certainly didn't consider myself to be evil, and look at what I had gotten myself into. Possibly Jim Lane had had the best of intentions when he led his army of thieves and ruffians into Osceola. Maybe he didn't know what they were really like. Possibly he thought he was going on a great military adventure with the intention of punishing a rebel army that was defending slavery. Possibly his intention was to free all the slaves in Osceola. Maybe he didn't know the nature of the men he was leading. It's possible that once they got there, the men had gotten completely out of hand. I know that even if I had tried, there was nothing I could have done to have prevented the bushwhackers I was riding with from robbing and stealing and killing people. In fact, there had been an occasional shot earlier than that, but whether anyone else had been killed, I didn't know because I stayed on my horse outside of the cabins. It was all too horrible to think about.

Thinking about this got me to thinking about the whole reason for the war in the first place. I know for the month or so before our family was destroyed, I had heard my father, Isaac, and Jacob discussing the situation. My father had felt that, given time, everything would calm down. It was not like he was trying to defend slavery. He said that he didn't support slavery but he did support the states' right to do what they wanted. Apparently slavery had been in existence long before the country was actually formed. America had only been a country since like 1790, I think, and there had been slaves there for a couple of hundred years before that. Apparently, as father said, you couldn't expect the country to change a custom in such a short period of time. He seemed to feel that, given enough time, it would take care of itself. He mentioned things like a cotton gin, which was a great work-saving device, and maintained that it decreased the number of slaves that were necessary to actually process cotton. He said that he thought within another twenty-five years, or so, slavery would not be a profitable institution anymore, and would die out on its own. He couldn't understand why people were so upset about it.

He would mention how his own father had been an indentured servant for seven years upon coming to this country. It was then that I remembered the discussion he had had with the stranger in Osceola who seemed to be offended that father would compare indentured servitude to slavery. With servitude, you were freed after a period of time. With slavery, you were only freed by death. I can remember how angry my father had been when we had returned from that church social the week before our home was destroyed. He seemed to feel that it was people like that who were causing all the problems and, if they were just calm about it, everything would be okay.

I now wondered just what Isaac and Jacob and Moses thought of this question. True, they weren't slaves and had never been slaves, but their father had been. From what my dad and grandfather had said, Abraham and his wife, Sarah, had been dear friends, more friends than slaves. I know my grandfather had often said that the only reason he could afford to buy Abraham was the fact that he kept running away so much that the plantation master decided he may as well sell him cheap as to keep paying slave hunters to track him down and bring him back. Then he would laugh about how funny this was. I know that when my grandfather had bought Abraham, he had promised him that, if he would work for him for a similar period of time that he had worked himself, he would make him free. I think Abraham believed him, because he never made an effort to escape after that, and then after he had served his time as a servant, he had been freed and my grandfather had given him forty acres of land to live on out of the land that my grandfather had settled and deeded.

This caused me to wonder about that situation. Forty acres of land was not anything you could actually make a living on. True, you could grow enough food to feed yourself and your wife and a couple of kids, but you really couldn't make a living on forty acres. So, even though Abraham was free, was he not more or less trapped? That made me think; maybe Isaac and Jacob were also somewhat trapped. Isaac had lived on the forty acres that his father Abraham had given him, and Jacob had lived in a little cabin across the river that my father had let him build but hadn't deeded him. They all worked in our fields and gardens and helped us to make a living on the land that we owned. True, my father had paid them cash money every year when he sold the crops, but were they not still, somewhat, trapped? Were they not still kind of slaves? That thought went through my head constantly as I rode northeastern throughout the day, but as I rode and thought, I would contradict what I had just been thinking. True, Abraham and his wife had lived on the forty acres and then Isaac had lived there. Abraham and Sarah had had several other sons and daughters, but all of them had moved on, just where, I had no idea. Apparently they usually went with my grandfather or father on those spring trips to the Osage trading post and just never came back, taking off on their own wherever they had gone. As far as I can remember, none of Abraham's other children ever returned. Maybe they were glad to get away from there.

However, Isaac had Abraham's place, and he seemed quite happy there, and I know Rebecca was, as she and mother were best of friends, helping each other birth their children and take care of them. I don't remember much about it, but my Dad always said that if I was hungry at the time, we would nurse from Rebecca and Abel would nurse from my mother. We had always been just like family. Still, of Isaac's children, only Jacob, Moses, Sarah, and Miriam had stayed around Osceola, and the rest of them had left. I finally decided that it had nothing to do with being slaves and being confined to the land, but rather it was just something that some people did. My uncle Aaron had moved off to the Osage trading post, and my other uncle, William, had moved off to some place in Texas. I knew I had aunts, but none of them had stayed around Osceola. It was all too confusing. Who could say why anyone stayed or why anyone left? The thing was, I know that all of Abraham's children had been free to do and go wherever they wanted. So, maybe there were not any hard feelings because their grandfather had been a slave at one time. However, this did nothing to settle the question of what the other blacks who were confined to slavery thought and felt.

I imagined myself being a slave, being made to get up every morning for work and being forced to work all day till dark. Well, that's pretty much what I did now. It's also pretty much what I had done ever since I was five or six years of age. It's what we all did. Even my younger brother, Jesse, would get up and come out and work in the fields with us. He had his own little hoe. This was one that had been filed down and sharpened so often that it was maybe a fourth the size of a regular-sized hoe, but yet he could manage and maneuver this. So, when we went out to work in the fields, he was always there, right alongside working—even working tobacco! He couldn't lift any of the tobacco, but when we staked it and put it up, he would carry stakes through the field, dropping them every few stalks so that we could come along and impale the tobacco. Then he walked back and forth along the lines to get more stakes. Mary and Elizabeth also carried stakes, and between the three of them, we had been able to move right along.

It seems like we had always been working, and I couldn't see a lot of difference between the work we did and the work the slaves were forced to do. However, it dawned on me that there was a definite difference. With us, if there wasn't much work to be done at that particular time of year, we were free to go hunting or fishing or swimming or just walking in the woods and exploring. I didn't suppose that any plantation masters ever let their slaves out of their sight, having them constantly under guard. Yes, I decided there was a lot of difference between working hard all your life and working hard for someone else and never being able to feel that you had any freedom or any time of your own. I resolved to ask Abel about these thoughts and questions when I saw him again.

I decided in my own mind that slavery was an abomination that needed to be abolished. While I rode slowly but steadily toward the northeast, I came to the conclusion that it was slavery that was the cause of all the troubles within the country at that time, and it was slavery that had caused the death of my family more so than this murderous, thieving robber, Jim Lane. The more I thought about it, the more I realized I no longer felt like killing Jim Lane, but the more I was resolved to put an end to slavery. How on earth a thirteen-year-old would do that, I really had no idea. Suddenly, reflecting on it further, I came to the conclusion that I should join the union army. That thought sounded ridiculous when it first seemed to burst into my head, but the more I thought about it, the more it looked like it might be feasible. I actually came across a plan. I rolled it back and forth in my mind as I moved toward the northeast and considered all the different possibilities. I would come up with one question after another and think of ways to deal with or answer them.

In the next day or two, I came across a small settlement. It wasn't more than a half dozen houses clustered together and a small general store, but the general store had a sign outside saying "Post Office" also. I dismounted, tied Pig to the railing, and proceeded inside. I shopped around and bought a few tins of beef and vegetables and beans and peaches. Then, I asked the lady if she had any paper and envelopes for sale. I bought two pieces of paper and two envelopes, and the lady graciously consented to allow me to use her pen and writing table. I sat down and wrote a long letter to uncle Aaron, front and back of one sheet of paper, and told him what my plans were. I then folded this and sealed it in the envelope and asked the lady if she would mail it for me. She was happy to do so.

I then went and sat down to try to write a letter for the recruiting station but couldn't seem to decide how to go about doing that. Finally I gave up and politely asked the lady how one went about writing one such letter. She replied that she thought I should write my name and address in the right-hand corner and then write "To whom it may concern on" the left side of the paper and then write the letter. I addressed it, "Aaron Everett, Osage trading post, Osage City, Missouri," and then wrote "To whom it may concern, dear sir." I wrote, "I would like to introduce to you my nephew, Thomas Everett. Thomas has been living with us here since his family was tragically murdered in the massacre at Osceola." I wrote, "Thomas is a good boy, strong and capable, and has a good sense of wits about him." Then I wrote, "He is sixteen years of age, and I feel he would be of benefit to your cause." I then addressed it, "Yours sincerely, Aaron Everett." I sat there and blew on the letter until the ink was dry, folded it carefully, and put it back in an envelope but did not address it.

Packing up my things, I went out, loaded up, and rode off. I now rode with a much greater sense of relief and determination. I headed continually northeast, planning on striking the Missouri river and following it toward the east. As I rode, I kept a lookout for union patrols or anything that might cause me trouble. I was fortunate in never encountering any. Possibly

I was already by this time too far east. One morning I came out to the top of a bluff, and in the distance ahead I could see a good-sized town. I had no idea what the name of this town was, but traveling more carefully, I skirted around to the south so that I could come up to it from the east. I struck a road on the east side of town and turned back to the west, and about a half a mile from the outskirts of town, I came upon an encampment of tents. There were union soldiers milling about in no apparent order. I stopped one of them and asked them what the name of the town up ahead was. He replied that it was Booneville. I asked him then who was in charge of recruiting here. He said that the lieutenant who was in charge of that was in town at that moment trying to sign up citizens for the cause.

I turned Pig toward town and rode in. Just in the middle of town there was a tent set up on the main street and a man sitting behind a desk out in front of the tent. I rode up to him and dismounted, and holding Pig by the reins, I walked up and introduced myself. He had been writing something in a ledger and had some papers scattered on the table in front of him, and he ignored me for a few more seconds until he finished what he was doing. Then he looked up and said, "How can I help you, young man?"

I replied, "I was there to join the union army."

With that, he looked at me rather skeptically. He looked me up and down and seemed to be sizing me up. He then said, "How old are you, boy?"

I told him, "I am sixteen," but I don't think he believed me. Then I reached in my coat pocket and pulled out the letter and handed it to him.

He opened it up, read it, looked up at me, and then looked back down at the letter and seemed to study it some more. Then he said, "It says here you're from Osage City."

I replied, "Yes, sir."

He said, "Why did you come all the way here if you wanted to enlist?"

This is one of the questions I had thought about while I was on my way traveling northeast. I replied that I had gone previously to the station in Jefferson City but the man had turned me down. I told him, "I then went back to Osage City and had my uncle Aaron write this letter." I replied that I had skipped Jefferson City, not wanting to run into the same recruiting man there, and had traveled on west looking for the next place. He asked me why I hadn't gone to Columbia, since that was probably closer. I replied that I couldn't figure out a way to get across the river and that I didn't think that Booneville was actually much farther than Columbia. This seemed to satisfy his curiosity.

He then took another look at the letter and looked back up at me and said, "Are you sure you're sixteen?"

I replied, "Yes, sir."

He said, "You don't seem to have any beard or any growth, not even a little fuzz on your face."

I replied that my grandmother had been Osage Indian and most Indians didn't have much in the way of hair. He seemed to be considering this for a moment when another man that had been standing by his left shoulder bent over and whispered something in his ear. I had noticed this man when I first rode up but hadn't paid any attention to him. My attention had all been concentrated on the man sitting behind the table. When this other man stood up straight, I took a good look at him and recognized him immediately as the sergeant I had met on our canoe trip to Osage City. For a moment my heart fell, and I thought that my efforts were to be frustrated, but at that time the lieutenant, which is what the man behind the desk was, spoke up and said "Well, Sergeant Shawnasee recommends you, boy, so I don't think I can do much better."

With that, I looked at the sergeant and gave him a smile. The lieutenant went back busying with his papers and ledgers and pretty soon slipped a piece of paper forward for me to sign. I bent over and taking the pen in my left hand (I was naturally right-handed), I printed out Thomas Everett across the bottom of the page. I had planned this out carefully.

Most adult men on the frontier weren't able to write or even print. The fact that my mother had insisted on teaching us how to write by reading and writing from the Bible came in very useful. However, by printing with my left hand, I figured it would throw the lieutenant off in case he wished to look at signatures and compare the handwriting on Uncle Aaron's letter. He did indeed look at the paper after I had signed it, said all was well and fine and then suggested I go up to town to sell my horse and gear. He said I wouldn't be needing a horse or that rifle in the army. Now, this was something I hadn't even for a moment considered. I began to hesitate and asked him how I was to get around without a horse. He said that I had signed up for the infantry and the infantry walked. He also related that a fancy gun such as mine was not used by the army and they wouldn't be able to supply me with ammunition for it. I hesitated, not meaning to argue, but I couldn't help but blurting out that the rifle had belonged to my father and it was the only thing that I had left. The sergeant spoke up then and said, "Give it to me, son. I'll take good care of it for you."

I thought that was probably the last I would see of the rifle, but I couldn't think of anything else to do, so I gave it to him. Then, by chance, the lieutenant spoke up and asked me if I would like to sell him my horse and saddle. He said I could sell it in town but he would give me a fair price for it. He said if I sold it in town, they would probably turn around and sell it back to the army and they would want to sell it for more than what they gave me. He offered me twenty-five dollars for the horse and saddle and bridle and rope. This was definitely more than I had paid for it, but still I hesitated, however just for a moment. The sergeant once again spoke up and said, "It's a fair price, son." So, I agreed.

I stripped off my blankets and my saddlebags and the sacks that had some of the canned food in it and the lieutenant said I should head back down the road to the camp and report to the corporal in charge. I felt such an intense sense of relief that I almost trotted down the road to the camp. I turned up and asked for the corporal of the guard or the corporal in charge, or whatever I had been told. They had directed me toward a man who was seemingly wandering idly around the camp. I walked up and told him that I had enlisted and that I was told to report to him. He escorted me to a tent in which he said I would be bunked and opened the flap while I bent and walked inside. Inside there were three men, all appearing to be around twenty or so. They all looked fairly similar to me. They were dressed in an odd assortment of leathers, woolens, and furs.

I introduced myself, and they all replied in kind. One of them pointed toward an empty corner of the tent and said I should make myself a place there. I went over, threw my gear on the ground, and sat on the saddle blankets. I didn't know what to do next. I asked the men how long they had been there and what had been happening and in general tried to come up with the news of the day. After a bit, I became curious about life in the camp. Everybody seemed to be just sitting around or walking around idly, doing nothing. One of the men replied, "Well, son, we wake up in the morning to the bugle and then throughout the day, whenever the bugle blows, we line up and do whatever we're told." That seemed to be about the gist of their daily activities.

About that time, the bugle did indeed blow, and we all moved out of the tent, walked to the center of the camp, and formed up in a line. The corporal I had reported to came up and handed me a stick about six feet long, which he told me was my gun. We then proceeded to march around the camp, formed line, and drilled. I learned that the men I was in the tent with were half the members of my squad, the other four members being in the tent next to ours. I lined up with the members in the squad. Besides the eight of us, there was one corporal. We marched about in single file, then formed the double files of a column and marched around some more. After going for about an hour, the bugle blew and we stopped. The corporal dismissed some of us to go back to the tent and delegated some of us to go help prepare the meal, and thus was life in camp.

CHAPTER 11

Every morning the bugle blew. We got up, formed a line in the opening of the camp, took roll call, and then were dismissed. When the bugle blew again, we went to breakfast. After we had eaten, we were free to relax a little bit until the bugle blew once more. Then we would usually drill and march around camp, left face, right face, form the line! We would do this for an hour or two, and then, when the bugle blew, we were dismissed, some of us being told to chop wood, clean up around the camp, or take care of the horses that the officers rode. After a bit, the bugle would blow again and we would go to eat a noon lunch. Then we would be free after lunch for a bit until the bugle blew, whereupon we would march around or do practice with the gun. Taking my wooden stick, I learned how to present arms and go through all the manipulations with the weapon. There were a few days when we practiced with a bayonet. Actually, this was just with the old stick gun, but we would take it and stab at each other, move our feet in the manner that the sergeant prescribed, and learn how to do butt strokes and other types of attacks with the wooden stick in lieu of a real gun.

We were there a couple of weeks, I kind of lost track of the time, and then one evening the lieutenant had announced to the whole camp that we would be leaving in the morning, so we should pack all of our gear together tonight because, after breakfast, we would be marching down to the landing on the river and boarding a steamer to St. Louis. I had seen steamers before but never had been on one, and the thought seemed like another great adventure to me.

The following morning after breakfast, we returned briefly to our tents, loaded up all of our gear, and when the bugle blew, assembled in the square and marched off down to board the riverboat. I found this exciting. We didn't have rooms on the steamer. Some men got inside and found a place to put their gear, but I stayed outside watching the water rolling by and looked at the bluffs and the shoreline. I walked around and around the steamer, stood in the back, and watched the wheel turn and watched the waves splash. Then, I went inside and wandered around. I ended up below deck down in the steam room, where I inquired briefly of the men just how a steam engine functioned. They directed me toward one man who was the engineer and who seemed less busy than the rest, who were feeding wood in the fire. He seemed to be constantly watching gauges and attending to things, but he didn't mind talking to me as he worked. He explained the different gauges and levers and the way in which the burning wood heated water, which made steam to turn the engine. I thought this was all fascinating.

Then, I wandered around through the rest of the ship and finally went and put my blankets and saddlebags on a spot under the upper deck and sat on the lower deck, leaning back against the housing. I stretched out my legs and watched as the landscape went by. Sure enough, just like on shore, it was the same on ship. Whenever the bugle blew, we gathered, but we couldn't drill and march on the steamer, so usually the bugle only blew when it was time to announce that a meal was ready for us. Then it blew again every night when we were to turn in. We traveled in this fashion down the river, seemed to go north, made a turn back to the east, and then came down to where the river suddenly seemed to triple in size. We were now on the Mississippi just above St. Louis.

I was rather confused as the boat seemed to turn upstream and move north. I had always thought that St. Louis was south of where the Missouri joined the Mississippi. I wondered if the pilot of the steamer knew where he was going. I asked some of the soldiers on the deck next to me, and they replied that it seemed we weren't actually going to St. Louis after all. Somewhere along the line while we had been traveling, apparently the decision was made to send us to a town called Canton, Missouri. I had no idea where this might be. The steamboat seemed to struggle and churned harder, making its way upstream against the current. It took another day of travel before the boat once again turned in toward the shore. It nosed carefully into the western bank and grounded. Ropes were tied, and the gangplank was lowered and we prepared to disembark. We were now found to be just above a small town on the banks of the Mississippi. Straight ahead of us was a little earthen-walled encampment.

It somewhat resembled my uncle's trading post with banks around it, but there was no palisade. We grabbed our gear and marched down the gangplank, up the embankment, and through a gate into the compound. As we marched through the levee wall, I noticed how the walls turned in for about thirty feet on each side and then opened up into a square compound that must have been about a half of a mile on each side. We were shown to what would be our tents. It seemed the majority of the rest of the regiment was already here. There must have been a thousand people milling around the place. It seemed that our fifty men would be joining this regiment to make up its maximum strength.

We were marched down to several tents arranged together. These tents were larger than the ones we had been in Jefferson City, and each was capable of holding nine to ten men. The sergeant who was leading the group assigned one tent for every ten men in the regiment in our group until all fifty had been stowed. I now found myself in a tent with, I won't call them a total group of strangers, but the three men that I had shared the tent with previously at Jefferson City had been assigned to another tent. I was by far the youngest of the group, naturally. It seemed that everyone else was from early to late twenties. I don't think there was anyone who was still younger than twenty.

If I had felt lonely and isolated before, this seemed to triple the feeling. I had noticed that when we were in the tent before, when we had breaks and a period of time in the evening, that I seemed to have nothing much to say to the other people in the tent. It's not that I was unfriendly; it's just that their talk seemed to be mainly about women, drinking, and other such things. Their language was often quite offensive. I know my mother would have been ashamed to have me associate with people such as that, and somehow I just didn't feel comfortable. I seemed to have gotten a reputation as being a sullen and gloomy character while we had been in Jefferson City, and now that I was thrown in with these older people, who were nearly total strangers, I seemed to find myself becoming more silent and uncommunicative.

It had been late afternoon when we had landed, and by the time we were escorted to our tents and arranged our gear, what there was of it, the bugle sounded and we went to evening meal. After that, since it was dark, there wasn't much to do except go back to the tent, arrange my gear, and lie down in preparation for going to bed. I always chose the corner in the back of the tent on the right-hand side because it seemed like people were always getting up during the night and making trips outside. I didn't like being stepped on and tripped over, so I arranged my ground sheets and blankets and laid down. It was pretty much totally dark in the tent. There were a few fires that had been lit outside, but these didn't provide any light inside. The other men in the tent seemed to lay there on their blankets or sit there on their gear and talk until much later. Often I would lay there and listen to these conversations, but usually I drifted right off.

When the bugle blew in the morning, we were up and off to breakfast and then had a bit of time to relax before the bugle sounded again and we lined up. Most of the rest of the regiment were taken off on drills or marches, which was fairly typical of military activity, but our officers and sergeant led us down to a long wood-framed building. Here, we were issued our uniforms and belts, buckles, boots, and other personal such items. We had been formed up in a long line that went through the front door and then passed single file through the room, where at different benches and tables soldiers behind of which sized us up and issued what they felt was the appropriate clothing and articles.

Standing in front of one such table, the man required me to remove my coat and, looking me over from head to toe, issued long underwear, pants, and a shirt. Then, we moved on down the line, where I got a woolen overcoat and a cape and a funny little square crumpled-looking hat with a stiff beak on the front of it. Then we came to a table where the man was issuing the boots. He looked over and said, "What size, son?" I told him I really had no idea. He looked down at my feet and said, "Take those stupid things off."

I took off my boots, and then he instructed me to take off my moccasins also. I stood there in my bare feet. He looked over and gave me a pair of boots and told me to try these on. They seemed to fit well enough. Possibly they were a little bit big, but I felt that was a good idea. I could always wear several pairs of socks to make up the difference, and as I was still quite young, I expected I would need larger sizes in the next few months anyhow.

I put on my moccasins and boots, gathered up all the gear I had been issued, and last, came to a table where they were issuing out the knapsacks and blankets and groundsheets. I stuffed everything I could into the knapsack, gathered up the rest of the gear, and carried this back to our tent. Here we disrobed and then dressed out in all the army-issued clothing. I put on my new boots and two pairs of woolen socks beneath them. After having dressed and packed all the rest of my belongings together in the corner, the bugle was blowing, and we lined up outside and marched off to drill.

We were there for about two weeks, drilling and marching and maneuvering. Some of the time we spent practicing with the wooden guns. We went through bayonet training and fighting with the wooden guns. We still hadn't been issued any weapons, and I was beginning to wonder whether we would ever be. The rest of the regiment did have weapons that I longed to ask to be allowed to examine, but I never got up the nerve. Any free time that we had, I usually spent it walking around the camp. The camp was basically one big square. There were two entrances at opposite ends, and at each corner, there was a redoubt that protruded somewhat from the wall, as the corners of my uncle's trading post had protruded, and on which small cannons were placed. There were no other cannons in the fort, just the four at the corners. It seemed that there was a permanent garrison to the fort that was separate from our regiment. These were based in some of the few wood plank buildings that there were on the base. The other wood plank buildings were for storage, and there was a small general store that was open to the soldiers. Some of the plank houses were homes for civilians who worked, in some capacity, around the fort, but most all of the regiment were housed in tents.

I found it interesting to walk around the top of the levee that made up the walls of our fort, looking out at the Mississippi and watching the steamers go back and forth. We were occasionally allowed time to go into the small town of Canton, but this only consisted of a couple of thousand people. It was smaller than Osceola had been and not nearly as appealing. It seems there was a meat-packing place there, and there was a smell that seemed to linger over the town constantly. It wasn't necessarily a bad smell, but it wasn't pleasant either. It seemed to be a combination of hog feces, blood, and smoke. It seems that the town specialized in butchering hogs and then canning the meat for sale. That plus the fact that the Mississippi

River had a smell of its own that was different from the smell of the Osage River, seemed to create a unique aroma. It was hard to explain.

We spent a couple of weeks of milling around, drilling, training, and marching back and forth along the road. One morning after breakfast when we gathered, the sergeant marched us off to a building where we lined up once again in single file and went through and were issued our rifles, belts, and other accouterments and our bayonet. With these, I now felt like a true solider; however, I was rather disappointed with the gun. I had seen that it was the same as the other soldiers had been drilling and practicing with, but I was surprised at how much it weighed and how clumsy it was. It seemed that the bore on the rifle was nearly as big as my thumb. In addition, the thing was exceedingly heavy and cumbersome. I supposed it must have weighed ten or twelve pounds. I had never imagined that they could weigh that much. The Pennsylvania rifle, I think, weighed probably half of that. It was also much harder to hold and aim because the weight of this thing seemed to drag your left arm down when you tried to steady it. One thing I had noticed is that whereas my Pennsylvania rifle had fixed front and rear sights, this had a ladder-type sight on the rear. I had never shot a rifle with such a sighting arrangement.

After we had gotten our rifles, we went back to our tents and adjusted all of our leather gear and accouterments. Then, we were marched out to drill and train. We went through the manual of arms with the new weapons, placed bayonet, and practiced stabbing at swinging straw dummies and butting and whopping them in general. I thought this was all great fun. The rest of the afternoon we were taken for a long march down along the river and back.

The following day, after breakfast, we were marched several miles upstream and then turned off onto a road leading to the west that crossed partway across the field up to some rather high bluffs. Here, we were marched down to an open field at the foot of the bluffs and stopped. The column that had been marching in single file was ordered to make a left turn, and there we faced across about fifty yards some straw dummies that had been set up, swinging and hanging from a wooden frame. I thought that we were probably going to have bayonet practice again, but the sergeant stepped forward, walked up and down the line, and gave us a speech. He told us that we were going to learn how to load and fire our muskets.

I thought that was rather strange. I mean, I thought everyone knew how to load and fire a rifle, but seems I was mistaken in that belief. I realized this when he started carefully going through the procedure to load and fire a weapon. Initially he told us just to stand and listen and do nothing. Then he went on to say, "First, you ground the butt of the musket on the ground. Grab the barrel with the left hand, reach into your pouch with the right hand, and take out one of your paper cartridges. Now feel the lead ball, in the head of the cartridge, between your thumb and index finger, and then carefully bite the ball off. Pour the powder down the barrel, crumple the paper, and shove the cartridge down the barrel. Now spit the bullet in the palm of your hand, wipe it on your blouse, stuff it in the barrel, and then pound it home with the ramrod." He went through this all very elaborately, slowly, step by step. He then said, "Be sure the ramrod is tamped down nearly to the end of it to make sure the ball is firmly seated in the barrel or else it may misfire or lose accuracy. Then, replace the ramrod, lift the gun up in the crook of your left arm, place the hammer on half-cock, reach in your pouch and extract a percussion cap, and place it on the nipple. Then, take a half turn to the right, put your left foot out, bring the rifle to your shoulder on command, take aim, cock, and fire when ordered."

He went through these instructions carefully, step by step several times with us all, standing in line, facing him. Then he, very thoughtfully, stepped around the head of the column and paced up and down behind us. He then said, "Ready, let's load now." Once again, he went through each step carefully, almost one word at a time. It was only then that I realized how difficult it was for so many of the people in our company, or whatever you called it, to remember to follow these simple commands. I think that probably half of them had never handled a gun of any type before. They seemed to be afraid of the guns or so intimidated by the sergeant's firm commands that they couldn't seem to remember what to do next. He went through the drill carefully, had us turn and step forward with the left foot, raise, and fire. He told us just to shoot in the general direction of these swinging straw dummies. I didn't feel there was any great challenge in just shooting straw dummies that big from fifty yards, but I did as commanded. I was surprised to see from the way the musket balls struck the bluff behind the dummies that it was obvious that very few people had actually hit anything.

We spent the rest of the morning going through the procedure of loading and firing slowly. We had been given twenty paper cartridges, and when these were fired, the sergeant once again stepped through in front of the column and gave another little speech. He had told us that by the time he was done with training us, we would be as good as the British troops that had beat Napoleon at Waterloo, whoever that was and wherever that was. He said the reason the British had been able to beat the French in every battle they fought was because of the fact that the British drilled with live ammunition and were trained to load and fire quickly. He seemed to brag how the British could get off three shots in a minute while the typical Frenchmen had trouble getting off two shots in a minute and that, in any battle with such weapons, the one who did the most shooting was the one who won. That all seemed pretty logical, no surprises about that, I thought. Then, he went up and down the line and asked each soldier to present his gun for him to inspect. It was surprising that when he ran his ramrod down the gun, he found several in which balls had been lodged and had not fired. I wasn't sure how that could actually happen. I didn't know whether it was because the person had forgotten to pour the powder in or what.

Later people around camp, when we had been marched back after practice, related that, if you only tamped the ball about halfway down, when the gun fired, the gases would not expand enough and would blow back; thus it didn't have enough force to dislodge the ball entirely from the barrel. Then, if you were to keep tamping balls on top of it, you could stuff the whole barrel full of balls that never fired. I didn't know whether that was possible, but I couldn't argue with anyone. That afternoon we got back in plenty of time to clean the guns thoroughly after the heavy firing and oiled them down good. We also had time to polish up our boots and our leather accouterments.

I had noticed in previous days when marching that the leather tended to let water in, and my feet seemed to get wet easily. I had decided to rectify that situation. We went to the evening meal when the bugle blew, and afterward I passed down to the little general store on base and sold off the heavy wool coat and pants and my moccasins and boots and my funny little hat and whatever else I felt that I could do away with. I kept the saddlebags for now, since they contained my Remingtons and my necessaries pouch. I bought some supplies in the store. I bought a piece of stiff black tanned leather similar to the knapsack I had been issued. I also bought some black leather cord. I bought some needles and some blue woolen cloth that matched my uniform so that I could patch it as needed. I also bought some beeswax and black shoe polish, and I bought a small, stiff pig hair brush for polishing the boots. I placed all of this in my saddlebags to use later.

The next several days we spent marching and drilling. We even went out several times with the rest of the regiment in its entirety and marched up the road, through fields, drilling and turning and marching as a whole regiment. We practiced getting in line of battle and all sorts of other maneuvers whenever the sergeants or officers called them out. One day a week or so later, the sergeant marched us off on our own again up to the field for target practice. This time he gave us a long and thorough discussion about how to actually aim the rifle so that you might hit what you were shooting at. He talked about elevation and windage and how to use the ladder sights. He went through this carefully like he had before, step by step, until it seemed to become rather boring to me. Then, once again, he walked around behind us and went through the actions of loading and then aiming and firing.

Once again, he told us just to aim at the straw-stuffed dummies swinging on the rope from the post. At this point, I had already determined that this was senseless. I would never be able to tell what I hit or if I even hit anything with all the rest of the men in the regiment, or actually we were about half of a company, firing at the ten targets in front of us. Five men firing twenty shots at one straw dummy would pretty much negate the ability to actually sight in your rifle. Instead, I aimed at the post that held the beam from which the dummy swung. I fired the first three shots, aiming what I thought was about three feet off the ground using the flat sights. I then raised it up to the first notch and fired the next three shots. Each time, I aimed for the same spot as I originally had. I then raised the ladder up to the next notch, aimed at my original first sight, and fired. I did this every third shot until we had shot off our twenty rounds, at which time we were marched back to the barracks where we cleaned our gear up and went to supper and then went to bed.

The following day we were given for leisure. A lot of the people in the regiment went into town. Others, I think, even went home because we had had the whole weekend off. It seemed to me that most of the people in the regiment came from in and around that area and were within probably twenty or thirty miles of their homes.

I spent the earlier part of the day after breakfast in the tent. Everyone else had taken off, and I was alone then. The first thing I did was take the piece of leather I had bought and punched two holes on each side. Then I punched two holes on each side, about two inches up, from the bottom of my knapsack. I took the black leather cord and ran it from the outside of the knapsack and through the corresponding holes on one side of the rough leather that I had purchased. I tied this on the one side. Then, I took out my Remingtons and placed them in a pouch that I had made from the lamb's wool that I had taken out of the woolen jacket before I sold it. I sewed this together to make one large mitten and placed the Remingtons in it, as well as the two extra cylinders. Then, in the bottom of my knapsack, I placed my lead balls, my percussion caps, my beeswax, and my brass flask. I then tied the leather cords on each side to make a false bottom in my knapsack. I then placed all my gear back in the knapsack, including the one extra powder horn. I felt quite safe now.

My Damascus-bladed knife, I placed in a sheath that I attached to the outside of my right boot. I punched four holes through the top of my boot and took the sheath for the knife and used the leather cord to tie it to where only the top three or four inches of the hilt of the blade stuck up above my boot. I kept my pants pulled down on the outside and over the boot so that my blade was entirely unnoticeable. I then took some of the woolen cloth that I had bought and made a pocket on the inside of my coat up over my left breast so that I could put one of my pistols in it if needed. I also made another pocket on the inside of the greatcoat down just above the waist on the right side. Then I made a hole in the pocket so I could reach the gun.

After having done all this, I stowed all my gear in the knapsack and took my saddlebags over and sold them at the store then walked on down to Canton. I had been there several times previously. It was a town of about two thousand people, but as I had thought previously, it was nowhere near as attractive as Osceola. There were some fine houses there, but most of the other houses were log cabins or wood-frame houses. It seems a lot of people that worked in the hog canning factory lived in town there, and they were not necessarily well off. In addition, the streets were all of mud, and due to the nature of the ground around the Mississippi, they never seemed to dry out. Because of the fact that there were about one thousand or fifteen hundred people in the fort and they liked to spend money on drinking, gambling, and other types of entertainment, a lot of the people on the street who you passed seemed rather coarse and rough. I had actually gone in a bar once and asked to buy a beer, which I had never had before, but the man had refused to sell it to me. This was despite the fact that I was wearing a union uniform and I couldn't see that I looked any different from any of the rest of the customers in the store, most of whom were all dressed as me and most of whom were drunk as skunks, but he had.

There wasn't anything I needed that I could see from the general store, so I simply walked up and down the streets and looked things over. There was a little church there that attracted my attention. I hadn't been in a church since the week before my family had died, so I went in there and sat for a while. I said prayers for my parents and my brother and Isaac and couldn't think of much more to say, so I just sat there for what seemed like a long time. It seemed to be starting to get dark when I got up and finally went back to the camp. Sunday they had church services on the base, as they had every Sunday that I had been there. But I had stayed in the tent throughout them, and that afternoon went out and walked up and down the levee looking at the river. I was tempted to buy line and try to go fishing and catch something, but then I thought, if I did, I didn't know whether they would cook it at the mess house or not, so I didn't bother with that. Instead I walked out to the target range. I inspected and measured out the groupings of my shots on the post I had used as target practice. The first three shots were three feet up, as expected. The next three shots were about four to five inches above that. The next group was about a foot up, and all seemed to be left of my point of aim. Then, about another foot up, was a fourth group that also was to the left of center. The last three groups continued to hit higher on the post, but always to the left. The gun definitely pulled to the left. But not having been allowed to step off any measured distance, I could only guess as to the trajectory and the windage.

That evening we went to bed as usual, and the Monday morning after that, we got up to drill once again. It seemed that we had been there—I had lost count— maybe five or six weeks. Thinking back on it, I don't remember just what day I had joined the army. After I had left Osage City to go to our homestead, I hadn't kept count of days, and as I had spent most of the next four or five weeks riding through territory, avoiding being seen, I had lost track of time. The day that I actually had signed up in Jefferson City, I hadn't thought to ask. So, I had no idea how long we had been in Canton or how long I had been in the service, but one day later that week, the colonel of the regiment called us all together and gave a speech on the parade ground. He formally introduced himself to all of us as Colonel David Moore and introduced his second in command, a Lieutenant Colonel Woodyard. He also introduced some of the majors and captains and lieutenants, but as he was parading his horse constantly back and forth in front of us, sometimes I couldn't catch names and never really paid much attention since I couldn't clearly distinguish the faces of the men he was naming from where I was anyhow. He said that we were now called the twenty-first Missouri infantry. He said that we had a fine reputation and named several previous battles that the regiment had been in before we had joined up. None of this had made any impression on me because I had never heard of any of the places or any of the battles he was talking about.

He said he was proud of us all and knew that we would obey orders, fight bravely, and make the regiment proud. He then announced that the rest of the day we should spend cleaning our uniforms, polishing our gear, and getting everything packed together because in the morning we would be marching out to go to war. It seemed the whole regiment was thrilled by this prospect, cheered, cried, and tossed their hats in the air. I didn't bother to toss my hat because I didn't know how I would find it afterwards, but I was excited as all the rest. This is what I had been waiting for. This is what I had signed up for. I think I had spent the last three months, or maybe more, preparing for this, and I couldn't have been happier.

When we returned to our tents, the fellow soldiers were all jubilant and excited, talking, planning, and preparing their gear and packing it up. We had the evening meal again, went back to our camps, sat around in the near dark of the tent, and discussed where we were going and what we might be doing. The colonel hadn't told us where we were headed, just that we were off in the morning, so after a short while, we spread out our blankets and groundsheets and went to bed.

The bugle sounded the next day well before daylight. We got up, rolled up our blankets and groundsheets, and attached them to the top of our knapsacks, which had already been packed the night before. I had slept in my uniform, all except for the greatcoat, cap, and cape, and had packed up all of my gear. Taking one last look to make sure that nothing was missing, I assembled out on the parade ground. We took roll call and then went off to breakfast. By this time, it was getting completely light, and we marched down and were assigned to different steamers that had nosed into the bank, grounded, and had been tied off. It seemed like there must have been ten or twelve steamers to hold the troops, officers, and gear. Of course, I kept my knapsack and all my equipment, but the tents were being loaded on, as well as cooking supplies, horses, and other such items for the army.

Once again, I stood on the outside where the air was fresh under the overhang of the upper deck, pressed against the wall, and tried to stay out of everybody's way. When everyone was on board and settled, the steamers all took off, one after another, and we headed downstream. I found out that today was March 18. That was interesting. I could tell that it was moving on toward spring by the way the buds were starting to form on the trees and by the slightly warmer temperature that we had been having. It also, with the warmer temperatures, seemed to rain nearly every day. That was always a sure sign that spring was coming.

CHAPTER 12

We passed on down the river it seemed like a lot faster than we had come up it just a few weeks ago. We arrived in St. Louis and were disembarked and put in at a barracks on the river. It was right in the heart of St. Louis. We didn't have hardly any time to see the town or even get adjusted because the day after we had arrived, we were told we would be moving on in the morning. We weren't told exactly where we were going, but once again, we loaded on board different steamers and went down the Mississippi. We traveled for a couple of days, moving along rather quickly, when the boat seemed to take a sharp turn to the left and enter into an even bigger river than the Mississippi. I thought that the Mississippi was the biggest river in the world, but it seemed like when we took the sharp bend, although from there on downstream the Mississippi widened out considerably, turning even further and heading up to the northeast was the mouth of what, I thought, looked like an even bigger river. I found out this was called the Ohio.

Just right around the bend, I noticed a military establishment and a small town just past it. The town seemed to be bustling with people, traffic, horses, and wagons. I don't know if it was the town itself or the fort that we were just then passing, but something gave off the worst smell I had ever encountered in my life. It smelled like an outhouse, only a hundred times worse. I made some comment to the soldier next to me, and he said that was Fort Defiance. He said the town was Cairo, Illinois, and that the fort and the town had been situated in such a manner that every spring, with heavy rains, the whole area flooded, which flooded out all of the pit latrines and toilets and produced this God-awful smell. I think this man was actually from some place upriver and previously had worked on steamers going up and down the river before he had joined the service.

We stopped briefly at a place called Fort Henry. This was at the mouth of the Tennessee River. We had been traveling on a line of steamers, and it seemed like the steamer that I was on was in the rear. Some of the other steamers had actually gone further up, but we stopped at Fort Henry and took on wood and supplies. I didn't even bother to disembark. Then, we were on our way again upstream, and later in the same day, we turned in to the right along the western shore of the Tennessee. We nosed into the bank at the foot of a steep bluff. The bluffs here appeared to be nothing but mud and dirt overgrown with scrub brush. At the top of it, there appeared to be a small town. There was a flagpole visible in the distance and a little log cabin next to it.

Once the boat was tied off securely and the gangplank lowered, we marched off down onto the bank, up a road, and to the top of the bluffs, passed through a little town that was actually bigger than I had thought from what I could see of it from the riverboat, and then turned off to the south and west and marched through a huge encampment of soldiers. I thought that I was in a big camp in Booneville. I had been surprised at the size of the camp at Canton, Missouri. Fort Defiance I had thought was astonishing, but this camp looked bigger than anything I envisioned before. For one thing, there were no fortifications around it, and tents seemed to be arranged in all different directions. It seemed as far as you could see, even into the distance, there were soldiers moving and tents being set up.

We continued to march off to the southwest for what seemed like a couple of miles and then were brought up short. Once again, I had lost track of the dates and the time, but I now found that we were being assigned a place to stay in the camp. Apparently we were joining up with General Prentiss's sixth division. Specifically, we had been assigned to General Peabody's first brigade. These were terms I had heard before in camp when we were drilling and practicing on the parade grounds and marching along the roads, but I had always found it hard to keep them straight. Apparently the army, as near as I could be correct, consisted of divisions, divisions being formed up of three or four brigades, a brigade having anywhere around four or five regiments, a regiment being something like ten companies, and a company being composed of something like ten squads of ten men. So, that thought went through my head that we were now part of General Prentiss's division and we were in the first brigade. I didn't know how many brigades were in General Prentiss's division. I had had the impression that was a variable number, but the thought went through my mind quickly that there must be something like ten thousand or fifteen thousand, maybe twenty thousand men here in our division. I felt quite secure, maybe even a little bit insignificant.

We were directed to an open area between two different regiments. The sixteenth Wisconsin was on one side, and the twelfth Michigan was on the other side. We marched up and were then disbanded and shown by our different company leaders to the specific tents that were assigned to us. We went in, and I, once again, placed my gear in the back corner of the tent and then went back outside and walked around the area. We had been told to stay in camp and not to wander off.

I talked to some of the people in the twelfth Michigan and the sixteenth Wisconsin and looked the area over around where we were now settled. It seemed that we were in a clearing surrounded by large areas of thick woods in patches. There were woods to our front and both sides. In front, facing toward what I think was the southwest, the woods were not so thick, so we could actually see through the woods fairly easily and out into a cleared area. This was only cleared for a short distance and then seemed to go up a slight incline to a ridge top that was at least partially wooded and then disappeared into the distance. From where we were, I could only see a couple of hundred yards in any direction.

Well, here we were, and now what were we going to be doing next? If it was anything like Jefferson City and Canton, Missouri, we would probably be here for the next month or two drilling and practicing. So far, I had been in the military only, looking back on it, something probably like three and a half months. During that time, I had done a lot of marching, a lot of drilling, and a lot of practicing with the wooden gun but had managed to fire only forty shots with my rifle. I had never been given another opportunity to try to sight the rifle in.

All of these thoughts were going through my mind, and I was feeling somewhat anxious, because we were finally close to the war and would soon be having some sort of activity. In fact, it wasn't much later that same day that I heard, in the distance, a flurry of what I thought were gunshots, but beings how no one else seemed to react, I determined that possibly it was just claps of thunder. Just what day it was, I really didn't know. I knew that the first of the troops had arrived from our regiment a couple of days before that, but just what the date was now, I had no idea.

As evening approached, the bugle sounded. We went off for our meal, and then I returned to the tent and spent what remained of the evening cleaning and polishing my weapons. I then spread my blankets and groundsheet and laid down for the night. I hadn't gotten to know very many people in the regiment. I was in the same tent with the rest of my squad, which had been designated part of I company. I think that was because our group of fifty men had been amongst the last to be recruited or at least to show up at Canton, Missouri. Of the people in my squad, I found that none had previously had any military experience, and most hadn't ever even fired a gun. However, in an army as large as ours, no one seemed to be particularly worried or afraid. I rolled over and fell asleep. During the night, I imagined that I occasionally heard gunshots, but being's how no one seemed to be alarmed, I paid it no mind. Also, it stormed all through the night, and it was hard to be sure.

The next day we awoke early to the sound of the bugle, had roll call, and went to breakfast. We returned to our camp, where people sat around outside the tents and talked and bragged about what they would be doing during the upcoming campaign, as they called it. Apparently we were heading some place south called Corinth, Mississippi. I had gathered this from talking to and listening to the soldiers around us who had been there for several days. It seems there was an important railroad complex at Corinth, and we were going to destroy it. It looked like to me that it would be a long time coming, because apparently this was thirty or forty miles away. Nobody seemed too anxious to be moving.

Thinking about it, I realized how incredibly complex it would be to have an entire army transferred here by steamboat or by marching or however they had all gotten here, to set up camp and get everything organized. It was absolutely astonishing the more I thought about it. Later that afternoon, we had heard some more gunfire off to the south and west. There seemed to be a little bit more excitement with people going back and forth than there had been, and I wondered what this was all about. Shortly after that, some of the officers came through and announced that Colonel

Moore would be leading a patrol out to check on the pickets who were apparently keeping guard down to the southwest somewhere.

Some of the different companies of the regiment were gathered up and marched off. I think there was maybe about half of the regiment that went. At least my company, company I, was left in camp. Several hours later about dusk, Colonel Moore returned with the rest of the soldiers they had taken out. Apparently they had seen nothing except hoof prints that they thought might be confederate cavalry probing and spying on us. They hadn't seen any troops or hadn't seen any cavalry, but apparently there had been a goodly number of tracks. I supposed it was natural that the enemy would be sending troops out to spy on us even if we were forty miles or so away.

After evening meal, we went back to the camps, sat around as always, talked, bragged, and discussed the leadership. People seemed to think that Colonel Moore was an excellent colonel, and they thought highly of Colonel Woodyard also. No one seemed to know much about General Prentiss. They said that Prentiss was one of the generals, along with Sherman and McClernand, and these generals all reported to General Grant. I had heard talk of these people previously. Grant apparently was exceedingly famous at this time because he had been in command of the army that had stormed and taken Fort Henry and Fort Donaldson, which we had passed on the trip up the Tennessee River. It felt good to be in an army commanded by such a famous general.

That evening when we went to bed, it was actually a fairly decent evening. The day we arrived and that night it had blown up a torrential rain. It had stormed, lightninged, and thundered, and the wind had thrown such that I thought it was going to blow our tent away, but tonight it seemed all was quiet and peaceful.

The following morning, I was awakened by definite gunfire. This seemed to be a little bit more intense and possibly a little bit closer than it had been on previous days. I don't know exactly what time it was, but it was certainly before any sign of daylight. It seemed a half hour or so after the first burst of gunfire that had awakened me, a commotion developed in the camp. Initially, I heard a lot of movement and rustling and just a lot of scuffling around. Then, the bugle sounded, still before daylight, and we grabbed our gear together and exited the tent to form up. I couldn't see just who was giving orders, but we were told that Colonel Moore had ordered the I company as well as several others form up, that we were going to be going out on a patrol to reinforce some pickets that had been placed previously. It seemed that there was some hint of trouble. I, like the rest of the men in our squad, had left my knapsack in the tent and had only grabbed my rifle, my belt for ammunition and other accouterments, and my canteen. It turned out that some of the men in our squad had forgotten to bring their canteens.

We marched off down the road, following Colonel Moore. It seems he had taken about half the regiment. As I remember having heard it, he had called out A, C, D, H, and I, or at least I knew for sure he had called out I. By this time, it was starting to get faintly light, and we marched off down what I felt was probably to the southwest along a road. It seems we hadn't even gotten warmed up yet by the marching when we starting meeting troops who were retreating back along the road. There were several wounded men. I don't suppose we were even a quarter of a mile from camp at this time. There was a discussion with Colonel Moore and some officers of the group of union soldiers who were retreating, and Colonel Moore ordered one of his officers to return to camp and bring up the rest of the regiment. By the time the rest of the regiment arrived, it was full daylight, and the sun could be seen starting to come up in the east. We marched off down the road, it seems but a short distance, and took a turn pretty straight west turn, judging by the sun coming up behind me.

We had only marched about maybe one hundred yards in this direction. Along the south side of the road there was a split rail fence, and as we were passing along a field out to the south, suddenly we were fired upon. I instinctively threw myself to the ground and could see soldiers lining the fence on the other side of the field. I took a shot at one, rolled over on my back, and loaded my rifle again while lying on my back, then rolled over and fired again. While I was reloading, several of the soldiers rushed toward the fence and knocked it down. There was a brief flurry of firing at some confederate troops across the field who were retreating back southward, I think, into some woods. They seemed to disappear into the woods and brush in the distance. I don't remember being scared or anything, other than excited at this time.

Someone gave orders that we tear down the split rail fence and form ranks in the field beyond which, now that I could get a better look at it, appeared to have once been a cotton field. The front of our line was along the northwest corner of the field stretching for a distance to the east and looking south. As our troops formed in a line along the field, which was slightly more elevated here than the southern end, we noticed the rebel soldiers obliging us by forming in a line across the field in the south. They had passed a distance out into the field, and Colonel Moore gave the order to fire. We let blast with one solid, roaring, thunderous volley from one end of the line to the next. I didn't need to be told what to do after that. I loaded and fired as fast as possible. My thoughts were only to try to get off three rounds a minute. I wished I had been able to sight my rifle better as the enemy lines I estimated to be a couple of hundred yards off. I really couldn't tell if my shots were having much effect, because everything seemed to go up in smoke. The black powder rifles put off a thick cloud of smoke, which smelled horribly of rotten eggs, and with nearly one thousand men lined up along the higher edge of the field and the smoke blowing uphill from the confederate lines, it seemed like we were fighting in the clouds.

I continued loading and firing as rapidly as possible and then, after about a half hour or so, things became quiet. About this time, someone gave an order that we were to retreat back down along the road we had come, which we did. Upon reaching the eastern edge of the field, we proceeded down it, down to the south; while across the field, opposite us, the confederates seemed to be emerging from the woods. Here we were on a knoll but had a good view of the field below and were on the edge of some brush and trees. I had reloaded on the run down the road. No one had taught me this trick. I think my father had talked about it and maybe I remembered it from him, or else it was just instinctive. By grabbing the barrel about two feet down from the muzzle with my left hand and letting the gun trail over my shoulder, I could fish my paper cartridges out with the right hand, bite off the bullet, and see the muzzle well enough to pour the powder down it. Then I crumpled the paper and stuffed it down, loaded the ball, and rammed it home with the ramrod, the whole time the butt of the rifle trailing along behind nearly brushing the ground. Then I brought the rifle up over my shoulder, and cradling it in my left arm, placed the cap on the nipple.

When part of the regiment had lined out across the top of the knoll looking west over the field, and part was still on the road, we let loose with a couple of blasts. The rebel army was emerging from the woods across the field to the west and coming straight on toward us. We fired away as fast as we could. It seemed that the rebels outnumbered us and the firing was so intense that I felt the safest place to be was on the ground. I dropped to the ground, lying somewhat protected behind a tree, and continued to load my rifle from the ground. I noticed about that time that some of the soldiers around me seemed to be so terrified that they were lacking in wits. One man was standing straight up with the rifle butt grounded and his left hand on the muzzle, standing erect and loading his rifle. I called out to him that he better lay down, the damn fool, but about that time he spun around, threw his hand up to his left chest and shoulder area, and began wailing pitifully. It seems like the rebels emerged from the trees, marched a distance, and then would fade back. How long this went on, I don't know, but I do know that I was able to get off another eight or ten shots.

Then we received orders to form up again and move back north along the field to the road where we were repositioned, looking back toward the field to the southwest. We had formed up facing kind of southwest going from across the little knoll on the east, across the road, and into some cover on the north. The troops who had been on the road were now positioned farthest north. I was beginning to feel somewhat nervous. There seemed to be a lot more rebel troops over across the field than there were of us. In addition, it seemed that there were some that were appearing directly west of us, straight down the road, and some even north of the road About that time another regiment or so, I suppose, of troops arrived. These were members of the sixteenth Wisconsin who I had noticed were encamped to the east of us along our original campsite. It didn't look like the whole regiment of a thousand men, but certainly there were several hundred. Some of the companies moved south, and some seemed to move north along the line to reinforce and extend our line.

Once again, the rebels seemed to be determined to advance. They came out of the woods, across the field, and down the road and along the woods to the north of it. Part of the picket fence was still standing directly in front of me, and I knelt down and blasted away between the top two rails. I was loading and firing as fast as I could. The smoke was blinding, and the musket fire was deafening. I suddenly became aware that people all around me were starting to retreat. I hadn't heard any command to retreat, but it was obvious that we were moving rapidly back down the road we had originally advanced on.

It seemed like we retreated back down along the road until we were somewhere in the vicinity of where we had originally met the pickets who were coming in. There was a slope and a fairly steep hill in this area. In addition, there was a small, shallow creek that flowed at the base of the hill. We formed into line along the top of the hill on the other side of the creek and no sooner had gotten into position, than the confederates appeared, coming down the road and through the brush and trees on both sides. The firing was even more intense here. It seemed like gunshots were coming from all directions. I had taken my place on the hill just over the creek and was kneeling down behind a tree that went up a couple of feet and then branched off and split in a fork. I became aware that every time I reached into my ammunition pouch, it seemed like there was less and less in the way of ammunition. It seemed to be getting very scarce! A man next to me went down, and I could tell that he was grievously wounded. I thought to myself that he wouldn't be needing his ammunition anymore, so I rifled through his pouch and took out all the paper cartridges that he had. My mouth was so dry, I could hardly spit, and my eyes were stinging and burning from the smoke and the grit that each blast of the rifle threw out. I wished I had time to take a swallow from my canteen to at least rinse my mouth, but I was too nervous to do that.

It seemed that the troops of confederates just kept coming, and I was determined to get off as many rounds as I could before they overwhelmed us. About that time, I noticed that the men around me in line had started moving slowly, but then rapidly, until they finally seemed to be one running mass of men rushing back down the road toward the camp. I thought it would be a good idea to join them, and away I went. It seemed like we all went running into our regional camp about the same time. A lot of the men just kept right on running, but now that we were back in camp, I felt more reassured. There were a considerable number of soldiers there who were just looking at us, seeming rather surprised to see us. Some had been still cooking breakfast, and most hadn't even bothered to have their guns with them. That soon changed as they scattered in all directions, I thought most going to their tents to get their weapons and gear, but some seemed to just take off following the members of our two regiments who were headed down the road as fast as they could go.

There were officers screaming for us to form up and fight, so I felt a little more comfortable. I took time to rinse my mouth out and drink about half the water that I had. I was, at that time, not seeing any confederate troops, and so I poured some coffee that was brewing over a campfire to fill my canteen up and top it off. I also inquired where I could get more ammunition, but no one that I asked seemed to have any idea. About that time the confederates were seen coming out of the woods and started to cross the field in the distance. They were probably less than one hundred yards off at that point and slightly downhill. I lined up behind a tree and started firing, once again as rapidly as I could. There were some people who were just joining up alongside me who it seems had finally gotten their guns and gear together and were coming to the fight, but about that time it seems the fight was over.

There were rebels appearing to my left and my right amongst the tents. I took off, and the thought went through my mind that it would be a good time if I had my knapsack and my pistols. I could remember dodging through the rebels, and dodging between the tents until I found the tent where we had been bivouacked. I knew the road that we had gone marching out on and that our tent had been eastward from where it joined another road that went on the diagonal across the plateau that we had been camping on. I ran down this road to where our original campsite had been, got my knapsack with my other weapons, and began retreating to the northeast through the woods and then across a field. It seems like the main confederate advance had been along the road that we had initially reconnoitered along. So once I had cleared the camp where they had come storming in, by moving to the southeast and away from the initial confederate advance and gotten my weapons, by retreating to the northeast, I was headed back toward the landing like most everyone else in our regiment had been. I was beginning to think I really didn't like being in the army so much after all.

I could see some fellow union soldiers around me, but everybody seemed to be moving to the northeast. Thankfully, I wasn't seeing any confederate troops at the time. Now, my only thought was to keep up with the other union soldiers. This means basically that I had to run like hell. I had been moving in a generally northeastern direction, crossed a cleared field on the one corner, and hit a well-traveled road. This seemed to go straight north, so I was able to run even faster. I followed this up until we hit a junction with another road, crossing roughly east and west. There were a lot more union troops here. There were actually some camps that had been set up, but I continued, as everyone else, just moving right on through these camps. A short distance beyond there, it seems that the officers were arranging troops. As I was heading by, on a dead run, back toward the river where we had landed, suddenly someone grabbed me by the arm, spun me around, and told me to form up here. I don't know who he was, but I did as I was told. It seemed like there were a good number of officers who were trying to stem the panic-stricken retreat, and we were being forced into a line along another road. This road was a rough-cut thing. It was apparent that there wasn't a lot of traffic along it. In places it had grass growing up in the center. I fell into line and moved somewhat further down this road as I had been instructed.

I hadn't moved far in that direction when I ran into some people I recognized from our original camp. These were people from the twenty-first Missouri regiment. I think there were a couple of privates I recognized and at least one corporal. He told me I was going the wrong direction, that we were the other way along this shallow road. I felt much more reassured to be back among my original regiment and considered myself to be quite lucky. We moved along the road and formed up. Looking straight out from the road where I was now taking cover, I could see that there were a few scattered trees and light brush directly in front, but then it cleared out. I couldn't tell at that time that there was actually a road that went up intersecting our lines at nearly a right angle off to the west of me. Off to the left of where I was, it was extremely wooded and so dense that I could not see in the distance.

Directly in front of me along the road were the remnants of a split rail fence. I left my gear there and ran quickly out and grabbed two rails at a time and drug them back to where I was along the road. I made several trips. Then, I took two of the rails and pointed them directly straight out from my position in the road toward where I anticipated the enemy might be coming. I took another two rails and laid them on top of these just about a foot from the edge of the road, which was actually sunken or cut away into the earth. There was an embankment no more than three feet high where I was. These two rails I laid about a foot from the edge of the embankment and put another rail across on top of them. Then, I pulled out my bayonet and cut away the edge of the embankment to shallow myself out a little trench so I could lay comfortably and look out underneath the railings. Then, I went through my knapsack. I removed my two Remingtons and laid them inside the woolen mitt with the two cylinders next to me on the ground. I also placed the brass powder flask next to them. I took the capper with my percussion caps and placed a string around my neck. I stuck the capper down the front of my shirt.

Things were quiet for a moment, and I quickly ran a patch through my rifle. I checked my ammunition pouch and found that I had about twenty rounds left. We had originally started off with sixty, and with what I had gotten previously, probably around another forty, I figured that I must have fired seventy-five or eighty rounds already that day. I was beginning to feel quite nervous. I didn't know how long this was going to go on, but I sure didn't want to run out of ammunition. I cleaned my musket rifle and reloaded and was lying there waiting to see what would happen next. I was beginning to feel a little more confident as I could see that troops were coming up from further back and displacing themselves to right and left along the road where I was positioned. I had no idea what time it was.

It seems these troops had no sooner gotten in position, in fact some still seemed to be moving up, when directly ahead across an open field it appeared that about a regiment of confederates emerged and made a head-on assault across toward us. We opened fire and blasted away rapidly. Their line seemed to falter and then withdrew back across the field and into the edge of the woods in the distance. I thought that the rebels must be getting cold feet because now it seemed to become rather quiet, at least in front of us. I could still hear cannon fire, it seemed, off especially to the right of where we were. There was some occasional firing off to the left, but where we were, it seemed that the confederates maybe had given up. Possibly they found us too tough to handle.

About this time a whole battery of cannon came up and positioned themselves, somewhat to my right and behind me. I felt much better now. In fact, it seemed that most of the people around me had begun to feel relaxed. Some people were getting up and walking around and conversing. The war was a thousand miles away. As I laid there on my left side watching across the field, my thinking was suddenly interrupted by a familiar voice. "So, there you be, my boy," I heard.

I recognized the voice instantly. It was the sergeant. I had seen him off and on throughout the last several weeks but hadn't talked much with him. Then, he said, "I thought you might be needing this."

I rolled over on my back and looked up to see that he had in hand my father's Henry rifle, which he was offering to me. I told him, "Well, thank

you, sergeant, sir, but I think you might be needing that more than me."
And with that, I reached over and lifted up my knapsack and spread the
woolen mitten apart to reveal my two Remingtons.

The sergeant laughed rather happily and said, "I always thought there
was something more about you than you let on."

This caused me to laugh rather hysterically for a moment or two.
I suddenly laughed and said, "Why, I hope there's not too much more
about me, because otherwise some confederate would probably shoot it,"
meaning that I was still rather small in comparison to others. This brought
a great chuckle from the sergeant. I told him he ought not to be standing
there like that, someone might take a straight shot at him, and he said he
needed to go inspect the lines and encourage the other soldiers and just
check out the position of what troops we had left and he would be back.

He walked off further toward the west up past where the cannons were
being positioned, and I felt thankful to hear that he would be coming back.
In anticipation of this, I took my bayonet and immediately behind me
whittled and leveled out a notch in the top of the embankment so that the
sergeant's position could be there and he also could see under the rails that
I had piled in front of me. Things were quiet for a while still. The cannons
managed to get themselves in position, and about that time the sergeant
came back and laid down on the edge of the road next to me. Suddenly
the cannon behind us opened fire across the open field into the woods on
the other side. I could tell there were troops moving back there. They were
so far away I couldn't make much out, but the cannons had no difficulty
in smashing through the trees among them.

My initial thought was this was great and would teach those rebs for
attacking us, but they were soon firing in return. Apparently there were
confederate batteries across from us, and they opened up on us. A number
of the men who had been standing and talking in the road were blown
apart by cannon fire. One of them wasn't too far from me, off directly
in front of where our own cannon were. Feeling quite evil and almost
sinful, I crawled down the road toward him and rummaged through his
ammunition pouch. When I returned, the sergeant was looking at me. I
didn't know whether his gaze was distasteful or not, but I replied, "I was
nearly out of ammunition."

His look changed immediately, and he said, "Good thinking, boy." I had no sooner gotten back in position than, looking out across the field, I could see confederate troops forming up.

It appeared there must be at least two to three thousand men over there. They formed up in two long lines that seemed to disappear into the distance, both to my right and left. Then, they started across at a trot. When it appeared that they were about halfway across the field, the cannon behind me, to the right, opened up on them. Still, they kept coming. They came still closer, and I opened up on them with my rifle. Then I would roll over on my back and reload as fast as I could and fire again. They kept coming and just kept coming. They didn't seem to slow down. I think that the force of the cannons blasting into them and the firing of our troops around me put up a wall of lead such that they had to force their way forward against it. They looked like they were leaning forward into a storm with high winds I think I got off three, maybe four, rounds until they were so close that I decided to fix my bayonet, and then I dropped the rifle on the ground beside me. I picked up my Remingtons, one in each hand, and as they got closer, probably no more than thirty feet away, I raised up on my left knee, right foot braced on the road and cut loose with both revolvers at the same time. I could see my shots having effect, and the troops seemed to slow and almost stop. I became aware that, immediately next to me, I could recognize the distant cracking of the Henry rifle, which was much different from the loud, booming noise of the rifled muskets, and then it seemed that they were gone.

I emptied both revolvers, and the smoke was so thick that I really couldn't see much in front of me, but I couldn't make out any movement and couldn't recognize anything to shoot at. I bent over and peered under the rail fences, still carefully watching as the smoke cleared. I became aware that there was nothing moving beyond me. Initially, I heard only moaning and groaning and rustling noises. The smoked cleared further, and I could recognize in front of me nothing but piles of wounded and dead confederates. They seemed to extend both left and right of my position up and down along the sunken road on which we had taken cover. There were horrible screams, piteous whines and moans, and now and then, you could tell that someone was moving and making attempts to crawl back toward the woods from which they had come.

While I laid there on my back relaxing for a moment, I reached over and took my powder flask. I capped the nipples of my Remingtons and began to reload. I looked up at the sergeant who was lying there and said, "Maybe you ought to reload that Henry too, sir."

I reached into my knapsack and brought out the small cloth bag that held the remaining thirty-some shells from the one box that I had opened to load it initially. I had carried the Henry for a couple of months, but I had never shot it. I asked the sergeant how he liked that gun. I told him, "I have never shot it and I wonder how well it works."

He replied, "I am glad that I have it."

I said something like, "I knew it would come in handy." I gave him the shells, and he reloaded. I hadn't even finished reloading one of the Remingtons by the time he finished reloading the Henry.

Things had been quiet up to now. I had finished reloading the pistols and stuck them back in my lambskin pouch, and about that time noticed movement off to my left. In that direction it was fairly wooded and scrubby, but there were definitely troops moving in the woods, and they were headed toward our lines on the left. Suddenly an intense firing broke out to the left of the line. I could look back down the sunken road for a distance and see that people were firing into the scrub brush there. I could now and then make out what I thought was an individual person, so I directed my rifle that way and fired where I thought I saw movement. The cannon opened fire also, and the sounds were deafening. The sergeant reached out and tapped me and said, "There's no sense firing, boy, you really can't hit anything at this distance." I decided that he was correct and ceased firing. About that time I noticed that the battery of cannon initially behind our lines had moved out in front of the line and across the road. They seemed to be firing toward the wooded area and scrub brush. They had stopped firing, and things became quiet. Then, looking straight out across the open field, I noticed that the confederates were forming again quickly along the wood line, and about that time they immediately came running back across the field screaming a strange, undulating yell. The cannon fired several times, and we opened fire on them as rapidly as possible. The confederates kept coming until they had actually swarmed around the cannon and seemed to be trying to drag it off back to their own lines.

Suddenly, union troops off to my right rose up and charged out across the field and battled with the rebels around the cannon. From where I was, I stayed hidden and fired across at the rebels who were behind the cannon and seemed to be clustering in an attempt to storm back and take them. I noticed as troops, both union and confederate, used bayonet and clubbed at each other. Finally, the confederates retreated back across the field, leaving their dead and wounded. Fires had broken out in places on the field. There was a good deal of undergrowth, brush, and brambles that were maybe knee high in places. Flames rose in the smoke and along with the gunfire, thankfully, blinded my eyes from the scene before me, and deafened it also. You could hear a horrible screaming, and a wailing, piteous cry coming from the field, and I knew there were wounded soldiers being burned alive in the blaze. It seemed that the flames died down and the smoke blew away, but no sooner had I noticed that then I could tell on the other side that the confederates were coming back again. They managed to cross maybe to within a one hundred yards, and probably no more than fifty, before they were again blasted back.

I don't know how many times I fired that musket, but I suddenly realized that my arm was so bruised and painful that I flinched every time I pulled the trigger. I understood now that it was causing me intense pain to fire that damn heavy gun, yet I continued doing it. As the smoke cleared and the last of the rebels seemed to disappear back into the tree line, I once again noticed there was fairly intense firing from off to my left in the woods there. I watched intently but never bothered to fire again. The sergeant had said it was much too far, and I agreed with him.

I was beginning to feel fairly confident now. I had lost track of how many attacks had been thrown directly forward toward me and the sergeant—at least I felt they were coming straight for me and the sergeant. I noticed there had been several attacks off to the left and intense firing in that direction fairly close to our position and there was a lot of firing off to the right, but it seemed like the hottest action had been right directly in front of us. I think there had been about four attacks straight at me personally. In addition, I could tell that there had been attacks further up and down the line. It seems like the entire day, except for the one brief period just before the cannons were brought up, had been nothing but shooting, screaming, smoke, and disaster. But now things seemed to be quiet, but only for a moment.

It must be getting somewhere late in the afternoon, I thought, and about that time an unbelievable thunder and roaring sound started to cross the field in the woods in the distance. I could hear strange whistling noises, and suddenly explosions were right and left, in front and behind me. I had thought that God must be throwing down thunder bolts, aiming them at me, but I realized that the confederates must have brought up at least a hundred cannon and were blasting away, all at the same time, and it seemed like they were aiming straight at me. All up and down the road, to right and left, cannon shots burst and whistling fragments of shells screamed up and down the sunken road. I was wishing that this would stop and that the confederates would charge us again. It seemed much safer to see men charging across the field and planning to kill you than not knowing when some shell might burst overtop you and take your life.

This intense cannon fire seemed to go on forever, but then suddenly it was quiet for a moment and then, again I heard that rebel yell that seemed to echo from all positions. Again, the rebels came storming out and across the field. There was intense firing off to the left, and soon I could see rebels coming across the road down to the left of me and even to the right of me. The sergeant said, "Boy, it's time to get the hell out of here," and I took one Remington, shoved it down the front of my greatcoat into the pocket, shoved the other one into my belt, threw my necessaries pouch around my neck, grabbed my knapsack, and took off behind the sergeant. Once again, I was running like a rabbit. As fast as I ran, I could barely keep up with the sergeant. I knew I couldn't have kept up with him, but he kept stopping frequently to help me and even took my knapsack to carry it for me.

Away we flew back toward the north. We were making our way through woods that were fairly thick and scrubby. At one point in time we came out on a road and joined in with troops who were fleeing down it. I could hear considerable firing in the distance. It seemed to be moving right along with us. In fact, it seemed to be inspiring us and pushing us to move even faster. I realized that some of the units that had been with us in the line were making a fighting retreat. I think they had actually started their retreat before we realized it because, by the time the thought came into my head that we should retreat, the confederates were already swarming across the road. But anyhow, now we were on a road that seemed to run straight toward Pittsburgh landing and making plenty good time.

I could make out in the distance the main camp that we passed through when we originally landed there at Pittsburgh. Then, I could actually see some of the buildings that composed the small town. At that time, we seemed to bunch up into a crowd of fugitives, and there were officers I didn't recognize who were trying to make some sort of order out of the chaos. I was staying as close to the sergeant as possible. I thought he knew what he must be doing, but I'm not sure that he actually did. It simply gave me great relief to be near the man. An officer of some description grabbed the sergeant by the arm and stopped him. He told the sergeant, "Take command of these soldiers here and form them into line," and indicated a place on the slope of a ridge on the edge of the camp that was built around the landing.

We gathered up stragglers as they passed by, and when we had formed up about a dozen or so of them, we took our place between two roads just west of the landing. We were in front of the second road and behind the first, situated on the slope of a hill that, behind the second road, rose steeply before entering woods. Off to our left, about a half mile, was the edge of the steep bluffs that overlooked the river. I was so exhausted that I simply dropped where I was. I took my canteen of weak coffee and rinsed out my mouth, which was so dry that I was having problems swallowing. My whole throat seemed to be swollen shut from the smoke and the taste of gunpowder in my mouth. I rinsed my mouth several times and drank about half the canteen and then gave it to the sergeant. He had either lost his canteen or forgotten it throughout the day, and he rinsed his mouth several times and drank down the rest of it. Then, he set about organizing the men he had gathered up. It seems they were from all sorts of different regiments and even different divisions, but we lined them up on the slope. Then we drug some logs and brush together and placed it in front of our position and snuggled in.

The sergeant looked the men over that he had gathered up and said, "I'm going off to get some water and some more ammunition. You men stay here, and this boy here is in charge till I get back." With that, he took off.

I looked at the men rather astounded, but none of them seemed to resent the fact that a boy probably half their age was in charge. I thought it was only because the sergeant knew me and didn't know these men and didn't know which of them he could trust. I thought if he put one in charge he didn't trust, he might take off and the rest might go with him. So, I just stood there and looked at these men. I felt a little bit nervous, and so, for some inexplicable reason, I spread my greatcoat so that they could be aware of the Remington stuck in my belt. No one seemed to say anything, and certainly no one objected. The sergeant was gone for maybe a half an hour or more and then returned with several canteens of water and some biscuits and even some canned meat. He passed this around to the troops, passed out the water, and passed out the ammunition. Everybody tore into what food that he had brought back, and in moments it was gone. I don't think anyone had eaten anything since that morning at breakfast. Thinking back on it, I wasn't sure I had even had breakfast then, and certainly throughout the day I think I'd had one canteen of water to drink. I felt so intensely relieved and relaxed, but then at the same time so incredibly tired, that I didn't think I could even stand if a confederate showed up. I thought I would just have to surrender, but the sergeant ordered that we clean our rifles and make sure that everything was loaded up.

For lack of anything else to clean it with, I stood up, made sure the hammer was down on the nipple, and then peed down the barrel. I stuck my finger in the barrel and sloshed it back and forth several times and then poured out the thick, almost gummy residue. I still had enough urine left to fill the barrel up again and sloshed it back and forth several times to loosen it up before I dumped it out. It was a little bit thinner but still pretty thick with black junk. Looking back on it now, I'm surprised the gun would even fire because it was so severely fouled. I hadn't even noticed how difficult it had been to load because of the fouling.

The sergeant had gone back down to the landing and returned with another load of canteens of water. I drank down another canteen nearly as fast as I could, then saved only a mouthful to wet a rag to swab the barrel of my musket with. It seemed like the gun was finally starting to get clean. By this time, I had managed to produce enough urine that I was able to fill the barrel one final time. I let it sit, sloshed it back and forth, dumped it out, and then swabbed the barrel again with a cloth on the end of my ramrod. The sergeant made a third trip back and forth with the canteens, and this time I took a canteen, took a small drink, and then poured some water down the barrel and swabbed it out. I did this a couple of more times, pouring just maybe a fourth of the barrel full with water and swabbing it until it came back clean. Then, I took a little bit of the solvent, swabbed the barrel out, picked the nipple clean, and let it sit to dry.

During this time, it was very quiet all around us. There was some firing off in the distance but nothing that raised any concern to me. I was beginning to think how silly I had been when we first came into camp.

They had been firing nearly like this for the first couple of days, and any time I heard it, I jumped up looking about, expecting to see rebels emerging, but now I could tell that it was off in the distance and that we were still safe. I talked to the men around me and found that there were men from some regiment from Michigan and one from Wisconsin and others from other divisions, including Hurlbutt and Vetch. We talked briefly about what had happened to us during the day, but no one seemed to be interested in talking much. I think everyone was simply too tired and exhausted even to want to think about it.

I was still exceedingly hungry and still somewhat thirsty, even after having finished nearly three canteens, but I was more tired than anything. I took my blankets and groundsheets, spread them, wrapped up in my greatcoat, and laid down to go to sleep. The sergeant was there looking over us all, and for some reason, I felt entirely safe. What, if anything, happened during the night, I have no idea. I think that if the rebels had attacked, they probably would have awakened me the next morning lying right where I was, just to inform me that I was now a prisoner. When I awoke the next day, I was surprised to see that during the night someone had posted artillery all up and down the road immediately behind us. I hadn't even been aware of that.

Sometime during the night, a cold rain had started. I hadn't even been aware of it. I had placed one groundsheet on the ground, two blankets over me, and the third groundsheet covering me entirely. I had covered up from head to toe. I hadn't even been aware that it had rained in a downpour for several hours during the night with lightning, thunder, and harsh, driving wind. Possibly, I kept thinking in my sleep that the battle was still raging all about me. I don't remember even having dreamed. Anyhow, when I awakened, everything was wet. It had stopped raining, but the wind was still blowing, and cannons had been mounted all up and down the road immediately behind us. The sergeant approached just about then. Where he had been, I don't rightly know, but once again, he had canteens of water and things for us to breakfast on. I ate hard tack and canned meat and even some bits of sausage. There wasn't much else. While we were there resting, we could hear increased activity off to the south and east. Then, horrible, thunderous volleys of muskets and cannons sounded off to the right in the southwest. What was happening now, I didn't rightly know and, in all honesty, I couldn't have cared less.

Sometime about mid-afternoon, I think, everything became quiet—at least anywhere close to us. During this time, the sarge had stayed there with us, helping us to feel encouraged, seeing to it that our guns were clean and loaded, and seeing to it that we were well watered. His presence, I think, served also to keep any officers, moving up and down the road behind us, from questioning what we were doing there. I think they respected the sergeant, or at least were intimated by him. He was, after all, quite a large man, being over six feet tall and robustly built. Plus he had a reassuring, almost jovial, way about him that even officers found appealing. Sometime about noon the sergeant disappeared back toward Pittsburgh landing, and when he returned, he had a wooden bucket that he had filled with hot stew. We all took our tin cups, scooped out stew, and drank or ate it from the cup. It had been a fairly large bucketful of stew. I think the sergeant had already eaten while he was in the main camp, so we each got about two cups and then a little bit more. Then, the sergeant passed around some crackers and sausages, and we feasted again. Throughout the rest of the day, we stayed where we were, resting. Shortly after I had eaten, I rolled up and slept again and was oblivious to anything that went on around me.

Later that evening, the sergeant roused me. He had been into town and had fetched more food for us. How he managed to convince anyone to let him have the food, I wasn't sure, but I had thought I wouldn't want to be the person who tried to say no to the sarge. The following day, we awoke once again at dawn. The sergeant roused us all. We loaded our gear up and marched down to the landing. Here, we had our first real breakfast in something like three days. I couldn't seem to eat enough. I had several cups of coffee to wash it all down with and even managed to get some honey to sweeten it with. This was a gift from the sergeant.

The sergeant and I went down toward the landing and a little bit south of it, and here there were several tents set up where survivors of our regiment had been gathering. Here, I learned that Colonel Moore had been severely wounded and had had to have his leg amputated and that Colonel Peabody, who we had originally been assigned to, I don't think I actually met him and didn't know who he was, had been killed on the first day of the fighting. There had been nearly a thousand men in our regiment the morning the fight started. It seemed like we had had men killed and wounded ever since we had gone out on the patrol and as we retreated back from it and to the camp and to the sunken road. I actually thought that the sarge and I were the only two people left of the whole regiment.

We stayed here for the next couple of days, eating and refreshing ourselves, and gradually more and more members of our regiment were found and relocated. I realized as I watched more and more people gather that the vast majority of people in our regiment had merely kept running once we had started to once the confederates had breached our main camp and during the fighting among the tents that ensued. Now, watching the troops gathered together, I realized that most of the soldiers were still there. I think that we probably had lost three or four hundred men and what, with all the fighting, screaming, shelling, smoke, and fires, I considered that almost miraculous.

We hadn't had to leave camp in the last few days, but people who had not participated in the actual battle had been sent out in burial details, and they returned with horrible stories of the carnage of the battle and estimates of how many people had been killed. From what I could gather, they felt like we had lost about two thousand men, which was shocking to me. I would have thought it would have been several times that number. They said that the confederates probably lost at least five thousand—at least those were the guesses I was hearing from people who reported on the number of corpses they had buried. One elderly man who had been working with the burial detail said that was probably only half the number of people who would die because certainly there had been a great many more wounded, and even if they made it off the field, they would probably die later.

This made me think about Colonel Moore who had had his leg amputated. I asked the old man about that, and he said that most people that had limbs amputated didn't survive. It was actually rare for anyone to survive an amputation, and with those encouraging words, I expected never to see or hear from Colonel Moore again. I remembered thinking how excited I had been to go off to war, thinking to free the slaves from their horrible plight and to avenge the death of my family, and all this seemed like such nonsense now. I thought to myself that, if there was any way I could change my mind and undo all of this, I probably would. But I had volunteered, and here I was. The sarge was here, and that was the main reason I elected to stay—that plus the fact that I didn't know how I would get back home anyhow. The thought kept going through my head—what would we be doing next? No one seemed to be in charge here of the survivors of the twenty-first Missouri, and since Sarge had been ordered to hold the line where we were first camped, we kept returning there.

CHAPTER 13

For the next several days, it seemed like no one knew just what to do next. The day after the big fight, there had been some sort of activity off to the south and east of where we were. This was in the distance, and we received no orders, so we merely stayed where we were and listened. The day after that, there was a little bit of gunfire off in the great distance, which was barely heard. I actually wasn't sure whether it even had been gunfire. Still, we received no specific orders. The sarge would go back and forth to the landing and return with buckets of stew or other types of food, and we pretty much stayed where we were, behind the fallen tree that we had propped up in front of the road where we had been told to stay. We had, out of precaution, gone through the woods and gathered more fallen limbs and had converted this somewhat into a lean-to. It was on a slope and was actually built in the reverse manner of what I would consider a usual lean-to, but the idea of this was to prevent enemy soldiers from shooting at us, and so the roof of the lean-to was on the downhill side and fairly strongly covered. Days went by. Still, we hadn't received any specific instructions.

The day after the big fight, I had noticed that my arm was so sore that I couldn't raise my hand above my elbow. It hurt to move the arm in any direction. The sergeant had been concerned that I might have been wounded, but I had reassured him that I hadn't been. He insisted on taking a look for himself. I took my overcoat and shirt off and was surprised to see that my right shoulder was intensely bruised extending all the way over to the base of my throat, down to my nipple line and down my arm all the way to the elbow. I wasn't sure how I could have received such an intense injury, but the sarge seemed to be relieved and actually said he was "most grateful to the dear Lord," as he said it was only bruising from the rifle. One of the other men from our little lean-to had replied something about me being "one murderous little bastard," as he put it, but at one angry look from the sergeant, he made no further comments.

I recalled then thinking how during the fight I had noted how badly that rifle had kicked and realized that I was flinching before I pulled the trigger on each shot. However, I was much too excited not to keep shooting. We went on down into the camp to see the docs. We had to wait in line for a considerable period of time, as it seemed that the surgeons had been overwhelmed for the last two days since this fight had started and had a lot more seriously injured patients than me to concern themselves with. The area around the hospital tents and buildings were full of injured people who moaned and cried piteously. There was a horrible smell that seemed to fill the air and permeate one's clothing. I had been told that there were piles of amputated limbs, arms and legs, and that these were just now being disposed of. I found the whole scene of such intense pain and suffering to be more than I could bear and chose not to wait there for any doctor to get enough free time to take a look at my bruised arm.

I had a thought and suggested to the sergeant that we wander over to the trading post. At the trading post, I asked the man if he knew of any healing women in the area. He mentioned a few and gave us some directions as to how to find their homes. Then, the thought struck me and I asked him if he had any witch hazel leaves or bark and whether he had any balm of Gilead salve. He replied that he didn't have any of these, but he did have some petroleum jelly, and so I bought that. Then, we went to the home of a lady who sold herbal remedies and lived there in town. She happened to have some balm of Gilead and witch hazel, and I gave her the petroleum jelly, and as she boiled up the leaves and stripped the bark off the twigs to make a salve, I sat and waited. The sarge had gone off and returned, making a couple of trips, and had procured a couple of fifty-gallon wood barrels from down at the landing that had been empty. I think only because he was a sergeant was he able to get away with this. He brought these back and made several trips, heating up cauldrons of boiling water and dumping these in the barrels. When he filled the barrels, he had me disrobe and sit in the one barrel up to my chin, soaking in the nearly boiling hot water. The sergeant said that was good to relieve aches and pains and the bruising in my shoulder. Also, he said he thought I needed a good bath.

After soaking until the water started to cool, I sudsed and scrubbed myself off, jumped in the other barrel and rinsed off, and covered myself in a blanket. When I went back inside, the lady thoroughly rubbed my shoulder down with the salve that she had made. She seemed to massage it, work it in, and manipulate my arm up and down. The soreness seemed to be greatly relieved. She then put a thick layer of the salve on my shoulder and wrapped a light linen dressing around it. I then redressed and was ready to go. The sergeant, meanwhile, had taken a bath in the two barrels, and when we got back to our lean-to, he suggested to the other men in our pieced together squad that they go down and take a bath too while the water was still warm. This, they hurried off to do but they returned a short time later. It seems that the lady had taken up our idea and was now charging soldiers to take a bath and a rinse. They said there was a goodly line outside of her house at the moment. This almost caused me to laugh thinking that, even in a horrible war such as we were involved in, when common people found it hard to acquire food and make a living, for an enterprising person, there always seemed to be a way to get ahead.

Our life in camp was beginning to seem almost pleasant and certainly a lot more relaxed than I had ever thought it could be. However, all good things must come to an end, I suppose. On the fourth or fifth day after the battle, some officers came by trying to make an effort to sort out and reunite people with their original squads and companies. When they approached our group, they asked confusing questions, something like what squad, what company, what regiment, what brigade, or what division. This made me feel intensely stupid, but I was relieved to note that most of the other people in our put-together squad had no idea what he was talking about either. The only thing that I knew was that we were in the twenty-first Missouri regiment and that I had been in I company. We had only been in the camp for a couple of days, and I don't think anyone really knew what division or what brigade we had been assigned to, but the sergeant did. The sergeant said that we had been in the sixth division, first brigade under General Prentiss' command. Well, that seemed to please these officers who were trying to straighten things out. It seems that the other people in our hastily patched together little squad didn't know much more than I did about what division or what brigade they had been assigned to. They were all privates like I was and apparently hadn't paid any more attention than

I had to where we had gone or who we had been assigned to, but these officers who were there to straighten things out pointed us off in different directions and told us who to report to and where we would be assigned next. This broke up our little group. We had to gather our gear, abandon our little shelter, and head off.

The sarge and I headed back away from the road on which we had been posted for the last several days. We moved somewhat south and east back onto the top of the plateau where we could actually look down over to the east and see the Tennessee River. Here, we found a camp thrown up, and I recognized some of my companions from the old squad in I company. There were other members that I recognized as having seen in the twenty-first Missouri regiment. Apparently it had taken so long after the actual battle had ended before anyone took any effort to try to organize the army up again. I think for the first day or two afterward, the entire army had been afraid that the rebels were going to attack again and attention was more directed toward using the troops that were still organized and hadn't been involved in any fighting to form some sort of a defensive line and to fortify this, but it seems that the confederates had all taken off, headed back down south from wherever they had come from, and now we were trying to patch things back together. Possibly also it had taken so long because it seems that Colonel Moore, who had commanded our regiment, had been severely wounded and had his leg amputated. It seems also that the colonel commanding the first brigade had been killed in the first day's fighting. Also, General Prentiss, who had been in charge of the whole division, had been captured, along with several thousand troops.

At that time, I didn't know how many soldiers were in a division, but it seemed that our whole division had been pretty much wrecked, but now we were being patched back together. However, I think that, because of the fact we suffered such intense or extreme damage, we had been moved back away from the main defensive works the army was putting up and were being rested and rejuvenated a short way behind the main line. For the next several days, we didn't even drill or do any type of practicing. We simply sat around the camp, ate three meals a day, and rested. What, with all that was going on, I'm sure the generals had much more on their minds than us, and maybe that's why it took a while before we finally received new officers to command the regiments and the companies and even the division.

A day or two after, we were given some free time in the evening to go into town, such as it was. I had been put back together with some of the other members of the I company, and there were even a couple of people I recognized as being members of our original squad, but when we were reassembled, I don't think anyone paid too much attention to organization on the squad level. Whatever had happened to the corporal of our squad, I never did find out, but I was assigned to a squad with a new corporal. There were two or maybe three people who had been in my original squad, but the other five people were strangers, although a couple of them I seem to have recognized from them having been in other squads in the company. I realized then that, even though I spent two to three months together with most of the people in my squad, I hadn't really gotten to know any of them.

I thought back over the last few months. Initially, I had been in Booneville and been in a tent that I shared with three other men. The other members in our squad had been in a tent next door. I hadn't made any attempts to talk with any of the men in the tent next to ours and had very little conversation with the other three men I shared the tent with. When I thought back on it, I believe that I was actually intimidated, possibly even scared by these people. They were all considerably older than me. In fact, I think they were at least twice my age. I can't say that anyone was ever unkind to me, but they certainly always seemed to be a little bit coarse and rough and vulgar. I realize now that several people had made attempts to talk to me, had made jokes and tried to find out a bit about me. However, I had never seemed to want to talk to any of them. I think that part of the reason why I felt intimidated is that they would realize, if I got to talking too much, just how much younger I was than they were. I also felt that I might let something slip. I had this inner fear that, even though I had signed up and was there, that if anyone found out that I had actually had only been twelve years of age, they would have sent me home. So, I had kept pretty much to myself.

There were some people who had expressed enough concern as to ask where I was from and about my family and other things, but I had been afraid to get involved in telling any of them about myself. For one thing, I couldn't talk about my family. Whenever I thought about it, I would get a tear in my eye, and that wouldn't do for a soldier to let other people see him crying. So, when anyone approached me or tried to make small talk or conversation, I pretty much ignored them. After a while, it seemed that no one made any effort, and I certainly didn't make any effort on my part to get to know any of them either. I know now that they considered me to be strange.

So, when we had been formed up into a new squad, I realized that there were two of the people there who had been in my previous squad going all the way back to Booneville. Whatever happened to the third, I never found out. In addition, there was definitely one person I could recognize from the other tent from our original squad. So, we had been put back together, and it seemed that some other squads had lost significant numbers of their original members. Of the ten members in my new squad, five of them I hadn't seen before, and when we had started out, we had ten squads in our company I, but now we only had eight. I made the decision that I was going to try to get to know some of the people in our squad and even get to know people in the company better than I had before. And so, when our squad was given leave and told we could go into town a day or two later, I asked to go along. I think this surprised a couple of members in the squad, but as half of them had never met me before, no one hesitated. And so we headed off for the evening to town.

When we got to town, we seemed to break up into smaller groups, and each of us went his own way. I had decided to follow the two people who had been originally with us in Booneville, and so we hung together. No one seemed to know exactly where they wanted to go. We had already eaten in the camp before we left, but there was a tent set up in which some civilians were serving food. We went in to see what they had, and I was delighted to see that they had several different types of pies still. They had one pie that was made from apple and dried cherries. I ate a couple of pieces of that and drank some coffee that I had put honey in, and we laughed and joked and thoroughly enjoyed ourselves. Then, we wandered over to the trading post, and then the general store in town, and looked around to see what they might have left for sale. I bought some more needle and thread and some more blue woolen cloth fabric to match my greatcoat, but there didn't seem to be much else that he had for sale. I would have liked to have found some more wax to treat my boots, but items were scarce. They certainly didn't have any other ammunition or black powder or anything like that for sale. I did buy a small, dried smoked salami, but there wasn't much else.

Then, we wandered around through the town and the tents that had been set up around it. On the bluff overlooking the river, there was a log cabin that seemed not to have been there when we first arrived. It was roughly and shoddily made, but seemed to be quite busy. We entered and found that it was packed fairly densely with soldiers of all different companies and regiments. The building was probably about fifty feet long and twenty-five feet wide. Looking around on the inside, it struck me that about half of the room had a plank floor and log walls and a log roof with a loft over it, but the other half had rough hewn logs for a wall, and a canvas roof over the frame. I think that it had once been somebody's business establishment, possibly had been damaged by some sort of fighting around camp, or at least it had been modified, so that at this time about half of the building had been added on to in a very rough and tumble type manner. At each end of the building planks had been set up on barrels and stretched across the end of the room.

There were a few tables with bench seats around them, but most everybody was standing around inside. It was extremely noisy inside, a lot noisier than any other gathering of soldiers that I had been in before, and I soon realized why. The soldiers kept pushing up to the counters at each end of the building and having their tin cups filled up with some good old-fashioned liquor. We three made our way up to one of the counters and demanded a drink. The man behind the counter never hesitated when we held our tin cups out but poured us all a nice shot in the bottom of the cup, and one of the men I was with gave him a dime and told him to keep the change. I curiously sniffed at the tin cup and didn't think I liked the smell of it, but I took a tiny sip, which seemed to burn my mouth and lips, and swallowed it on down. It seemed to burn all the way down to my stomach, which seemed to glow with warmth and also seemed to want to make me cough, but I did not. I smacked my lips like I appreciated it and stood there listening to the men as they talked around me.

It seems the man that had bought the drink was a Jack Willoughby. He had enlisted in Booneville with the original ten members of my squad. The other man was a Benjamin Wright. They had both lived in and around Booneville. Willoughby had worked as a teamster hauling freight up and down between Booneville and Jefferson City and other towns in the area. Benjamin Wright had worked on the riverboats, loading and unloading and taking occasional trips up and down the river. Their families still lived in and around Booneville. Neither one had been married and seemed to have been at least a little over twenty. These were two men who previously

I had been rather intimidated by. I had always thought they were rather coarse and vulgar, but I now realized there was nothing bad tempered or mean about either one. It seems that's just the way people on riverboats and teamsters talked. They laughed and joked, especially the more they drank. They had another drink of whiskey that Benjamin bought. I hadn't finished my first, but they said, "Well, it's your duty to get the next round when we're ready for it," and I didn't hesitate to say, "You bet."

They laughed and told stories about where they had been and things that they had done. Then they asked me about myself. I told them truthfully where I had come from. It seems that neither one of them had ever heard of the place before. They asked me if I was looking forward to going back after the war, and I said I doubted it since the whole town had been burned to the ground. This surprised them. They didn't recall having heard anything about it. Then, one of them said, wait a minute, that he had heard something about a battle being fought at Osceola, but he hadn't heard anything about the whole town being burned. I said, "Well, I suppose that isn't all that surprising what with all the other excitement going on during the war." We moved on to another topic. I think that they possibly sensed that it was a good idea to change the topic because no one asked me anything further about my home or family.

It was time for me to buy the next round, although I was still sipping on the first. I gave the bartender a dime, and he seemed quite appreciative. The more we sipped and talked, the louder we seemed to become. I hadn't finished my first dose in the tin cup yet, but I was feeling quite talkative, warm and relaxed, and happy. About that time the sergeant showed up. He also seemed to be talkative, warm and relaxed, and happy. I hadn't noticed, but he had been drinking on the other end of the building. I think he had come in a short time after we had. Maybe because it was the sergeant who was drinking with us, but the other soldiers, Ben and Jack, seemed to feel that we needed to talk more soldierly. The conversation turned to the battle of the last couple of days. I suppose it was because he was a sergeant and it was his job to know such things, but he seemed to know a lot more about what had actually happened than I did. To me, it had just been one confusing mess of shooting, reloading, shooting, running, stopping, shooting, and running some more. Where we had been, what we had done, I could not have told, but listening to the sergeant tell of the last few days of the fight, it seemed that we had been right in the thickest of it. Well, I certainly thought anyhow that we had been in the thickest part of it, but to hear the sergeant tell it, we had taken most of the brunt of the fight.

When we had gone out scouting that morning, that had been the actual start of the confederate attacks. We had fought and had been driven back and through the camp but had borne the brunt of the initial attack and slowed it. Then, indeed, there had been attacks on the right, especially upon General Sherman around a church that had been off in that direction. Apparently this had been nearly as bad as the fight we had been in, and General Sherman had been pushed back too. According to the sergeant, there hadn't been too much fighting on the left end of our line. Then, when we had been reformed in the sunken road, it seemed that the rebel army had spent most of their time trying to break the center of our line, possibly because the two flanks, as the sergeant said, had rested on deep creeks that they were unable to swim or wade across. In the sergeant's mind, General Prentiss and the sixth division had saved the entire army. This brought loud cheers from all across the cabin. It also brought some jeers and boos from some soldiers who apparently had been with General Sherman and some from General Hurlbutt's troops, but everybody seemed to be happy and cheerful at this time. There were calls for "three cheers for General Prentiss," and "three cheers for General Sherman," and "three cheers for General Hurlbutt."

For some reason, I was finding the name Hurlbutt to be extremely funny. Whenever we were cheering his name, I was calling out loudly "Hurl Butt" with the emphasis on Butt. Jack and Ben found this extremely funny also. Ben asked me what I had been doing during all this fighting. I said, "Well, as near as I can remember, I would rise up and take a shot, then pull my head down and try to make myself as small as possible." Everybody thought this was exceedingly funny, me, making myself as small as possible. I hadn't meant it to be funny, but I guess it was. Someone asked me what I thought of the battle and what I had done, and I said, "Well, it seemed like to me we would take a bunch of shots, duck down, shoot some more, and then run like hell." This provoked loud cheers and howls also. I hadn't meant that to be funny either. It just seemed like what we had done.

The sergeant said, "Well, you should have seen us in the sunken road there next to Hickenlooper's battery. "

By this time, Ben had bought the fourth round and I was starting to sip on my second cup. I found Hickenlooper to be a very funny name also. I yelled out "three cheers for General, or maybe it was Colonel Hickenlooper." Everybody cheered for Colonel, maybe General, Hickenlooper. Then, people seemed to get a little more sober and solemn. Someone suggested that we toast General Prentiss and Colonel Hickenlooper and Colonel Peabody. It seems that these three officers had been in charge of the regiments in the sixth division as they fought in the Hornet's Nest, as people were calling it, and had either been killed or captured.

By this time, it was getting to be fairly late. I had finished off two of my tins of whiskey, while Ben and Jack had finished off several. I think I bought three different rounds, and to my way of thinking, that meant that we had had nine different rounds of whiskey, although I was still sipping on my second. Jack and Ben were getting to where they could hardly stand up, and I noticed when I went to walk outside to pee, I had a difficult time keeping my balance. I went back in and bought another round, which made my fourth that I had bought. I think I bought the last one also. I suggested that we head back to camp. Jack and Ben and I took off, and I noticed that the sergeant came right along. That was probably a good thing, because I'm not sure the three of us could have found our way back to the camp. Sarge had been back and forth several times and seemed to know the way quite easily.

I was a little unsteady on my feet, but Jack and Ben were positively reeling, especially Ben. Sergeant put one shoulder around him and took his arm, and Jack was on the other side, and I was following slightly behind them as we made our way back. And as we did, I finished off my third tin of whiskey. Sarge lifted up the flap and helped Jack and Ben stumble through, falling over some of the other people who had returned even earlier, and I tried my best not to step on anyone as I ducked my head through and made my way back to the corner where my knapsack and bedroll had been set up. I laid down on top of the blankets and the bedroll, not bothering to take my greatcoat off, and bunching my cape up around my head for a pillow, I laid back and went to sleep.

CHAPTER 14

When the bugle sounded in the morning, it seemed to jar me awake. I woke up feeling still extremely tired, and I felt a dull ache in my head and was somewhat weak in the knees when I went to get up and march out for roll call. However, I was up and out and lined up with the rest in no time. This was because I was still dressed from last night. We had been allowed to rest and recuperate and reorganize and now, once again, we began marching and drilling up and down the roads and across the top of the plateau, and it seems like that's all we did for the next couple of weeks. It seems that being in the army takes a considerable amount of planning before anybody can decide what to do next. I had been told we were on our way marching down to a place called Corinth originally, which people said was thirty or forty miles to the south of where we were now. If that had been our original objective, I would have thought we would have been right back on it. True, we had fought a horrible battle and had whole divisions pretty much destroyed, but one thing that I was certain of was that we had done a lot more damage to the rebels than they had to us. I thought that if we had been headed toward Corinth in the first place, why weren't we moving out now? The rebels had definitely taken a worse licking than we had. They had waited to look things over after the battle, but then seemed to disappear as quickly as they'd come.

As we marched and drilled, I began remembering things from the night before when we had been in the saloon. I remembered expressing the opinion that we should be off and chasing them down, that they were running like rabbits and it would be a turkey shoot or something to that effect. It seems one of the men who had been with us in the little makeshift squad we had had a few days before that had been there. I had heard him spout up—although I had never seen him, I recognized the voice—as he called out, "I told you he was one bloodthirsty little bastard."

I was still laughing about things that we had said last night in the bar. Anyhow, we marched and drilled around camp and waited. It seems that one reason we were still waiting was that General Grant was no longer in charge of the army. A General Halleck was coming down to take over. I thought that General Grant had done a magnificent job, myself. I didn't know who he was and wouldn't have recognized him if he came up and slapped me on the back just then, but I thought he had been the general in command of the army when we had been attacked and we had won; the confederates had definitely retreated off as fast as they could go. Things had been hot and hectic for a while, but we had put together a line after we had been forced to retreat originally. That line had been reinforced. We defended it well, and although we had to retreat again, we had formed another line, and the confederates had been seen off. Whoever had been directing all that, I supposed it was General Grant, had done a magnificent job, so he should be given the credit. I didn't know how backstabbing officers could be, but apparently some were complaining that he had done a poor job of it. Anyhow, General Halleck was coming, and we were just waiting until he got there. Well, what did I know about things anyhow?

General Halleck eventually did arrive, and when he did, for a day or two after that, it seemed there was a lot of talk about planning. Ben and Jack would speculate with the sergeant and me as to what we would be doing next. The sarge said he had heard that we would be moving out soon, headed down to Corinth to take the railroad depot there. I had asked him what was so special about Corinth that we were going there. He said it was a juncture of two railroads. One came from the west and moved east and another went from the north down south. We needed to take that to stop the confederate army from being able to get supplies and moving troops. Well, that seemed like a great idea to me. So, under General Halleck's command, we started off a day or so after that.

We had loaded up all of our gear and packs. It was somewhere up around the middle of April, I think. The weather had been rather cold and chilly and had rained frequently but had recently seemed to dry off a bit. The ground, which had been almost continuously muddy, was now merely damp. In fact, it was getting to where it was almost too warm to be wearing my overcoat. This I found worrisome, because I had my Remingtons concealed in the one pocket in the chest and the other in the belt at my waist. I was afraid I wouldn't be allowed to carry them. Officers and sergeants sometimes had revolvers, but I hadn't seen any of the common privates carrying any. I didn't know if they would let us. So, I spent one day making a pocket on the inside of my blouse. I made this over the left breast using the dark blue woolen cloth. It was obvious when you stood to attention and snapped up straight that there was something under my blouse, but I was hoping no one would be curious enough as to demand to take a look and see what it was. I came to the idea that I would try to offset this obvious bulge by making another pocket over my right breast and chest area. I stuffed this with my woolen cap that I had brought from home and my two coyote fur mittens. Now, I looked almost symmetrically deformed. I had conceived of this idea, putting padding over my right shoulder and chest area because of the way that damn old rifled musket kicked. It had taken most of the last two weeks and two jars of liniment from the herb woman until my shoulder had gotten to where I could actually raise my arm up to scratch my ear again.

So, I had packed up my overcoat and all my other things together in my knapsack and had been prepared to move out the morning that we had been instructed to. We got up early at revelry, had breakfast, and then watched from where we were as the rest of the army gathered up and went marching back down the road that we had fled up just a couple of weeks before. From where we were on the top of the plateau, I watched the troops as they marched down in a column of four and into the distance, disappearing down one ridge into a low ravine, coming up the other side and moving down to where they were probably about where our camp had been on the day the fight had started. I saw them go out of sight across the field that we had found full of rebels attacking the camp and disappear into the woods on the other side. I was thinking it was time that we would be marching out, but the order never came. Now, I was seeing the end of the column clearing our original camp and marching off across the field. Soon they were out of sight. Still, no order came for us to move out.

The day passed, and we stayed where we were. The sergeant didn't know what to make of it either. We spent the day there in camp, and the following morning when the bugle blew, we had breakfast, formed up again, and waited. I suppose it was nine or ten o'clock before we were ordered to move out again. We went marching off down from the plateau, across the road at the edge of town, down a ravine, up a ravine, passed another road or two, and pretty soon we were marching through where our original camp had been under Colonel Peabody, then across the field, which now had fresh mounds of heaping dirt where bodies had been buried. We marched into the woods and down the road near to where our original fight had been with the pickets, and there we found the tail end of the columns that had marched out the day before. They were just disappearing from a long row of trenches that went east and west from where we were. We were ordered into these trenches, and that's as far as we marched that day.

It seems our whole division spread out to the east and the west in the trenches that had been dug, and we watched and listened for activity away to the south. An hour or so later, some officers came back and ordered that we dig the trenches down about a foot and pile the dirt up on the north side back toward the camp we had just left. Then, we leveled off the mound of dirt that was in front of us to where it was about half of its original size. We were now in a trench that had dirt facing both north and south in case we were attacked in either direction, but there weren't any sounds of gunshots, bugling, or anything else that I could tell. After we had dug the trench out and filled it in from the other side, we were allowed to sit around and rest for the rest of the day. We ate some of the cold rations that we had been sent out with and waited. That evening, we took and set up some of the two-man tents we had been recently issued. It seems now that we were moving away from a main camp and were on an actual campaign, we would be sleeping in these. Each man who was in our company had been given what looked like a groundsheet to me but which could be fastened together to make a tent that would house two men. Jack and Ben had known each other from Booneville and put their groundsheets together to make their tent, and I found another man to share my canvas with. His name was Jacob Maitland. He had been in the twenty-first Missouri regiment when we had landed at Pittsburgh Landing before the battle. He was younger than most of the other people I saw in our squad, or even in our company, but was several years older than I was.

We fixed our tent together and set it up and spread our other groundsheets inside, and then we sat on our knapsacks out in front of the tent overlooking the trenches that we had just modified. He had asked me about the fight we had had a couple of weeks before that. He seemed to be ashamed of the fact that after the fight that we had in the field of old cotton to begin the day, once we started retreating back to the camp, he hadn't hesitated. He hadn't gotten his knapsack. He ran through the camp and just kept running all the way back to Pittsburgh Landing. He said that he had gone down the bluff next to the water and was trying to clamber onboard some of the steamers that were there. He said there were a lot of people in the regiment who hadn't stopped running until they got to the steamers. He said if they had been able to make the steamboat captains take them onboard and head down the Tennessee all the way back to Missouri, they would've, but the steamboat captains threatened to shoot anyone who tried to get onboard the boats. He said they had gathered at the base of the bluff next to the landing and demanded to be taken on and taken away from there. He said at one time an officer had come by and threatened that if they didn't calm down and behave themselves, he would have them all shot by the armored steamboats that were out in the river. He seemed extremely ashamed of himself and seemed to feel the need to talk about this. He actually felt embarrassed that I was willing to share the tent with him. I told him I don't know why he should be embarrassed, that if the sergeant hadn't grabbed me by the arm and pulled me into line, I would have probably been right there with him.

It was then that I heard talk about how, of the thousand men in our regiment, most had fled all the way back to Pittsburgh Landing. Only a couple hundred had managed to gather together to form up and fight the rebels in the sunken road, and of these couple of hundred, most had been captured. It seems like the sarge and I and only about fifty other, or maybe sixty, so the rumor went, had been involved in the fight from the start to the finish. Apparently most of the people in the regiment now knew who we were. This made me feel almost famous, but I knew it was all nonsense, and I said so to Jacob. I told him I hadn't known what to do anymore than anybody else and that, if it hadn't been for the sergeant stopping me and gathering us together, I think everyone would have been back to the river. I told him it seemed to me just only a strange quirk of fate that, depending on where you had been, how it had affected your whole action for the rest of the day. Anyhow, he seemed to feel more relieved and not nearly so embarrassed. We kept talking then until we were bugled into bed about what was going on and what the generals could be thinking. I figured they had to have had some sort of plan in mind. I didn't think someone could get to be a general for no good reason at all, but we slept there that night, probably no more than four miles from where we had started out.

The next day the bugle blew. We had had our cold rations and were up and ready to march, but no orders came. Probably a couple of hours later we were ordered to form up and march down a road in columns of four and after having gone about two miles at the most, I suspect, we came to another line of trenches and were ordered to divide and march both east and west along these trenches, where we once again started digging out the bottom and piling the dirt on the north side and leveling it off on the south side. Then, we set up our tents and made camp again for the night. We couldn't have been more than two miles from where we had started. I felt like pacing back and measuring off to find out for sure how far we had come. And there, we spent our second night on the march and the third night of the army's march. This repeated itself over the next couple of days. On about the fifth day of our march, we were once again digging out the trenches, and soldiers began to start making jokes and comments. Someone called out that he thought this General Halleck was planning on digging his way all the way to Corinth. Someone else called out, no, he thought he was planning on digging his way all the way to Richmond. I had begun feeling more talkative these days and I called out, "No, he's just having us dig graves for all the rebels we are going to kill."

Someone whose name I had never gotten to know, but that I recognized, called out loudly, "I told you he was one bloodthirsty little bastard." Everybody started laughing again. It dawned on me then that a lot of people in my company knew who I was, even people I had never met or talked to previously.

Well, we dug out the trench, then filled in the trench, then set up our tents and spent another night on the road to Corinth. The next couple of weeks passed in similar fashion. We dug trenches, filled them in, and each day moved a mile or two closer to Corinth. Then, one day, out to the front just about sunset, we heard a round of cannon explosions, a few scattered musket shots, and thought that maybe we had finally reached Corinth. The sounds soon frittered away, but it left us with a feeling of intense excitement. This time, we dug the trench maybe a little bit deeper, and I packed the earth a little bit more solid on the north side, and I even went so far as to notch out the top of the earth and pack it down tight over an area of a couple of feet and laid a small log over this. Then, if we were attacked from troops circling around to the rear, I could lean down with my head below the log and fire behind me. I also formed up the trench similarly in front of where I was at in case we had troops attacking from the south. We set our little two man tent up again on the north side of the trench and retired for the night.

The following morning before the bugle had even blown, we heard a brief flurry of cannon shots, a scattered musket shot or two, and then all was quiet. I got up and scrambled to the trenches but nothing further happened. We ate our cold rations and packed up our gear again and waited for the order to march out. It was afternoon before the order came, and we marched off down the road and entered into Corinth, Mississippi. It had taken us about three weeks to get there. I had heard that it was thirty miles; some people said it was forty miles. I don't know how far it actually was, moving as we had a couple of miles a day, I thought. However far it was, it had taken us over three weeks to dig our way here and now we were there and there wasn't a rebel in sight. It seemed that the army was ordered to set up their camps in different parts of the town of Corinth, and our division was ordered to go into camp north of the town but just south of the entrenchments that the confederates had made. Here, we gathered together and, when the pack trains starting coming up, they set up the larger tents that would hold a whole squad and we made camp.

While the camp was being set up, Jack, Ben, Jacob, and I went wandering through the confederate entrenchments. As we walked along, we had noticed that there were some logs protruding from redoubts that had been stripped of bark and painted black. Around some of these were scarecrow-type people gathered and erected. On one that I passed, someone had painted a face with a big wide open smiling grin. We all seemed to notice this about the same time and laughed almost hysterically. Then, talking to other troops who had been with the leading brigades of the army, they related that when they first marched into town that morning, there had been no fighting whatsoever. It seems the night before the confederates had fired several barrages of cannon at the troops as they were moving into their entrenchments on the hill nearest the confederate fortifications, but that we hadn't attacked them since it was late at night and we all expected a severe fight in the morning. However, they said that throughout the night, the confederates kept cheering. They could hear trains coming and going, the campfires kept blazing up higher and higher, and they had the feeling that the confederates were being reinforced and that this morning would bring one horrible fight.

So, when the sun started to lighten the skies in the east, we fired off an artillery barrage lasting for about fifteen minutes, but no one had replied at all to our cannonading. Then, thinking that was unusual, they had sent out a few patrols to sneak and probe their way into the confederate fortifications and had found them entirely abandoned. It seems they weren't being reinforced during the night, but they were retreating. This, they had managed to do, having gotten all of the confederate army out and even all of the civilians, it appeared. The town was totally abandoned. Except for union troops, I hadn't seen a soul. We looked again on the smiley-faced scarecrows and all broke down with intense laughter. It seemed these rebels had just as good a sense of humor as we did.

We wandered through the fortifications on top of the ridge that the rebels had built and then wandered back down into our camp just below. The squad-sized tents had been set up, and we searched around and found some more of the people in our squad and found the corporal of our squad, who was unpacking his gear in a tent that he had selected for ours. Someone said that it was now May 30. I think we had actually spent over three weeks digging our way to Corinth. I didn't know what day we had been ordered to start out. I determined then to try to keep a better idea of what day it was. Growing up where I had, we had never paid any attention to dates, other than my mother trying her best to keep track of which day was Sunday so that once a month we could go to church and meetings. Otherwise, days had had no significance to us. We went merely on seasons and sign of the moon for planting. Now, I realize that to some people dates and time had considerable importance.

Anyhow, today was May 30. We had taken Corinth, and I hadn't seen a single rebel personally, but I learned that we had taken a couple of thousand confederate prisoners. Either these were men who had been so badly wounded at Shiloh that they had been unable to be moved, or else they were sick. It seems there were hardly any of them who were able to be out and about. Therefore, they had been abandoned when the army had withdrawn. Well, we were here, and I didn't know what to do next. We wandered around through camp until the bugle blew. We gathered and went for evening meal and wandered around talking some more until it was time for taps. We had gone to bed having not done much else that day except wander around and talk.

The following day, we gathered again for revelry and roll call and marched off for breakfast, and then we returned to camp. I wondered where we were going to be going next and what we were going to be doing. I think General Halleck had no idea where to go next or what to do either, and for lack of a better idea, he decided that, since he had dug his way to Corinth, now that he was here, he just may as well go ahead and dig up the whole town too. The confederates, to my way of thinking, had a perfectly good set of trenches and redoubts on top of the hill to the north and west of town, overlooking the junctions of the two railroads. I think one went from Memphis to Charleston, South Carolina, someone said, and the other one went from Columbus, Kentucky, or someplace in Kentucky, down to Mobile, Mississippi, or was it Mobile, Alabama? Anyhow, the reason we were here was because of these two railroads intersecting, and now that we had taken the town, we had to keep it, and General Halleck decided to do this by digging trenches on the east side of town and trenches on the south side of town and trenches on the west side of town, and even another whole set of trenches between the trenches the confederates had dug on the north and between the town itself. The man liked to see his soldiers dig, I'll say that for him.

CHAPTER 15

We had gotten to Corinth on May 30, but once again I had lost all track of all time. I didn't know what day of the week it was, much less what day of the month. It seemed like we had been boring ourselves by digging and making up fortifications. The weather had gotten so hot, it was nearly unbearable. I had thought that when we first got to Pittsburgh Landing, because it had been so rainy and cold, that I was going to fight the war wearing my great overcoat the whole time. It seemed like I had a horrible time keeping warm, but I had long since abandoned the greatcoat. It was carefully stowed in my knapsack. I had even wished several times that I could shed these heavy woolen pants and my heavy woolen blouse, but we had been issued no other uniforms, so we were stuck. You couldn't have the army running around in their long underwear. However, it was much too hot. It was almost unbearable.

A number of troops had started coming down with sickness. They had strange fevers and diarrhea. I blamed the diarrhea on the nasty-tasting water. There were a few shallow wells in the town, but these had rapidly gone dry with all the people drawing water out of them. We had been forced to go for several miles away from town to get water from the creeks and rivers. However, that water seemed rather stale and certainly was most definitely muddy and had a horrible, nasty taste to it. I had thought that's why so many troops were getting sick with diarrhea and fevers. The doctors didn't seem to be able to do much to relieve the troops. This made me think of the herb lady back in Pittsburgh landing, and it made me think also of Rebecca and my own mother. We hadn't had any doctors around, but they had always seemed to have a plan for treating almost any type of ailment that could come up amongst a family. Thinking back, I tried to remember what my mother and Rebecca would have done.

It was now, I think, about the middle of June. In the middle of June, I think mother would have been out looking for alumroot. This was a spindly, almost stick-like weed that grew on the edge of the woods. They would usually gather the leaves and brew up hot water to make a tea from it. They used this for diarrhea, like the troops were suffering from. Also, they might use black-eyed Susan flowers and leaves. They usually used those for when they thought we might be inflicted with worms. Black-eyed Susans would be in blossom about this time. If not actually blooming, they certainly would have leaves. They also might be using boneset. They used both the flowers and the leaves to make teas from, and all of these, I thought I could recognize. I had also seen them use what they called Christmas fern, which was easily recognizable. They gave this usually for fever. And one thing I thought that I would have no difficulty in finding were dogwood trees. Dogwoods had already bloomed out, but the trees were easily recognizable and the bark could be scraped and used to make a tea that my mother always said was a good tonic.

So, as I had leave for the day, I wandered around through the woods and hills just outside of Corinth. I was occasionally questioned by troops who were on picket and guard duty, but people pretty much left me alone, although I think they kept an eye on me and I was careful not to make any attempt to get out of sight. I was able to find some, I thought, of each of the things that I was looking for and gathered up a whole gunnysack full of leaves, stripped bark, and flower petals. I took all this back to camp and threw it all in a big cauldron and set fire beneath it and boiled it all up. The sarge and other people in the squadron were curious as to what I might be doing and kept watching intently as I proceeded. After it had boiled for a good hour or so with me stirring it and adding more of the nasty-tasting water, I let it cool. Then I poured the brew through a shaped muslin cloth to filter it and gathered the, what I called a tonic, together in a coffeepot. We passed it all around to the members in the squad, and they didn't hesitate to drink a cup, or two even, of the tonic. Most everyone commented about how horrible it tasted. There were a few comments that they thought I was trying to kill them all. I think that most people decided that, if I was going to kill them, it wouldn't be on purpose. Besides, I was drinking it too.

Surprisingly, over the next three or four days, we continued to make the tonic, and the people in my squad seemed to improve, while most of the other companies continued with their problems of intermittent fevers and dysentery. We soon had several members from each squad inquiring about the various ingredients that we had put in the tonic, and I never hesitated to show them and explain what the herbs looked like out in the forest or pastures and would readily accept contributions from other people. Sometimes I couldn't positively identify the things that they brought in and would never add anything that I wasn't sure I could identify. The tonic had no special secret formula. It was basically just anything that turned up that I knew wasn't poisonous and in which I had learned had some specific benefits. These were all combined in the brew and never necessarily in the same proportion.

Over the next several weeks, we continued making our tonic, and it seemed that we developed somewhat of a reputation. We had more and more people from different companies bringing ingredients and had to increase the production. Initially we were using a small, about a ten-gallon kettle, but after a couple of weeks, we were cooking up as much as fifty gallons at a time. Our reputation seemed to grow. I think that after a couple of weeks of this, we had managed to stir up some animosity, even jealousy and envy, amongst the surgeons treating the regiment. I could remember hearing comments on several occasions about how the doctors were unable to make much headway with their remedies, if they could even find anything to prescribe, whereas our little home brew was thought to work miracles.

One day, I was surprised to find a rather crotchety old physician inspecting our ingredients and watching as we brewed up our potion. He was probably approaching sixty, was still tall, although had obviously been taller and stronger. Now, he was somewhat stooped and bent. He had whitish hair with still a touch of gold in it and a reddish golden mustache that had mainly turned white. He had a rather sharp, pinched nose and rather beady bluish eyes with protuberant eyebrows. He watched while we cooked up our brew and then, as he departed, made the rather caustic comment that the only thing that was of benefit was that we were boiling the water before we drank it. He said he had been trying to get the company commander to do that for the last two weeks. Most of the soldiers around just seemed to feel like he was jealous.

Over the next few weeks, the corps remained quiet there in Corinth—quiet, as far as there was no activity to speak of against the rebels, but certainly not quiet as far as their own soldiers were concerned. People seemed to be becoming increasingly restless and resentful. We had managed to dig our way to Corinth and then dig up the town but hadn't done much else in the last couple of months. Our life in Corinth was pretty much confined to doing picket duty and keeping lookout on the civilian homes and properties. I think this sparked as much animosity as anything. Most of the soldiers seemed to be of the opinion that, since we had fought these rebels and suffered all the hardship of marching down here, that anything the rebels possessed should be ours.

The generals had taken to posting pickets to watch the civilians' homes and properties. When we had first taken the town, we had been posted in tents and lean-to shelters. The soldiers felt there were perfectly fine homes in town that we could be barracked in. In addition, we continued on our usual diet of beans and bacon and hardtack. I think that soldiers felt that there were better food supplies kept hidden in houses and cabins, smoke houses, and root cellars throughout the city, and then again, I suppose that a lot of the bigger houses probably had silver or other items that could be taken and sold for a goodly sum. The fact that we had been threatened with arrest, whippings, or even being shot for ransacking these homes didn't sit too well with a lot of the troops.

The weather, when we first started out to Corinth, was rather cool, rainy, and sometimes downright cold. Over the next several weeks, it gradually warmed up so that soon it became extremely hot, dry, and nearly unbearable. Throughout the month of June, it seldom rained. We had had to depend on civilian wells and public water sources initially, but without rain, these soon dried up. The engineers brought in drills and began drilling wells around town and around our bivouac areas. They were having to go down two to three hundred feet to bring up water, and surprisingly, when they got it, it was still as nasty as the water that we had to begin with. It seemed that they couldn't drill wells fast enough to keep up with the water needs as the summer progressed and rains continued to hold off.

We had to be making round trips six to eight miles to bring back water in barrels for the troops. Plus, as the weather warmed, nature had other unpleasant surprises in store for us. Soon, there were great clouds of mosquitoes covering the whole town and the camps. Starting from dusk and going till complete dark and then from first sign of sunup until it was blazing bright and hot, the skies would almost be darkened with clouds of mosquitoes. I think the creatures must have had some means of communicating, because I think every mosquito for hundreds of miles seemed to flock to where the army was encamped, and if the mosquitoes weren't bad enough, the chiggers were worse.

Where I had lived along the banks of the Osage during the summer, ticks would become a real nuisance, but they were nothing like the chiggers. You could usually see ticks, but you really couldn't see chiggers. All you would get was a reddish, itching spot that would soon seem to boil up, and like the mosquitoes, the chiggers just seemed to continually increase in their vigilance. Soon, nearly from knee down to ankle, our legs were one continuously red, itching, weeping sore. I would gladly have traded off my uniform for some buckskin britches and moccasins. We had been able to keep the ticks off by tucking our britches in down to our ankles inside the moccasins, which we brought up and tied over our calves, but there was nothing that could be done to keep the chiggers from crawling up our boots and under our woolen pants, and that was the other thing. It was exceedingly hot and unbearably dry. We were being eaten alive by mosquitoes and chiggers and suffering from lack of water, especially any good water, and still we were forced to wear these heavy woolen uniforms.

The troops became more and more angry and discontented. At one point, some of the men in the squad started hatching a plot to break into some homes, ransack them for anything of worth, and split off from the army. They had made the comments that they were entitled to some of that wealth that the confederates had accumulated and they deserved it for pay, for having to suffer through these conditions and also because of the fact that the little monthly stipends we had been promised always seemed to be late, and at this point, several of the companies hadn't received anything for months. Some of the troops remarked that we had been there for weeks, probably a couple of months, and very few civilians had ever bothered to return, and they gave their opinions that the civilians would never return as long as the town was held by union forces. I offered my opinion on the subject, relating that not all the civilians who lived here necessarily supported slavery or even agreed with the rebel cause. The fact that they lived here meant nothing. If someone had lived here all their life and it was home, it would have taken a tremendous amount of courage to have packed up and abandoned everything that they owned to move away, so I thought that you couldn't say that their property or possessions should be confiscated as contraband unless you knew who they were and what their actual views on the war were. This didn't seem to impress anybody much.

However, about the time the discontent reached its boiling point, Colonel Moore returned, minus his right leg. For a couple of weeks, this seemed to quiet the discontent. I think that the troops felt remorseful whenever they saw him hobbling by on crutches, thinking that they had talked so badly of the cause and of the leadership and had even thought about rebelling; but only for a couple of weeks. We continued to stay in Corinth, nothing further seemed to happen, and the troops became restless again. The army did send out troops in one direction or another on patrol looking for rebels to fight, but nothing else much happened. It got hotter and hotter and drier and drier. The troops were thirstier and thirstier and the bugs more ravenous.

General Halleck at some time had been relieved and sent off somewhere. I had heard different reports that General Grant was now back in command and soon we would be off after those rebels, but this didn't seem to make much of a difference either. Then, we heard that a General Rosecrans was in command, but I could see no change in the situation. Some time, about a month after Colonel Moore had returned to the troops, we awoke to the news that during the night nearly a whole company of the twenty-first regiment had been arrested for mutiny and rebellion. I had known that things were moving toward some sort of a climax but had tried to avoid any groups that I felt were being affected by the more discontented and troublesome soldiers. They had hearings and held court, and this seemed to quiet things down as people listened carefully for the results of the inquisition, as some troops called it. Most of these soldiers were returned to their squads, but a half dozen or so were convicted, and I'm not sure whatever happened to them. There was some talk that they were taken off to prison, and some people speculated that they were taken off and executed but that no one had wanted to tell the rest of the regiment that because they thought it would inflame passions even more.

As the summer passed and started into fall, it became slightly cooler, and we had fewer problems with water as the engineers had managed to drill wells pretty much all over town, and then again activity seemed to have picked up in our area. There seemed to be more and larger patrols going out in different directions, and there seemed to be a lot more activity. Just what was happening, I couldn't really say. I guess you can't expect colonels and generals to tell every soldier in the corps what they're thinking and planning. If they did, I'm sure that in no time the confederates would have found out our plans. Therefore, days came and went, and we had no idea what was happening for sure. It just seemed that there was an increasing tension and increasing frustration that seemed to be passing through the army gathered there. Then, one afternoon the word came that we would be moving out.

We cleaned and readied all our gear and loaded it up in our packs, expecting to march out of Corinth the next day. Where we were going, we really had no idea. However, we were to be somewhat disappointed. The following morning, part of the troops did indeed march out of town, even a couple of the companies of the twenty-first Missouri left, but most of the army stayed where we were in Corinth. Patrols were increased, and sentries were increased. Some companies were even detailed to stand guard in the entrenchments that we had dug all around Corinth. It seemed that the generals felt that, with a third of the army out marching, looking for the enemy, those of us who were still here were at increased risk of being attacked. Anyhow, we were much more vigilant.

After a couple of days, we still hadn't heard or seen any sign of rebel troops in the area, and it seemed that another three or four days later, we heard some rumor that the troops we had sent out had fought a great battle with confederates. The story was that once again the union troops had been victorious and that the confederate troops had skedaddled out of there as fast as they could, fleeing off somewhere to the southeast. I thought that surely we would be loading up and marching out after them, but again nothing seemed to happen for the next couple of days. Then, gradually the troops that we had sent out probably a week before that, maybe more, began marching back into town.

Our couple of companies of troops from the twenty-first Missouri eventually returned to our camp, and we gathered around in groups to listen to the stories of the events of the last week. They had gone out in two different army groups, one led by a General Rosecrans and one led by General Ord. They had split up someplace around a little town called Iuka, General Ord being instructed to circle around to the north and attack the town from the north while General Rosecrans came in from the southwest. Unfortunately, the attack had been made by General Rosecrans, but General Ord had never shown up. The confederate troops had been beaten and driven off, and the union troops had occupied the town. According to our boys, General Ord had sat with his army five or six miles north of Iuka and done nothing. They were extremely disappointed. The boys from the twenty-first had been with General Ord and were itching for a fight. They were quite irritated and violently outraged by the incompetence of the generals. They had marched all that way, split forces to surround the town and attack it from two sides and trap the confederates, but then, for some reason, half of the army hadn't even been engaged in the battle. And what was worse, here they were back in Corinth.

Well, I reasoned that since they had beat the large confederate army, the generals must be planning on getting all the troops back together and that soon we would soon be marching out once again en masse. However, nothing happened. The weather, which had been getting cooler, changed, and it got considerably hotter. We remained in our camp just north of town and south of the new trenches and emplacements that we had fortified. We were posted to the northwest of the town where we had been for the last three months. No, come to think of it, it was more like six months. Even I was becoming exceedingly sick and disgusted with this place and couldn't wait for something to happen or for us to move on to someplace else. I didn't think that any place could be as bad as this. I guess you should be careful what you wish for.

The camp seemed to have a buzz of excitement running through it over the next couple of days. There were some rumors of confederate troops being seen in the area. We were placed on a higher degree of watchfulness. Patrols were sent out more frequently, and it seemed they went farther in different directions. Colonel Moore, who had been out on patrol someplace northwest of town, returned very early one morning. I had been sleeping peacefully, as well as most of the people in our squad, when the colonel came back into town. There was a buzz of excitement as the companies that had been out with him marched into the tents, but things quickly settled down as they broke up and went to catch what sleep they could for the remainder of the night.

Barely had we gotten back to sleep when we were aroused from bed by the jarring blast of artillery somewhere just north of town. Everyone was up quickly, gathering their weapons and their equipment together. We assumed that this meant some sort of action was about to commence. The men in my squad and I gathered outside the tent, awaiting further developments. We had already dressed and gathered our gear when the bugle started blowing. We marched to the center of our camp, gathered in line, and went marching off toward the sound of the guns. Once again, I was reminded of how important marching and drilling was. It seemed like so much boring nonsense until something happened, and the fact that we knew what to do and where to go and what we were expected to do when we got there by simply following the orders of the officers sincerely impressed me.

We went marching off to the northwest, following the route of the Memphis and Charleston railroad, up to a battery of cannon. We took up position to support the battery and were quite anxious and alert, keeping a watch in all directions for signs of confederate troops or movement. It seemed we were there for several hours, and nothing further happened. We could hear artillery fire off to the north, and now there were some sounds coming from the northeast and then again from the northwest, but still we failed to see any troops or any activity around us. This seemed to cause me even more anxiety. It seemed like that's the way it had been at Shiloh, that there had been sounds of gunfire and cannon all around, but no one in our front and then suddenly there they would be. I don't think I had ever been more alert.

Then, Colonel Moore came up on his horse and ordered that we were to form again in a line and move out on the railroad, again toward the front. We formed up and marched out, following his lead. We marched about two miles or so and came to a high ridge there in front of Corinth on the northwest side. Here, we were ordered to break off and march down to the left. We marched past troops of the sixteenth Wisconsin, and I felt a strange sensation in my gut. When Shiloh had started, we had been fighting next to the sixteenth Wisconsin, and here we were again. This definitely caused me some uneasiness. We continued marching on down along the top of the ridge and took up position on the extreme left of the line. It seemed as if we were in another fight for our lives.

There had been some trenches and fortifications in this region, but these had been allowed to deteriorate. We manned and fortified our positions as well as we could. The rebels came out, and with a yell and a rush, they charged upon our left front and left flank, and I reverted to form, biting off bullets, loading, and firing as rapidly as possible. The stinking clouds of black-powdered smoke arose over our heads, but as we were on the top of the ridge, the smoke from these seemed to blow away rapidly. However, the fire from the confederate soldiers as they advanced seemed to hide them in a cloud of obscurity at the foot of the ridge. I had loaded and fired and loaded and fired as rapidly as possible. I vaguely remember seeing Colonel Moore's horse fall and the colonel going down again, but still we continued to load and fire. I can't say that I was actually aiming at any one soldier in particular. The smoke obscured the slope of the hill too much for that, but it seemed that we could see movement of a line of troops advancing and that I would fire as fast as I could into that. And then the rebels were in and amongst us. It seemed that they had come around the left flank, which was open and were now striking the left front of the line also.

We gave way down the hill, stopping and firing as we went. I had placed one Remington in my belt and the other in my inside blouse pocket over the left shoulder before we marched out. I stopped and turned around now. We had been forced out of our shallow entrenchments and were backing down the hill, and some of the confederate troops were feeling the urge to chase us. I turned around and emptied the Remington at these, stuck it back in my belt, and caught up with the rest of our troops. Major Moore, who apparently had taken over after Colonel Moore had gone down, was there riding back and forth, and he managed to gather the troops together to form another line in the open on the reverse slopes of the hill. We reformed and fixed bayonets. I fixed my bayonet but reached in and switched the Remington from my belt, placing it in my pocket on the inside and having the fully loaded revolver ready to hand.

As Major Moore rallied the troops and we turned to rush back up the slope, my eyes were drawn to a tight group of three, no four, rebel soldiers just off to my left. They seemed intent on rushing the artillery that had been behind us to the left but now was nearly in line with me. I raised my revolver but, as I did so, the ground shook and a sudden burst of red mist obscured my vision. It reminded me of Fourth of July fireworks bursting; then my vision was blocked by a thick cloud of sulphurous, stinking black smoke. When it cleared, there were no rebels to be seen. I couldn't believe that they could have run off so fast. But as we charged back up the hill, it became obvious that they hadn't. Small pieces of them lay scattered in all directions. I felt queasy, and I had a strange, disgusting feeling in my stomach, as I tried to step and tip-toe over what, seconds before, had been four living souls I suddenly remembered talk of our casualties after the battle at Shiloh Church. People had mentioned the number of killed, wounded, and missing in action. I had vaguely supposed that that meant troops that had run off, never to be seen again. As I looked on the ground around me and carefully hopped and skipped through the carnage, I had a sudden realization of what "missing in action" really meant!

With a yell and a scream that we thought outdid anything we had ever heard from the confederates, we charged back up the slope. We hadn't given them much time to settle in to the entrenchments and certainly no time to fortify their positions by building up a wall on the back of the shallow ditches. We were back among them in a heartbeat. I emptied the Remington, firing right and left as quick as I could, and then took the bayonet to some of the troops as they scrambled up and out of the trenches and back down the hill the way they had come. Ordinarily, you would think someone would hesitate about attacking a man from behind, but I felt no qualms about prodding a few backsides with a bayonet to get them back out of our position.

We were back in where we had started. It seemed that the confederates had run all the way back down to the bottom of the hill. I rapidly reloaded my rifled musket and then undid the ties on my knapsack and switched out the cylinders for the revolvers. Something told me I didn't have time to reload the cylinders that were in the revolvers themselves, so I simply switched them out. It was a good thing that I did, because it seemed that I had no sooner finished readjusting the cylinders when we could see the rebels reforming at the foot of the hills and coming back up. It seemed that they never got more than halfway up this time. We held our fire and then set off a volley altogether that stopped them cold and sent them back down the hill. They reformed and came back, reformed and came back, and each time we would blast them away.

It seemed that the confederates in our front were becoming leery of us or possibly just weary of running back up and down the hill. They seemed to come slower each time. However, off to the right the firing was much more intense. I believe that confederate artillery had been positioned to blast the line to the right, especially along the railroads. Looking back to the right, back to the north, we could see as union troops begin scurrying down the bed of the railroad back toward town. It was obvious that they had been overwhelmed, and from the looks of things, they weren't going to be rallied. The confederates to our front began marching back up the hill, and once again, I went quickly, searching for a paper cartridge to bite and pour and reload the musket, but couldn't find any in my pouch. I looked around for fallen soldiers next to me, planning to ransack through their pouches for ammunition, but there weren't any in the immediate vicinity and I didn't dare leave my position to go searching up and down the line. About that time Major Moore went riding by on the reverse slope of the hill ordering us to form up and fall back.

Once again, all that marching and drilling paid benefits as, with the confederate troops over halfway up the hill, we formed up, marched back down the hill and intermittently, on orders of Major Moore, turned and fired a blast. Since I had no cartridges for my rifled musket, whenever he ordered us to turn and take aim and fire, I turned, drew my pistol and let fire with it. It was probably at too great a distance for the pistol to have much accuracy, but I figured the more lead flying and the more noise and smoke, the better. It might dampen the enthusiasm of the rebs and keep them back.

We marched back in, past the main entrenchments and fortifications we had labored on for the last several months, and were ordered back off to the southwest along the line. We marched off down there and took position around some big old buildings that I had been told previously had been a college. We were on a high ridge on the extreme west end of town, looking down over a road and into the distance. We marched up, got into the fortifications there, and waited. We had had no breakfast, and now troops came up bringing some food and water for the regiment. Mainly all that was available for us was hardtack.

Once we had gotten in position, we listened intently for further sounds of fighting. There were some occasional artillery off to the north and northeast and occasionally some vigorous bursts of musket fire. By and large, by the time we got into position for the rest of the night, things were quiet. Throughout the night, we listened and watched intently. You couldn't say for sure when something might develop, but nothing ever did. I was anticipating that at about daylight we would have vigorous fighting as we did at Shiloh. There, it seemed like it was still dark, just showing a sign of light when the fight commenced that lasted pretty much all day, but I was surprised the following morning that there was only some light sounds of activity, again off to the north and northeast.

It must have been nearly midmorning before anything serious started. The artillery thundered nearly constantly, and the sound of rifle fire was pretty much continuous. Still, to our south and west, we saw no signs of activity. We held our position, watching, and listening intently for any sign of movement to our front. We even became somewhat convinced that the artillery and the rifle fire had gotten farther south than we knew our batteries and main fortifications were and we thought that we might possibly be retreating.

Things seemed to slow down, cease for a few minutes, and then move off back to the north. What had actually happened, who could say? We were doing our best or maybe worst to imagine the fighting that was taking place off to the north beyond where we could see. We asked each other for information. Any officers, who went riding by, we stopped and begged to know what had happened, but I'm not sure that they knew anymore than we did. We were simply told to stay where we were and man our positions.

Afternoon came and went. The temperature increased, and we became quite thirsty and nearly unbearably hot. I think it may have been as hot as any other day that we had been there. I suspected it was at least one hundred degrees, maybe more. The thought went through my head that all that firing, flashes of gunpowder, smoke, and flame from the cannons possibly could have been enough to even heat the whole town and the atmosphere around it. All I knew was that it was unbearably hot and dry. I had the good sense to take my canteen with me that morning when we lined up, but several people in the squad hadn't thought that far ahead. I drank from my canteen and passed it around. I suspected that we would have water brought up throughout the day by officers and others, but there never was. It seems they had more to worry about with the fighting to the north than they did with supplying us with water in the southwest.

The fight seemed to trickle down and gradually stopped. I can't say that I actually realized when it stopped. There had been lulls throughout the day, and I suspected this just might be a period of quiet before all hell broke loose again, but I suddenly became convinced that it was truly over. This made us even more worried, I suppose, that we should be keeping an eye out to the south and the west. Maybe the tricky rebels were trying to sneak around and come at us from another direction since, once again, we had stopped them in what was probably their main effort.

About this time, the sergeant showed up again with some soldiers he had put together to go back to camp to bring us canteens of water. He had four or five men with him, and I think each one carried ten or fifteen canteens. They came passing these out along the line. I had somehow found myself on the extreme southwest of the line, and I think he had been bringing water all afternoon but running out at companies farther north of where we were. The sergeant was always quite eager to inform us as to what he knew, or at least as much as he thought he knew of the situation. Apparently the rebels had exhausted themselves, taking and retaking Battery Robinette, which was alongside the Memphis and Charleston railroad, pretty much in the center of our fortifications. This was not too far from where our original line of tents had been. They had been beaten back, and everything was quiet now, but he said that the generals were expecting them to attack again in the morning.

We slept somewhat fitfully in the trenches that night. I don't think I ever closed my eyes but continued watching, listening, and sniffing the air, but nothing occurred to arouse my suspicions. Early morning came, and the skies to the east lightened slightly and still there with no sound of activity. It came to full sunup, the sun arising above the trees off to the east, and still there was no activity. There was some noise way off to the north that we speculated was the enemy, either forming up for an attack or forming up to withdraw. Sometime, it seemed about midmorning, we were given the order to form up and march off to the northwest, following the road that ran on the south side of the Charleston and Memphis railroad.

We had nothing for breakfast again other than hardtack and water. We formed up and marched off as ordered and throughout the day saw only an occasional trace of the enemy. We came upon wounded stragglers and discarded equipment. There was only an occasional gunshot somewhere off in the distance, whether it was them shooting at us or us at them, I had no idea. We marched off for I don't know how many miles, and we seemed to me to be unduly cautious. We marched, I felt, somewhat slowly, with riders and skirmishers out in front probing for the enemy. It seemed that we marched quite carefully, but in vain. That day it seemed, way off in the distance to the north and west, there was a considerable amount of firing, but that abated. Just what had happened, I really could not have said.

We continued to advance slowly but steadily to the west for the next couple of days. Then, we were ordered to halt. Initially we kept in line, but after a few hours, we were allowed to fall out along the side of the road. Most of the troops merely sat off along the side of the road, but I busied myself by dragging logs together, looking west and to the south in case trouble should show up. Nothing happened. We remained there for the night and the following day were ordered to return back to Corinth. It seemed we made much better time going back than we had going out, and before the day was over, we were back in our original camp, behind the main fortifications along the railroad from Memphis to Charleston and maybe a little more tired but no worse for the wear of marching for the last three days.

Once again, the soldiers were somewhat discontented. For the first week or so, we had been quite elated, joyous, and excited. Boys in the regiment bragged that we had been in three battles with the confederates, and each time we had whipped their butts and sent them packing. We were beginning to think that the twenty-first Missouri regiment was something special. However, I never bothered to point out to any of the other boys in the regiment that at Shiloh we had been pretty much decimated, that the army had won but most of our regiment had fled the lines back to Pittsburgh Landing as fast as their feet would carry them. At Iuka, some of the companies had been there but had never actually been involved in the fight. This wasn't their fault. It was the fault of the generals who were commanding the troops that day that they never managed to link up both of the armies in the attack on the town.

Rumors seemed to start spreading through the camps that once again this had been another screw up on the part of the general, his officers, and his staff. It seemed like when our army had gone out from Corinth, pushing the rebels back to the north and west, that we had troops stationed in and around Pocahontas, and some other places, that could have cut the rebels off. The one day we had indeed heard fighting was when the rebels had run into General Hurlbutt and his troops, and had been brought to a halt there. There was some talk that we had him trapped between several large commands but, for some reason, inexplicably General Grant had ordered General Rosecrans to halt and return to Corinth. Well, I didn't really know the truth to any of that. Certainly, we had marched for three days and had not seen any confederate troops, so I couldn't have any idea of where they were. They may have slipped off to the south. Possibly General Hurlbutt had run into only a few of the confederates who were trying to escape. Possibly these confederates had gotten lost or separated from the rest? I mean, I had no way of knowing.

One thing that I became convinced of is that the generals liked to argue, fight, and backstab each other as much as they did the enemy. Well, once again, we were back in Corinth, and Lord help us, but I wished we could be someplace else. So we had fought a great and glorious battle at Corinth, Mississippi; we had chased the rebels off to the west, where once again they managed to slip away and no one knew where they were now. It seemed like Iuka before. These rebels had a way of showing up fairly unexpected, fighting a battle that they always seemed to lose, but then just as mysteriously disappearing into the woods that covered most of northern Mississippi along the border with Tennessee. Where they were now, we seemed to have no idea, but we knew where we were; we were back in Corinth. We came to truly loathe that place.

It was not nearly as hot anymore since we were well off into the month of October. It had been just over a year since Osceola had been ransacked and burned and my family had been murdered. The chiggers and mosquitoes were not nearly as bad as they had been. In fact, the mosquitoes had pretty much ceased. We didn't seem to require as much water since the weather was definitely colder. It even started to rain some. This helped greatly as we made every effort to collect as much rain water as possible. The water that we got from the wells and the streams was still as nasty as ever.

Once again, our life consisted of drilling, marching, standing sentry duty, and sending out patrols intermittently. In other words, it was boring as all get out. In fact, one evening I had a horrible nightmare. I'm not one who was ever inclined to have nightmares, and considering all that had happened to me, it's surprising that I couldn't remember ever having had one previously. But on this night, it had been raining. There was lightning and thunder booming, and perhaps this reminded me of Shiloh. The nightmare was exceedingly horrible. I dreamed that I had been wounded in the battle of Shiloh and left injured on the field, unable to help myself. While I lay there suffering but unable to move, I had been attacked and eaten alive by hogs. Perhaps this was a memory of how I had disposed of the bodies of the raiders back in Osceola. Perhaps it had been caused by rumors that I had heard, spread by union soldiers after the battle of Shiloh, of having seen hogs across the creek in the ground between our entrenchments and the confederates' positions. They reported that in the flashes of lightning that they had been able to make out hogs moving across the field, devouring the dead and wounded on the other side of the creek. One man had even reported that he would take shots in that direction whenever he was able to see something outlined by lightning. He said he wasn't concerned whether he actually hit the hogs or not. He was thinking the sound might suffice to scare them away, and if he was lucky, he would hit the wounded and put them out of their misery.

Anyhow, the nightmare was quite intense and terrifying. I dreamed that I had finally died there in the fields of Shiloh and because of my behavior, been sentenced to hell and was now suffering in Corinth, Mississippi because of my evil deeds. I woke up in a cold sweat and was actually quite relieved to find out I was awake and not dead, but somewhat devastated by the fact that I was indeed still in Corinth. And so, time passed for the next couple of months, and then one day, quite joyously and unexpectedly, we were told that we should clean and load our gear up because we would be moving out in the morning. We had expected we would be off to pursue the confederate army wherever it was located at the time but then were somewhat disheartened to find out that we would actually be marching back up through Shiloh to Pittsburgh Landing and were going back down the Tennessee River to the Ohio and down to Memphis, Tennessee. Well, at least we were leaving Corinth, and that was good enough for me.

CHAPTER 16

The following morning revelry sounded. We lined up for roll call, had breakfast, and then marched out on the road north. We spent two days marching over the path that had taken General Halleck nearly five weeks to dig his way through. We reached Pittsburgh Landing, having marched past the scene of our previous battle. The place looked much improved in this period of time. There were large mounds with crosses indicating where soldiers of both sides had been buried. Most of these were where the fighting had been thickest. We marched close to the position we had fought from in the sunken road. I recognized what had once been the thick stand of scrub oak and brush that had been east of us. The oak trees that had been twelve to fifteen feet high were rather uniformly cut off about thigh high. It reminded me of the corn field back home, in the fall, after we had chopped the stalks off. What had once been an almost-impenetrable stand of small trees and brush was now just stubble. I had noted it that spring, but somehow its significance hadn't registered. To think that the lead flying back and forth between the combating armies could be so thick and devastating was appalling. We marched back through our entrenchments on the bluff around Pittsburgh Landing and down to the landing itself, where we lined up and waited turns for the different transports to load. Since it was now nearly December, I hurried to get indoors and found a place inside where I could deposit my gear and sat on my knapsack. The steamer disembarked, and down the Tennessee we went.

It was past dark on the second day after we had left Corinth when the ships took off downstream for the Ohio. I soon got tired of trying to watch the scenery as it went by. We had whatever it was they could find for evening meal, and I sat back, leaned against the side of the steamer's cabin, and fell asleep. The journey down the Tennessee and down the Ohio was uneventful. We passed around the junction of the Mississippi, where the Ohio joined and headed downstream to Memphis. Shortly below the junction of the Ohio, the Mississippi seemed to triple in size. It was December, and it was doing a lot of raining, and I suppose the water was considerably higher than usual.

In a few days, we reached Memphis and disembarked. Where we were going, we seemed to have no idea, but we marched into camp. Again, we quartered in eight-man tents that were crowded as we fit the whole squad in. During the day, we woke up for revelry, breakfast, marching, and drilling, and time seemed to pass rather uneventfully. About this time, we received word that some of us would be going back to Missouri to recruit new members for the regiment. I was somewhat surprised one evening when the sergeant came by and instructed me that I should clean and pack all my gear to be ready to go in the morning because I was going to accompany him and our squad back to St. Louis. Other sergeants and lieutenants with their squads had been selected to return for the recruiting effort also. I was intensely pleased that our squad had been chosen to go. It was not that I was desirous of getting out of any fighting or tired of being with the rest of the regiment, but I thought they would probably just be quartered around Memphis until we got back, so I felt this would be a nice break.

So, the following day after revelry and breakfast, our squad, led by the sergeant, headed down to the river, and together with three other squads, we boarded the steamer and headed north. The steamer was not crowded. We had ample room to stretch out and enjoy ourselves. We passed the time watching the shore go by and eating good meals for a change and walking the decks of the steamer, talking, and making plans about what we might expect once we got to St. Louis. We reached the landing at St. Louis and disembarked, at least the sarge and our squad did. One of the other squads disembarked also, but the steamer that we had been on put back out and headed upstream intending to do their recruiting at Canton, Missouri.

We milled around on the banks for a while, and about a half hour later, the other squad was ordered to embark on a steamer, and once they had, it backed away with the big wheel churning and turned and headed up the river, I was told to Booneville, Missouri, where they would be doing recruiting. Then, our squad, led by our sergeant and a lieutenant, marched down the bank a ways, turned up toward the town, and marched off to Benton barracks. There, we were shown to a wooden barracks that actually had two wood-burning stoves, one at each end. In the barracks there were some new recruits that apparently some other officers of the twenty-first Missouri regiment had gathered over the proceeding several weeks. It seemed like their few weeks in the army had been similar to mine had been in Booneville. They were still dressed in civilian clothes and had been marching and drilling with wooden guns. We found bunks, deposited our gear in a wood chest at the foot of the bunk, and began to make ourselves feel at home.

At one end of the barracks was a small, private room that the sergeant entered. He deposited his gear and then, shortly thereafter, returned. He called us to attention, and the new recruits lined up at the foot of their bunks. The sergeant had us form up opposite, looking directly across at the new recruits. He welcomed them, each and every one, to the twenty-first Missouri. He went through and gave a brief history of the regiment. He ended up by praising our participation in the recent battles of Shiloh, Iuka, and Corinth. He related how we had been in the great and glorious battle of Shiloh, how we had held the center of the line and how General Prentiss and Colonel Woodyard had been captured, saving Grant's entire army from defeat. Then he mentioned how we had been with Halleck when they had marched down and conquered Corinth. He mentioned the battles of Iuka where the twenty-first Missouri had been part of the two divisions sent to confront confederate General Sterling Price's army, how they had defeated the rebels and forced them to retreat so fast we hadn't been able to keep up with them. He then mentioned the glorious fight at Corinth, Mississippi, where we had been attacked by confederate armies and in two days of severe fighting, had seen them off as well.

Well, I had been there through all of these things, and listening to him recount it, it certainly did seem great and glorious, but to my recollection, it had been mainly marching, digging, sweating, and being vermin bait. And then the sergeant finished up his little speech by going down the line and asking each and every one of us to step forward as he introduced us. I was certainly shocked. I wasn't aware that the sergeant even remembered my name, and I had no idea that he knew the names of each and every one of the other men in the squad as well. He had certainly never called me by name. Whenever he would address me, it had always been as "son." I thought that he probably called everyone of the recruits, son, since he was probably twice as old as anybody else there except for the other officers and sergeants. We stepped forward, stood erect at attention, and stared straight ahead as he called our names. Then, we stepped back into line. The sergeant then dismissed the new recruits and us, and I went and sat again on the chest at the foot of the bunk I had selected.

I sat there thinking for a few minutes over what had just transpired. Then, feeling rather intimidated, I walked over and knocked on the door to the sergeant's room. He called loudly, "Come in," and I entered. The room wasn't really all that big. I don't suppose it was more than seven or eight feet wide, and its length ran along the width of that end of the barracks. There were two bunks, one at each end of the room, and at the end of the bunk was a typical wooden chest. In the corner where he was, there was a wooden table that served as a desk and a chair. I asked him if I might have a word with him. The sergeant replied, "By all means, pull up a seat." Then, he pulled the chair away from the table and sat down facing me. There was a chair at the other end of the room, but I pulled his wood chest away from the bed and sat on the corner of that.

Now that I was here, I seemed to be at a loss for words. The thing that was on my mind that had caused me to ask to have this conversation finally came blurting and stuttering out. I said, "Sergeant, sir, I have been with the regiment for nearly a year now, and we have spoken a few times, but I wasn't actually aware that you even knew my name."

He laughed and replied, "Well, son, I try to know the names of all the men in my company, and I know the names of a good many men in the rest of the regiment also." Then, he went on to say, in a most friendly and talkative manner, "You see, son, that's part of my job being the company sergeant. My job is to check on all the men in my company, look out for their worries and needs, and keep informed of the situation in the company. The company sergeant reports almost daily to the officers in charge of the regiment, and the corporals of the various squads report almost on a daily basis to the other sergeants, but most particularly to the sergeant of the company. I like to feel that I know what each man in the company is doing, how well he responds to orders and commands, whether he keeps his gear cleaned and his guns polished, and especially whether he is disenchanted with the military in general." I took this to be a reference to the near mutiny that we had had just that last summer.

Then, when the sergeant had taken a brief moment to rest and collect his thoughts, I blurted out, "Well, I was just surprised. I had no idea that you even knew who I was, much less anything about me."

He laughed again and said, "Well, son, I've been keeping my eye on you pretty much since you got here." And, then he laughed and said, "By the way, how are your brother and sisters and your uncle Aaron?"

Then, I had to laugh as I replied, "Well, sir, they're doing just fine the last time I heard."

The sergeant said, "I knew you must have made it down river to the trading post in safety." He said, "I figured that out as soon as I saw you there in Booneville. You didn't have any further trouble, I take it."

I replied, "No, sir, we made it just fine. My aunt and uncle and cousins were delighted to see us, and I spent several weeks there as my family settled in and got acquainted."

I neglected to mention my adventures going back to Osceola, and I was too ashamed to mention my thoughts of going into Kansas, and then I was surprised again at the memory of when I had enlisted there in Booneville. Of course, I had recognized the sergeant immediately when I had actually taken enough time to take a good look at him. That distinctive brassy dark reddish hair was one certain giveaway, but he was quite noticeable also because of the exceptional size of the man. He also was well over six feet tall, as my own father had been, and he had that distinctive, as I now knew it to be, Irish accent. When I thought of this, I again blurted out that I hadn't been aware that he had recognized me when I enlisted there at Booneville.

He smiled and laughed again and said, "Son, I knew who you were as soon as I saw you. I have never seen hats and boots like those on anyone else before or since."

That made me blush with embarrassment. Then I said, "Well, you hadn't said anything."

He said, "Son, that was not my job to talk to you. I was standing there assisting the lieutenant, but if I hadn't recognized you, you would never have been accepted and allowed to enlist." He said, "You know, the lieutenant didn't much believe you and wasn't inclined to let you enlist, despite that letter from your uncle. It was only because I recommended you to him that he let you enlist. I told him I knew you to be a fine and outstanding young man and that you would be a more than capable soldier."

Once again, I blurted out, "You did what?" Then, I said, "How could you know that?"

He said, "I figured anyone who could take his family down river in a canoe for several hundred miles alone on over a week's journey in the middle of wartime with raiding and bandits of all sides on the loose was more than capable of taking simple orders in the military." Now, that made me laugh!

We sat there and talked a great deal longer. It seemed the sergeant was in a mood to talk. I think that most of his conversations with the officers, other sergeants, and corporals had all revolved mainly about military matters and morale in the company, but now we were just simply sitting there talking. The sergeant told me how the lieutenant had liked that horse I had sold him. He said that the lieutenant had decided to keep the horse as his own. He said that the lieutenant had grown particularly fond of the horse and had made the comment, on various occasions, that it was the "goingest horse" he had ever had. I guess that after all that time with Pig, trying to keep his head up to keep him from mulching grass as he walked and continually keeping him kicked up in a trot, I had finally instilled in the horse a desire to see the countryside on his own. The sergeant related that the lieutenant said that whenever he got on that horse, it just seemed to want to take out and was ever ready to travel. I laughed and laughed at that.

By that time, it was getting late, and when the bugle blew, we went down for evening meal, and upon return to the barracks, the sergeant advised us that before we went to bed that evening, we should polish up our weapons and our uniforms, because he wanted everything bright and shiny for in the morning. He didn't tell us why. The next morning, the bugle blew us out of bed, and we lined up for roll call and revelry. Then we went down and had breakfast and once again were given a brief period of private time after breakfast until the bugle blew, once more, and we lined up on the parade ground. I thought we would be doing further marching that day. Members of other companies had lined up until I think that probably a whole regiment of people were there. Our little squad was the only squad from the twenty-first regiment, unless you counted the new recruits.

A colonel came out in front of the regiment and made a small speech. He welcomed the sergeant and our squad there to participate in recruiting new members for the regiment and for the further drilling and training of the regiment. Then, he called out the sergeant's name and presented him with a medal. I was quite excited and proud to see the sergeant so recognized. The colonel mentioned that the sergeant had seen distinctive service in the battle of Shiloh with General Prentiss' sixth division and had held the line while the rest of the army was reinforced and entrenched along the sunken road. But then, what was even more surprising, after the sergeant had received his medal and had marched back and taken his place at the head of the line of our squad, the colonel went through and called out the names of each and every other man in our squad. Our corporal was named, and, as he stepped forward, it was announced that he had been promoted to sergeant of the squad, and he was likewise given a medal. And then I was even more shocked as the colonel went through the list, calling out the names of all the remaining members of the squad, including me.

We had all been promoted to corporal and were likewise given medals for service in Shiloh and Iuka and Corinth. I hadn't actually been at Iuka, but I didn't feel like speaking up then and telling the colonel that I hadn't been there. The

general concluded the presentation, and we were marched off back to our barracks. We were only given a brief break then until the sergeant came back from his office, called us to attention, and marched us off for a long walk down the road and back, by which time lunch was ready. We had another short break, and then that afternoon we went for a march and drilled around the parade grounds. After evening meal, we gathered around, talking about what had happened to us that day in the barracks. Our old squad had taken the bunks at one end, somewhat separate from the rest of the new recruits. The sarge came out of his office and asked if we might all step in for a few minutes. When we did, he told us that we should sew our new stripes on and that we should make more of an effort to mingle with the new recruits, talk to them, get to know them, and put their minds at ease.

Then, he went on to explain to us what our new responsibilities would be. I had never really understood the arrangement that the military had for looking out for the soldiers until then. It seemed that maybe the sarge was getting more experienced. I had learned that he had only been made sergeant of the company on the recruiting trip when I had first encountered him at Booneville. Since he was new at the job, maybe he wasn't exactly sure how to go about it and possibly it was through his own trial and error that he came up with what he felt was the proper way for a company to be managed. He explained to us that he, as sergeant of the regiment, reported daily, or every few days anyhow, to the colonel of the regiment and to the different captains and majors and lieutenants.

To this day, I'm not sure just how many officers a regiment has. It seems that there are usually two colonels, one who is in overall command and a second in command. Then, they usually have at least one major and usually a couple of captains. It seems that every company has its own lieutenant and sometimes two. Then, it seems there is one sergeant for a company whose job is to watch over the corporals and the other sergeants of the company and report to his lieutenant and even to the captains and majors. It seemed that usually there were three other sergeants in a company and that there was usually one corporal for each squad. Usually there were ten squads in a company. But of course this arrangement seemed to only work about half the time. Especially after Shiloh and some of the other battles we had been in and even throughout times that we had been in barracks or digging our way to Corinth, the number of troops in a squad and a company varied. In Corinth, in particular, there had been a lot of sickness, and at any one time three or four, even half the people in some squads, were unable to report to duty.

One thing I found particularly interesting was that officers never seemed to last very long. Our division had lost General Prentiss to capture and Colonel Moore had been wounded and Colonel Woodyard also had been captured. I had never known any of the names of the lieutenants, but it seemed like at least half of them had been replaced in the weeks after the battle. I also learned that I was going to be made corporal over the squad that was to be directly supervised by the newly made sergeant. The other men as corporals would all be directly in charge of their squads. Then, the sergeant dismissed us. He told us in leaving that we should be sure and sew on our new stripes, and as I left, I almost rushed to my footlocker to get into my knapsack for the needle and thread.

I had never thought it particularly strange that a man should be able to sew. I had often helped my mother and two sisters as they repaired our clothes and made new ones, so I was somewhat shocked to see that nobody in the rest of the squad even had needle and thread. It was late enough that they didn't think they could acquire any, and even if they had, it seemed like none of them knew how to sew. I don't know whether they were razing me or whether they were being honest, but it seems that I ended up doing all the needle and thread work that evening. After I had sewn on my stripes, I fixed up the new sergeant's uniform, and after having stitched the stripes on two of the corporals' jackets, I realized I didn't have near enough thread to do everybody else's. It seems like they were all quite eager to volunteer to go out in an effort to find more thread, and I took a break until they returned.

I used this time to go and knock on the sergeant's door, and as previously, he called out quite happily, "Come on in." I entered and again made myself comfortable on the wood chest at the foot of his bed. I told him that I had another question, and he said, "Fire away." I said that he had mentioned that we should make an effort to get to know every man in the squads that we were commanding, and he said that he thought it was quite important that we do that. I then related that I felt somewhat embarrassed to say that I had never gotten to know any of the men in the squad that I had been with originally. He said that was really too bad. He said, "You know, things there had been a little bit different. In Booneville we had had tents for only four men, so that made it somewhat hard to get to know the members of your squad if they were camped in another tent." He also related that the corporal of our squad had lodged in the second tent and that possibly he hadn't been particularly wise in spending all of his time in one tent. He speculated that he thought maybe the corporal should have split up his time from week to week and moved back and forth between tents.

He then asked me how well I actually knew Sergeant Wright. Indeed, this was the name of our newly promoted sergeant. He had been our original corporal of the squad from Booneville. And thinking about it, I realized that I couldn't tell him anything about Sergeant Wright. I didn't know where he was from. I couldn't even remember his first name at that moment. Then, thinking about it, I realized that there were eight other privates in our squad, but only four of those had been with us at Booneville. The other three had either been killed, taken sick, or gone missing in combat. Counting me, there were only the five of the eight privates from that squad still there. I was even more embarrassed then to think that, although I knew the names of these men, I knew nothing else about them. This caused me to blush and become even more embarrassed. I think the sergeant noticed that immediately and he said, "That's all right, son, that's all right." He said, "Sergeant Wright kept me abreast of your development. Despite everything he could do to engage you in conversation and from what the other members of your tent had said, you were not easy to get to know. In fact, the sergeant thought that you were somewhat of a mental case. He said you were sullen, morose, and withdrawn. He said you refused to engage in any conversation and seemed to prefer to sit in your back corner of the tent in the shadows where you couldn't be seen and that you seemed to ignore the rest of the members of the squad."

I thought about that and realized that it had indeed been true. I tried to explain to the sergeant that I had felt rather intimidated by most of the men who were considerably older, but not only that, that I always had this inward fear that if I ever talked too much, I would somehow let slip how young I actually was or that, if they got to know me, they would realize that I probably had no business being there. He said that I should relax, that everyone had known pretty much immediately how much younger I was, and that, according to official military policy, I shouldn't have been there. But he said we did have quotas to get for recruits and the military couldn't wait forever for us to fill them and that in his opinion, if you find a ready, willing, but most importantly able recruit, age shouldn't matter that much. He said, "Besides, once you were in, no one was going to kick you out." I laughed wholeheartedly at this comment, and I think the sergeant had a good laugh also.

About that time there was a knock on the door, and Corporal Anderson appeared. It seemed that they had managed to find some more needle and thread but still no one knew how to sew. The sergeant just laughed wholeheartedly again and said, "You know, son, as long as they can talk you into doing the sewing, they'll never learn." And with that bit of advice, I returned to the barracks, took up my seat on the wood chest and had the remaining corporals pull their chests over as I showed them the difficult and tedious procedure in threading a needle and sewing on stripes. I sewed on another set of stripes and then turned the needle and thread over to them, and in no time at all, every soldier had his new stripes on his blouse.

We went to bed again just after it had gotten good and dark and the following morning supervised as the new members in the company, which now numbered fifty-eight, went down and were fitted out for their new uniforms. We then returned back to the barracks building where the troops spent the rest of the morning outfitting in their new uniforms. After lunch, we went for a nice long march down the road and back and returned to the barracks just in time for evening meal and some free time after that before taps.

Once again, I went and politely knocked on the sergeant's door. His hearty bellow of, "Come in," echoed, it seemed, through the whole barracks.

I entered again and said, "Sarge, might I have a word with you, sir?"

It seemed I had been picking up some of his strange way of talking. I had never before said might instead of can. The sergeant laughed, pulled out his chair, and once again I sat on the chest at the foot of his bed. Once again, I didn't know quite how to begin, and so I just blurted out, "You know, I was embarrassed to say that I didn't know much about the other men and I didn't know how to go about telling you that after all this time I still didn't know really who they were. But now I don't know how to go about talking to them and admitting that I don't know anything about them."

The sergeant just laughed and said, "Why don't you go ask the other men to come on in and tell them I want to have a word with them?" This, I did and they all assembled in the sergeant's room. The sergeant said, "Make yourselves at home, boys," and they struggled to do that. He said, "You can have a seat on the bed and drag the other bed over too." So, we rearranged the furniture and sat around in a group with the sarge in the one corner next to his desk. Then, the sarge said that he would like to see us get to know the troops better and that, in order for us to know them better, we should know ourselves better also. So, he asked us to start with the sergeant, John Ben Wright, and go around the room and introduce ourselves and tell us a little bit about each other. I had thought this was a brilliant idea that I had to go in and talk to the sergeant and confess to him that I really didn't know the other troops in our squad well. I was thinking that he would just fill me in since, by this time, I was coming to the conclusion that the sergeant knew pretty much everything. I hadn't expected this. So, we proceeded around the room with the men giving just a little brief talk about themselves.

Sergeant Wright spoke first. He said that he had been born just south of Keokuk, Iowa. Apparently his father had once been in the military and had been stationed in Keokuk. He had moved from there down and settled in northern Missouri not far from Canton. He said that his father had then taken up farming. When the war started, he felt an obligation, like his father, to serve in the military and had gone down to enlist. He related that he had been in the military for two years now, having served with Colonel Moore in the original regiment that had been formed into the first northeast Missouri home guard.

Then, Corporal David Mencks spoke up. He had recently joined about the time I did and had been from St. Louis. His father had been a German immigrant and worked in a brewery there in St. Louis. He had trained with my group at Canton, but we had never gotten to know each other.

Corporal Mike Anderson spoke up. He had been from around Memphis, Missouri. I was surprised to know there was a Memphis in Missouri. His family had also been farmers, like mine. He had served originally in the first northeast Missouri home guard and knew Sgt. Wright well.

Then Steven Rowe spoke up. He also was from St. Louis, and his family was of German descent. His father had worked in some capacity for the city. I think he did pretty much whatever his boss felt that he needed him to do at the time, whether it be cleaning streets, digging ditches, or whatever a city employee was needed to do. He had signed up at age nineteen and had trained at Canton the same time as me. I had talked to him some previously. He looked younger than nineteen, and I felt more comfortable around him. But we had been in different tents, so I didn't know him well.

Lewis Vonn had been one of those men who had been in my tent in Booneville. He had come from someplace pretty much straight west of Booneville, this being a small town called Marshall. It seems that his family, like mine, had done farming in that area. Lewis had enlisted about the time I did, having been somehow involved in skirmishes around Lexington, Missouri, and along the Missouri river there. Apparently confederate troops had come through and done a lot of damage in the area, and as a result, he had been inclined to join and fight for the union.

It seems his story was actually somewhat similar to mine. He hadn't lost any family or close friends, they but had been robbed of possessions and especially crops they had harvested.

Then, there was Sergeant Earnest Francis Smith. We had often joked with him, calling him E. F. Smith, since one of the generals at Pittsburgh Landing had been a C. F. Smith, but there was no relationship. Earnest was a young man who came from around Hannibal, Missouri. His father had been a clerk in the store there.

William Jones had enlisted at Booneville. His family had lived there, and as a younger man, he had worked on the docks along the river and occasionally had gone downstream on the steamers and even keelboats.

Then, there was a Don Callahan who had lived outside St. Louis in a town called St. Charles. He, like the sarge, had a rather thick Irish accent. His father had come over as a young man and somehow made his way to St. Charles.

Then there was a Jacob Koontz. Jacob was probably the oldest man in the squad. He was older than the sarge, but not much. He liked to talk a lot. I thought, from what Jacob had always said, that he was extremely old, and indeed he certainly looked much older. He had been born someplace in western Illinois and had crossed over into Missouri somewhere around Canton. He had worked on ferryboats going back and forth, taking passengers across the Mississippi when necessary, but had spent most of his time hunting and trapping along the Mississippi and the rivers in that area. Jacob was a rather crusty old pioneer type. Even in his new uniform and stripes, he still somehow looked disheveled and dusty. He had a great long beard and rather long hair. I thought he was probably the only man in the regiment who had not been bothered by chiggers and ticks in Corinth since he probably had been totally familiar with them all of his life. About the only thing that looked clean and polished about Jacob was his rifled musket. From the care he bestowed upon that weapon, I knew that he was quite capable of using it.

Then there was me. I had listened rather intently to what they had said as they had taken their turns talking about themselves. Most of the men kept it short, and so did I. I told them that I was from Osceola, Missouri, which had been burned early in the war and that I was an orphan, my parents and other family members having been killed, and that's pretty much all I had to say. Then, the sergeant dismissed us for the evening.

The following day after breakfast, we went down to the armory where the nearly sixty men who had been gathered were issued their weapons and accessories. We spent that morning as the new recruits cleaned and polished their weapons. After lunch that day, we went out for drilling on the parade grounds. The recruits learned to handle their weapons, shoulder arms, port arms, and present arms and spent the afternoon marching around the parade ground. The next couple of days were spent in further drills and long marches up and down the roads. One evening after supper, the sarge called me into his office. He told me to make sure that I had my weapon cleaned and polished, because tomorrow we were going to take the troops out for their first round of target practice. He told me that he wanted me to put on a display of loading and firing the musket. Apparently the sarge had decided to improve his instructions to the troops on this particular topic.

I was excused and went out and sat on the chest at the foot of my bed. I considered what I was going to do as far as going through the routine of carefully loading and discharging the weapon. I expected the sergeant wanted someone to demonstrate, as he called it, how to get off as many as three shots in a minute. I had my own ideas on how to improve this and politely knocked on the sergeant's door, and when asked to enter, I requested leave for the rest of the evening, asking the sergeant if I could go out to the range to look it over. He seemed rather surprised by that, but I could tell by the glint in his eye that he had decided I was up to something and he wasn't going to ask what.

I hurried off and went over to the hall where we ate our supper. A few troops were still there cleaning up the meals and doing dishes. I borrowed some old flour sacks from the sergeant of the mess hall, as well as some chipped-up wooden platters. I told the sergeant I wouldn't be bringing these back, as I had need of them. These were somewhat chipped up and cracked. Some had also suffered from being too near the stoves and were partially charred. He didn't seem to feel that he would mind being rid of them but asked me to replace them with new ones from in town so that he might not get in trouble if anyone questioned this. I promised to do just that and hurried off. As I did so, I picked up some burned wood from the ash of the fireplace outside and placed it in one of the white muslin flour sacks. I also acquired some twine from outside the mess hall that had been used to bind up some of the sacks.

Then I hustled on out the few miles to the target range and prepared my targets for the demonstration tomorrow. I got back just slightly before the bugle sounded taps and went promptly to bed without mentioning anything to anyone where I had been.

CHAPTER 17

It dawned sunny and slightly warmer than it had been. We lined up for roll call, and after breakfast, we returned to the barracks and loaded up with our gear and our rifles. We marched out from the barracks to the practice range. As we marched up to take position, I noted the sergeant expressed a brief look of surprise when he glanced toward the straw-stuffed dummies dangling from the posts. It was possibly only because I was looking for some type of reaction that I noticed this, but most people didn't seem to mind. The sergeant gave his usual speech about the superiority of the British army and the fact that they never lost a battle with the French under the Emperor Napoleon. He also praised their ability to fire three shots in a minute and emphasized the different steps in loading a musket. He went through this several times slowly, step by step, and quite explicitly. And then, at the end of his talk, he announced that Corporal Everett would now demonstrate for us.

I stepped out from line and marched up next to the sarge, stopping about fifty yards from the row of straw dummies. I stood there rigid at attention. The sergeant announced that on his count I would load and fire as rapidly as possible. He again emphasized that we should just simply aim at the straw dummies and not to bother about accurate fire, the intention was to get off as many shots as possible. I nodded and shook my head, and on the command, "Now," I grounded the butt of the musket, grabbed the barrel, pulled a paper cartridge, bit off the ball, poured the powder in and crumpled the paper and stuffed it in, spit in the ball, rammed it home, brought it up and placed the cap on the nipple, aimed, and fired. And now my little surprise for sarge and the new company was revealed.

I had come out the night before with the five wooden plates and the five white flour sacks. I had placed the plates in the sacks and tied them, suspending them from the rope that held the straw so that they were sitting right on the shoulders of the straw dummies. On each white face, I had drawn eyes and a nose and a big wide grin with the charcoal that I had picked up from the dining hall. I had thought in Corinth when we first got to the fortifications that the confederates had an incredible sense of humor with their smiling dummy heads on top of their fake cannons. And now, there were five smiling dummy heads on top of the straw sacks.

I had loaded and fired as rapidly as I could and blew away each smiling face. I was loading and firing as quickly as possible, but taking only enough time to make sure that the smiling faces disappeared with each blast. I blew away three smiling faces and speeded up as much as possible, and just as the sergeant yelled, "Time," boom, the fourth smiling face disappeared. I snapped back to attention with the rifle on my right shoulder. The sergeant looked at the assembled squads up and down and replied, "Well, well, boys. Now you see what a real soldier can do." Then, he ordered me back into line. We had roughly sixty men in the newly formed company by that time, and the sergeant ordered them forward in one line. Then he and the rest of the new corporals took up position safely behind the new recruits, and as he called out slowly each step involved in loading the rifles, we paced up and down the line, watching carefully as the troops went through the drill. The first six shots were tediously slow in coming. Then the sarge picked up the pace slightly for loading and firing the next six shots. Then he picked up the pace even faster for the next four or five shots. For the last three shots fired, I could tell that the sarge was hoping to see that he could get some of the new recruits at least to manage three shots in a minute, but that never quite happened.

After having delivered the twenty shots that we had been allocated, we turned around and marched back to the barracks and supervised as the new recruits went through carefully cleaning and oiling down their rifled muskets. After lunch that day, we went out again on a long march up and down the road. After supper that evening, the sergeant invited me into his quarters. For a moment, I thought that I might be in some sort of trouble, but after entering and shutting the door, the sergeant smiled widely and said in a pleasant voice, "Wherever did you come up with that idea?" I told him that I had gotten the idea from the confederate smiling-faced dummies at Corinth. He chuckled loudly and said, "Yeah, leave it up to those Johnny Rebs. They have got a fine sense of humor. It's almost a shame to be fighting them." Then he said, "That was indeed a good idea, but wherever did you learn to shoot like that?"

I explained to him that where we had grown up we had been loading and firing rifles from the time we were knee-high. He said that he thought we needed to make a better effort in training the troops to shoot. The sergeant said a lot of the new recruits had never carried a gun before, much less loaded or even fired one. I found that strange and hard to believe, but he insisted that, until he had joined the army himself, he had never owned or fired a gun, and he said that most of the recruits we had picked up and would be picking up from the St. Louis area had probably never owned or fired a rifle either. He said, "That's why I have to be so careful and meticulous about explaining how to load a musket. If you had never done it before, it can be quite challenging." And he said that in combat, he had noticed that some people forgot even the simplest of things, couldn't concentrate, and ended up putting the ball in first, the powder on top of it. Then they were not able to fire and then poured in more powder and put in more balls until the musket was totally jammed full and incapable of being fired. That surprised me, but if the sergeant said it was true, I'm sure it was.

The sergeant then said that he had thought I had done a very commendable thing because he said that in the morning he would be announcing to the different squads who their corporals were going to be, and he said he had felt somewhat hesitant, thinking that some of the new recruits might resent someone so much younger than them being placed in command. He said he was sure now that nobody in the company would resent having me as a corporal. I could only smile and say that I hadn't even thought about anything like that. "I just thought it would liven up the demonstration."

He laughed and chuckled again and said, "Well, it certainly did that." He said, "I was quite surprised when I saw those smiling faces looking back at us, and I knew at a glance what you had been up to the last night."

Then, he made as if to dismiss me for the evening, but I felt bold enough to ask him a further question. "Sarge," I said, "might I talk with you a bit more?"

He said, "Sure." And so again, I sat on the chest at the foot of his bed while he sat on his chair next to the table he used for a desk. "Go right ahead."

I looked up at him and said, "Well, Sarge, you know all about us, but I haven't any idea about you." I said, "I know, at least I picked up, that you were an Irishman, but well, I was just kind of wondering if, well, could you tell me more about yourself?"

I could tell that the sergeant was momentarily taken aback, but then he relaxed and leaned back in his chair some and said, "No, I don't mind at all."

Then, he went on to tell about his life. He had been born in Ireland, that much I knew, but he had come from a small village in the north central part of Ireland. His father had worked as a groomer and farrier for the lord's horses. It seems his father's main job was to look after raising, breaking, training, and in general caring for the lord's horses. He related that his father had never particularly adjusted well to the job. It seems that at some point in time, a couple of hundred years before, his ancestors had actually owned the land that the British lord now claimed. In fact, according to the sergeant, the British lived in their ancestral home, a rather large cut stone manor house with a slate roof. I had no idea what slate was, but apparently, as the sarge explained to my question, it was a type of soft stone that was easily slabbed off and could be used to put a roof on buildings.

According to the sarge, his family had laid claim to several hundred acres of land, but when the British had taken over, they had all been displaced. The sarge related that, since there wasn't much else for an Irishman to do, in his own country, that his grandparents and father had stayed on and worked for the lord of the manor. Apparently this was a rather humiliating situation. The sarge related that he had watched his father work at a job that his father had always considered to be beneath himself and how his father had never been happy, drank too much, and was often at odds with the British lord who now owned their property and for whom they were forced to work. He said his father died, he thought of unhappiness, at a relatively early age, having married young and fathered seven children, five sons and two daughters.

Being's how he was the second youngest of the sons and had older sisters and several older brothers, all of whom were living in the same small one-bedroom stone hut with a straw thatched roof, he determined as soon as he was old enough, he would move on. Apparently he decided there wasn't much future in Ireland. He said his older brother had replaced his father, being in charge of caring for the raising and breeding of the horses, and his other brothers worked cutting hay, thatching grain, and whatever else that the British lord found for them to do. But he had decided he didn't wish to continue in that line, having seen what it had done to his father. So he talked to the parish priest, who had gotten permission from the lord for him to immigrate to America, and when he was a little over fourteen, he had set sail for New York City.

He said he had gone to live with an Irish family who had agreed to sponsor him and upon arrival in New York, had taken up residence with these people. They lined him up with a job working on the docks, unloading ships, and that initially he had been quite happy and thankful for that. He said that over the next couple of years, he had grown rather disenchanted there. He said the family was exceedingly nice and as fine a couple as you could hope to have been sponsored with, but that the job down on the docks grew to be more and more unpleasant. He related that he had left Ireland to get away from the British lord, but upon arriving in New York, he felt that all the opportunities for advancement and all the political power and control of the city were in the hands of wealthy Englishmen who had come to America years before and who now were entrenched in the local politics and controlled the good jobs in the city.

He related that considerable tension had developed between the native-born New Yorkers and the Irish immigrants and that most of the Irishmen in New York belonged to one gang or another who served to look out for the interest of Irishmen and to organize a political opposition to the New Yorkers. He related that it wasn't much different in New York than it had been in his home of Ireland, where the Irishmen were continually looked down upon and treated with a mixture of disrespect and distrust. And so, unlike most of the other Irishmen working on the docks, he had avoided the taverns and the bars, where he said they seemed to eat and drink to excess, and had saved up his money and moved west. Apparently he had gone across New York and into Ohio, and after reaching Cincinnati, Ohio, had come down the Ohio River and ended up in St. Louis. He said that he lived in St. Louis for a couple of years working along the docks and at a packing plant. He said that St. Louis was not a bad town. People were much friendlier than they had been in New York City. There didn't seem to be any disrespect for Irishmen, as there were a lot of people of different nationalities in St. Louis. He told me that St. Louis at one time had been founded by the French, and then one time it had been controlled by Spaniards. I didn't know all of this and found it rather hard to believe, but if the sergeant said it, it must be true. Then he said that once it became American, people of all nationalities had seemed to flock there. He related there was a large German population and a good many Irishmen also.

So, he felt pretty much at home in St. Louis, except for the fact that he missed small towns. He said he had lived in a relatively small village all his life, and he liked being around horses and open country. So, he had seen an opportunity to move north to Canton, Missouri, and had. He said he had taken up a job at the pork packing place and had rented a small house. He told how he had met and married a blond-headed German girl. He said her parents had come over from Germany when she was quite small and that she was a couple of years younger than him. They had married and had been exceedingly happy. Apparently they had five children. The sergeant said that he wasn't aware that life could be so good and everything was progressing well. He said they had managed to save up enough money to buy a small house and move out of the tenement. Their house had been just south of the town of Canton. Then, about five years before, a fever had struck the town. His wife had sickened first and then the two daughters and the youngest son. The sergeant related how they had suffered with high fevers, abdominal cramps, and diarrhea and that, despite what the doctors and their neighbors had been able to do, had died.

As I listed to this, I could see that the sergeant's eyes filled with big tears that he held back. His voice shook, and his hands seemed to tremble some, but he was able to control himself with the greatest of effort. He said that after that his two sons were boarded each day, when he went to work, with the woman who lived next door. Apparently she had several sons and daughters and they had all been sick with the fever also, but none of them had died. Surprisingly, her husband, who he thought had been the strongest of the whole family, had not survived his fever and dysentery. He said that the neighbor lady had taken in laundry and sewing and would board his two sons for a small amount of money. He always felt that she hadn't charged him enough to take care of his sons, but he thought that she was hoping that she might land herself a new husband through this arrangement.

He said he continued to work at the pork-canning factory for a couple of years after that, but then, after the war had broken out, he had been one of the first to sign up. He said he had been posted to the usual training camp like we were doing now and had been with the regiment from the time it was first formed. He said that he had left his two boys living with the widow lady from next door. He said he had sold the house they had bought and given her half the money if she would continue to raise his two sons, and away he had gone. He said a few months after that he received word from the lady that the youngest of his two sons had come down with the same type of fever that had killed the other members of his family and had not survived. Here, again, his eyes seemed to water up, and his voice shook. The sergeant said that he had been off somewhere around Kansas City at the time that he received the word and hadn't even been able to get back for his son's funeral.

Then, he went on to tell how his oldest son, who was about eighteen, had signed up for the military, like he had, and been assigned to a different regiment. Apparently he was one of the few people killed in some skirmish along the Mississippi River around southeast Missouri. Now, my eyes filled with tears and my voice seemed to crack, my hands seemed to tremble, as I looked at the sarge and asked a silly question , "Were you then all alone in the world?"

The sergeant seemed to stiffen up and said that, no, he still had family left in Ireland but that he had never heard from any of them after he had left. He said it had been probably thirty years since he first left and he had never written and they had never written him. I think that was one reason why the sergeant had been so adamant before that one should keep in contact with one's family and why he had insisted that I write my uncle and sisters and brother and let them know what I had been up to.

Since I had been back at the Benton barracks, I had sent two different letters. I hadn't yet received any word from them, but I figured it was only a matter of time until I did. Of course, I couldn't be sure that they ever received any of my mail either. Then, the sergeant said, "You know, son, I don't think I have ever told anybody any of that." And he said, "I'm not sure just why I told you."

I said, "Well, it was probably because I asked."

He replied, "Well, even then, I didn't have to tell it all." Somehow I felt quite proud and pleased that he had. I excused myself and went back out into the general barracks and prepared for taps.

The next day after breakfast when we returned to the barracks, the sergeant announced that he was going to form up the squads we had so far. We had sixty-something men by this time. The sergeant went through and assigned one squad of men to Sergeant Wright and made me the corporal of this squad. Apparently I would be reporting to Sergeant Wright, and he would have the ultimate command of the squad. There were eight other men in our squad, with the sergeant and I making ten. He then assigned the five remaining squads to the other corporals of our original company.

Then we had gone out marching, drilling, and hiking the roads. Sergeant Wright and I were at the head of our new squad throughout the next several days. After a day's training and drilling, I would make it a point to go through my squad, as I felt it to be, and try to get to know the men better. There were several Germans in the new squad. There was a Johnny Applebaum, an Otto Kerner, a Christian Nichols, and a Hans Verner. These men had all come from the immediate St. Louis area. Their fathers had all recently immigrated from Germany, although they had all been born themselves in the St. Louis area. Then, there was a Robert Cantrell, a Michael Francis, a Frank Martin, and a Tom Sinclair. They all lived in small towns but had been recruited in the St. Louis area, having traveled, according to them, distances of anywhere from twenty to fifty miles just to enlist.

Most evenings I reported to the sergeant. Usually other corporals were there as well, but I would often try to have a few words in private. One evening I approached the sergeant's door, knocked politely, and on hearing his cheerful "Come in," entered. I asked if I might have a few words with him, to which he immediately replied, "Absolutely. What's on your mind?"

I had been thinking about our first battle at Shiloh, and I had been wondering why General Grant had been relieved. We had been discussing this in the barracks earlier in the evening. Some of the recruits had stated that there had been reports in the newspapers that Grant had been drunk and that we were caught unawares and nearly defeated. Some said we had been saved only by the timely arrival of General Buell. I voiced my opinion that I thought General Grant had done a fabulous job! I said I knew nothing about a General Buell, and I certainly didn't think we had needed saving.

I related all this rather speechlessly to the sarge. He just laughed and said, "Well that's the way it is with these generals, sometimes they're the army's worst enemies. They never want to share the credit or let anyone else get the glory."

He went on to explain that he thought that General Halleck was merely jealous. After all, General Halleck was in overall command, and General Grant had been too successful. Grant had been victorious at Fort Henry and at Fort Donelson and then had fought the rebels to a standstill at Shiloh and sent them packing. That was too much for Halleck, who felt his subordinate was outshining him. "Son," he went on, "that's why Halleck had to come down and take over. He just couldn't sit by and let Grant get all the glory. It's probably also why Halleck was so timid in his advance on Corinth. After having criticized Grant, and humiliating him in the press, Halleck couldn't afford to be caught off guard."

I thought about that and decided it made sense. Besides, I had to admit that although it had taken us weeks to dig our way to Corinth, we had made it and never even had to fight for it. But then I thought more of it and said, "Well, indeed we took Corinth, but what good did that do? We were then further south than we had been, but the rebels were free to move around behind us. We hadn't known where they were, and when they attacked, they came from the north. What kept them from attacking north as we attacked south?"

This brought a great bellow of laughter from the sergeant. "Well nothing, I suppose," he said.

I then went on to surmise, "Maybe taking towns and railroads isn't that important. Maybe we should concentrate on finding the rebel troops, fight them, beat them, and destroy them."

The sergeant had listened to all this with a merry twinkle in his eye and now laughed again and said, "I totally agree, maybe we should make you general."

Now it was my turn to laugh. "Imagine, me a general."

We continued talking late that evening before I excused myself and went to bed in the barracks. As I laid there trying to sleep, I chuckled softly to myself. Me, a general! But who knew? I was already a corporal and barely thirteen.

CHAPTER 18

I made it a point to try to be as helpful as possible with the men. After one day of marching in cold rain and muddy roads, several of the men complained about their boots leaking and their feet being cold and wet and nearly freezing throughout the march. I immediately went to my chest, got out the beeswax I had carried with me throughout the previous campaign, and showed them how to warm the boots over the stove and to rub the beeswax in good and let the boots sit and warm and soak up the beeswax. I told them that this would help to repel water. Then, over the next several days, we continued to apply several more coats of beeswax and polish to the boots. They were surprised how well this worked.

I had also noticed how, especially the Germans, had difficulty with their muskets. As the sarge had said, none of them had previously ever held a gun, and they found it exceedingly difficult to go through the simple procedure of loading the weapons. So, in the barracks without actually using any paper cartridges, we practiced going through the steps involved in biting the ball off, pouring the powder and stuffing the paper, and ramming it all home. I would call off the steps and they would respond, and we kept at this, faster and faster, until I was satisfied they could have gotten off at least three shots a minute. Then, they remarked at how impressed they had been that I could shoot the heads off the dummies. They said they weren't sure they even managed to strike the sack at all. I then went through explaining, minutely, about how to line up the front and rear sights, and then I explained to them how the rear sights could actually be raised and lowered depending on the distance. I would actually draw them little diagrams of front sight and rear sight and the proper alignment.

Then, we would sit around the barracks and take the empty muskets and aim at specific objects to line up the sights. This was something that I had done with my own rifle when I was young. There was nothing like just practicing, whipping the gun up to proper firing position, and lining up the sights so that it became almost automatic. There is nothing like practice to make you good. So, we had gone through practicing, pantomiming loading the gun and pantomiming raising, aiming, and firing. I knew the next time we returned to the target range they would be functioning better than any other squad in the company.

We continued marching, drilling, and practicing, and gradually more and more men arrived from recruiting stations around the St. Louis area, until finally we had ninety men. Then, one day the recruiter had come in from Booneville. He had managed to get ten men. It had taken him all of this time to do that. It seems that people were not so enthusiastic about signing up for the war anymore. In fact, there was some talk that the government might actually have to force people to join up. I didn't see how they could do that. I'm sure my father would have been extremely offended with the idea that a country that prided itself on liberty and freedom would resort to forcing people into the army. I thought that it would never happen. Surely not!

Some evenings I spent gathered with my squad. We were becoming quite close. I had gotten to know them all and knew a lot about their families, homes, and prior life. They were often eager to hear my thoughts on the army and the war. This evening, they were complaining bitterly about all the marching and drilling. I surprised myself by trying to defend this; after all, I had felt the same way. I told them how at Shiloh we had marched out to investigate the commotion off to the south. I described how we had come into contact with the rebel troops and how Colonel Moore had ordered us to form up and fire on the confederates and how, when more confederates had appeared, Colonel Moore had directed us to form up and retreat. Then he had marched us into another position, where we turned to face them again. I described how we had been outflanked and the order had been given to form up and retreat again. As I remembered it, we had then reformed on the slope, on the other side of a creek, and fought fiercely from there until being formed up a final time and ordered to retreat.

I think that I only now realized that all this had been accomplished with remarkably good order. We had marched back into camp with the troops in control. It was only then that we became thoroughly confused as the rebel army burst into camp. I described how, in the mad panic that ensued, some officers had managed to rally the troops and reform us in the sunken road. I said I believed this was only possible because of all the drilling we had done, and because we had been trained to follow orders without complaint. As I talked, I came to realize that without all this training, an army could never be brought together to fight.

I was surprised how my squad listened quietly to my every word. Even some members of other squads had gathered, without being noticed, and had been listening. Although the soldier who had first christened me "one bloody little bastard" was long gone, the reputation had stuck, and I was surprised that the troops looked on me as their special little bastard.

In the days that followed, my squad, and indeed, it seemed, the whole company, came together to march, drill, and parade with a special pride.

Whenever I wasn't spending evenings with my squad, I looked forward to spending time with the sergeant. He never seemed to tire of our talks. I knew that he had a lot of responsibility, so I hated to bother him too much, but he never hesitated to spend some time with me when I requested. Tonight, when I knocked on his door, I could tell he had been anticipating my arrival. He happily called out, "Come in." When I had seated myself next to his desk, he asked, "What's on your mind?"

I had been thinking about the sergeant, and I said "Well, I was just wondering what Ireland was like."

He seemed surprised by that question and hesitated for a moment and then said, "Well, let's see. What I remember most about Ireland is the greenness of the land. Ireland, you know, is called 'the Emerald Isle' because of it. The weather is milder than here. We usually get some snow in the winter, but not like Missouri, and seldom is the weather so cold or the wind so harsh. In the springtime, the rains come and the pastures and meadows take on such an intense green color that it is breathtaking. Then as it warms up a little more, the clover and wildflowers bloom and everything turns purple, red, or white. The villages are made up of stone cottages, and the fields are divided by stone walls, since there's not a lot of forest. But I can only speak of county, Monahan, never having seen much of Ireland myself." I asked the sergeant what a county was, and he seemed surprised. He said "Well a county is, a county, you know."

I said "Not really."

"Well," said the sergeant, "I guess a county is a potion of land that the government designates so that they can appoint officials to manage it. You know Missouri has fifty or sixty counties, and they elect representatives to report to the governor in Jefferson City, so they can manage the state. How do you think they can maintain law and order otherwise?" Then he asked me "What county do you live in?"

I told him "I have no idea." I just knew that we had lived on the banks of the Osage River, upstream from Osceola.

The sergeant said "And how much land did you farm?"

I thought about it and replied, "Well Dad always said that we owned about a thousand acres."

And Sarge said "And that's because the county set it up so you could get title to it, and then the government protects you so no one else can come and settle on your land. And they do that by appointing and electing local judges and law officials to keep the peace."

That all made sense to me, so I changed the topic back to Ireland. I was curious and asked if he ever missed home and if he ever thought about returning. He smiled sadly, I thought, and said no, never. He was happy here and had no desire to return to what he had left. I felt stupid then because I could see that he was thinking of his wife and children who were gone, but also somewhat relieved. Although the sergeant appeared so jovial with his troops and was always ready with a kind word of encouragement or advice, I had the sudden feeling that he was deeply lonesome. Maybe that's why he seemed, like me, to enjoy our evenings together so much. I think we had both found our new homes in the army. I excused myself and returned to the barracks. Tomorrow would be another long day. After the last squad had come in, the next day we went down, and they were issued their uniforms. For some reason, the last three squads that had joined prior to theirs were still in their civilian clothes and marching with dummy guns. I guess there was something about taking just ten men to get uniforms at a time that maybe the quartermasters of supply didn't appreciate. It was only after we had the last forty men in the new company that we could go down and get them uniforms. Either that, or they didn't even have any on supply to hand out. So, now we were all dressed up in our new uniforms. I anticipated that in the next day or two we would probably go down and acquire the new weapons for the recruits.

And so, once again after evening meal, I knocked on the sergeant's door and asked if I might have the evening off to run some errands. I usually spent a portion of every evening going in and sitting and talking with the sarge. It amazed me what he knew, and I liked to hear stories about Ireland and other European countries. He readily agreed and then smiled and said, "You know, we won't be going to the target range for a few days yet."

I said, "Well, that is just as well."

I told him that I had in mind trying to get some cappers for the men in my squad. I told him that the idea of reaching in the pouch trying to pick up an individual cap to place on the nipple of the musket was time consuming and rather clumsy and that I thought if I got a capper for each of the boys in the squad, they would probably be able to get off four shots a minute or more. He thought that was a fine idea, and I think he was pleased to see that I was no longer quite as sullen and morose as I had been previously. In fact, he related that a good sergeant or corporal always thought of his men and how best to help them and care for them. He said, "You know, these are still just boys, and a lot of them are still homesick and unsure of themselves. A little bit of kindness goes a long way." I thought how true that was.

So, that evening I marched all up and down the streets of St. Louis inquiring about where I could find cappers. There were a few stores that had them, but they had become exceedingly hard to find. I managed to come up with three. Then, as I was heading back to the camp, since it was probably getting close on to taps, I went past a store window and looked in. The man in the shop was a silversmith. There were a few silver candlesticks and some silver plates, and I entered. The man said he was just closing up for the night, I but asked him if he could spare just a minute. He looked rather surprised, but agreed. I said, "Looking about the shop, it looks like business has been rather slow."

He replied that, indeed, it truly had. Silver was becoming scarce, and he couldn't hardly get enough on hand to work his craft on. When he had gotten it, it seemed to be slow on selling because people weren't much interested in buying unnecessary luxury-type items. He said most of what he had on display had been there for months. Then, I asked him if I could show him something. I reached around my neck and pulled out the string with my little brass capper on it. I told him how I had been looking for these for the men in my squad, and he gave me a rather strange and surprised expression. I told him that I had had a difficult time finding any. I asked him if this was something he might be able to make, and he smiled and said, "You mean out of silver?"

I said, "Well, of course not. Possibly make it out of copper or brass like these."

He looked at it and thought about it for a bit and said, "You know, that wouldn't be very difficult." He took a fine screwdriver, took it apart, looked it over, and said that, certainly, he could make those without a great deal of effort. I asked him if he might be able to make up five for me, since I had managed to find three already, and he said he could but that it would take him a day or two. I told him there wasn't really any hurry. Then, I said, "You know, I think I'll talk to the sarge and see. Maybe we should have some for the whole company."

That seemed to give the man an idea. He said that he might come with me to talk to the commander down at the barracks and that the military wasn't issuing these, that possibly he could even supply every company that came through and trained there. So, I told him I would be back in a couple of days to pick up the cappers and I told him I would let the sergeant know that he might be coming by to talk to him, and then I hurried on back to the barracks.

We had about a week's period of time where the temperatures warmed up and it began almost to feel like springtime, but then once again it became quite cold. We had some icy rain followed by a fairly heavy storm. We got about a foot of snow. This kept us in the barracks for the next three or four days. We spent the time talking to the new men in the squad and explaining how to sight in a rifled musket, how to aim, and just discussing other things that I felt were pertinent and helpful about life in the military. I told the recruits about the fever and dysentery that we had had at Corinth and how the tonic had really seemed to relieve the disease and the symptoms. I also mentioned to them what the old regimental surgeon had said about simply boiling water. I talked to the recruits about keeping their boots waxed and polished to help keep their feet dry and talked to them about the troubles we had had with chiggers and how this could be minimized, although not entirely prevented, by keeping their drawers stuffed inside some long socks that came up to about the knee and suggested on the next trip into town on holiday that they should look to find some of these knee-high socks. I talked to them about how the best things to prevent blisters with all the marching was to keep the socks straightened out and pulled up and, if the boots were loose fitting, to wear even two pairs of socks because anything that rubbed would cause a blister.

We talked about the experiences at Shiloh and since I had been in the army for over a year now and had actually been involved in three what I now found to be fairly famous engagements, I realized that the new recruits in the squad actually listened carefully to anything I had to say. I talked to them about Shiloh and my thoughts on it, such as they were. In looking back on it, I realized that I had indeed been terrified most all of the time. I also realized that I had instinctively been obeying some of my father's previous commands about hunting. Namely, to take advantage of any cover that was offered, never show yourself anymore than you had to, always to listen, smell, and look, and let these govern your actions but above all, never to react in just a blind panic. Always try to be aware of events around you and think before reacting. This now seemed to me to be a particularly good piece of advice.

As I remembered, the whole camp we had retreated into the morning of the battle of Shiloh had packed up and ran. We had been attacked by a goodly number of confederates, that's true, but the total number of men in the camp actually far outnumbered the number of confederates that came storming in. There is something about just a panicked reaction that is contagious, and even in that situation, if people had kept their heads and had looked the situation over and thought before they reacted, the various companies in camp there would have simply held their ground and fought off these confederates since we actually had outnumbered them, at least two and maybe three to one. It amazed me how looking back and talking about things seemed to help clarify what had happened and made me see things through a different light. It also amazed me that the new recruits seemed to hang on everything I said.

The next day it was warmer, and we went out and drilled on the parade ground. That afternoon when we were dismissed before supper, I went into town and checked with the silversmith who was making the brass cappers for me. I bought the five that he had prepared and asked him how things were going. He said he had been in to town to see the commander of the barracks and, although the officer hadn't been able to purchase these to supply all the new recruits training in the barracks, he had advised the silversmith that he would suggest to the different company commanders that they should go there, and if the recruits individually wanted to purchase cappers, that he thought that would be a good idea. The silversmith related that he was currently working as rapidly as he could to produce new cappers.

I got back into the barracks just in time for supper that evening, and the sergeant asked me to come in and talk with him again after we had gotten back to the barracks. He said that we would be going out the day after tomorrow to train the new recruits in musket drill and that in the morning they would all be issued and pick up their new weapons. He said that as soon as we had finished training the last of the new recruits, we would be ready to ship on back to the front lines. The next day, we escorted the last of the new recruits down to the armory, where they were issued their new rifled muskets and accessories. We then spent the day drilling on the parade ground with them. That afternoon, I went back to the cookhouse and got some more flour sacks and wooden plates and went out to assist with preparing the straw dummies for musket practice in the morning.

The next day after breakfast, we returned to the barracks and the troops picked up their gear. We lined up in front of the barracks on the parade ground and marched out to the target range. The sergeant gave his usual training speech on loading and firing the rifled muskets and then asked me to step forward and give a demonstration of how a good soldier was able to load and fire. This time, I had succeeded in breaking the fourth smiling face before the sergeant called, "Time." As I turned to walk back behind the troops, I couldn't help but notice the big smile the sarge gave and his cheerful wink. Then, as the sergeant called off the instructions to load, aim, and fire, we paced up and down behind the forty remaining recruits to see how they were doing. This still surprised me to see how much the troops struggled with simply loading a musket, but after they had fired their twenty rounds, the sergeant had the older recruits line up in two groups of thirty and had the new groups watch as they practiced going through their loading, aiming, and firing of their twenty paper cartridges. We instructed the new recruits then to watch carefully each step that the older recruits took in going through the routine, and by the time the two groups of thirty had fired their twenty paper cartridges, I was thinking that the whole company would be ready for action.

Over the next three to four weeks, we continued marching and drilling the company. The weather had been quite cold and exceedingly windy for the last three weeks but was beginning to warm up slightly. It was sometime around the first of March when the sergeant announced that we would be returning shortly to service. There was an air of excitement that went through the whole barracks. The men made a special effort to wax and polish their shoes and their leather accessories. The recruits, whenever they went into town, took special care to purchase any extra socks or wax or other items they felt like they might need. It was impossible at that time to find any Henry rifles or Remington or Colt revolvers, but I had managed to find another two boxes of cartridges for the Henry as well as an extra fifty rounds of precast lead balls for the Remington revolvers. We went out to the target range again, and the new recruits went through their second round of twenty shots with the muskets. They were beginning to be able to handle them nearly as well as the "old vets," as they called us. It seemed like they were actually looking forward to getting into action.

That evening sarge had talked with me, as we often did, in his room after supper. It seemed that he was somewhat disappointed. He had heard only that afternoon that we might not be rejoining up with the twenty-first Missouri regiment. It seemed that the other companies had already left from up at Canton, Missouri, and had gone down the Mississippi a day or two before that. They were heading down to Mississippi, and we would be going down ourselves in the next couple of days. However, the news that he found disturbing was that someone had decided that the twenty-first Missouri would now have all the new recruits that were needed and that our new company of one hundred men was being assigned to another regiment entirely. The sergeant, it seemed, was more upset about this than I was. I can't say that I really knew anybody else in the regiment. True, there were some people I knew in the company, but I didn't think that I would particularly miss their presence. However, it seems the sergeant had grown to know a number of the other sergeants and lieutenants fairly well. He also knew several of the privates and corporals, and I think he was somewhat disturbed also since most of the entire regiment had come from the same part of the country where he lived. He didn't really know anything about the thirty-first Missouri regiment, but it seemed as if he really didn't have any choice.

I suppose I could request transfer back to the twenty-first, but it would mean leaving the men that we had been training for the last couple of months. I guess if I had to make a choice, I would rather be with this company than to be assigned to another company, even if it was in the twenty-first Missouri regiment. I could see how he felt. I think he had had a lot to do with training most of the companies in the regiment, but this was the most recent company, and I think he was taking a special pride in the fact that he had been able to develop a closer bond with them; at least I certainly felt much closer to the men in the squad that had gone with me to become corporals and train the new recruits. I also felt a lot closer to the other eight men of my squad than I had ever felt to the eight men in my previous squad. Everything considered, I knew that I would definitely prefer to be with these hundred men of this new company than to go back to the twenty-first Missouri regiment, and I tried to explain my thinking to the sarge. We sat and talked until taps before I returned to my bunk with the rest of the men in the squad.

The following day after breakfast, we went for a long march down the road and returned in time to take a quick break before lunch. After lunch, when we returned to the barracks, the sergeant made an announcement that in the morning we would be meeting a steamer down on the landing and would be heading down the Mississippi to Memphis or beyond. The soldiers all cheered and were especially pleased to find out that they had the afternoon off. They were instructed that they could use it in any fashion they chose, but to make sure that their boots were polished, their clothes were cleaned and laundered, and their rifles cleaned and oiled down, because, according to the sergeant, after breakfast we would return to the rooms, pack up, and march down to the landing. That afternoon, I spent my time cleaning up my gear and getting all my uniform and underwear laundered. Then, I packed up my knapsack with all my gear and was ready to go before the bugle blew for supper.

When we returned to the barracks that evening, I took out the brass cappers and went through the squad, handing them out individually to each of my soldiers. They knew what it was and were quite pleased to have it. I told them to keep it on a leather throng about their neck and keep it hid inside their uniform, since they weren't actually military issue. I also told them that they should keep it quiet, since I had none for the rest of the men in the company. I think this made them each feel quite special. Just the thought that their corporal would take the extra time and spend his own money to buy them something individually, I could see was quite touching. I had made the similar suggestion to the other corporals of our company, and some had actually conveyed this suggestion to the people in their individual squads. Some of the corporals had bought cappers for themselves, and some of the new recruits in the other squads had taken advantage of the suggestion and had bought their own. But my men were especially pleased to think that I had taken the time to get them a little gift at the completion of their training. Before taps that night, every man had loaded his knapsack and put his gear together, and by the time the bugle blew, they were ready to march off at a moment's notice. The next day would find us on our way down the Mississippi to Memphis.

CHAPTER 19

This was the life, I thought, again, as I stood on the bow of the ship in the early morning sunlight and watched the shore on both sides of the Mississippi go by. The sun was just starting to show above the hills to the east and cast the western banks of the Mississippi into bright sunlight, but the eastern banks were still concealed in shadows. We had boarded the steamer while it was still dark, and I had dropped my pack and rifle on the floor of the cabin and immediately made my way up on the deck. It was toward the end of March, I don't know exactly when. Time has a way of slipping past, especially when the days all seemed to be filled with the same routine. I suppose we were on our way down to the Ohio. For some reason, nobody ever seemed to know just exactly where we were headed. It seemed the officers liked to play some sort of a game and liked to keep us in the dark.

We were on a smaller steamer, nothing to compared to the ones on which we had gone up the Ohio on our way to Shiloh before. There was certainly plenty of room for the hundred men of our company and their gear, as well as a large amount of supplies, but there was plenty of room in the cabin, and I could have been inside if I had wanted to. It wasn't rainy or particularly cold, although we seemed to pass in and out of banks of fog that were lying close off the surface of the Mississippi waters. I was wearing my greatcoat, cape, and forage cap. It wasn't cold enough for a scarf or wool mittens. I preferred standing out on the deck and watching the shores go by. Once again, I thought that this was the life. I thought that after the war was over maybe I would like to work on a keelboat. Then, I remembered that there really wasn't much use for keelboats anymore except maybe on

273

the Osage River. I thought it would be great to work on a riverboat and watch the shore go by. I thought it would be even better to be the pilot of a steamboat. Then, I thought, what was the point of making plans for after the war when who knew how much longer this war would last or if I would ever live to see the end of it.

The sun rose gradually higher and began to shine more directly on the water, and now I was able to see both banks in fairly good light. Where we were at the moment on the river, there were fairly high bluffs and banks on the western side. Sometimes through the trees that were still bare of leaves, you could see sandstone and limestone bluffs. Occasionally these were several hundred feet high, but usually forty or fifty feet high. In other areas, there didn't seem to be much in the way of rock cliffs, but there seemed to be high bluffs of dirt. On the eastern side, it seemed that everything was flat and rather swampy looking, with cultivated fields interspersed with thick patches of forest. You could see, off farther in the east, higher ridges that were probably similar to those on the west side of the Mississippi.

Questions would run through my head, and I considered trying to store these up and later discuss these with the pilot of the steamer. I wondered why it was that the river flowed here and not farther east. Looking at the ground, there didn't seem to be much difference. Then, the thought went through my head as to just why the Mississippi flowed this way and not the other. The Osage river flowed, I knew, north to hit the Missouri, which seemed to flow east, and the Mississippi I knew flowed to the south, but having traveled most of this territory, I couldn't say that I could tell a difference in the elevation of the ground. I wandered up to the pilot's cabin and thought that I might be able to talk with him. On previous trips, the riverboat pilots had seemed quite eager to talk about the ship and their job, but when I knocked on the door of the cabin and asked if I might talk with him, he rather abruptly ordered me out.

I returned to the lower deck and stood again on the bow of the ship and watched as the ground went by. I made a point of watching the river and the currents as I had when we had canoed. I occupied my time watching the banks, the shore, and the river flowing south. The day seemed to pass slowly, and when it became dark enough that you could no longer see, I went and laid down, using my knapsack as a pillow, and slept through the night. Sometime late the following afternoon, early evening, the boat pulled into the shore, and we disembarked at Milliken's bend. This reminded me a lot of Fort Defiance by Cairo, Illinois. There were large earthen levee fortifications around the camp, and as we crossed over the levee and down to the camp, you could see that along the levee walls were a lot of plank lean-tos with plank roofs. These pretty well covered the entire inner walls of the levee. In the center area, there were plank barracks buildings and a few tents. We marched through the fort to the far side along the northern levee and were shown a long, lean-to type barracks to occupy.

The floor of the barracks was dirt, but since it was built up higher on the levee wall than the level ground inside the fort on the levee wall, it was relatively dry, that is in comparison to the parade ground, across which we had marched, which was mud, probably six inches deep. The old fort smelled, if possible, even worse than Fort Defiance had as we passed by it previously on our trip up to Shiloh. It looked like there must have been fifteen or twenty thousand men stationed in the fort and around it. What with all those people, the pit latrines, and the general waste and bustle of an army confined there for a period of time, it created a very unpleasant-smelling situation.

After evening meal, we returned to the barracks, since that time of year it was quite dark early, and lit a few candles to talk before taps. The door to the barracks suddenly opened with a crash, and a rush of stumbling men poured in. Most of them were wearing either sergeant's or corporal's stripes, but probably half were simply privates. It seems that they had learned there was a new company of recruits for the thirty-first Missouri regiment to which they belonged, and they were eager to make our acquaintance. They shouted out until they had located the sarge, who had placed his gear opposite the door on the one end of the barracks. We had pressed around as close as we could to the group that was forming. A few bottles of liquor were brought out and passed around. The sergeant exclaimed in his best Irish accent, "Boys, you know I don't approve of drinking in barracks, but maybe just this once." There were several cheers and considerable laughter as a portion of liquor was poured into the tin cups the soldiers stretched out until the bottles were empty. It looked like sarge got a pretty generous share.

They were quite eager to tell us about everything that had transpired while we had been away recruiting, it appears. It seemed they had been there since well before Christmas, and they were quite anxious for the spring to come so that we could be moving on. The loudest and most boisterous of the bunch was a sergeant about the same size as Sergeant Shawnasee. It was he who brought the biggest jug and seemed the most eager to talk.

"Yes," he said, "we no sooner arrived here than General Sherman decided to try to take Vicksburg all by himself. We had gone up the Yazoo River to land at the foot of Vicksburg. We disembarked the division into the swamps at the foot of the bluffs and marched away from the river into open ground at the foot of the bluffs. It seemed that on both sides there were trees and swamps, but where we entered, the ground seemed to form a big, open triangle. They formed us up at one end of the triangle where it was pointed right at the river, and we were ordered to march across the swamps and up the embankments into the confederate fortifications. You could take one look at the installations those old rebs had built on the top of the bluffs and tell it wasn't possible. I don't know where these generals get their education, but they certainly are rather lacking in intelligence. You could look at it and tell at one glance there wasn't any way we were going to be able to take those fortifications. The bluffs looked like they were nearly straight up and down. They were made out of dirt and mud. There was hardly anything that could be used for cover, and what's worse, the bluff sloped toward us on both sides. One look at it, and you could tell that we would be marching into a trap where the rebels on the bluffs could shoot at us from three sides. Still, what could you do? Orders were orders.

"We went marching across the open ground and then went stumbling and splashing through the mud up to your knees. There was no way to even fire a shot since the rebels couldn't be seen on the top of the bluffs. We were about halfway through the swamps before the artillery started opening up, and after that, it seemed the safest course was to clear the swamp as soon as possible. The boys gave a great cheer, and we went stumbling and rushing through the swamp as fast as possible. We reached the base of the bluffs and started up. It was nothing but mud, and you could hardly walk on it, but yet we were determined to do it. At times, you were on your hands and knees crawling up through the mud, grabbing at clumps of grass or small bushes to try to pull yourself up. The bluff got so steep that it seemed like we were looking straight up. You couldn't see any rebels, nothing to shoot at. I don't know how they managed to see us, but they kept up a perfect hail of musket fire and rolled cannonballs with lit fuses down the hills at us. The one thing about old General Sherman, the guy's determined. He kept at it and kept hurtling more troops forward throughout the whole day. Finally, after it got to be dark, we felt it was safe to go traipsing and splashing back through the swamps to get the hell out of there. And ever since that, they have had us engaged in digging up the whole countryside." This provoked howls of laughter.

Sergeant Shawnasee said, "Yeah, these officers sure like to have the men dig. We dug our way all the way from Shiloh to Corinth," and the new sergeant, whose name happened to be Flanders, said that he wished there was some way we could dig our way into Vicksburg, but we hadn't even been digging at Vicksburg. He said they had come up with some great idea to dig a canal across the point of land where the Mississippi made a big bend in front of the bluffs at Vicksburg so that they wouldn't have to try to go past that artillery on the hills. It seems that the Union generals were afraid they would lose too many steamboats and have too many people drown in the Mississippi trying to run a fleet of boats past the bluffs. So, they tried to dig a canal across the point of land to connect the Mississippi above and below and be able to bypass the town of Vicksburg. It seems they had dug for months on this before the river broke through the dam at the one end and flooded the whole thing.

Then, they had been involved in digging another canal to join the Mississippi to Lake Providence. Apparently this was somewhere to the west, and the thought was that they could dig a canal to the lake, they would be able to go down through the rivers and the swamps that ran out of the lake and joined the Mississippi below Vicksburg. They dug and dug and spent several weeks digging this canal, but then once they had gotten to the lake, they found that getting out of it on the other end was impossible. Apparently the rivers ran through great stretches of Cyprus trees and they had to try to cut these trees off ten feet under water to try to clear a path for the steamboats to get through. He said he thought there were still some people trying to cut the trees, but they had abandoned that idea also. There seemed to be a continuous hum of conversation going on. It became louder and louder, and the tin cups were filled and refilled. I thought that they had only had four or five bottles of liquor when they first came, but it seemed like it kept miraculously re-supplying itself.

One of the corporals said he had a story that topped all yet. Apparently some other troops had been involved in an attempt to get behind Vicksburg from the east. Why we just didn't march down from Memphis on the eastern shore, no one seemed to know, but he said that they had loaded up troops and gone up north on the Mississippi and had blown a huge hole in the levee there. It seems that there had been a river connecting up there previously that the confederates had blocked off with a huge earthen levee. He said that they had blown a huge hole in the levee and flooded the whole countryside, and then had gone by steamer through the flooded land to try to hit the waterways east and come down from above. But once again, the steamers hadn't been able to find their way through the swamps and the forest on that side of the river either.

Then, one of the other sergeants said, "I have the best story yet." It seemed that Sherman had taken one of the divisions of troops stationed at Milliken's bend and had marched through the swamps on the east side of the river to an opened bayou that apparently connected to the Yazoo river somewhere below. They had all then embarked on several steamers and had gone through the swamps here following Admiral Porter's ironclad ships. He said they wound their way through the bayou and through the forest and down some small streams that became even tighter and more closely packed. He said at one point in time you could look front and back and see six or eight boats at the same time that all looked like they were within easy musket shot, and all of the boats seemed to be facing different directions. He laughed and chuckled and said some were going south, some were headed north and some were going east and west, but we were all following one another in line. It was the damndest thing you ever saw.

Apparently the ironclads were somewhat smaller than the steamers that they were on and were able to get farther ahead, but the steamers had to cut off tree limbs and hack brush out of the way to make any progress at all. He laughed and chuckled and said the worst part of it were that the trees were alive with snakes, rats, mice, coons, possums, and other sorts of vermin. He said bumping up against the trees knocked the critters loose, and they showered down on the boats and went scuttling up and down the decks. He said, "They actually gave us brooms and sticks to beat and knock the nasty things off the boat." He said it must have been like Noah and his ark. Worst of all, there were a couple of times that skunks ended up on-board. He said no one wanted to try to sweep them off, but the things didn't like being on the deck and didn't want to be in the water and there were crewmen all over the decks, so it was a regular stampede of people around and around the ship to try to avoid the skunks before they managed to get them over the side. He said eventually it got to the point where they couldn't go any farther. Admiral Porter and his ironclads had gotten far enough ahead and had run into trouble from confederate troops. The way forward was blocked and trying to back their way out of there was a lot harder than going forward. He said that the rebels were surrounding the ships and were in great danger of sinking the whole fleet until Sherman had ordered several hundred of the troops to go to the aid of Admiral Porter. They had been ordered to disembark from the ships right into the swamps and had managed to wade and splash their way forward to drive off the confederates so that the Admiral could back his ships out of there.

Everyone seemed to think that this had been great fun. Nothing really much had happened in the way of battles or excitement, just a lot of digging and idiotic boat trips. We were having a great time being filled in on the details of the commanding general's disappointments, but we were soon interrupted by the bugle announcing taps. Sergeant Flanders and his comrades excused themselves and made their way rather unsteadily back to their barracks in the fort. We went to bed that night wondering what further brilliant plans they could come up with for us. It seems they tried digging their way past Vicksburg on the west and the east and I was wondering where else could they find for us to dig. But as it turned out, they had made up their minds to quit digging. We were only in camp for a few days before we were ordered to make our gear and be ready to embark in the morning. We were going to run the river. We were on our way to Vicksburg.

CPSIA information can be obtained at www.ICGtesting.com
Printed in the USA
LVOW110106160212

268877LV00001B/44/P